A Dark Dividing

A Dark
Dividing

Sarah Rayne

FELONY & MAYHEM PRESS • NEW YORK

All the characters and events portrayed in this work are fictitious.

A DARK DIVIDING

A Felony & Mayhem mystery

PRINTING HISTORY
First UK edition (Simon and Schuster): 2004
Felony & Mayhem edition: 2011

Copyright © 2004 by Sarah Rayne

ISBN: 978-1-934609-80-4

Manufactured in the United States of America

Printed on 100% recycled paper

Library of Congress Cataloging-in-Publication Data

Rayne, Sarah.
A dark dividing / Sarah Rayne. -- Felony & Mayhem ed.
    p. cm.
Originally published: London : Simon and Schuster, 2004.
"A Felony & Mayhem mystery" --T.p. verso.
ISBN 978-1-934609-80-4
1. Journalists--Great Britain--Fiction. 2. Twins--Psychology--Fiction.
I. Title.
PR6118.A55D37 2011
823'.92--dc22
                              2011000750

The icon above says you're holding a copy of a book in the Felony & Mayhem "Wild Card" category. We can't promise these will press particular buttons, but we do guarantee they will be unusual, well written, and worth a reader's time. If you enjoy this book, you may well like other "Wild Card" titles from Felony & Mayhem Press, including:

BONNIE JONES REYNOLDS
The Truth About Uniicorns

For more about these books, and other Felony & Mayhem titles, or to place an order, please visit our website at:

www.FelonyAndMayhem.com

or contact us at:

Felony and Mayhem Press
156 Waverly Place
New York, NY 10014

ACKNOWLEDGMENT

The poem quoted in several chapters, and specifically in Chapter Twenty, by the Mortmain children, is from *A Shropshire Lad* by A. E Housman, and was written in 1896.

A Dark Dividing

CHAPTER ONE

WRITING AN ARTICLE on a newly opened art gallery in Bloomsbury was the very last kind of commission that Harry Fitzglen wanted.

Slosh down over-chilled wine and sandpapery savouries in company with a lot of smug females with too much money and not enough to do? It was hardly in keeping with the image, for God's sake! Harry observed, with some acerbity, that covering arty society parties was a female thing, and then was so pleased with the disagreeable nature of this remark that he repeated it in a louder voice to be sure no one in the editorial department missed hearing it.

'You're really just a sweet old-fashioned romantic at heart, aren't you?' said one of the sub-editors, at which point Harry threw a reference dictionary at the sub-editor, and went off to his editor's office to point out that he had not joined the staff of the *Bellman* to report on fluffy Bloomsbury parties.

'It's not until next month,' said Clifford Markovitch, ignoring this. 'The twenty-second. Six till eight stuff. The gallery's called Thorne's, and it's the latest fling of Angelica Thorne.'

1

'Oh God,' said Harry, and demanded to know where Angelica Thorne had got hold of the investment capital to be opening smart Bloomsbury galleries.

'I don't know, but it's one of the things I want you to look into,' said Markovitch.

'It's probably guilt money from some ex-lover.'

'Well, if he's a front-bench MP with a wife and children in the Home Counties, we'd like to know his name,' said Markovitch at once. 'The thing is that Angelica's reinvented herself as a purveyor of good taste and of Art with a capital A, and the gallery opening's worth a few columns on that alone. What I want is—'

'Names,' said Harry, morosely. 'Celebrity names. The more celebrity names the wider the circulation.'

'It's our golden rule.'

'I know it is. It's carved over your office door like the welcome to hell line in Dante's *Divine Comedy*.'

'You know, Harry, I sometimes wonder if you're quite suited to this place,' said Markovitch doubtfully.

'So do I. Let's get on with this, shall we? I suppose this gallery opening will be packed with the great and the good, will it? Angelica Thorne knows half of Debrett, in fact she's probably woken up in the beds of a good few of them.'

'Yes, but I don't want anything libellous,' said Markovitch at once. 'Gossip, but not libel. Oh, and you'd better have a look at the exhibits while you're about it. Up-and-coming paintings on the one hand, and futuristic photography on the other, apparently. The photography's the partner's side of things, by the way.'

'If they turn out to be exhibiting displays of dismembered sheep pickled in formaldehyde you can write the copy yourself.'

'You have *met* Angelica Thorne, have you?' demanded Markovitch. 'No, I thought not. Dismembered sheep and Angelica Thorne aren't words that occur in the same sentence.' He considered for a moment, and then quite suddenly leaned across the desk and in an entirely different voice, said, 'It's Thorne's partner I'm interested in, Harry. She's down on the PR hand-out as Simone Marriot, but I've been delving a bit.' Markovitch loved delving. 'Her real name is Simone Anderson.'

Silence. Markovitch sat back in his chair, eyeing Harry. 'Now do you see what this story's really about? And why I've given it to you so far ahead of the date?'

Harry said slowly, 'Simone Anderson. But that was more than twenty years ago Are you sure you've got the right person?'

But Markovitch would have the right person, of course. He had a complicated card index system of events that might be worth saving up in order to disinter them in ten or twenty years' time. Harry would have bet next month's rent that the wily old sod had been gloating over these particular notes for at least a decade. The *Bellman*'s critics said, loftily, that reading it was like eating reconstituted leftovers, but Markovitch did not mind this in the least; he said the *Bellman* did everything in good taste and took no notice of people who said he would not recognize good taste if it bit him on the backside every morning for a fortnight.

'Simone Anderson,' said Harry again, thoughtfully.

'You do recognize the name, then?'

'Yes.' Harry said it with supreme disinterest. Never display enthusiasm for a job. Hard-bitten Fleet Street hack, that was the image. A reporter who had come up the hard way, and who rode with the knocks on the journey.

'We'll run the Thorne Gallery thing, of course,' said Markovitch. 'But what I really want you to do is delve back into the Anderson story. Properly delve. I don't just want a cobbled-together re-hash—'

Harry observed that this would make a change for the *Bellman*.

'—cobbled-together re-hash of the original facts,' said Markovitch firmly. 'I want some new angles. Now that Simone Anderson has turned up in the world again, so to speak, let's try to find out what she was doing while she was growing up—school, college, university if any. Boyfriends, girlfriends, lovers of either sex. How did she end up in photography? Is she any good? How did she come to link up with Angelica Thorne? I daresay you can manage all that, can you?'

'I might.' As well as never sounding enthusiastic, never sound optimistic, either. Always sound as if there's a bottle of Chivas Regal in your collar drawer, like a sleazy American private-eye. 'If I agree to do it, I suppose I might come up with one or two angles,' said Harry unenthusiastically. 'I'm not a bloody research assistant, though, you should remember I'm not a bloody research assistant.'

'I know you're not, but something odd happened within that family, Harry. I can remember the whispers, and I can remember three-quarters of Fleet Street trying to ferret it out. It was twenty years ago but I can remember the buzz. People died and people disappeared from that family, Harry, and although most of us suspected something odd had happened, no one ever got at the truth. There were rumours of murder covered up and whispers of collusion within the medical profession.'

'Collusion? Collusion over what?'

'I don't know. None of us could find out.'

'And you think I'll find out, twenty years on?'

'You might. But even if you don't, an update on Simone Anderson—Simone Marriot—will still make a nice human interest story.'

The *Bellman* specialized in nice human interest stories. It liked to tug at heartstrings and it liked publishing rowdily illustrated triple-page spreads about celebrity couples, and minor royalty. Sometimes it ferreted out an injustice and mounted a campaign to put it right, or petitioned for the release of some wrongly convicted criminal.

Harry suspected that Markovitch selected the injustices and the wrongly convicted criminals more or less at random, but he had never said this because he needed the job, in fact he needed any job, and so far he had managed to steer clear of drafting appeals to clear the names of old lags, which was one mercy.

'Oh, and keep a note of all your contacts. I want them on the computer, *and* on the card-index.' Markovitch did not entirely trust computers. 'In another ten years' time there might be another follow-up on this one. I'll save it up.'

'Don't save it up for me. I won't be here in ten years, in fact I won't be here in five, in fact you'll be lucky if I'm around this time next week. Now that I think about it,' said Harry, disagreeably, 'you might as well give the whole thing to somebody else here and now.'

'I'm giving it to you.'

'Well, I don't want it.'

They often had this kind of discussion but it never got to the 'You're fired' stage, because Markovitch could not forget that Harry had worked in the upper echelons of Fleet Street before the messy and acrimonious divorce that had eventually led to him being sacked, and Harry could not forget that he needed the money after Amanda's perfidy over the joint bank account and the house.

'You can have a by-line.'

'I don't want a by-line,' said Harry. 'I don't want my good name attached to the drivel your paper serves up. But I'll tell you what I will have, I'll have a bonus if that week's circulation goes up.' He would not get one, of course, because nobody on the *Bellman* ever got bonuses. So he got up to go, but before he reached the door, Markovitch said, 'Harry.'

'Yes?'

'It's the mother I'm most interested in.'

'I thought it might be.'

'She might be dead by now,' said Markovitch. 'She vanished completely, and we could never find her.'

'Was she nice-looking?' Harry had no idea why he asked this.

'She had a quality. Something that made her stick in your mind.' For a moment Markovitch even sounded wistful.

'She'd be mid-forties now, presumably?'

'Maybe even a bit more. Melissa Anderson, that was her name. I would very much like to know what happened to her, Harry. What you need to do is find a pathway into the past, that's what you need to do.'

'You don't want a reporter on this job, you want an orienteer,' said Harry crossly, getting up.

'Where are you going?'

'To the pub to find the magnetic north,' said Harry.

Extract from Charlotte Quinton's diaries:
28th October 1899

Tonight during dinner, I suddenly wished there were pathways into the future so that one could know what lay ahead, and sidestep awkward situations.

But at least Edward v. pleased at confirmation that it's almost definitely to be twins in January as already suspected, and is already talking about moving to a bigger house after the birth. This house dark and gloomy—dark houses no place for children (don't I know it!), and anyway, there will have to be extra servants, have I thought of that? Surprisingly enough, I have.

Has told everyone we know that we are expecting twins (in fact has told some people several times over), and is expanding delightedly like a turkey cock all over London. Suppose he thinks that appearing to have sired twins emphasizes his virility.

Dr Austin has promised that I will be given something to help with the birth—expect that will be chloroform, which they use for royal births nowadays, although Edward's mother, who came to dinner tonight, disapproves of the practice, and says it's God's will that children come into the world through pain and suffering. Pointed out medical science now strongly in favour of alleviating pain of childbirth—better for both mother and baby—at which she said I was being indelicate and supposed it came of mixing with writers and artists in Bloomsbury.

Suspect Edward of being of the same opinion as his mamma. He has a lot of opinions, Edward—most of them disagreeable. Wish I had known about all his opinions before marrying him.

10th November 1899
We have been discussing names for the babies, although Edward's mother says it tempts Providence, and that pride goeth before a fall.

Still, Edward thinks George and William will suit very nicely, since these both good English names, none of this foreign rubbish. Sounded exactly like Mrs Tigg when she orders in household supplies. A nice saddle of English lamb for Sunday, madam, I thought that would suit very nicely, she says.

At a pinch, Edward will concede George and Alice for the twins, since a daughter always a pleasant thing to have, and if the name Alice good enough for Her Majesty's daughter, good enough for a Quinton.

Asked him what about Georgina and Alice, to which he said, Oh nonsense, my dear, you're built for bearing boys, anyone can see that. Hate it when Edward is bluff and head-patting! Pointed out crossly that am actually quite slim-hipped and strongly object to being regarded as brood mare anyway, to which he wondered huffily what the world was coming to when a wife could make such a very unbecoming remark, and said his mother had been quite right when she said I was indelicate at times. Told him I thought it unbecoming and indelicate for husband to discuss wife with mother.

Sulky silence all through supper as result of this. Would not have thought it possible for anyone to sulk while eating steak and kidney pudding and steamed treacle sponge, but Edward managed it.

Question: What am I doing married to a selfish and self-centred turkey cock who sulks at supper?

Answer: Being revenged on Floy. (Who does not, I fear, give a damn what I'm doing any longer.)

Answer adjudged correct in all particulars. And if there really were pathways into the future, I would never [underlined three times] have succumbed to Floy's silver-tongued seduction.

CHAPTER TWO

Except that the drinks were better than he had expected and the food more plentiful, the opening of Thorne's gallery was almost exactly as Harry had predicted. Expensively voiced people milling around and murmuring things about paintings. Females covertly pricing each other's outfits. Good lighting and nicely grained wooden floorboards.

There were no dismembered sheep or flayed corpses, and no unseemly displays of avant-garde or existentialism, in fact some of the paintings were rather good.

Whatever the house had been in its previous incarnations it lent itself very well to its present existence. It was a tall narrow building and either Angelica Thorne's taste was more restrained than her legend suggested or the London Planners had wielded a heavy hand, because the outside had hardly been tampered with at all. The paintings appeared to be grouped on the ground floor with the photographs upstairs. Harry made a few suggestions to the photographer he had brought with him, and then left him to get on with it.

There were quite a few decorative females around—Harry spotted Angelica Thorne early on. She appeared to

9

be embracing the Bloomsbury ambience with the fervour of a convert; either that or someone had recently told her she resembled a Burne-Jones painting, because the hair was unmistakably pre-Raphaelite—a corrugated riot of burnished copper—and the outfit was suggestive of flowing cravats and velvet tea-gowns.

Of Simone Marriot, or anyone who might conceivably be Simone Marriot, there was no sign. Harry propped himself up against a door-frame and scribbled down a few semi-famous names more or less at random to keep Markovitch sweet, and to let people know that he was press and might therefore be expected to behave errati-cally. After this he helped himself to another glass of Chablis and went up to the second floor.

There were not so many people at this level. That might be because it was still early in the evening and they had not yet permeated this far, or it might be that the wine was still flowing downstairs, or it might even be that the wine had flowed a bit too well for most of them already and the narrow open stairway presented an awkward challenge. ('Break my neck by falling downstairs in front of Angelica Thorne's upmarket cronies? Not likely,' most of them had probably said.)

But even after several glasses of wine Harry nego-tiated the stairway easily enough. He came around the last tortuous spiral and stepped out on to the second floor which had the same pleasing Regency windows as downstairs. There was even a view of the British Museum through one of them. Nice. He began to move slowly along the line of framed prints.

There were two surprises.

The first was the photographs themselves. They were very good indeed and they were thought-provoking in rather a disturbing way. A lot of them used the device of illusion, so that at first glance an image appeared to be ordinary and unthreatening, but when you looked again it presented an entirely different image. Nothing's quite as it seems in any of them, thought Harry, pausing in front of a shot of a darkened room with brooding shapes that might have been shrouded furniture, but that might as easily be something more sinister. The outline of tree branches beyond a window formed themselves into prison-bars and one branch had broken away and hung down, giving the false image of a coiled rope, knotted into what might be a hanging noose. Harry stared at this last one for a long time, the noise of the party fading out.

'Do you like that one?' said a voice at his side. 'It isn't exactly my favourite, but it's not bad. Oh—I should explain that I'm not trying to pick you up or anything. I'm Simone Marriot and this is my bit of Thorne's Gallery so I'm meant to be circulating and making intelligent conversation to the guests.'

Simone Marriot was the second surprise of the evening.

'I thought you looked as if you might be easier to talk to than most of the others,' she said. 'I'm not sure why I thought that.'

They were sitting on one of the narrow windowsills by this time, with the sun setting somewhere beyond the skyline and the scents of the old house warm all around them. The party downstairs seemed to be breaking up, and Angelica Thorne's voice could be heard organizing some of them into a sub-party for a late dinner somewhere.

Simone had longish dark brown hair with glinting red lights in it, cut in layers so that it curved round to frame her face. She wore an anonymous dark sweater over a plain, narrow-fitting skirt, with black lace-up boots, and the only touch of colour was a long tasselled silk scarf wound around her neck, in a vivid jade green. At first look there was nothing very outstanding about her, she was small and thin and Harry thought she was very nearly plain. But when she began to talk about the photographs he revised his opinion. Her eyes—which were the same colour as the silk scarf—glowed with enthusiasm, lighting up her whole face, and when she smiled it showed a tiny chip in her front tooth that made her look unexpectedly *gamine*. Harry found himself wanting to see her smile again.

'I like your work very much,' he said. 'Although some of it makes me feel uneasy.'

'Such as the barred window and the tree that might be a hangman's noose?'

'Yes. But I like the way you identify the darkness in things, and then let just a fragment of it show through. In most of the shots you've disguised it as something else though. A tree branch, or a piece of furniture, or a shadow.'

Simone looked pleased but she only said, 'I like finding a subject and then seeing if there's a dark underside.'

'Isn't there a dark underside in most things?'

She looked at him as if unsure whether he was baiting her. But she seemed satisfied that he was not; she said, 'Yes, in almost everything, isn't there? That's the really interesting part for me: shooting the darkness.'

'Can I see the photographs again? With you as guide this time?'

'Yes, of course. Hold on, I'll refill your glass first.'

She hopped down from the windowsill. She was not especially graceful, but she was intensely watchable and Harry suddenly wondered if she had inherited the quality that had put that wistful note into Markovitch's voice when he spoke of her mother.

They moved along the line of framed photos together. 'I like comparing the kempt and the unkempt as well,' said Simone. 'When I was doing this sequence over here—'

'National Trust versus derelict squats.'

'Yes. Yes. When I was doing those I saved the really decrepit shots for the last. Like when you're a child and you eat the crust of a fruit pie first and save the squidgy fruit bit for last. This one's Powys Castle. It's one of the old border fortresses and parts of it have hardly changed since the thirteen-hundreds. It's beautiful, isn't it? Ruined but glossily ruined, and the ruins are being nicely preserved so there's a bit of the past that's caught and frozen for ever.'

'And then to balance it you've got this.'

He thought she hesitated for a second, but then she said, 'That's a seventeenth- or eighteenth-century mansion. It's meant to illustrate the past dying—the place has been neglected for years, in fact it's decaying where it stands. Actually, it's a vanity thing to have included that one—it's a shot I took when I was about twelve with my very first camera and I always felt a bit sentimental about it. But I thought it was just about good enough to include as contrast in this sequence.'

'It is good enough. Where is it?' said Harry, leaning closer to see the title.

'It's called Mortmain House,' said Simone. 'It's on the edge of Shropshire—the western boundary, just about where England crosses over into Wales. I lived there for a while as a child.'

'Mortmain. Dead hand?'

'Yes. Somewhere around the Middle Ages people used to transfer land to the Church so their children wouldn't have to pay feudal dues after they died. Then the heirs reclaimed the land afterwards. It was a pretty good scam until people tumbled to what was happening, so a law was drawn up to prevent it—the law of dead man's hand it's sometimes called and— Am I talking too much?'

'No, I'm interested. It looks,' said Harry, his eyes still on the place Simone had called Mortmain House, 'exactly like the classic nightmare mansion.'

'It does rather, doesn't it?' Her voice was just a bit too casual. 'I haven't exaggerated its appearance, though. It really does look like that.'

'Filled with darkness? With nightmares?'

'Well, nightmares are subjective, aren't they? We've all got a private one.'

Harry looked down at her. The top of her head was about level with his shoulder. He said, '"I could be bounded in a nutshell and still count myself a king of infinite space, were it not that I have bad dreams."'

'Yes. *Yes.*' She smiled, as if pleased to find that he understood, and Harry wondered what she would do if he said, 'We all have a secret nightmare, but what you don't know, my dear, is that I'm here to see if I can wind back Time or find a pathway into the past...'

He did not say it, of course. Never blow your cover unless it's a question of life or death.

He said, 'Is it a particular quality of yours to see the darknesses in life?'

Simone hoped she had not banged on for too long about darknesses and Mortmain House and everything, to the journalist from the *Bellman*. But he had seemed to understand—he had quoted that bit about nightmares—and he had appeared genuinely interested.

So it was vaguely daunting when Angelica, conducting a breathless post-mortem on the opening two days later, reported that Harry Fitzglen had phoned to ask her out to dinner.

'How nice.' Simone refused to be jealous of Angelica, who was giving her this terrific opportunity. People hardly ever mentioned Angelica without adding, 'She's *the* Angelica Thorne, you know—one of the real *It* girls in the Nineties. Dozens of lovers and scores of the most extraordinary parties. There's not much she hasn't tried,' they said. But one of the things that Angelica was trying now was being a patron of the arts, and one of the people she was patronizing was Simone, and for all Simone cared Angelica could have tried necromancy and cannibalism. She refused to be jealous because Harry Fitzglen was taking Angelica out to dinner, even when Angelica, smiling the smile that made her look like a mischievous cat, said they were going to Aubergine in Chelsea.

'If he can afford Aubergine, he must be pretty successful.'

'I like successful. In fact—Oh God, is this the electricity bill for the first quarter? Well, it can't possibly be right—look at the *total*! We can't have used all that heating, do they think we're *orchids* or something, for pity's sake!'

They were in the upstairs office in the Bloomsbury gallery. Simone loved this narrow sliver of a building, tucked away in a tiny London square, surrounded by small, smart PR companies, and hopeful new publishing houses, and unexpected bits of the University or the Museum that seemed to have become detached from their main buildings and taken up residence in convenient corners. The office was small because they had partitioned it off from the rest of the attic floor, wanting to keep as much gallery space as they could, but from up here you could see across rooftops and just glimpse a corner of the British Museum, a bit blurry because the windows of the house were the original ones and they had become wavy with age.

Simone liked the scents of the house as well, which despite the renovations were still the scents of an earlier era. In the late 1800s and early 1900s Bloomsbury had been the fashionable place for what people called intellectuals—writers and painters and poets. There were times when she had the feeling that it might be possible to look through a chink somewhere and glimpse the house's past, and see them all in their candlelit rooms, discussing and arguing and working—No, it would not have been candlelight by then, it would have been gaslight. Not quite so romantic.

Still, it would be nice to trace the house's history; Simone would love to know the kind of people who had lived here when it had been an ordinary private house. She and Angelica might set up a small display about it: they might even find some old photographs that could be restored. Would Harry Fitzglen have access to old newspaper archives and photographic agencies? Could Angelica be asked to sound him out about it? Angelica was enthusiastic about Thorne's but the enthusiasm might not stretch to discussing marketing strategies with a new man.

Simone studied Angelica covertly. Today she was wearing the newly acquired glasses with huge tortoise-shell-framed spectacles. She did not need them but they were part of her new image. Simone thought they made her look like a very sexy Oxford don; she thought only Angelica could have managed to look both sexy and studious at the same time, and she suddenly wanted to make a portrait photograph of her, to see if she could show both moods at the same time. Would Harry Fitzglen see these two aspects of Angelica when he took her out, and if so which one would he prefer? He would prefer the sexy side, of course. Men always did.

Or would he? He had been far more intelligent than he had let on at the opening and much more perceptive; Simone had known that almost straight off. Even without that Shakespeare quote about bad dreams he had seen the darkness within Mortmain, although anyone with halfway normal eyesight would probably have done so. But that question he had put about Simone herself seeing the darkness had put him in another category altogether because as far as she knew no one else had ever sensed the presence of darkness in her own mind.

No one had ever known about the little girl who watched her.

She had been four years old when she became aware of this inner darkness, and she had been a bit over five when she began to understand where it came from.

The other little girl. The unseen, unheard child whom no one else could see or hear, but who lay coiled and invisible inside Simone's mind. Simone did not know her name so she just called her the little girl.

To begin with it had not been anything to be especially frightened or anxious about. Simone had not even known that other people did not have this invisible companion to talk to. And she quite liked having this other little girl around; she liked the sudden ruffling of her mind that meant the little girl was there, and she liked talking to her and listening to some of her stories which were really good. Simone liked stories; she liked people to read them out of books, although not everybody read them in the right way.

Mother always read them in the right way. Simone liked listening to Mother, and she liked watching her when she read. Her voice was rather soft and everyone thought she was quiet and gentle—people at school said, Gosh, what a great mother to have, isn't she a pushover for things?—but Simone's mother was not a pushover at all. She made rules about not watching too much television, and about homework and bedtime at seven o'clock every night, but everyone said this was what most mothers did. And Simone was pretty lucky not to have lots of boring relations because you had to be polite to them, and sometimes there were cousins who came to stay and you had to give up your bed, or uncles who had too much to drink and aunts who got cross. It was not so great having lots of family.

But Simone would have quite liked some family, and so when the little girl said, 'I'll be your family,' she was pleased.

The other little girl did not have to do the same things as Simone. She did not seem to go to school although she had lessons at a table and she had to learn a lot of things by heart. Simone did not get to know this all at once; it came in bits, like a series of pictures coming inside her head, or like the nights when she could not sleep and kept hearing snatches of the television from downstairs but not enough to know the programme or recognize the voices. She always knew when the little girl was there, because there was the feeling of something ruffling her mind, like when you blew on the surface of water and made it ripple.

Once she tried making a drawing of the little girl. This was a bit spooky because it turned out to be much easier than Simone had expected. As she drew, the girl's face got steadily clearer, like polishing the surface of a smoky, smeary old mirror until at last you saw your reflection.

The girl's face looked straight up out of the paper. Simone thought it was what people called a heart-shaped face, and she thought the girl ought to have been quite pretty. But she was not. She had a sly look, which made Simone feel uncomfortable and even a bit frightened. Until then she had been quite pleased with the drawing but when she saw the sly eyes she scrunched the paper up and threw it in the dustbin when Mother was not looking. But even then she had the feeling that the eyes were still watching her through the thrown-away bits of food and tea-leaves.

Extract from Charlotte Quinton's diaries:
30th November 1899
Edward points out that if calculations are all accu-

rate, the twins may be born on 1st January 1900, and thinks this a good omen. Has even gone so far as to make a little joke about that night in March after your birthday dinner, my dear, which is the kind of remark he normally regards as rather near. Clearly I'm being viewed with indulgence at the moment. It will be God's mercy if it lasts.

But a new year and a new century and two new lives, Edward says, pleased at having coined this neat phrase by himself. He adds, expansively, perhaps a new house, as well, what do I think? Some very nice villas out at Dulwich.

Saw copy of Floy's latest book in Hatchard's while shopping this morning. Horrid shock since dozens of them were displayed in the window, and especially a shock since photograph of Floy in middle of it all. He looked as if he had been dragged protesting into the photographer's studio for the likeness to be taken. Highly upsetting to come upon image of ex-lover staring angrily out of Hatchard's window.

Came straight home and went to bed, telling Edward I felt sick and dizzy. Felt dreadfully guilty when he insisted on calling Dr Austin out, since could hardly explain real reason for sickness and dizziness in first place.

Had to endure excruciating examination, although must admit Dr Austin v. gentlemanly and impersonal. It will teach me not to tell untruths, however. He prodded around and measured my hips, and asked some questions, then looked portentous, but said, oh nothing to worry about, Mrs Quinton, and he would send round a mixture for the sickness.

Edward's mother to dinner tonight (third time this month!), which meant one of Edward's mother's homilies. This one was to the effect that I am racketing about town too much, and rest is important in my condition.

Told her high time science found a less inconvenient and messy method of reproducing after all these thousands of years, and was accused of being Darwinian and having peculiar reading habits—also of scamping on housekeeping since first course was eggs in sunlight, and the tomato sauce was pronounced too acidic. Not surprising I feel sick if this is the kind of dish I allow on my dinner table... And on and on.

Went to bed in bad temper. Will not buy Floy's book, absolutely will not...

Later
Sent out to Hatchard's for Floy's book on principle that better to read it and be prepared before anyone tries to discomfit me by telling me about it. Have always suspected that Wyvern-Smith female of trying to sink her claws into Floy on her own account, and do not trust her not to drop the subject into dinner-table conversation out of sheer malice. Edward's mother says she dyes her hair—Clara Wyvern-Smith that is, not Edward's mother. Would not be at all surprised, although wonder how Edward's mother knows.

6th December 1899
Think something may be wrong. Dr Austin downstairs in earnest conclave with Edward earlier, although when I asked if anything wrong, all Dr Austin would say was that he thought the twins were a little quiet, considering how near to the confinement we are.

However, Edward has gone off to his managers' meeting as usual, telling me not to wait up since he may be late. He may be as late as he likes for all I care.

9th December 1899

Floy's book brilliant. Have had to read it piecemeal and in secrecy in case anyone sees and wonders, and it is not the kind of book that should be read like that. Should be read in one glorious sweeping read, so that you shut the rest of the world out while you walk through the landscapes that Floy unfolds, all of which are like glowing jewel-studded tapestries unfurling silkily across your inner vision. It's about lost loves and relinquished passions, and a heroine who struggles between duty and love... Have not dared wonder, even for a second, if Floy wrote it after that last agonizing scene, when I told him I must stay with Edward and he called me a middle-class provincial-minded conformist, which is about the most stinging string of epithets Floy can bestow.

(I'm lying, of course. I spent the rest of the night wondering furiously if he wrote it after we parted.)

But whenever it was written, Floy has—and always will have, I think—a gift for making his readers feel that he has invited them into a soft, secret world, glowing with dappled afternoon sunlight or golden lamp-light, with siren songs humming under old casement windows, and sexual stirrings and erotic whisperings everywhere. And that the reader is there alone with him, and that it's a wholly enchanted place to be...

Refuse to apologize for that burst of sentiment, since if cannot be sentimental about a lost love, not much point to life.

12th December

What a delight to have an excuse for handing over the Christmas and New Year preparations to Mrs Tigg and Maisie-the-daisie! Also to avoid unutterably tedious dinners with Edward's business colleagues— 'Dreadfully sorry, don't quite feel up to formal entertaining this year. What with the birth imminent— feeling wretchedly tired—sure you'll understand.'

'A quiet Christmas,' Edward has told everyone. 'Charlotte is not feeling quite the thing.'

Charlotte is feeling very much not the thing, especially when it comes to interminable dinner parties with eight courses and the conversation exclusively about politics, banking, or scandalous behaviour of Prince of Wales. Last Christmas one of Edward's managers stroked my thigh under the tablecloth.

Ridiculous and pointless to wonder how Floy will spend Christmas. Do people in Bloomsbury have Christmas, one wonders? Or do they sit around earnestly and paganly discussing life and love and art (or Art), like they did on the one occasion when Floy took me to someone's studio, and we all ate Italian food and drank Chianti, and somebody asked to paint me only Floy objected because he said the man was a bad leftover from the Pre-Raphaelites, and I was so beautiful no painter in the world could possibly capture my looks...

All flummery and soft soap, of course, I know that now. Even so, spent most of the evening remembering Floy's house in Bloomsbury, with the scents of old timbers and the incense he burns when he is working because he says it stimulates his brain...

And the night he lit dozens of candles in his bedroom and we made wild love there, with the sounds of London all around us and the distant view of the British Museum from the window.

Wonder if Floy will be stroking anyone's thigh under tablecloth at Christmas?

Later

Am increasingly worried about that remark of Dr Austin's that the twins are a little quiet. Do not want them leaping around like the Russian ballet, but would feel better if they were a bit more assertive.

If everyone's calculations right, only a couple of weeks left now.

CHAPTER THREE

SIMONE WAS NINE when she discovered the word 'possession', which was not a word she had ever heard before. She asked Mother about it, doing so in a carefully casual voice, and Mother said that once upon a time there had been a belief that a person's mind could be taken over by another person's mind, but it was not true, of course, and where on earth had Simone picked that one up?

'Um, just in a book. It isn't true, then? About people's minds being taken over?'

Mother said it was very definitely not true. It was simply an old-fashioned superstition, and Simone did not need to be thinking or worrying about such things.

Mother was pretty clever, but Simone knew she was wrong to say that possession was only a superstition. She knew that the little girl who lived partly inside her own mind was trying to possess her. Sometimes she appeared in scary dreams, and took Simone's hands and tried to pull Simone into her own world.

'For company,' she said. 'You'd be my friend, and I'd never be on my own again. Wouldn't you like that? We'd be together for always.'

But Simone thought she would not like it at all because each time the dreams came she had glimpses of that other world, and she had glimpses of the place where the little girl seemed to live. It was a bit puzzling; there were cold stone floors and grim-faced people, and clanging iron doors that were locked at precisely the same time each night. In some complicated way the little girl seemed to have lived in the black cold place for practically her whole life. Simone did not really understand this, because she did not think people lived in houses like that these days.

To begin with she had thought the black stone house might be a prison, but then she thought that children did not get put in prisons. It might be a hospital, except that hospitals were clean sharp places, full of light and busy brisk people; Simone knew that on account of once having to go to hospital when she fell off her bike. She had had to have her leg stitched up and they had given her an anti-tetanus shot, and the nurse who had done it had said, in a bright voice, Dear goodness, what were those marks on her left side, they were surely not scars, were they?—and in an offhand voice that Simone thought she was not meant to hear, Mother had said something about a difficult birth. But she had thought later on that the nurse was a bit dim not to know about birthmarks, which Mother said lots of people had; it was not a particularly big deal although it was probably better to be a bit discreet about when Simone went swimming or changed for games at school.

The black stone house where the little girl seemed to live was not bright or brisk, and the people who lived there did not talk in that over-bright, slightly false kind of way. But wherever it was it was becoming gradually clearer to Simone, just as the little girl was becoming gradually clearer.

It was quite difficult to imagine what it must be like to live in one place all your entire life. Simone and Mother had moved around and lived in quite a lot of different places, and each time they went to a new house Mother said, 'There, now we're nicely settled,' but they never were, and after a time—it might be quite a long time but sometimes it was only a few months—the frightened look came back into Mother's eyes and they were off again, looking for somewhere else and packing things up, and choosing another town.

The little girl knew about the moving around, because she knew about most things Simone did. She did not wholly understand this part of Simone's life, but she said that if Simone moved so often one day she should come to live near her. Simone could fix that, couldn't she? It was usually pretty easy to fix things with grown-ups. There was an impression of some strong dislike about this— Simone thought the word was contempt, as if the little girl did not much like grown-ups. As if she liked getting the better of them.

'Yes, I do like getting the better of them,' she said. 'If you come to live here, I can tell you properly about that. We can be really together then. That would be extra specially good, wouldn't it?'

The little girl lived in a place called the Welsh Marches, she said—it was the part where England began to be Wales. Simone had never heard of it, and she was not sure if she wanted to live as near as all that to the little girl; she thought she might be a bit frightened of her.

But she looked up the Welsh Marches in her school atlas and asked a question about it in geography one day. It sounded pretty good. There had been a lot of battles between people who wanted to protect Wales and people who wanted to take it over, which was interesting. And the Welsh people had written a great many ballads and poems and beautiful music about their history, said the teacher, pleased with Simone's interest. They might have a lesson specially about it next week, and they might make it their term-project as well if everyone agreed. Simone had done very well to raise such an interesting topic.

Simone told Mother about the project, and about thinking it might be a good place to live one day, and Mother said, vaguely, 'Oh, I don't think we're going to move again, Sim. I really think we're all right here, don't you?'

Simone knew they were not all right; she knew that one day Mother would start to get the anxious look again, and she would start glancing through the windows of their house after it got dark as if she was worried that somebody was watching, and asking Simone questions about whether there had been any strangers roaming around the school gates. It might not happen until next year, or it might happen next week, but it would happen in the end because it always did.

Harry Fitzglen finished the article on Angelica Thorne's gallery opening, and smacked the printer crossly into action.

He had praised the gallery, referring to 'the newest, but potentially most successful toy of ex-socialite and *It* girl, Angelica Thorne'; had mentioned the attractive ambience of the Bloomsbury house and had even added a couple of sentences about Bloomsbury's academic provenance, along with a deliberately off-hand reference to William de Blemont's original thirteenth-century manor of Blemondsbury. This was intended to make the *Bellman*'s readers feel pleasantly intellectual, although to balance things out he had also sprinkled the article with mentions of the famous and the rich who had been present, and had even sent photo-proofs to the *Bellman*'s Women's Page editor, so that the outfits worn by the merely infamous and rich could have the correct designer labels attached to their outfits. To gratify Markovitch he had woven in the names of a few of Angelica Thorne's former lovers, although he had omitted to mention the disgraced MP and the multi-millionaire press baron, since both were currently bringing writs for libel against several newspapers.

After this, he had put in a couple of paragraphs about Simone Marriot's photographs, which would probably be subbed out but which were the best part of the whole thing. As the printer churned out the pages he wondered what had happened to his own idealistic self of ten or twelve years earlier: the young man who had read John Donne and Keats, and planned to write a Booker-winning novel. He fell in with the wrong females and then he fell into the slough of despond, that's what happened to him, remember? He drowned in a vat of Glenfiddich, like Richard III's brother in the malmsey butt.

Still, the article was well-written, he knew that without any false vanity. Once upon a time he had been a very good features writer, he knew that without any false vanity as well. Dammit, he had been better than good. He had believed in what he was doing and he had liked his life and thought it worthwhile, until the day he had come home early to discover a letter from Amanda propped up on the mantelpiece, saying she was leaving him, she was in love with someone else, and she knew Harry would not want her to live a lie any longer. It was better to have truth between them, wasn't it, and she knew he would want her happiness.

This was such all-out and overwhelming balls that Harry had crumpled up the letter in fury, thrown it across the room, and headed for the bottle of Scotch. It had only been when the bottle was almost empty that he had retrieved the letter and smoothed it out to read that Amanda would allow him to divorce her for adultery, and that to defray her current living expenses she had drawn a cheque on their joint deposit account. The cheque, Harry later discovered, was for almost the entire amount in the deposit account and was apparently intended to help Amanda to live through the difficult weeks between the divorce and the remarriage. That she elected to live through those weeks in a flat in an upmarket part of Hampstead did not come as any particular surprise.

What did come as a surprise was that everyone except Harry himself had apparently known who was sleeping in his bed, never mind waking up to eat the porridge. Half of Fleet Street, it seemed, had been sniggering over what Goldilocks was doing, and most of them could have supplied a list of who she was doing it with as well, in fact quite a few of them were actually on the list themselves.

That had been the point at which Harry had gone on that spectacular month-long binge, missing most of his deadlines, and turning up half-cut to interview some blonde airhead starlet who was not so airheaded that she did not know how to complain to a managing director and get Harry fired from the more-than-reputable Sunday broadsheet where he had worked for five years, and where he had been due to be made assistant features editor with a breathlessly eager assistant of his own and a share in a secretary.

But like the famous women's lib anthem, he had survived. He had made of Amanda's new husband a figure of ridicule. Absolutely inorganic, he told people. A Trivial Pursuit. And even though he had hit rock bottom hard enough to crack the cement he had eventually started the long climb back into a career, although it was a pity the climb had had to begin on the staff of the *Bellman*.

Since then he had steadfastly avoided beautiful females who thought their looks absolved them from worrying about intelligence or personality or sensitivity, and who invariably ran off with richer, more satisfactory lovers.

But if they were talking about beautiful females with rich lovers...

Harry thought he would have been less than human not to get a kick from walking into Aubergine with Angelica Thorne. She was wearing a mulberry velvet outfit with a very short skirt, and her legs, which were extremely good, were encased in black stockings. No, they would be tights, not stockings. Or would they? It was to be hoped this did not prove a distraction; Harry reminded himself firmly that this was a ruse to find out about Simone and therefore a working dinner, and was rewarded by an inner derisive hoot.

The waiters recognized Angelica of course, and leapt to provide menus and wine-lists, and to enquire whether the table was satisfactory. Would another table be preferred? No, it was no trouble in the least. I'm spending money like a drunken sailor, thought Harry, and what's worse, I'm spending money I haven't got.

Angelica talked enthusiastically on the gallery and on the run-up to its opening. 'For one thing it took ages to find the right place, you can't imagine the prices of property in London, well, I daresay you can—where did you say you lived? Oh, I see. Oh, rather fun out there, I should think.'

'A riot. Tell me about finding the house.'

'Well, it had to be the right part of London, because—oh, they're doing partridge au choux tonight, let's have that, shall we?—because the thing is that you can't have a gallery in the East India Dock Road or Whitechapel, can you? Well, I know there's the Spitalfields concerts these days and they're very successful, but I think that might be an exception.'

'But you found the Bloomsbury house,' said Harry.

'Simone found it. She said we absolutely had to have it, never mind what it cost. As a matter of fact,' said Angelica, 'she was quite intense about it.' She broke off to eat the pâté that was the first course. She ate with a kind of hungry sensuality; Harry watched her and remembered the black stockings. He waited, and after a moment Angelica said, 'I don't mean to go all Edgar Allan Poe or Susan Hill about her, but at times I wonder if Simone might be—well, wired in to something the rest of us aren't.'

'You don't mean drugs, do you?'

'No, not drugs, I'm fairly sure she doesn't take anything. But she picks up atmospheres and things.'

'Atmospheres?'

'Yes. I think she's a bit telepathic as well—that can be frightfully disconcerting sometimes.'

'I should think it might.'

'I've always supposed it comes of being a twin,' said Angelica, and Harry looked at her. After a moment, he said, in a voice carefully devoid of all expression, 'She's a twin, is she?'

'Yes, although she never mentions it. I don't know what happened to the twin—I think she—or it might even have been a he—must have died.'

People died and people disappeared, Markovitch had said.

'I've sometimes thought Simone feels a bit incomplete because of it,' said Angelica, and Harry, who had been re-filling the wine glasses, glanced up, because this was an unexpectedly shrewd remark.

He said, carefully, 'Twins do have an amazingly strong link, of course.'

'Yes, and— Oh, this is very good wine, Harry. And Simone was right about the house, of course. It's absolutely perfect. In fact she wondered—'

'Yes?'

'I do hate to mix business with pleasure,' said Angelica semi-apologetically, and Harry smiled at her and thought, Oh, no you don't, my dear. You'd mix anything you felt like mixing.

'Simone wondered if you might be able to dig up something about its history,' said Angelica. 'It's smack in the middle of where the aesthetes used to gather, isn't it? In the eighteen-nineties and the early nineteen-hundreds. Earnest young men with soft shirts and brooding eyes and metaphysical conversation. I don't mean we want to nail up labels saying Isadora Duncan danced on this table or a plaque saying Oscar Wilde slept here, but Simone thought if anything interesting had happened in the place or if anyone famous had lived there she could set up a display. Old photos and newspaper cuttings and so on. She's very good at that kind of thing, you know. The past shadowing the present.'

'I know she is.' Finding out about the house's past would mean another link to Angelica and—more to the point—to Simone herself. Harry said, 'I'll see what I can find.'

'Would you? We'd be so grateful.' Angelica managed to make it sound as if her gratitude might come in a very alluring form indeed. Harry mentally calculated how much his credit card was good for and ordered a second bottle of wine anyway.

'Did you actually buy the house?' Because if Angelica had been able to outright buy a house in that part of London she must be even wealthier than the tabloids said.

'No, we took over a lease. The freeholder's one of those property management companies—all very efficient, but hydra-headed, and so faceless. Can you be hydra-headed and faceless both together?' She studied the dessert trolley which was just being trundled past.

'Do have whatever you'd like,' said Harry.

'As a matter of fact,' she said, resting her chin on her cupped hand and gazing at him with sudden intensity, 'what I'd really like is to adjourn to my flat for coffee.' Harry stared at her. 'What do you think?' said Angelica and her voice slid down an octave into a sexy purr. Harry felt as if she had stroked the inside of his thigh with a velvet-covered hand. Angelica smiled. 'Or would you rather stay here for pudding?'

'I think,' said Harry, finally disentangling himself from the smile, 'that I'd rather go to your flat.'

'For pudding?'

'Perhaps for a just desert.'

Angelica set a pot of coffee to filter as soon as they got into the flat, and put out a bottle of brandy and two glasses. The kitchen was so small that avoiding physical contact was impossible so Harry did not bother to avoid it.

She was clearly delighted at the approach. She was taller than most girls (those legs), and she moved forward at once so that they were pressed hard together. Her mouth opened under his, and for several minutes they stood locked thigh to thigh in an increasingly passionate embrace, and then Harry began to slide his hands questioningly beneath the luxurious dark red velvet. Angelica gasped with delight, and reached down to pull at her skirt. There was the snapping open of buttons, and a rustle of sound as the skirt slid to the floor. She stepped out of it and kicked it out of the way—Harry retained just enough mental equilibrium to think it took terrific style to treat designer clothes like that. And practice, said a sneaky voice.

It was stockings after all, rather than tights. They were held up by garters and she was wearing silk underwear.

As she pulled him back into the living-room, towards the deep sofa at one end, he was aware that the coffee had filtered and switched itself off. But presumably they could always drink instant coffee afterwards.

It was almost three a.m. before he went out into the odd half-world of the extreme early morning. He picked up a cruising taxi near Holland Park which took him home. In the morning—the real morning, when the world was up and about its lawful occasions—he would send flowers to Angelica. 'Thank you for a memorable evening,' he would say on the card. She would smile the wry cat-smile at that.

After he had done that he would tell Markovitch that he was following a number of promising leads and that they had better regard his working hours as flexible for a week or two, and then he would see what he could find about the Bloomsbury house and its previous owners. Angelica had said that Simone had been 'intense' about leasing it for Thorne's. 'She picks up atmospheres,' Angelica had said. What had Simone picked up about the house that had made her so passionate about it? As he got into bed he was aware of Angelica's scent still clinging faintly to his hair, but it was not Angelica he was thinking about as he switched out the light; it was Simone.

It ought not to have given him such a jolt when Angelica had made that reference to Simone being a twin.

CHAPTER FOUR

Twins. IT HAD given Melissa Anderson a consider-
able jolt to hear the word, but it had been a very pleasurable
jolt. *Twins.*

'And first off, as far as we can tell, they're both developing at a normal rate,' said Martin Brannan, regarding
her from behind his desk. He was rather nice-looking:
dark-haired and with a kind of enthusiastic intensity, and
he was a lot younger than Mel had expected. He might be
in his early thirties, but no more than that.

'But?'

He had not moved, but he looked as if he might
mentally be taking a deep breath, like a man about to
plunge into something dark and cold and unpleasant.
Mel waited, and then in a voice that managed to be both
professionally detached and humanely compassionate,
Martin Brannan said, 'Mrs Anderson, they're joined.'

Joined?' Mel did not immediately take this in. 'I don't— Oh.
Oh God, *joined.* You mean—like Siamese twins, don't you?'

'Well, we don't call them that any more. We call it
conjoining.'

Mel did not care what it was called. She was aware
of a rushing sound in her ears, but she fought it back

because she would not faint like some helpless wimp, she absolutely would not—

The thing to do was establish the facts—even to write everything down. Joe would want to know details when she got home; he would ask a great many questions and be annoyed if Mel could not supply the answers. The trouble was that she did not think she could hold a pen at the moment, never mind write decipherable notes.

But after a moment she was able to say, 'You can do something about it, can't you? There are operations—' You heard about the operations on TV. Lots of publicity, heart-breaking photographs, newscasters talking in hushed voices, and gruesome reports of eight- and twelve-hour operations. Sometimes one child died at the expense of the other. Sometimes both of them died. And all of it unbearable for the parents. But now I might actually be one of those parents. And Joe? said her mind uneasily. How is Joe going to react to this?

Martin Brannan said, 'We can't see as far ahead as an operation, yet. Don't let's jump any guns. I expect you know that identical twins develop from a single fertilized egg, don't you? And they're always same-sex children for that reason. One theory for conjoined twins is simply that the developing embryo starts to split but stops before the split is quite complete.'

Mel supposed she did know this, in a general sense.

'We don't know why that happens yet—although one day we will. Your GP had a suspicion that something wasn't quite as it should be, which is why he sent you to me. It's why we've done the scan a bit earlier than normal, as well. So, now, the scan indicates that your twins are joined at the chest, fairly high up. That's what we call thoracopagus twins.'

'They're face to face?' Mel had a swift mental image of the twins curled tightly into a silent embrace.

'No, not exactly,' he said. 'The join is at the side. Fairly high up—around the ribcage.'

'Side by side.'

'Yes. The images show that the limbs are all separate and free, though. Does that make you feel any better? It should do, because it makes me feel a whole lot better, I promise. And there seem to be two heart shadows, so they aren't sharing a single heart—that's always a massive concern with thoracopagus twins.'

'How good a chance that there are separate hearts?'

'A lot better than good.'

'And the bad side of things?' I'm doing quite well, thought Mel. I'm being calm and logical, and I'm not embarrassing him with hysterics or faints or anything. But she was aware of a churning panic, and she thought that panic, after today, would smell of the lavender air-freshener somebody had sprayed around this office and the geranium plants that somebody had put on the windowsill to catch the sun.

Brannan took a minute to reply. 'There's some fusion of the scapula,' he said. 'Around the clavicle—about here.' He indicated the area just inside his shoulder. 'It's not a large area though, and we ought to be able to deal with it. They'll both have a massive scar afterwards, of course, but we might do a skin graft when they're older.' He studied her thoughtfully, and Mel was deeply grateful to him for talking as if it was a foregone conclusion that the twins were going to survive the birth and have the operation, and that they were going to grow up to reach ages where skin grafts could be done.

'It could be so much worse, you know.'

'It could?'

'Oh yes,' he said, and there was such conviction in his voice that Mel believed him, and did not want to know all the so-much-worse things that she might have had to cope with.

'Will you—you will be able to separate them all right, won't you?'

'It'll be a difficult and dangerous procedure,' said Brannan. 'Because there's some bone involved—possibly tendons and muscle as well—the separation might leave some damage to one of them. Not necessarily, but possibly.' He leaned forward. 'Listen, though, you're going to hear all kinds of conflicting statistics and stories over the next few months—try to ignore most of them, or ask me for the real information. And remember that thoracopagus twins are by far the easiest to deal with, and that as a rule of thumb more than seventy-five per cent do survive separation.'

'Both twins?'

'You're jumping guns again,' he said, and then, before Mel could deal with this one, said, 'D'you want to know the sex of the twins, at all?'

There, not for the first time, was the faintest trace of Irish in his voice. Nice. 'Are you allowed to tell these days?'

'The ruling is that we're not required to tell, but we can use our discretion. But we've got the amniocentesis results, so we do know what they are.'

Mel considered, and then said, 'I'd like to know if I could.'

'Of course you would. Let's make them into real people for you. For both of us.' Again the smile. 'Two girls,' he said.

Two girls. Two *girls*. *Exactly* what I hoped for. Two tiny girls, lying like furled-up buds, clinging on to one another, but their limbs whole and free, and probably each with their own hearts, beating in exact time together.

Mel said, carefully, 'Two girls,' and despite everything felt a delighted smile widen her mouth. 'Oh, thank you.'

Joe reacted exactly as Mel had expected.

At first he turned red-faced with annoyance, and then he went off to ring a number of people up—mostly business associates or fellow Town Councillors whose wives or sisters had had children fairly recently. He returned from the phone armed with several names, and said it was just a question of finding a proper specialist to deal with the matter. Mel should have found that out at the consultation, but of course she would have been upset. He understood that. His tone said he was allowing for her being upset. There were times when Mel thought he did not live in the twentieth century.

Harley Street figured in several of the names on Joe's list. Mel managed not to ask how Joe thought they would pay for Harley Street specialists, or even how they would pay for private healthcare at all, when people were not really queuing up to buy the dolls-house homes that Joe's company built: two-and-a-half bedrooms, £1,500 deposit for first-time buyers and a twenty-five-year mortgage.

But he seemed pleased that the twins were girls. Very nice indeed, he said indulgently. And all this nonsense about them being joined up would be sorted out; Melissa would soon see, and then there would be two little girls. Two pretty little dolls that he could spoil and cosset, said Joe. (Two pretty little accessories who would look good on newspaper photographs of Councillor Anderson attending civic events and local charitable functions...? That was a dreadful way to think!)

Mel wondered how Joe could think the babies would be pretty, when she was very far from pretty herself, and Joe was no oil-painting either. It did not, in fact, matter if the twins were pretty or not: Mel would rather they had character and kindness, and happy and interesting lives.

The truth was that she should never have married Joe in the first place. Isobel, who had known Mel longer than anyone, had been right when she said Mel was out of her tree to do so. The trouble was that Mel had been fed up with being on her own and being broke and being in a dead-end job, and she had been fed up with being nearly

thirty and never having had a proper long-term relation-
ship— It was a lot of fed-ups, and they had added up to
her falling into the trap of any marriage being better than
no marriage, which very likely went to show that she was
not really living in the twentieth century either.

Mel was trying not to acknowledge how much she
had come to dislike Joe, because dislike should not have
any place in marriage. She was trying even harder not to
acknowledge that the dislike was sliding into something
even more worrying.

Fear. It was a bad thing to discover you disliked your
husband, but it was much worse to discover that you were
frightened of him.

For a lot of the time now, Simone was quite frightened of
the little girl.

The problem was that she was hating, more and more,
the glimpses she got of the little girl's world—the world
with the black stone house. Simone did not like that place,
she did not like the feeling that the little girl was trying
to pull her deeper and deeper into the world where the
house was. Or did she? A tiny, rather horrid voice, whispered that wouldn't it be exciting to know more about
that world?—that not-quite-real place where the little girl
lived...? To even step into it, just for a little while, like
people in books stepped into other worlds...?

The little girl said that one day they would be able
to share all their secrets; she was looking forward to that
because it would be an extra-specially good thing to do.
But Simone did not think it would be extra-specially
good at all, and she did not have many secrets anyway.
She thought she would try not to listen to the little girl's
secrets, although this might be difficult because the little

girl seemed to be getting stronger all the time. Once or twice Simone had had the feeling that she was being made to look down into the little girl's mind, which seemed rude, like snooping on somebody's conversation. Simone always saw thoughts and feelings in pictures, and seeing down into the little girl's mind was like peering over the rim of a deep old well that did not smell very nice, and glimpsing the memories and the secrets lying at the bottom. It might be better not to look too closely at some of those secrets.

Shortly after Simone was ten Mother began to get the anxious look in her eyes, and after a little while she said they would be moving again.

'You mentioned the Welsh Marches just recently, didn't you?' she said. 'You did a project on it at school, and you seemed quite keen. Would you like us to live there?'

This was unexpected. Simone had not thought that she might be able to choose something so important as where they lived, and she was a bit worried by the thought of being so near to the little girl. 'Is it a place where we could live?'

'We can live anywhere we like,' said Mother, and Simone heard that although her voice was bright, underneath she was anxious. 'We're secretly gypsies, didn't you know that? We probably had a great-great-grandmother or something who danced to a tambourine and lived in a painted wagon.'

'Not really?'

'No, but I'd sometimes like to know how you can be so fey.'

'What's fey?'

'It means you might know what other people are thinking.' She smiled at Simone, but Simone saw that when Mother drew the curtains that evening, she stood at the window for a long time looking out into the street.

Mother found a house in the Welsh Marches quite soon afterwards, in a place called Weston Fferna.

'Nearly but not quite Wales,' she said as they drove along the roads, with the car piled high with suitcases and records and china, and things Mother said the removal van could not be trusted with. 'It's lovely countryside, isn't it? This was a good idea of yours, Sim; I think we'll like it here.'

Simone hoped so too. She had not seen the house that Mother had found for them to live in, because Mother mostly did the house-hunting by herself, but she had seen photographs and it looked pretty nice.

'And we'll be together, Simone... We'll really be together at last...'

Simone sat very still in the car, because the little girl's voice in her mind was much stronger and it felt much closer than ever before. It was pretty spooky to think she might get to meet her at last, but it was quite exciting as well. I might find out who she really is, and how she gets inside my head and then I might not be so frightened of her, thought Simone hopefully.

They turned off the main road and went down a windy little lane, and that was when Simone looked across at the fields on their left. There were lots of fields, mostly with sheep in them, and lots of trees, and there were gorgeous smudgy mountains straight ahead. Here and there was a farmhouse or a little group of cottages or a church spire.

And across the fields, set a bit above the road and frowning down at the cars, was an old, old house. Simone glanced up at it, and instantly felt as if somebody had punched her stomach.

The house. The black stone house where the little girl lived. The place of clanging doors that were locked every night at exactly the same time, and of angry despairing screams. The place where you ate your meals at long scrubbed-top tables, and where there were sour smells of despair and loneliness, and where the rooms smelled of sick and dirt and some of the people smelled of sick and dirt as well.

'Are you all right, Sim?' This was Mother, not looking at her, concentrating on the unfamiliar road but picking up that there might be something wrong in the way Mother sometimes did pick up other people's thoughts. 'You're not feeling car-sick, are you? We're almost there now.'

'I'm, um, OK.' Simone was not OK, of course. But she said, 'I'm just looking at the old houses and things on the road.' She twisted round in the front of the car, trying to see through the rear window, watching the black house get smaller and smaller as they drove away from it. There was no mistake; Simone knew exactly what the house looked like; she knew about the door at the centre like a square grinning mouth, and the straggly little bits at the back which were called sculleries and the underground rooms where people were sometimes shut away.

She even knew about the old trees that grew around the house, because the little girl had told her about them. She had said to Simone that they were bad old trees: if you looked at them for long enough you saw wicked faces in the trunk: horrid evil faces that looked as if they were a thousand years old, and that stared at you out of withered eyes. Wizard oaks, they were called. There was a poem about them; it told how on some nights the evil old wizard woke up and parted the branches, and peered into the room to see if there were any little children he could snatch up and carry away.

Simone stared and stared at the house. It was scary to find it like this, all by itself in the middle of fields, but the really scary part was that even from here—even with Mother's little car bowling smartly along the road—she could see that the house was a very old crumbly building, with gaping holes where the windows had been and birds' nests in the chimneys. Worst of all was that she could see that it was empty, and that nobody could possibly have lived in it for years and years, especially not any children.

They reached their new house quite soon afterwards. The furniture van was there already, and things were being unloaded and carried inside. It was a pretty nice house, a bit like a large cottage. There was a pointy roof and flowery things growing up the walls, and a tangly garden that would be great for games. The rooms all had nice scents that made you think of orchards on warm afternoons.

After the furniture van drove away there were about a million things to do, so Simone forgot about the black stone house for a while. There was unpacking and beds to be made up; Simone's bedroom was right at the top of the house and it had a padded window-seat so you could curl up and look out over the fields if you wanted to. She could not see the old house from her window, which was one good thing. And after she had unpacked her books and cassettes and CDs the room felt really friendly, and then after supper a large ginger cat wandered in from some-where to investigate them and had to be found a saucer of milk. And what with all this going on Mother did not seem to notice that Simone was being so quiet.

She did not dare to tell Mother about the black old house in case it meant there was something wrong with her. If you heard voices that other people did not hear, and if you knew what places looked like before ever you saw them it might mean you were mad, and mad people were shut away and never let to go out into the world.

CHAPTER FIVE

THE BLACK STONE house was called Mortmain
House, and people who lived there were hardly ever
let to go out into the world. Sometimes they were shut
away inside it for years and years—children as well as
grown-ups.

But one of the really bad things about it was not knowing
who to trust. The children who lived there could not tell
whether the men who came to visit were nice, ordinary men,
interested in hearing about lessons and about the food that
was served, or whether they were the other ones: the ones
with the treacly voices, who were the baddest people in the
world. If you had known how to tell the difference, the little
girl said to Simone, then you might have been able to do
something about it when they came. Hide somewhere or put
a chair under the door-handle so they could not get in, that
would be one way. But as it was, nobody could tell.

Simone asked who the treacly voiced men were, and
the little girl said the children called them the Pigs. They
had nasty piggy eyes, greedy and sly, and thick fingers
that prodded at you. After they had looked, they quite
often smiled and nodded to one another, and said you
were good enough to save up for a while.

Save up for what?

But the little girl only laughed when Simone asked this, and even though the laugh and the voice was still inside her head Simone heard that it was a horrid kind of laugh, pitying and smug, as if the little girl thought Simone was stupid. You know, she said. You know what I mean, and so Simone pretended that she did know, really.

Mortmain meant dead-man's hands. It was French, and the little girl had explained it to Simone. 'It's always been called that,' she said. 'Mort is French for dead, and main means hands. I don't suppose you'd know that, though.' There was a faint air of I'm-better-than-you, which was one of the things Simone hated. So she said she was just starting French at school, and she knew what Mortmain meant perfectly well.

But it was a pretty spooky name for a house—even for that house. Spookiest of all was Mortmain's crumbliness, because you had only to see it once to know that people had not lived there for years and years.

'It's a famous ruin,' Mother said, when Simone asked about it one day. They had been at Weston Fferna for several weeks, and they were getting to know some of the places and some of the people. Mother had made one or two friends, mostly other parents at Simone's school. 'It's quite a prominent local landmark,' Mother said. 'I read about it in the library—they've got some quite good books on local history there. I'll take you to see them one Saturday.' Mother liked things like local history and local legends; she liked Simone to know about them as well.

'But what was it really? I mean years ago—when it wasn't all broken up?'

'A workhouse. That's a place where people in the past had to go if they hadn't got any money. Workhouses were dreadful places, not much better than prisons, and it was regarded as very shameful if you were taken into the workhouse; it meant you couldn't pay your way in life.

And then I think that later on Mortmain was used by the army in the war. For the soldiers to live.'

'World War Two.' They had learned about this a bit at school; Simone had always hated the sound of it, because it must be pretty horrid to have the whole world at war all round you, and bombs being dropped all the time. Simone had made some drawings of soldiers and air-raid shelters, and then Mother had found some old photographs that had been her mother's—that was Simone's grandmother, whom Simone had never met because she had died when Mother was quite small.

But the photos were great; they showed young men in uniforms, and girls with their hair pinned up in rolly shapes on top of their heads. Simone loved photographs better than anything, even better than drawings. She loved seeing how people looked against different backgrounds—trees or houses or the sky—and how the trees and the sky could look different according to what time of day it was, or whether it was raining or sunny, and whether the people themselves looked different because they had a storm-sky behind them, or sunshine, or black wintry trees. She pored over the photographs for hours, until Mother said if she was as keen as all that perhaps she would like a camera of her own, what did she think?

'I'd like that a huge lot,' said Simone. She added, 'I'd extra-specially like it,' then wished she had not said 'extra-special', because that was one of the little girl's expressions. Mostly she tried not to use them, but sometimes they seemed to sneak out by themselves. She said, 'I'd really like it. When could we do it?'

'Next birthday? It'll be quite expensive, so it can't be like buying just an ordinary thing. But we'll go into some shops beforehand—it'd probably have to be somewhere like Oswestry, or maybe we could drive further into England to Chester. You've never been to Chester, have you? It's nice. We could get some brochures to look at and you can think about what sort of camera you'd like.'

This was one of the really good things about Mother. She understood that if there was going to be a particularly exciting treat you wanted to think about it and discuss it before it happened. Simone would like to have a camera of her own very much. She said carefully that she would quite like to take photographs of Mortmain House. Would that be possible?

'What a funny little horror-comic you are,' said Mother. 'Yes, of course we'll go out there if you want to, although we'd better make it a Saturday afternoon when there's lots of people around. I think tramps sometimes doss down in the ruins, and gypsies. Real gypsies, I mean, not us.'

'Oh, I see. Um—would we have to ask someone first?'

'I don't think so. I don't know who owns it—I don't think anyone does know. That's why it's been let go so badly, I suppose. But I can't imagine why you want to photograph it. It's a gloomy old place.'

The little girl did not think that Mortmain was especially a gloomy old place; but Simone supposed that if you had never known anywhere else—if you had never known about huge, sun-filled rooms, and schoolrooms where people talked a bit noisily about lessons, or places like cinemas or swimming pools where everyone shrieked and laughed, you might think that Mortmain was pretty good.

But gloomy old places could be splendid for games, and one of the games that the little girl told Simone about was a game called the dance of the hanged man. There was a song that went with it: Simone was not sure if she had understood it properly, but it was something about, 'The morning clocks will ring/And a neck God made for other use/Than strangling in a string.' Then came the chorus that everybody had to join in, which was about the gallows-maker building the frame and then the hangman leading the dance, and everyone had to do all the movements about building the gallows and hammering in the nails and fashioning the gibbet. Then they had to jig round the yard in a line for the dance. Simone thought she understood that that by 'the yard', the little girl meant a sort of playground.

She did not properly understand about the hanging game and she did not properly understand about the other children who seemed to be part of the game, but she thought it sounded hateful, and the little girl sounded hateful as well when she talked about it. Sly and giggly and as if somebody was being hurt in the game, and as if she found this exciting. Simone was not absolutely sure what a hanged man was, except that it had something to do with murdering people.

She was not sure who was being murdered or whether it was only a game anyway, but she thought it might all have something to do with the men who came to inspect the children, and who were so extremely bad and cruel, even though they looked normal and ordinary.

'Think of them as normal and ordinary,' said Martin Brannan on Mel's next visit. 'It's what they are, you know. You'll see that when they're born. It'll be a C-section, of course. You're all right with that, are you?'

'If that's the best way.' Mel did not mind how the babies were born providing they could be born safely and with the best possible chance of surviving.

'It is the best way. We'll probably do it at thirty-seven weeks. Full anaesthetic as well, I think, rather than just a spinal epidural. You'll go to sleep quite comfortably, and when you wake up it'll all be over, and a cup of tea waiting at your bedside.'

'You can't make it a gin and tonic, I suppose?'

'That'll come later.'

'In a minute you'll pat my hand and say, *Trust me.*'

He gave her the smile that seemed to hold such intimacy and liking, but that he probably used on all his patients. 'I don't need to. You do trust me. You'll have to come into St Luke's a few days before the procedure. That means everything will all be calm, and nicely planned ahead. It's a very civilized way of giving birth. I wonder now—'

'Yes?'

'I wonder if it would help you to know a bit more about other cases of conjoining,' he said, speaking slowly as if he was considering the idea for her.

'You mean, like the real Siamese twins?' Mel had been trying not to use this word, but she used it now. 'The first ones?'

'Chang and Eng. Yes. They led an odd life, those two, but they were quite separate personalities and they achieved a degree of normality, even in their time. That was the early eighteen-hundreds. They died in eighteen seventy-something, as far as I can remember it. They were never separated, but they both married and fathered several children.'

Mel said cautiously that this must have been a bit bizarre for all parties, and Martin Brannan said, Yes, and bizarre was hardly the word was it. This time the smile was more of a mischievous grin, sharing the small joke with her. It was remarkable to think that this man already knew her body more intimately than anyone else ever had or ever would, and that in a few weeks' time his hands would be inside her womb, cutting and slicing, and detaching two tiny living creatures... It was something you ought really to share only with your husband, that intimacy. She wondered if Martin Brannan had any children, and then she wondered whether he was married, and supposed he was.

'There's a wealth of stuff written about these cases,' said Martin. 'Oh, listen, though, keep off the medical side, won't you? It's graphic and distressing at times, and you won't have the necessary detachment. And it can be confusing. Concentrate on the personalities and the successes. The twins who were separated and lived normal lives—even the twins who weren't separated and still lived reasonable lives.'

'I'd quite like to do that,' said Mel thoughtfully. 'If I knew about other cases—other parents—I don't think I'd feel so isolated.'

'Mel—' In some subtle way they seemed to have travelled beyond the Mrs Anderson/Mr Brannan stage by this time, although Mel had not quite ventured to call him Martin yet. 'Mel, you aren't isolated,' he said. 'Nor are the twins isolated.'

'Simone and Sonia,' said Mel, suddenly aware of the inner delight again at remembering the girls' names. 'We're going to call them Simone and Sonia.'

'Nice,' he said, giving her the sudden smile. 'Simone Anderson and Sonia Anderson. I like that very much.'

Joe thought Mel was being morbid, reading up all those accounts of joined twins. Dear goodness, he said, why must she bury herself in the lives of all those sad grotesque creatures, most of whom had lived in the days before medical science was really developed? To his way of thinking it was downright dismal; his mother had said exactly the same thing as a matter of fact. Nature had a way of taking care of things, Mel would see. They would wait for the birth, and the chances were that everything would be all right.

'But it can't be all right,' said Mel. 'All the scans and the tests show that the twins are definitely joined. They aren't going to become unjoined.'

But Joe had no opinion of scans and tests, and he had no opinion of clever young doctors who frightened people half to death. What Mel needed was cheering up, he said. Would she not like a little shopping trip to one of the big department stores for baby outfits? They might go along this very morning. Marks & Spencer, or British Home Stores. They would have a bite of lunch in the BHS coffee shop.

Mel looked at him, and thought, I wanted a soul-mate, a sensuous impetuous lover: someone who would plunder the love-poems of the centuries and quote rose romance verse to me by passion-filled firelight, or whisk me away to Paris's Left Bank or Samarkand or the Isles of Avalon at a moment's notice. What did I actually get? Joe Anderson, who gives me verbatim reports of town planning meetings, and thinks the height of dissipation is lunch at British Home Stores.

She said, 'If you don't mind, I'd rather stay here, I think.'

Even if she had wanted to fight Saturday-morning shopping crowds she did not want to go shopping with Joe, who was apt to be embarrassingly bluff with shop assistants, and tell them his name with unnecessary loudness in the hope that they would recognize him as a prominent member of the local Council. What she really wanted to do was to stay in the warm, well-lit study, and read the books she had borrowed from the local library about all those other twins who had beaten the odds. She wanted to try to visualize them, and to imagine how their parents had felt and behaved and reacted.

'I do wish you'd read some of this for yourself,' she said. 'It's very reassuring. A lot of those twins managed to lead really interesting lives—remarkably so—and most of them adapted in extraordinary ways. It's only comparatively recently that medical science has been able to cope with this condition, of course, so most of them had to stay joined. But there were twin girls who appeared in films in the twenties in America: Daisy and Violet Hilton they were called. They were put in freak shows as children, and they had a dreadful life until they managed to escape from their guardian. And Chang and Eng Bunker—those are the really famous ones, of course. The real Siamese ones. They married two sisters, and fathered several children. And then in the twelfth century there were the Biddenden Maids. They were quite rich and they did masses of good works, and there are cakes baked depicting them even today, apparently.'

But Joe did not want to hear about the Biddenden Maids, and he did not want to hear about Daisy and Violet Hilton or any of the other conjoined twins who had managed to lead almost-normal lives. He did not, in fact, think that Melissa should dwell on these cases and he was rather surprised at this man Brannan encouraging it. In fact his mother had said only yesterday—

'But doesn't it make you feel better to know that our twins aren't—well, freaks?' said Mel, who did not want to know what Joe's mother had said. 'That it's just a—a sly trick of nature, and that if they can be separated they probably won't even be disabled at all?'

Joe's face twisted with sudden, rather frightening anger, but he mastered it almost at once, and said that Mel was becoming quite whimsical nowadays—a sly trick of nature indeed!

Mel had known, as soon as the word *disabled* came out, that it had been a mistake to use it. But once you had said a word you could not unsay it; it lay on the air between you, puckering the air with its ugliness, just as a thought, once formed, stayed stubbornly in your subconscious. Even a dreadful deformed thought that kept sneakily asking if you might have done anything that could have contributed to the twins' problem. Or even if Joe might be somehow to blame. No, that was a truly ridiculous thought, in fact it was positively Victorian.

Anyway, whatever thoughts might pad softly and treacherously through your subconscious mind, the words *disabled* and *deformed* must never ever be allowed to be part of them.

Extract from Charlotte Quinton's diaries:
1st January 1900
Had no idea that chloroform made one so *sick*. All very well to talk about, No pain, Mrs Quinton, far better to do it this way; what they don't tell you is that although the stuff knocks you out for the entire birth, you spend the whole of the next day retching miserably at regular intervals.

It's slightly peculiar knowing the twins are here after all the waiting. Have not yet seen them, but Dr Austin says they are both girls. Edward will not like that very much—he wanted sons—but I shall love it. I shall love having two daughters, and I can't wait to meet them.

2nd January: 10 a.m.
Oh God, oh God, can hardly bear to write this. Dr Austin has just told me that the babies are joined to one another—they're *joined*. They're growing out of one another like some dreadful creature in a freak show. That's why they weren't brought to me when I came out of horrid chloroform.

I said, 'When can I see them?' and Dr Austin looked surprised, as if he had not expected me to ask this. He hrmph'd a bit and eventually said, Well, perhaps a little visit to take a look might be in order, perhaps after lunch when I had had a nap.

Do not want a nap after lunch, and do not want any lunch either. But did not dare to argue with Dr Austin in case he banned me from seeing the babies at all—not sure if doctors able to do this, but would not put it past Edward to be quietly having all kinds of sinister discussions behind my back. He knows a lot of people, my husband, Edward.

My husband. Edward. It's curious, but I put those words together, and they never seem quite to fit.

He has not yet been to see me, although flowers were delivered—red and white carnations. Expensive and eye-catching, because he would want the nurses to see them and say, Oh, how beautiful! What a generous husband! Wonder if Edward knows the superstition that red and white flowers mixed together presage a death?

It's almost twelve o'clock. Two hours to get through.

2nd January: 1.30
I can hear Dr Austin's voice in the corridor outside, and I can hear the sound of a bath-chair being brought for me. It's rumbling along the bare floors. Ridiculous to think that it sounds like the beating of two hearts, twined inextricably around one another...

CHAPTER SIX

For SOME TIME the only sound in the small operating theatre was that of the measured bleep from the monitors. There was a scent of oranges, from the sweetened orange juice that Mr Brannan sometimes sipped when he was operating.

'H'm,' said Martin Brannan's registrar. 'As well the lady opted for a general anaesthetic, isn't it?'

'I didn't give her any choice. Rosamund, if you'd tilt the light this way, so that I can see—'

'I'm sorry, Mr Brannan,' said the very new, very young, theatre nurse. 'Is that better?'

'It is. Wait now, here's the amniotic fluid— More swabs, please— And suction— Yes, that's more like it. All right, everyone? Here we go then. Incubator ready?'

'Yes.' This was the paediatrician.

'Now then, gently as a velvet whisper at midnight—' His hands moved delicately but surely.

'Oh God,' said the new young nurse, one hand flying up to cover her mouth.

'Thoracopagus,' said the registrar, half to himself.

'Yes. But we knew that anyway.' Martin held the two tiny creatures in his hands for a moment, and then handed them to the paediatrician who was waiting at his side. 'And it's not as bad as it might have been by a long way. I don't suppose you've ever seen an omphalocele baby, have you, Roz? If you had, you'd be thanking all the gods that these two have all the organs growing inside their bodies and not outside. I'm delivering the placenta now—' He worked for a few minutes. 'That's fine now. We're ready to close the uterus. How are the girls?'

'Still a bit blue,' said the paediatrician who was bending over the incubator. 'The heartbeats are pretty good though, and the weight's quite good as well. Eleven pounds six ounces together—not absolutely half-and-half, I don't think; one of them's just an ounce or two lighter. Difficult to be precise.'

'Breathing unaided?'

'The smaller one's a touch tachycardic—she still needs a bit of help. The other one's all right though. She's starting to look a better colour as well. But as you said, Mr Brannan, all in all, they're in far better shape than we'd dared hope.'

Martin straightened up, aware for the first time of his aching back and neck muscles, and gestured for the orange juice. His other hand was still on Mel's anaesthetized body, half-possessive, half-protective.

An indignant wail broke through the ticking monitors, and the team relaxed and smiled. 'Hear for yourself,' said the paediatrician. 'That was the stronger twin.'

'She's called Simone,' said Martin. 'And the other one is Sonia.'

The first thing that Mel saw as she came up out of the soft darkness of the anaesthetic was the slender-stemmed bud vase on the table at the side of her bed, with a single rose in it—creamy-pale and in the half-open stage. Lovely. Mel smiled hazily. Joe would always do the conventional thing, of course, but this was unusually sensitive of him. *Perhaps I misjudged him. Perhaps there's some romance in him after all.* There was a card propped up against the vase. She turned her head to read it.

'Sorry it can't be the gin and tonic yet,' said Martin Brannan's slanting hand. 'But we'll drink a double together at Simone and Sonia's eighteenth birthday party. In the meantime, enjoy this.'

Mel was lying back on the pillows, considering the implications that this seemed to suggest—all of them good—and wondering when she would be allowed to see her babies, when the nurse brought in a pink basket filled with dark red carnations and bright green asparagus fern, and tied up with pink satin ribbon.

'Gorgeous, aren't they? They're from your husband, Mrs Anderson.'

'Really? I would never have guessed,' said Mel.

Joe Anderson had initially been pleased at the news that Mel was expecting twins, and while he would have liked a son, the image of two pretty daughters who would form a frame for his dazzling career had been very acceptable. His mind had flown happily ahead to paragraphs in the press. *'Mr Joseph Anderson, the newly-elected Member of Parliament, celebrating his by-election victory with his family...'* This was not in the least fanciful: it was practically a settled thing that he would be adopted as candidate for the next by-election, wherever it might be.

Later on, if things went well, there would be even grander items. *'Joseph Anderson seen escorting his daughters to a private reception at No. 10...' 'Together with his twin girls, hosting a reception at his constituency for the Prince of Wales...'*

A larger house would be needed, but once he had been elected they would most likely have to move anyway. To something gracious and mellow—eighteenth-century, perhaps. Large gardens and velvety lawns for the twins and their friends. Even a small tennis court, and a paddock for a pony. Two ponies. *'Joe Anderson, who is tipped for a place in the next Cabinet reshuffle, caught in a happy, off-duty moment with his twins at the local point-to-point...'*

And now these delightful visions were meaningless and false. Really, it was too bad of life to play such a trick.

Or was it? How would it be if one took this thing on board? Even turned it to advantage? He considered the possibilities carefully. Once the twins had had the operation to separate them all news value and sympathy value would go, of course, but while they were still joined he might get quite a lot of mileage out of it. He could talk worriedly about the ethics of separation and his own religious convictions and he could disclose his own agony at having to put the babies at risk. That was all the kind of thing that voters would go for.

He might even start to work for one or two children's charities as a result of the twins' condition— *'Mr Joseph Anderson, whose life holds a deep sadness, but who works tirelessly for children's charities...'* Ah, now that *was* a good idea. He could talk modestly about the twins' tragedy guiding him into those areas, and people would speak of him as a caring man. *'Joseph Anderson pictured outside Buckingham Palace, after receiving his OBE for services to children...'* He would ask around at the Council offices to find out about suitable charities. If you were going to do good, you wanted to be sure that everyone knew about it.

Joe was so pleased with all of this that he went off to order two dozen carnations for Mel. He asked the florist to deliver them in a pink and gilt basket, since it would not do for anyone at St Luke's to think that Councillor Anderson (almost certain to be the Right Honourable Joseph Anderson very soon) was a penny-pincher.

In the tradition of all good newspapermen Harry was starting his research into Simone Marriot's family by checking archived newspapers. You did not neglect your own terrain, and providing you took a balanced view newspapers were a primary source for research, although you had to read and analyse both ends of the spectrum. You had to get at the facts. This last sounded like a nineteen-fifties American police series. I'm here to get the facts, just gimme the facts, Mack. Hero lights up a Sobranie, tips hat to rakish angle, turns up raincoat collar, and adopts a macho pose under a handily positioned street light. Harry Lime in *The Third Man*, or Bogart's Philip Marlowe, sneeringly cynical. Great role models, both.

Giving Harry this commission, Markovitch, wily old wordsmith, had used an unexpectedly picturesque phrase—pathways into the past. It conjured up the dusty purlieus of ancient files and curling-edged letters and mediums' trances, and Harry suspected Markovitch had employed it calculatedly to snare his interest. He ate a makeshift meal in the small kitchen of his flat, dumped the dishes in the sink, and in the absence of the Sobranie and the hat poured himself a large whisky and sat down at the computer. The portals of the internet might not be as romantic as fading photographs and sepia-inked diaries but they opened up the past a whole lot faster. You see, Mr Wells, after all we discovered a time machine to take us back. But we call it an internet search engine. What do you think of that for a good science-fiction title, H.G., or can I call you Herbert?

He found the announcement of the twins' birth easily enough. Just over twenty-two years ago it had been, and Simone's twin was called Sonia—the name had a faintly foreign, slightly exotic ring to it which Harry rather liked. The journalists of the day had pounced on the story, of course, and splattered it across their pages. *'Conjoined twins born in North London...' 'Wife of by-election's front runner gives birth to Siamese twins...'*

But the story had got going in earnest when Joseph Anderson had unexpectedly adopted religious scruples over the operation to separate them. Harry, reading the articles critically, had no idea if this was genuine or assumed. Given Anderson's political aspirations, which were mentioned several times, it might very well be a convenient pose. He tried to think if the anti-sleaze movement had got going at the start of the 1980s, and thought it had.

But whatever Anderson's motives, the whole thing had made for terrific copy. Part sob-story, part ethical dilemma, part ordinary people propelled into an extraordinary situation. Markovitch, vampiric old hack, must have revelled in it at the time. Hell, it sounded as if most of Fleet Street had revelled in it.

'Siamese twins' dad says, "When God deals a bad hand we have to grin and bear it,"' That was the *Mirror*, of course. The *Telegraph* had assembled a few comments from Church leaders, with one or two bishops rather guardedly observing that there was a duty to the newborn and medical science was a wonderful thing, and Rome coming down strong on the side of the unborn, and pointing out that the sanctity of life must always be paramount.

The Times, with the dignity it usually considered incumbent on its position, had run articles written by a few eminent gynaecologists, most of whom had taken up several column inches to describe the exact process of the surgical procedure that was envisaged for the Anderson twins, and also several other surgical procedures that, as far as Harry could make out, had bugger-all to do with the case in question.

The *Mail* had been quite sympathetic to Joseph Anderson, ('*The agony of a father...*') but the *Sun* had been distinctly derisory, and had managed to get hold of a particularly bad photograph of Anderson looking predatory at a ballot-box. The sub-editor had positioned it alongside a very smudgy shot of two small babies who might have been anyone, and who were probably not the Anderson twins at all. To round things off there were several snide observations about innocent and defenceless newborn creatures, and even a quotation from Pope about the trusting lamb licking the hand that was raised to shed its blood, although God alone knew where the *Sun* had got hold of a Pope quotation.

This was all so far, so good. Harry saved several of the articles for future reference, typed up some notes for possible sidelines for inquiry, and jotted down likely-sounding sentences as they occurred to him. After an hour of this he leaned back, massaging his neck to ease muscles cramped from bending over the keyboard for so long.

He would have to pursue the twins' lives as far as he could, of course. He would have to find out about the operation to separate them. Simone appeared to have survived all right, but how about the other one? Sonia. Who is Sonia, what is she, that all our swains commend her? More to the point, where is Sonia? Harry scribbled a note to check the marriage and death columns for her name. He would have to look up details about the father's political career as well. He had never heard of Joseph Anderson, but that did not mean Anderson had not finally got himself into Westminster, and walked the corridors of power at some stage.

And what about the personalities of the twins themselves? Angelica had said Simone was sometimes fey, and that she had been strongly attracted to the Bloomsbury house, to the extent of saying they must have it. Why? What was there about the house that had so deeply affected her? Harry had a deep suspicion of females with a 'must-have' streak. They were usually enormously untrustworthy and monumentally self-centred, as well as being acquisitive to their eyelashes. Amanda had been a must-have in its highest form and because of it Harry had had to sell the London flat so that he could give her the half-share that Amanda said she must have, it was nothing less than her right and her solicitor had confirmed this. Harry's solicitor had unwillingly confirmed it as well. After the building society had taken its cut of the sale proceeds, and after the lawyers had taken theirs, and after erratic house prices had diminished the property's value by about ten per cent, Harry had been left with a measly thousand quid. Not enough to buy so much as a broom cupboard. So there you go, life's a bitch, especially if you've married one.

He poured himself another whisky, rummaged the bookshelves for a London telephone directory and the address of HM Land Registry office, and sat down to compose a letter of inquiry about the Bloomsbury house's previous owners.

Even with the cards stacked so strongly against them, even lying inside the incubator, Simone and Sonia were beautiful children; Mel saw that at once.

Little russet-brown caps of silky hair. Small, sweet faces, with mischievous eyes. Like something out of a nineteenth-century fairytale, or that scene in *Midsummer Night's Dream* about the bank with the nodding violet and the sweet musk-roses. She would see if Joe would agree to adding Violet and Rose as second names. There had been something of a fashion for flower names around the turn of the century; Mel had had a great-aunt, born around that time, who had been called Lily. And in one of the books she had been reading there had been a brief mention of conjoined twins born to someone called Charlotte Quinton a few minutes after midnight on 1st January 1900. The timing and the date—the very start of a new century—was probably the only reason they were mentioned and there was nothing about the twins' lives, or whether they had ever been separated. But they had been christened Viola and Sorrel, which Mel found rather attractive. Viola and Sorrel Quinton. Had their mother thought they resembled mischievous, curled-up flowers as well?

Charlotte Quinton's diaries:
2nd January 1900: 10.00 p.m.
The beating of the invisible heart that I thought I had heard was inside my own head, of course. Panic, sending the blood thudding through my body, because despite what I said earlier, I really was frightened about seeing the twins.

We went through horrid, soulless passages, and Dr Austin's nurse, who was pushing the chair, tried to make bright conversation along the way, the silly creature. Or was she really so silly? Difficult to tell, because the pounding was all around me, and there was a huge suffocating weight pressing down on my head. A fine thing if I were to faint just as we reached the babies' room. Edward's mother would never let that one go unremarked! Poor Charlotte, no stamina. Always has to make a scene. No breeding, you can always tell.

So I managed not to faint, purely so as not to give the old bat the satisfaction.

But the hovering darkness was with me as we went along, like a huge black bird, beating its wings relentlessly and uselessly against prison bars. The wheels of the chair screeched and scratched on the stone floors, like the sound made when somebody draws a nail across a slaty surface, and the wheels sang a sinister little song to themselves like train wheels. *You'll-never-cope... You'll-never-cope...*

Yes-I-will... Yes-I-will...

And then we were there, entering a room painted an unpleasant dark green, and the nurse was pushing the chair across to a wide hospital crib in one corner, and I wanted to get out of the shameful chair and walk across the room to meet the twins properly, but I was still sore and aching from the birth, and light-headed from the chloroform.

The light from one of the narrow windows slanted across the crib and their eyes were shut tight against the unfriendly world, and if Dr Austin had not explained to me that they were joined together at the waist, I would just have thought they were lying cuddled close together. The one nearer the window had turned her little face to the sunshine as if she was absorbing its golden warmth through her skin, and I wanted to snatch her and her sister up, and take them out of this dour place where people thought it acceptable to put babies in depressing dark green rooms.

It was suddenly enormously important to give them names, to make them into real people. I looked at them for a long time, seeing all over again how they were clinging to one another, almost as if they were trying to draw strength from one another.

Clinging. I remembered that I had wanted to give them fashionable flower names.

'Ivy,' I said aloud, trying it out. 'Ivy and Violet.' And then I looked back at the small shut faces and knew those names were quite wrong. Ivy was a creeping, clinging plant; Violet was a shy, shrinking name. The twins would need all the strength they could get: vital not to give them creeping, cowering names. So I said, 'No, not Violet—Viola.' Viola had been one of Shakespeare's nicest heroines: she had been a twin as well, and she had triumphed over all kinds of adversities.

'Viola. That's very pretty.' The nurse bent over to write it on a little tag around one of the tiny soft wrists. 'And Ivy for the other one, did you say?'

'No. Ivy's a parasite. Sorrel,' I said, without realizing I had been going to say it. Wood sorrel had grown in the garden at home when I was small; it was pretty and hardy, and even remembering the name made me think of autumn woods and the purple mists of harebells.

'Viola and Sorrel.'

'Yes.'

Viola and Sorrel.

They left me alone for a very long time with the twins. As long as you wish, they said. We shan't disturb you. Are you comfortable in that chair? There's a cushion here if you want it.

So I stayed in the room on my own with the babies, and when the nurse had gone I reached both hands down inside the cradle, one hand to each of them, and they each curled a tiny hand around one of my fingers in the way babies always do, only this was different, because they were mine. I stayed with them for a long, long time.

And now I'm lying awake in the high, narrow bed in my own room and I can suddenly see that the nurses and the doctor, who were so emphatic about leaving me there on my own, had been more than half-hoping I would pick the cushion up and place it over the helpless little faces. Quick and clean and merciful. Except how could I *possibly* have murdered my babies? How could anyone?

Later
Have no idea yet how I am going to face Edward. All the recriminations: told you not to go racketing around Town all those months, told you to live quietly, even offered to rent a country house for a few weeks, but you always know best...

(Would Edward have wanted me to use that cushion tonight? If I believed that, I would have to leave him. But of course he would not have wanted it.)

But it's not just Edward who has to be faced, there's his mother as well, and oh God, how am I going to face Edward's mother who never thought I was good enough to marry her son anyway, and who will now say, darkly, that she is not in the least bit surprised things have gone so disastrously wrong, what can you expect...

But I *will* cope and I *will* face Edward, and somehow I will face his mother as well.

4th January 1900
So. So after all, there is to be no coping, and there is no longer any need to worry about facing Edward, or even his mother.

They have died. My two beautiful scraps of humanity, Viola and Sorrel, who clung to one another so determinedly and who clung to my hands that night, have died.

They told me this morning, Dr Austin standing at the foot of my bed, Edward next to him, a nurse in attendance in case I succumbed to hysterics. Something about lungs not fully developed, something else about heart too weak to stand the strain.

It was Edward who said, Blessing in disguise. Of course it was.

But that was when I collapsed in floods of stupid helpless tears, and Edward had to be hustled out, red-faced and trying not to be angry at me for making a scene…

8th January
Edward suggests I stay away from funeral—everyone will understand, no one will expect it, and what if I start crying again, embarrassing for everyone, have I thought of that?

Yes, I have thought of it and I don't care. Will be there if I have to be carried.

10th January
Day before funeral, and peculiar to be back at home. Curtains all closed at the front of the house, and Mrs Tigg alternating distractedly between emotional tearfulness and bustling culinary activity. 'Oh, those blessed angels, madam, how can you bear it, but they

say God takes the little children unto himself, and not for us to question— Now, I've ordered a nice ham to bake in time for the funeral, and what do you think about lobster salad as well?'

Maisie-the-daisie is round-eyed at the solemnity of everything, and scuttles out of the way if I enter a room. Mrs Tigg says she has taken up with the fishmonger's boy, and fears the worst since he is a bit of a Lothario on the sly and Maisie a bit too easily impressed, if you know what I mean, madam.

We are going to have the baked ham and lobster for the wake (Maisie's young man can deliver a couple of live ones on the morning), and Mrs Tigg will do a nice tureen of soup as well, since likely to be bitterly cold day, and you don't want to catch your death of cold at the cemetery, madam, what with you not yet fully recovered from the birth.

Cannot help thinking that if I had been married to Floy we would have been helpless with grief in one another's arms by now, and he would not have cared if I saw him cry, and perhaps he would have found something to read to me—some poem or sonnet or some fragment of philosophy that I might have clung to until I could drag my way back up into the light.

Question: Would it be easier to bear losing Viola and Sorrel with Floy at my side, and music and philosophy, and crying in his arms and all the rest, than with lobster salad and closed curtains, and Edward and his mother, and all the admonitions about, Please don't make a scene at the church, Charlotte, and, I don't think that outfit is really suitable for the service, do you?

Answer: No idea, but do know that Floy would not have cared if I had made fifty scenes at the church, in fact he would probably have joined in.

Am going to wear the black crêpe de chine with the bell-shaped skirt for the service. Very stylish, very *belle époque*. Edward can disapprove all he likes, and his mother can droop and drone over grave in her widow's weeds and grisly mourning brooches until the Last Trump for all I care.

I will bid farewell to my babies with as much style as I can manage.

CHAPTER SEVEN

Charlotte Quinton's diaries:
12th January 1900
Twins' funeral, and certainly the most dreadful day of my life.

Edward had not wanted me to go, of course, and his mother had not wanted me to go, either. Should I not be resting on my bed, especially since only twelve days since birth? Said I felt perfectly capable of attending my daughters' funeral, and anyway, Chinese peasants in rice fields return to work within *hours* of giving birth. Was accused of having peculiar ideas and supporting socialism, in fact Edward's mother would not be surprised to find I was an admirer of Keir Hardie and the Independent Labour Party, although in her view they will never amount to much.

Church was full, of course—mostly ghouls and snoopers as far as I could see—and Edward's family out in gloomy force. His mother arrived late (suspect this was planned in order to create an effect), positively *enshrouded* in the weediest of black and exuding attar of roses. She walked sombrely to a seat, leaning heavily on ebony-tipped stick, clattering it on the marble floor as she went. (When did the old witch start using a walking stick? First time *I've* seen her with one.)

Edward had chosen the hymns—'The Lord is My Shepherd' and 'The Day Thou Gavest Lord is Ended'—and the vicar talked about the cruel taking of new lives, but pointed out that the ways of the Lord were mysterious and wonderful, which I thought unhelpful. Edward's brother read a poem by Robert Louis Stevenson about the departed ones not being dead but only gone a few steps ahead, and waiting to meet their friends again face to face. Quite admire Stevenson, but found this monumentally inappropriate, given the circumstances.

Tiny coffin standing on flower-decked trestle at front of church. *Far* too elaborate, with brass handles and brass plate and polished mahogany, but of course it dominated the proceedings. I tried to hold on to that moment when the twins were only a few hours old, and when their tiny fingers curled around my finger—if I can keep that memory I can keep a little part of them with me for ever. But it was so difficult because I kept imagining them lying inside their coffin, still in that pitiful embrace. 'In death they were not divided...' That's an uncomfortable quotation if ever there was one.

Wished Edward had consulted me about the funeral details, since would have preferred things very simple, with small posy of violas and wood sorrel on coffin instead of stupid pretentious hothouse lilies and white hyacinths. But I managed not to cry, which was one in the eye for Edward's mother.

Followed the coffin down the aisle fairly composedly, with the organ playing Handel's *Largo* and everyone walking after me. Edward v. solicitous, holding my arm, bending over to ask if I was all right every forty seconds, which was irritating.

And then, just as we were reaching the side door, which led out to the cemetery, and just as I was thinking, I've managed quite well, I haven't broken down and at least nobody will be able to say I caused a scene, I caught sight of the man sitting at the back, in a corner of the church near to one of the soaring stone arches. He was not joining the exodus into the churchyard, and he was so quiet and still and so deeply in the shadow cast by the stone pillars that he ought to have been unobtrusive. He ought to have gone unnoticed, except that once I had seen him I found it impossible not to go on seeing him.

He looked like a tramp who had strayed into the church by mistake, or possibly an Irish tinker who had parked his gypsy caravan outside for a moment. He was watching me, and the deep shadow was suddenly pierced by a shaft of sunlight that came in through the stained-glass window above him. With the harlequin-patterned light on him the tramp-image vanished and he looked more like a cross between one of the early Christian ascetics and the villain of a melodrama.

But he was neither, of course, and he was certainly not a tramp. And so far from taking part in villainous romances he was more likely to write them, and while he knew, in theory, about asceticism, he had never, to my knowledge, practised it.

The darling of the Bloomsbury set. The much-fêted, frequently copied, endlessly envied young man whose admirers said his prose was written with a pen of iron, the point dipped in diamonds, but whose detractors held that his work contained no more merit than the erratic, flickering-candleglow emotion of a dream-clouded mind.

Whatever the truth about him, today he looked what he was. Man of letters, Oxford and Winchester. Lunatic, lover and poet. And the dreams were not erratic at all, any more than they were drug-induced: the dreams were always with him, as much a part of him as the shape of his eyes or the way his hair grew. And there had been a time when he had pulled me into those dreams with him and when I had wanted nothing more than to stay in his dreams.

He could never be unobtrusive, and he could never go unnoticed, no matter the company he was in.

Philip Fleury. Floy.

It simply had not occurred to me that he would walk into the church, and join in the service, as composedly as a curious cat, but it was what he had done.

I managed a half-nod of acknowledgement, and then we were outside, Handel's music trickling after us, the rain that ought to have acted as background to the service starting in earnest at last, sliding relentlessly down from suddenly leaden skies, dripping from the trees and plunging the churchyard into a dark dismality, depressingly reminiscent of every elegy ever penned by every mournful romantic. The gravestones jutted up like jagged grey teeth, shiny with rain except the really old ones, which were weather-scarred and crusted with moss.

Tried to focus on the twins again, but all through the brief burial I was dreadfully aware of Floy standing a little way off beneath one of the old trees, his coat collar turned up, the rain misting his black hair.

Later

Extraordinary to discover the truth of the old adage that helping with someone else's troubles takes your mind off your own.

The wake, which has just dispersed, was as dismal a gathering as any I ever attended, despite slightly overeager, goodwill-to-all-men that pervades any after-funeral assembly. Edward's aunts clustered in corners, jet-beaded bonnets busily nodding, discussing suitable inscriptions for the gravestone. Someone was suggesting 'Not dead but only sleepeth', and when I said I could not imagine a grislier inscription for a gravestone they looked at me with shock, and then with a kind of tolerant pity. Poor Charlotte, the tragedy, you know. Would not be surprised if it had affected her mind.

Was just going along to scullery to make sure Mrs Tigg coping with things (lobster salad was being particularly well received), when heard Maisie in downstairs lavatory near back stairway, retching her poor little heart out.

It's the fishmonger's boy who's the culprit, of course, and from the sound of it he never had any intention of marrying her. Poor little daisie, she gasped out the sorry tale between bouts of sickness and tearful apologies, and please not to tell anyone, mum, especially not the master, him being so particular.

To me, the saddest part of the whole thing is that the poor creature doesn't even seem to have derived any pleasure from the act, in fact, am not even sure if she realizes exactly what caused the conception. Gather it happened one night after he saw her home from the Girls' Friendly Society, and she succumbed to his blandishments up against the scullery wall (NB. v. unromantic for them both; virginity should always be given up in beautiful setting and after appropriate and not-too-vehement rebuffs, and *not* yielded messily and awkwardly within sound and scent of Mrs Tigg's preparations for tomorrow's Sunday roast beef).

But at least this has turned my thoughts in another direction, since am determined Maisie not going to be thrown out on to the streets by Edward spouting righteous Victorian rodomontade about, Never darken these doors again, and, Take your shame and leave my house, you strumpet. This is the twentieth century, for goodness' sake, and Maisie-the-daisie not some rapacious Piccadilly street-walker, or even one of those saucy baggages who entertain parties of gentlemen in smoking rooms! Would not mind betting that Edward knows more about *those* ladies than he has ever let on! But the behaviour of his own household must be irreproachable, of course, and would not put it past him to summon up the smug moral rectitude of the eighties, and throw the daisie out into the storm.

So have told her not to worry, we will work something out, and have now decided that best plan will be for me to go on long visit to my family, and take the daisie with me. Edward has already said I ought to have a holiday, and why not go away for a few weeks—South of France or Kitzbühel very nice at this time of year, and Thos. Cook could make all the arrangements. But Shropshire and the Welsh Marches are very nice at any time of year—even now, with snow frosting the meadows and sharpening the leafless trees—and Weston Fferna sufficient of a backwater that even Edward's mother cannot accuse me of *racketing*.

More to the point, there is a place just outside Weston Fferna called Mortmain House that acts as hospital and orphanage, and where girls in Maisie's condition can have their babies discreetly and (I hope) without an atmosphere of disapproval, and can then leave child to be brought up by Mortmain Trust.

There are four or five months to the birth as far as I can make out, and it should be easy enough to find her some sort of temporary work in the area (large farming community there, so always glad of honest, hard-working girls for kitchens and dairies), and then explain to household on return to London that she has taken a new post in Shropshire. Quite understand that she will hate the idea of leaving child behind and entirely sympathize but cannot see that she has any other choice—she is much too young to pose as a widow, and (have to say it) not really sufficiently bright to lie convincingly about husband killed at Mafeking or Ladysmith. Not sure she would even know where Mafeking or Ladysmith are anyway.

So tomorrow morning I shall tell Edward that I am taking his advice, and am going to Weston Fferna for a few weeks, taking Maisie with me.

Question: Am I doing all this because by saving Maisie's baby and giving Maisie some kind of new life, I believe I am in some way redressing the balance on what happened to Viola and Sorrel?

Answer: Yes, perhaps.

Conclusion: Does it matter, anyway?

'Does it matter anyway,' said Joe slowly, 'if the operation isn't done?'

The afternoon sunshine had been streaming into Mel's hospital room, and Joe's arrival had pulled her abruptly out of a warm drowsiness. She did not, for a moment, take in the meaning of what he had said.

'I don't think they want to do it absolutely at once. Mr Brannan says the surgical team will probably prefer the twins to be about six months old because—'

'I meant,' said Joe a touch impatiently, 'does it matter if it isn't done at all?'

This time the words did get through. Mel stared at him, and thought, Surely he doesn't mean he's against the separation? Oh God, I think it's just what he does mean. After a moment she said, as temperately as she could, 'But we can't let them grow up as they are. They won't be able to—well, go to an ordinary school for instance. Or if they do, they'll be pointed out as—as freaks. And they won't be able to have boyfriends or get married—' And that's what you want, she thought suddenly, looking at him in horror. You want to keep them in a sort of hothouse, because that'll get you sympathy. Poor Joe Anderson, what a tragedy, but isn't he brave and selfless, devoting his life to those poor girls... This is all about helping you to win the by-election, you selfish monster? thought Mel. My God, I'll have to find a way of talking you out of this! Joe was explaining that to start with they would buy a larger house. 'Somewhere with a bit more privacy for the twins. I think we can afford it, especially now it's almost settled that Faraday's applying for the Chiltern Hundreds. Everyone says I'll stroll through the by-election.'

'I'm sure you will,' said Mel, automatically responding

to her cue. 'But look here, the twins must have the operation as soon as possible! Of course they must!'

'I don't say that in the future—' He was using his I-am-a-reasonable-man, and-this-is-a-reasonable-argument voice, but Mel heard the steely note beneath. She sought for an argument to use against him—something that would not antagonize him, something that would flatter him—but found nothing.

'I don't want to be embarrassing about this,' Joe was saying very solemnly, 'but it's a religious thing, Mel. I've thought very deeply about it. I've been hoping you'd understand.'

Impossible to say that the only religious convictions Joe had were bound up with his own egotistical ambitions. Pointless to lose one's temper or even show any emotion at all. Mel said carefully, 'But the operation wouldn't be contrary to any kind of religious ruling, would it? Martin Brannan says it's quite a straightforward procedure. The risk's very small indeed. I think we should trust him.'

Joe's eyes snapped with annoyance for a moment. He said, 'I don't know why you can't see that Brannan is a—a publicity-seeking ladder-climbing philanderer. You've only got to look at his record with females!'

'I don't care if he's keeping an entire harem!' said Mel, sharply, and then realized this had come out too aggressively. Damn. She sought for something to say that would smooth things over, but Joe was already standing up, preparing to leave. He did not want to tire her so soon after the birth, he said solicitously. And he knew she was finding this upsetting, so they would discuss it another time. But Mel should remember that he was perfectly capable of looking after his family. No matter what happened, the twins would always have every care, every luxury. They would have a splendid life.

Except, thought Mel, the ordinary normal life that

they ought to have. She lay back on the pillow, her mind working.

Between 1898 and 1915 the house in Bloomsbury had been owned by someone called Philip Fleury. Harry had obtained this information with surprising ease, receiving a reply from the Land Registry Office within a week. Fleury, whoever he had been, had apparently sold the house shortly after the outbreak of WWI to one of the smaller War Office departments. This might have been due to patriotism, or it might have been due to the house having been requisitioned. It might even be that the owner had simply wanted to get the hell out of London before the Zeppelins turned up.

And then in the mid nineteen-twenties Angelica's faceless property company had acquired the house, since which time it had presumably had a series of tenants.

The Land Registry search had given Philip Fleury's former residence as Oxfordshire, which might mean anything, but had stated his profession to be a writer. A writer. One of Angelica's earnest young men with soft shirts and brooding eyes? Harry did not think it would have been possible to live in Bloomsbury and be a writer and not be part of the intellectual set of the era to some extent. The Fabian Society and the Pre-Raphaelites. Ruskin and Millais and Aubrey Beardsley, and various Movements, and idealism in all its different guises. Had Philip Fleury been part of all that? What sort of writer had he been? Poems? Novels? Twee little articles about Free Love or rebellious leaflets calling for a League of Nations to be set up? Whatever he had written, this was surely the sort of stuff Simone had been wanting to find. How likely was it that any of Fleury's work had survived? Not very likely at all, but still—

Harry left the *Bellman* offices early and once in his own flat flipped the computer on and requested it to search its spider-filaments for Philip Fleury's name. He could have made the search at the *Bellman* but he felt oddly protective about it. Sure you aren't just scared of being exposed as a hopeless romantic? demanded his mind. Oh shut up.

There were a couple of genealogical sites with Americans trying to trace their antecedents and proudly mentioning Huguenot ancestry, but there were no Fleurys that would fit even remotely with the man who had lived in Bloomsbury. Harry had not really expected there would be. But if Fleury had written books—

He began to work through the listings of antiquarian bookshops. More of them had websites than he had expected; clearly sellers of rare and out-of-print books were moving out of the mustinesses of the Dickensian era and into the world of modern technology. He went doggedly through the lists of their stocks.

It took a long time. It took him through most of the evening, with a break to phone out for pizza and then to eat the pizza, and it took him through half a bottle of single malt whisky as well. In fact he was starting to think that he would have to give up and take to the streets of Hay-on-Wye or tramp up and down Charing Cross Road, when the name suddenly came up. Philip Fleury. Harry's heart leapt with anticipation. Found him! He had the absurd compulsion to grab the printed name on the monitor in case it vanished into the chancy, nebulous ether of cyberspace.

There was only one book listed—*The Ivory Gate*—but there was a note describing Philip Fleury as a prominent member of the Bloomsbury set, and a close friend of many notables including Henry James, Rebecca West and Aubrey Beardsley. There followed a catalogue reference number for the book, a publication date of 1916 (this edition), and a brief note advising all inquirers that the book's condition was moderately good although there was some foxing. The price was £95.

Ninety-five pounds. For pity's sake, thought Harry, it's hardly a first folio Shakespeare, or a Byron autograph.

And then he saw that against the price was a further note. 'Flyleaf inscription. Believed to be by author.'

The bookshop appeared to be situated somewhere near to the Welsh border, just outside Oswestry. Harry would not have cared if it had been situated on the farthest reaches of Katmandu or in the middle of the Barents Sea. He had to have Philip Fleury's book. He had no idea if it was because he wanted it for himself, or if he wanted to be able to present it to Simone in the manner of Lancelot putting the Grail into Guinevere's hands, but whatever it was the compulsion said to grip certain people at auctions or in casinos or on race-tracks seized him by the throat.

He completed the Order Form on the bookshop's page, typing his credit card number into the appropriate box for payment and then pressed 'Submit'. Then he sent another email to the bookshop confirming the order and explaining that it was extremely important that he buy this book for primary research. If it had not been half past eleven at night he would have phoned them as well. As it was, he rang them at five minutes past nine the next morning to make sure they had received his order and his email, and that they would send him the book at once. Yes, it was important. Yes, of course he would pay for Special Delivery or Courier Service or any damn thing they liked. Oh—could they tell him the actual words of the flyleaf inscription?

There was an agonizing wait, and then the voice at the other end said, 'Yes, I can tell you. It says, "For C, and for Viola and Sorrel. Floy".'

'Floy?'

'Yes.'

'You said author's inscription,' said Harry accusingly.

'I can't help that, this is what's in our catalogue. We can't guarantee that it is the author, of course.'

'I thought his name was Fleury. Philip Fleury.'

'It is,' said the voice, this time a touch huffily. 'But if your name was Philip Fleury, don't you think you might accept a soubriquet of Floy? A proliferation of ffs and lls, isn't it?'

Harry considered this and found it reasonable. 'Do you know where the book came from? I mean, is there any provenance?'

'No. It's quite old stock. I've been here for twelve years and it was here when I came. But it'll more than likely be from around these parts. A house-contents sale. A private library. We do quite a lot of those—well, we used to. Most of the big houses around here are gone now or turned into council offices or posh restaurants.' The Welsh lilt that had been just discernible earlier came a bit more strongly. 'The publishers are listed as Longmans Green & Co if that's any help.'

It was not really much help at all, although Harry had a vague idea that this was a now-defunct, but once-prestigious publishing house.

'So there's no indication whatsoever as to where the book came from?'

'None at all,' said the voice. 'I told you, the stock's quite old. Did you say you'd pay the extra three pounds ninety-five for twenty-four-hour delivery, Mr Fitzglen?'

CHAPTER EIGHT

EVEN IN HER very wildest moments Mel had not thought that Joe would talk to the reporters who had gathered outside the hospital after the twins' birth. She had not thought for a second that he would make a statement to them without consulting her.

But incredibly, there it was on the late evening news just as Roz Raffan came in with a mug of hot milk and the offer of a sleeping pill.

'I thought you were in theatre tonight. Are you moonlighting, or do you double as drinks-server?' said Mel, who had been starting to feel sleepy but who was pleased to see the familiar face. It had been nice to strike up this small friendship with Martin Brannan's theatre nurse.

'I thought I'd look in to say goodnight before I go off duty. They were putting the drinks out in the ward kitchen so I said I'd bring yours in. You don't mind, do you? You're our celebrity, Mrs Anderson.'

'It's the twins who're the celebrities, not me. And I wish you'd call me Mel. Am I meant to drink that revolting stuff?'

'Not if you don't want to. I can pour it down the sink if you like. Is that the evening news just coming on?'

'Yes.' Mel had been half-watching the television in the corner of her room, and half-reading. 'Everything's so gloomy. Wars and famines and things.'

'They put out an item about the twins on the lunchtime news,' said Roz, pausing at the foot of the bed, her eyes on the screen. 'I saw it in the canteen. Didn't anyone tell you? I expect your husband would have OK'd it with our press office, wouldn't he?'

'Not necessarily,' said Mel dryly, and Roz looked a bit shocked.

'I'm sure he would, Mrs Anderson, I mean, Mel. He's so thoughtful always.'

'What did the news item say?'

'Only a brief announcement. And no names were mentioned, but somebody said the media were camping on the doorstep almost within minutes.'

'Oh, no.' Mel had not thought about this aspect.

'Well, it's news, isn't it? People are interested. They're concerned for you.'

'I'll bet the reporters aren't interested or concerned for me,' said Mel caustically. 'In fact—' She broke off as the newscaster said, 'The Siamese twins, born two days ago at St Luke's Hospital, are reported to be doing well and are breathing unaided. The twin girls are joined at the side of the chest, near the top of the ribcage, and although Martin Brannan, consultant gynaecologist in charge of the case, issued a statement that an operation to separate them would be reasonably straightforward, it seems as if a row could already be brewing. Over now to St Luke's and our reporter there.'

Mel started to say, 'What do they mean, a row—' and stopped as Joe's head and shoulders appeared on the screen, a microphone held up for him by the TV reporter. Joe had assumed his chin-tucked-into-neck look, that made him look jowly and righteous. Like a bullfrog, thought Mel. And he shouldn't have worn that terrible checked overcoat; it makes him look like a bookie's tout. But her heart was starting to race with apprehension because Joe seldom did anything these days without a calculating eye to its effect.

The interviewer said, 'We've heard, Mr Anderson, that you're unhappy with the prospect of the operation to separate your daughters.'

Joe took a minute to answer, and then said, in a frowning voice that implied that he was a man at war with himself, 'Yes, that's quite correct. Yes, indeed I am unhappy about it.'

'Can we ask why? Mr Brannan has already made a statement saying that the likelihood of the operation succeeding is high—'

'Mr Brannan is an admirable doctor, but he's not the twins' father,' said Joe quite sharply. And then, switching personas almost visibly, he said, confidingly, 'You see, I am a man of deep religious convictions, and one of those convictions is that we must accept the hand that God has dealt us.'

There was an awkward pause. Mel thought: that's thrown the interviewer. They'll edit that pause out if they run it on later news bulletins. Then the interviewer said, cautiously, 'Are you against medical intervention, then?'

'I'm not a Christian Scientist, if that's what you mean. I'm not against medical intervention *per se*. I was quite happy for my wife to be given a Caesarean procedure for the birth, for instance: I understood that it was necessary if she was to survive and that was the most important thing of all.' This was said with an air of what was very nearly complacency. 'But,' said Joe, 'there are medical statistics suggesting that in the severer cases—where it's necessary to sacrifice one twin—the survivor frequently dies as well, or cannot live free of a ventilator.' He spread his hands in a gesture of appeal. 'How can I submit my daughters to that kind of risk?'

'You referred to statistics just now?' The interviewer was clearly on firmer ground here.

'Yes, I have read several recent case-studies,' said Joe, and named his sources. One was a professor of gynaecology in the Seychelles; the other was a medical historian in Michigan. This was disconcerting; Mel had not expected him to be quite so well provided with information.

'But—forgive me, Mr Anderson,' said the interviewer, 'we understood that there was no suggestion of having to sacrifice one of the babies in this case. A joining at the chest—'

'Thoracopagus,' said Joe. 'Yes, that can be one of the less serious joinings. But there is some fusion of bone and tendon around the shoulders, so the risks are still high, you see. And the outcome could be a quite severe disability to one of them.' A pause. 'I wonder how many of your viewers would be able to face inflicting permanent disability on their own children?' he said.

Clever, thought Mel, her eyes never leaving the screen. Oh God, that one's going to be difficult to fight.

'However,' said Joe drawing his brows down, 'I should like to say this. Quite apart from statistics and medical history, when it comes to this dangerous and complex operation on two such tiny scraps of humanity— well, I have searched my conscience, and—' Here he broke off, and Mel could see that he was considering whether he might safely say, And I am not ashamed to say I have prayed. The interviewer would probably shrivel up if he did say it. But Joe appeared to decide that he had gone far enough in that direction, and he said, 'I don't wish to embarrass anyone with my faith. I'm aware that it isn't considered good etiquette to talk about religion. But I'm an old-fashioned man—' And now, thought Mel, he'll go into the simple, God-fearing-man routine.

He did go into the simple, God-fearing-man routine. He told the interviewer, who was clearly torn between wanting to nail down a really newsworthy interview and indecision as to whether his masters would approve of a religious slant, that life was a precious thing. You did not tamper with life or with nature, said Joe solemnly. If it was God's will that his daughters should face life with a handicap then he, Joe Anderson, did not believe he could set himself up against God.

'You won't give permission for the operation?'

Again the pause. Then Joe said, 'No. No, after a great deal of soul-searching, very regretfully I have decided to withhold my consent.'

'What about your wife? She can give her consent on her own, can't she?'

The question was sharp and incisive, but Joe said, at once, 'My wife and I are at one over this.'

Mel discovered that she was clutching a fold of the sheet between clenched hands. I must stop feeling like this, she thought. I've got to keep my temper, and I've got to appear perfectly calm. If anyone even half-suspects what I'm thinking—

There was a quick shot of the front of St Luke's, and then an item about the current stability of the pound started. Mel reached for the remote switch and turned the set off, her mind working. Joe had been far cleverer and far more adroit than she would have thought possible.

She turned to look at Roz, who had been staring at the screen. 'Did your husband mean all that?' said Roz slowly. 'About not tampering with nature, and about withholding permission for the separation?'

'It sounds like it.' Mel was thankful to hear that her voice sounded reasonably normal.

'But I don't think there is that much of a risk. Mr Brannan definitely said there wasn't, and he's so clever.' Mel heard a touch of hero-worship in Roz's voice and smiled inwardly. Roz was so earnest and also just a bit old-fashioned, so that Mel kept forgetting how young she was.

But she only said, 'Yes, I know he is. And I'm all for taking the risk anyway. The twins can't live like this.'

'No, of course not.' But there was some doubt in Roz's voice, and Mel looked up. Roz coloured, and said, 'I was only thinking that in a way they've been lucky. In the timing, I mean. Eighty or a hundred years ago they'd have been smuggled discreetly away to an institution and forgotten.'

'Yes, that's true.'

'They're going to be so pretty, aren't they?' said Roz unexpectedly. 'I go along to see them when I come off duty each night.'

'Do you really?' This was rather touching.

'I feel sort of proprietary about them. With being in at the birth and everything. When they're older they'll have lovely colouring, won't they?'

'They've got my mother's hair.' Mel found herself liking Roz for saying this, and for seeing the vagrant glint of auburn in the little, soft heads.

Roz said, a bit hesitantly, 'Mr Anderson won't really try to block the operation when it comes to it, will he?'

'I don't know.' Liar, said her mind. You know damn well he will.

'I'm sure he won't when it comes to it,' said Roz. 'But if you ever had to—well, take some kind of action—' She looked at Mel without speaking and Mel felt a jab of apprehension.

But she said lightly, 'What on earth do you mean, Roz? What kind of action?'

'Making them wards of court or anything like that—'

'Oh, I see. I don't think it'll come to that,' said Mel. 'I'm almost certain they can operate just on my authority.'

'Can they? Yes, I expect so. But I'd be on your side whatever happened, Mel. I'd do anything to help. I really would.'

It was said with slightly embarrassing intensity, and Mel was not quite sure how to respond. In the end she just said, 'Thank you very much,' and left it at that.

She could not tell Roz about the idea that was starting to form within her mind, and she could not tell anyone. If she had to go through with it, this quarter-formed plan, and if she succeeded, it could make her the loneliest person in the world.

But she would have the twins and that was all that mattered.

Roz Raffan was moderately satisfied at the way in which the friendship with Melissa Anderson was developing. You had to be careful about that kind of thing in this job, because when people were in hospital their values often altered and they sometimes formed emotional ties with nurses and doctors. It was all to do with dependency and with the lowering of barriers, of course; Roz had been told that during her training, and warned about getting too close to patients. But she did not think anyone could say the friendship between herself and Melissa fell into that category. She thought she was pitching it about right.

The aunt who had brought her up had always said that good fortune seldom went to the people who appreciated it, and Roz knew that this was perfectly true. Look at Melissa Anderson. You would have thought she would have been more than satisfied, more than happy with what life had given her, but you had only to talk to her for two minutes to see she was not very happy at all. And yet she had a husband who was quite well-off by a lot of people's standards, and a nice house to live in, and very likely an extremely interesting life ahead if Joseph Anderson became a Member of Parliament. Roz thought he was almost certain to do that: for one thing he had such very fine standards. Roz had been brought up on very similar standards herself, so it was gratifying to meet them in somebody else. Respect God and people will respect you. Always do what you know to be right, regardless of the consequences.

You had only to listen to Mr Anderson to know that he followed the same principles. You did not find many people these days who were prepared to stand up for their religious beliefs, but Joseph Anderson was prepared to and Roz admired him for that, although she knew he was wrong about blocking the twins' operation.

The twins. It was to be hoped that Melissa appreciated her good fortune at having them. Roz was not too sure about that. She had thought several times that Melissa had absolutely no idea how lucky she was.

She also thought Melissa might not realize how lucky she was to have such a good, reliable, God-fearing man for a husband.

Charlotte Quinton's diaries:
30th January 1900
Still cannot believe I have successfully deceived Edward, that good, reliable, God-fearing husband— also the rest of the household (including Edward's mother!), and that Maisie-the-daisie and I are actually on our way to Weston Fferna.

Am writing this in the train (not in the least bumpy except when we go over the points, so a good opportunity to bring diary up-to-date). Maisie has never been in a railway train before, and is sitting bolt upright, clutching the edges of the seat, and staring wide-eyed and fearful through the window. She wanted to bolt for home when we got to Paddington

Station, and had to be sat down and talked to calmly. I explained about power of steam (not sure I got that absolutely right), but in the daisie's defence, have to admit that place a seething hive of people and machines and huge sudden spurts of steam from trains, and all a bit daunting. Floy would have seen all kinds of images in the sight: he would have talked glowingly about iron and steel engines, breathing fire like modern-day dragons, and drawn analogies with some kind of Dante-like inferno, and then gone away to incorporate it all into a book. But I only saw the trains and the people and smelt the hot iron, and God alone knows what Maisie saw, poor little creature.

Mrs Tigg made us take a luncheon basket—'Because you can't go all that way without proper sustenance, madam,' as if the Welsh Marches were the end of all civilization—and Edward has arranged for a first-class compartment, since not fitting that his wife travel any other way.

Later
The lunch basket contains cold chicken and ham, brown bread and butter, egg-and-cress sandwiches, and some of Mrs Tigg's plum cake. Also two small bottles of Mrs Tigg's delicious lemonade, so we have had quite a feast.

The train is still jolting on its way through the countryside, and now we are skirting the ugly industrialist towns of the Midlands. There's a teary rain sliding down the grimy windows of our carriage, but I can see all the grey-roofed manufactories and the clouds of vapour that hang over them, and occasionally there are glimpses of narrow streets with huddled-together houses, where the ant-workers live, scurrying from their houses to the manufactories, and then back again. In and out and to and fro and round and round, like lemmings, like creatures on treadmills, hardly ever seeing daylight, poor souls. Perhaps one day someone—someone with vision like Floy's—will find a way to capture the greyness and the dreariness, and the rain-blurred figures.

Told Maisie how, as children, we used to make up little songs in the train to go with the constant clackety-clack of the wheels, but she doesn't understand because she didn't have that kind of childhood. I would have taught Viola and Sorrel those songs—or perhaps they would have made up their own—but that won't ever happen now. (But I have that one tiny memory—the little warm fingers curling determinedly around mine. As long as I can keep that, I won't have lost them completely.)

Keep telling myself there will be other children—doctors say no reason not to have other, perfectly normal babies—but somehow, cannot get enthusiastic about that. Edward says, heartily, we will look forward to sons, but have a dreadful suspicion that Edward's sons might take after him, which is v. depressing prospect.

Question: How am I to find the resolve to return to Edward after this business with Maisie has been sorted out?

Answer: I have absolutely no idea. But I know it has to be done.

We're almost there. It's been a long train journey and there was a tedious delay on the line a while ago that held us up for almost an hour, but the train's slowing down now, and ahead of us is the tiny halt just outside Weston Fferna. If I lean forward and wipe the damp mistiness from the window with my glove I can just see the light of the station-master's lantern signalling to our engine-driver. We're nearly home.

Home. So many memories go with that word. I remember, I remember, the house where I was born... Christmases and summers and springs. Roaring log fires and berries on trees, and buttercup-splashed meadows.

And the excitement of all the journeys—I *love* journeys. Going to London for shopping, for visits, for birthday parties in people's houses, for grown-up parties and dances later on, but always coming back to Weston Fferna. The train always used to sing its own little song when we came back, the wheels chanting, *Going-HOME, going-HOME...*

I remember, I remember, the roses, red and white... And the winding lane with the stile and meadow-sweet and lilac in summer. I was kissed for the first time on that stile—Father would have had a fit, and Mother would have been aghast. I was fourteen when it happened, and the boy was—somebody local; I forget his name. What a slut I am not even to remember who gave me my first kiss.

And blackberries in autumn, and the scent of apples. And the sharp coldness of November, when the air is like spun glass so that your nose prickles with it, and cobwebs in the hedges are spangly white, like lace. I lost my virginity on an afternoon like that, beneath the trees in Beck's Copse. It was a bit frightening and briefly painful and then it was marvellous, but I remember his name, and I remember that he was the son of one of our neighbours, and he was dreadfully upset afterwards because he said he had smirched my purity and committed a great sin against womankind, such nonsense, because I was as keen to do it as he was. (Although quite a revelation to discover later that not all men take three minutes flat from start to finish, and then sob with shame. Floy once told me that most men consider premature ejaculation something of a bêtise. And quite right, too.)

Still, that sharp cold afternoon under the beech trees—and one or two afternoons and nights afterwards (and let's be honest, Charlotte, four or five other lovers after that, as well!)—all meant I had to pretend with Edward on the wedding night. Edward would have been scandalized to his toes to think he had married someone who was not pure.

We're almost home, we're in the little pony-trap now that they keep at the tiny station, and it's jogging along the few miles to my parents' house. We're turning right at the crossroads—what the locals call the four crossways—and I can see the signpost pointing the way home. Across the fields I can see the church where Edward and I were married. It's rather a gloomy church; I never liked it much.

And now it's almost dark, but if I lean forward a bit, I can see the old trees on the hillside to the left.

I remember, I remember the fir trees dark and high… And the house that dwells behind those trees, and where Maisie and I must go very soon now.

Mortmain.

CHAPTER NINE

MEL THOUGHT IT was curious how a seemingly small event could be a catalyst, and how it could finally push you across a private and very personal Rubicon—a Rubicon with which you had been struggling for several months. Or did I cross that particular Rubicon a long time ago without noticing?

The twins were four months old when the Parliamentary seat that Joe had been hoping would fall vacant finally did fall vacant. His adoption as Party candidate for the by-election was officially announced, and he told Mel that they must give a party. There were a number of people who would be involved in the campaigning and it would be a way to thank them in advance for the work they were going to do to get him elected.

This was all perfectly reasonable; Mel had always known that if Joe really did make this bid for Westminster there would have to be entertaining and various semi-public functions, and on balance she thought she would quite enjoy it. But then Joe said, in a too-casual voice, that they might as well regard the evening as the twins' debut as well. Mel could buy them new outfits for the occasion—the cost did not matter, well, not within reason—and Joe would get some publicity shots taken of them beforehand. Now that he thought about it, they ought to invite a few other small children as company for the twins. It would look well on photographs afterwards, what did Mel think?

What Mel thought would not actually matter, because Joe would do what he wanted, regardless of her opinion. It was becoming obvious that the party for his campaigners was already taking second place in his mind, and that he was treating the evening as a major PR exercise to bring the twins to the attention of potential voters.

This was appalling. Mel would hate it for the twins, and the twins, who were already noticing people and responding to them, would hate it as well. It was unbearable to think of them being made use of, and to imagine them cast abruptly into the midst of other children— normal children—who would not understand about them, and who might stare at them or point. And I'd stare at all those children myself and feel resentful, and wonder why I couldn't have given birth to normal babies like those other women!

What was even worse was that this was probably only the start: Joe would thrust the twins more and more into the limelight if he thought it would further his cause. I can't let it happen, thought Mel. I can't.

Joe went on with his plans for the party, regretting several times that they had not yet struck out with the purchase of a larger house which would create a much better impression, although perhaps it was better not to appear ostentatious or nouveau-riche, there was nothing more calculated to put people's backs up. What had Mel bought to wear for the evening—? Oh my word, very dashing. Rather a bright green though, wasn't it? Still, if she thought she could carry it off— And doubtless she would find other occasions to wear the dress again so as to get the full value of the cost, would she? And what would the twins be wearing? Oh—pale green for Simone and pale blue for Sonia? Well, doubtless Mel knew best, but he had always thought that pink was the prettiest colour for little girls. Nonsense, their hair was not red at all, or only the merest hint; a nice sugar-pink would have been very suitable. You had to think how colours would come out in black-and-white press photographs. Was it too late to exchange the outfits at the shop?

Martin Brannan and the paediatrician had given the twins an almost-clean bill of health. Weight gain was on course; heart, lungs, kidneys were all working properly for both the babies. The twins' responses to stimuli were excellent—it was already apparent that Simone liked bright colours and Sonia liked sounds—and they were taking bright-eyed notice of the world around them, enjoying being talked to or sung to.

'Start giving them as normal a life as you can from now on,' Martin said to Mel. 'Take them out and about; let's toughen them up a bit. Wrap them up so that they aren't especially noticeable—we don't want them stared at by voyeurs—but let them get used to people and noise and shops and traffic. They mustn't live in a glass cage.'

Mel reported all this to Joe, and then, striving to keep her voice ordinary, said, 'They'd like to start assembling the surgical team for the operation. It'll take a little while to do that—to get the right people together all at the same time—but if they start the preparations now Martin Brannan thinks the separation can probably be done before Christmas.'

'Not a very pleasant time for a hospital stay,' said Joe. 'Two babies spending their first Christmas in a hospital bed—'

'They'd be home well in time for Christmas.'

'Even so, I think we'll leave things as they are. Certainly until after the by-election.'

His dismissive tone was so maddening that Mel had to beat down anger before replying. Then she said, We can't leave it much beyond six months. They're being very clear about that. Joe, I know you've got qualms, but I was hoping you'd have come round to the idea by now.' Pause. 'You haven't though, have you?'

'No.' This time there was no explanation, no it-is-God's-will stuff.

'That's a pity,' said Mel slowly. 'I was hoping you would reconsider. It would be much better if you would.'

Martin Brannan had said the twins must not live inside a glass cage, but if Joe had his way they might be imprisoned in that cage for most of their lives.

Had any other mothers of conjoined twins faced such a dilemma? There had certainly been a number of eighteenth- and nineteenth-century parents who had sold their children to freak shows—and how akin to that was Joe's behaviour now? It was rather disturbing to see parallels but Mel did see them. Still, most of the parents she had read about had seemed to be ordinary, more-or-less honourable men and women, who suffered agonies at their children's condition and would do anything to ensure normal lives for them.

What about Charlotte Quinton, so briefly mentioned in just one of the books on conjoined twins? Charlotte's twins had been born at the very end of the Victorian era, but the books did no more than list her name so there was no way of knowing whether her twins had survived, or, if they had, where or how they had lived. Mel kept wondering about Charlotte; probably because there had been just that brief, tantalizing reference to her and then nothing else. It made her a slightly mysterious, rather romantic figure.

It was actually quite odd that Charlotte's twins did not seem to have been written about in any more detail—or was it? Perhaps they had died and there was no story to tell. Or perhaps there was a story but it had been kept from the public, or simply not been thought sufficiently interesting. Or, twisting things around the other way, perhaps the story had been so interesting that Charlotte had left the country. Changed her name, and disappeared—

Changed her name and disappeared...

Thank you, Charlotte, said Mel silently. Whatever happened to you and your twins, I think you've been instrumental in showing me what I've got to do.

Charlotte Quinton's diaries: 31st January 1900
Breakfast with Mother and Father always a slightly peculiar event since marriage. Frequently feel relegated to maiden status again, and at times as if I have been summarily picked up and carried, willy-nilly, back into childhood.

But life here almost exactly as it always has been. Mother fussing over local politics—church fête, Lady Somebody's musical evening, worried because Queen's health giving concern—although what can you expect at her age, but such a pity if she dies in the summer with all the garden parties and people having to wear black, so unbecoming in hot weather...

Father tutting over world politics— Mafeking and Ladysmith in a fine old pickle although shouldn't believe all you read, damned newspaper fellows will tell you anything... Anglo-German alliance doomed, mark his words, that man von Bulow no use to them as Chancellor...

My two young sisters, just starting to be emancipated from the schoolroom, are allowed down to dinner now except when guests are invited. They giggle together over fashion books, and secretly play ragtime jazz on the piano when Father is not around... Caroline has learnt the steps of the mazurka, and promises to teach me...

I found it all extraordinarily restful.

After breakfast told Mother that Maisie was thinking of taking post in a church orphanage in North London because she wanted to help children. Said I thought of going out to Mortmain to let her see the children there.

Felt dreadfully guilty because Mother, dear unsuspecting soul, thought this so thoughtful and responsible of me—dear Charlotte—and remarked that kitchen-maids were unfailingly ungrateful, always wanting to leave just when you had trained them to be properly useful, although one could hardly object to such a worthy ambition on Maisie's part.

'And although I believe there are certainly orphaned children in Mortmain, they say that a good many of the other inhabitants are a touch wanting, poor souls,' she said lowering her voice, and then went on to remind me not to bother Edward with tittle-tattle about servants, since gentlemen never want to hear that kind of talk.

It's a remarkable thing, but I only have to be back in this house for half a day before all of Mother's precepts come flooding back. 'Gentlemen like to talk about their own interests and to be listened to without interruption...' 'A lady never makes a scene...' 'Do not respond or react if someone is impolite enough to make a coarse remark in your hearing...'

I told Mother that Edward never takes any interest in servants anyway, and only interested in dinner being on time and house decently clean.

(Note: Not sure this is entirely true, since just before leaving London, caught Edward eyeing Maisie's replacement, who's a bit of a sauce-box, I suspect.)

Mother then asked after Edward, and dutifully inquired about his mother, whom she cannot bear although we have to pretend otherwise. *So* comforting to hear Mamma being teeth-grittingly polite about the old bat.

Have been offered the use of the trap for the expedition to Mortmain, with Griggs to drive it—'Since you are bound to still feel in delicate health, Charlotte'—but I have said we do not need Griggs. Admittedly I have not driven pony-trap since marrying Edward, but do not think it's something one forgets.

Hope Mortmain House, close to, is not as forbidding as it looks from the road.

Later

Mortmain House is more forbidding close to than it looks from the road, in fact think it is the ugliest, most evil-humoured house I have ever seen.

We had to leave the trap on the roadside, with the pony loosely tethered to a tree, and then walk up the steep track. So much for delicate health!

The closer we got to the house, the more I began to entertain serious doubts as to my plan for the daisie's baby, because this did not look in the least like a place where a helpless child ought to be left, in fact it did not look like a place where anyone ought to be left. If Floy had been here he would have started to spin dark fantastical tales about the place and its occupants, and about the old trees with their knurled trunks that looked as if faces leered out from them, but I only saw the unsightliness of the black stones, and the smearily dirty windowpanes, and the unkempt bushes and unweeded paths.

But managed to assume cheerful manner for Maisie (who was looking more terrified by the minute), and said it was a great mistake to judge anything by its appearance: once inside, house most likely very cheerful and bright.

She did not believe me of course, and do not blame her. Bad enough to be facing prospect of giving birth to fatherless child, without prospect of leaving the poor mite in this gloomy place. Hope fishmonger's assistant was worth all this, but seriously doubt it.

The thick shrubbery screened quite a lot of the house's front and probably made most of the downstairs rooms horridly dark, although at least somebody had clipped parts of the bushes into a semblance of tidiness. But as we approached I had the eerie feeling that we had taken a wrong turning somewhere, Maisie and I, and that we had stepped out of our own Time and into a wholly different one. Remembered how I had once wished for a pathway into the future, so that I could foresee awkward situations and sidestep them, and half-wondered whether I had unwittingly found one this afternoon. Found this disturbing, but the most disturbing part was not that we might have stumbled out of our own Time (read Mr Wells's excellent book last year and would love to travel through Time, although not quite as far as the characters in *The Time Machine* did!). No, the eerie part was that I could not tell if it was the Past or the Present we might have stumbled into.

There was no door knocker, so I used my furled umbrella (v. useful thing, a furled umbrella), and rapped smartly on the door. We waited. And waited. The minutes ticked by and I was just thinking that if this was the Future it was not very efficient, when Maisie said, 'There's smoke coming from the chimneys, mum.'

'Where? Oh yes, so there is. Then I daresay it's simply that they didn't hear our knock. It's a big house, after all. I think we'll try the door, Maisie; we're here on perfectly legitimate business.' On reflection, do not think the word 'legitimate' entirely tactful, given circumstances, but Maisie did not seem to notice.

So I reached out to the vast iron ring-handle, and turned it. It protested a bit, and then it turned on its moorings, and I pushed open the door.

The hinges shrieked like a thousand banshees in torment, and once we had stepped inside the heavy old door swung back on itself, thudding into place like a tombstone being displaced on Judgement Day, and if that was the sound the inhabitants of Mortmain had to put up with every time anyone came in or went out, am not surprised that some of them are, as Mother phrased it, a touch wanting.

As the door closed we both froze, expecting people to instantly appear and demand to know our business, but nothing moved anywhere. There was a lingering smell of mildew and mice and everywhere was rather dark, with a dismal, depressed gloom that made me feel as if we had gone into a tunnel. But after a moment my eyes adjusted, and I could see that we were in a good-sized hall with some nice old panelling covering the walls, although it was a shame that no one had bothered to polish or even dust it. Several doors opened off the hall, and there was a wide staircase at the back, with sagging shallow treads and a beautiful carved banister.

Whoever had built the original Mortmain House had clearly been a person of some discernment. Have a half-memory of Father once saying that it was some seventeenth-century squire who speculated in one of the South Sea Bubble schemes and lost all his money, poor man, although Father never had much sympathy with unwise speculation, not the behaviour of a gentleman and think yourself lucky, Charlotte, that Edward so very reliable when it comes to financial affairs.

'We'll take a look round,' I said firmly to Maisie.

Now I admit that this was not the most sensible decision, in fact writing this entry in the privacy of my old bedroom (marvellous not to have to share a bed with Edward for a while!), I will freely admit that it was the action of a fool.

But we went in, Maisie and I, Folly and Innocence hand in hand into the lions' den or the devil's lair, whichever it was, and I called out to know if anyone was here. ('Always be polite, Charlotte, no matter the circumstances...') A horrid echo of my voice came back at us, exactly as if the place might be empty after all, and the poor little daisie cringed with fright. (Brought up in East End, one of a family of fourteen, and not used to so much empty space.) So to bolster up her courage (to say nothing of my own), I said we would take a look round.

Mortmain is a terrible place. The walls are damp and everywhere smells disgusting, and we had to step over puddles on the floors where the condensation had dripped off. At least, I pretended it was condensation—alternative explanations too revolting to contemplate. There's a maze of dark, dank corridors that immediately made me think about the labyrinth where the minotaur lived, arrogantly demanding a feast of virgin once a year. (Why are monsters in fables nearly always male, I wonder, and why was it always virgins they wanted?)

As we went through the corridors we kept hearing the clatter of crockery from somewhere unidentifiable and invisible, and several times we caught the scents of food cooking. Not very nice food from the smell of it either, in fact boiled cabbage and Lenten pottage if you ask me, but it was a note of domesticity that ought to have been cheering (something reassuringly down-to-earth about boiled cabbage). But it was not cheering at all, because every time we tried to go towards the sounds, thinking to at least find sculleries if we did not find anything else, we seemed to go deeper into the gloom. Like a nightmare where you can see the place you want to reach but you never manage to get close to it. I began to wonder if we should have brought a ball of twine with us, or at the very least a stick of charcoal to mark the blind alleys.

Was just thinking that in spite of boiled cabbage Mortmain must have been abandoned, when we rounded a corner where two corridors converged, and without warning saw a child. At first I thought it was a patch of shadow but then it moved and I saw that it was a child of perhaps ten years old. And the pity of it was that I could not at first tell if it was a boy or a girl, so thin and so raggedly clad and shorn-haired was it.

'Intruders?' said the little creature. 'Come to view us, have you?' It was not quite the local accent, but there was a faint lilt that reminded me that we were almost in Wales and that the Welsh make the most beautiful music, and I could not help thinking how, under different circumstances, this rough, suspicious little voice might have sung the wonderful Welsh ballads and love songs and war laments.

I said, as gently as I could, 'Certainly we have not come to view you. Only to visit. To see what kind of place this is.'

The child considered us, head on one side, and I suddenly ached to reach out to it, and hug some warmth into its suspicious face, and ruffle its short hair into silky curls and tell it that the world was a good place outside these walls. Did not do so, of course. Could hear Mother's shocked voice saying, But it might have *fleas*, Charlotte, or headlice. Did not much care if it had both, but had to fight sudden rush of emotion, and remind myself very firmly that if Viola and Sorrel had lived their childhoods would have been very different from this! Stupid way to think! Still, for several minutes I had to struggle not to show my feelings— 'A lady never makes a scene, Charlotte.'

The child was watching us closely. Then it said, 'But you want to know things about us as well, don't you? That's why most grown-ups come here. We know that.'

'There might be a little baby we would need to bring here to live.' But even as I said it I already knew I was not letting Maisie's child come here, not if I had to adopt it myself and defy Edward and his mother.

'Oh, a bastard,' said the child, in a dismissive, is-that-all, voice. 'They bring lots of those to live here.'

The off-hand use of the word and the tacit compre-
hension of its meaning ought not to have shocked
me, but it did. I said, 'Are there many children living
here?'

'Sometimes there's more than others. Some get
taken away, though.'

'To new homes?' Because if Mortmain was, after
all, an honest-dealing place where orphans were
found respectable places—

'Homes?' said the child scornfully. 'No.' It was
nearly, but not quite, Nah. 'Where've you been living,
missus? When we're old enough it's the men take
us.'

'The men? I don't understand—' Oh don't be naif,
Charlotte, of course you do!

The child was regarding me with pitying contempt.
'It's for the places in London. They buy children for
them. Don't you know anything?'

Brothels. Houses of ill-repute. But children? Yes,
children, Charlotte. You knew it went on, didn't
you?

I had known, of course I had. But I said, disbeliev-
ingly, 'People come here to—to take little girls away
with them?'

'Not only girls.'

'Boys are taken as well?'

'Some men like boys, didn't you know that?'

I let that one pass. 'But can't you do anything about
it?' I said. 'I'm sorry, I don't know your name—?'

'Robyn.' It was a boy's name, but from the way she
said it I realized that this was the feminine version.
This was a little girl whose hair ought to be in ring-
lets, and who ought to be dressed in ruffles and laces,
instead of this horrid no-colour, no-shape garb.

'Then, Robyn, isn't there someone here that you
could tell? About the men who come?'

'Who would we tell?' Again the note of scorn. 'They're all in the dodge anyway. So we don't trust anyone. Specially not visitors.' This last was said with contempt.

'You can trust me. Truly you can. Perhaps I could do something to help you.'

She looked at me thoughtfully, as if trying to decide how far we could be trusted. I thought she assessed my outfit and its probable cost as well, and I was absurdly relieved that although I was still wearing mourning for my babies, I had put on a plain merino wool costume of dark grey that afternoon, with a very unassuming hat. ('Always dress suitably for the occasion, Charlotte, never embarrass those less fortunate than yourself.')

'Anyway, we've found our own way of dealing with the Pigs,' said the child.

Pigs. Most children think pigs are rather sweet creatures—curly-tailed and daintily and pinkly fat like the fables and the fairytales—but when the child, Robyn, said the word it was filled with such loathing that I saw the men through her eyes: I saw their mean little pig-eyes and snouty faces. They would tramp through Mortmain's vastness, slyly pointing with thick fingers. We'll take this one today and that one, and those two we'll leave for a couple more years until they're ripe...

'What do you mean, "deal with them"?' I said. 'How do you deal with them?'

Again the assessing look. It was extraordinarily piercing and very disturbing. For a moment I thought she was not going to answer, and then she seemed to come to some kind of decision. She said, 'All right. I'll show you. But you must promise never to tell.'

I looked at Maisie, and said, 'I promise.' Maisie nodded, too afraid to speak, and I said, 'We both promise. You have our solemn word.'

'That's not enough. You got to promise on the thing you hold most sacred in the world. That's what we do in here. Usually it's our mothers if we can remember them, or a brother or sister. You got to promise on something like that.'

Without hesitation, I said, 'Then I promise on the memory of my two babies who died. I promise on the memories of Viola and Sorrel that I'll never tell.' I looked at her. 'That is the most sacred and most precious promise I can possibly make, Robyn.'

'All right. I believe you. But first,' said the odd little creature, 'we have to spit on our hands and press them together.'

It was a childish ritual, but Robyn somehow imbued it with such solemnity that I found myself doing what she asked, and making Maisie do it as well. After we had all spat and clasped hands, Robyn said, 'That means that you can't ever betray me and I can't ever betray you. We're friends now, and we're bound together for the rest of our lives.'

Bound together. I stood staring down at the odd ragged child with the huge intense eyes, and thought: so that is now four—no, five—people to whom I have become bound in the course of my life: I am forgetting Edward, and certainly I am bound to Edward—we were bound together in matrimony two years ago in the church across the fields behind Mortmain.

And I am bound to Viola and Sorrel, inextricably and for ever and no words are needed for that.

And Floy. No words are needed for that, either. Because if I am bound to anyone in the entire history of the world, I am certainly bound to Floy.

CHAPTER TEN

HARRY HAD NOT read more than three pages of *The Ivory Gate* before he realized that Philip Fleury had been an extremely good writer. Fleury had the ability to paint vivid, evocative word-pictures, and also an extraordinary ability to slide inside his characters' minds, scraping out their inner emotions, and then offering those emotions to the reader with a kind of uncaring arrogance. Take it or leave it, but this is how it was.

It was necessary to turn the pages of the book with caution because they were so extremely old and brittle, but despite this the story and the people—particularly Fleury's central heroine—came strongly up from the musty paper and took on substance.

As a baby, the heroine had been summarily taken to one of the dreadful institutions that scarred Victorian and Edwardian English life: as far as Harry could tell it was a cross between a workhouse and an orphanage, with the worst characteristics of both. He glanced at the publication date, but there was nothing about 'originally published...', only a publishers' note to say that this edition had been printed in 1916.

The child—her name was Tansy—had been taken to the institution shortly after she was born. Philip Fleury made a reference to her birth being 'shameful in the eyes of the pious, fraudulent world', and just as Harry was thinking this bland euphemism struck a discordant note against the image he had begun to form of Fleury, on the next line Fleury added, 'A love-child. By any other name, a bastard,' and Harry relaxed, because for some inexplicable reason, whatever else he wanted Philip Fleury—Floy—to be, he did not want him to be a prig.

But Floy was not a prig. So far was he from being a prig that, like Charles Dickens fifty or sixty years before him, he must have stirred up a good deal of resentment by his graphic descriptions of workhouse conditions in general, and by his scathing denouncement of the beadle-bureaucracy that had held sway. He must also have disturbed a great many of his readers by his accounts of the sufferings endured by the residents of his own mythical workhouse-cum-orphanage. Harry found it harrowing to read the book, but despite this he could not put it down. You were a spell-weaver, Floy, he thought. What we'd call today a page-turner. My God, I hope you got proper acknowledgement of your work. I hope you made a fortune out of it. I hope that 'C' and Viola and Sorrel, whoever 'C' and Viola and Sorrel were, got a share in it.

Floy's story was woven out of very dark strands indeed—at least, its opening was—and the small Tansy's story was perforce set in a dark landscape. From the age of four she was made to pick oakum in what was called the Women's Workshop, which meant unravelling old lengths of rope in order to scrape out the tar. She lived and slept with the adult women, and ate with them in the long, wooden-floored refectory; most days the food consisted of thin gruel and occasionally salt pork, and coarse bread, with water to drink. I still hope you made a fortune, Floy, thought Harry, but I'm starting to hope you'll give Tansy a happy ending. Or were you one of the morbid writers of your era, immersing your readers in angst and weltschmerz and whatnot, without any glimmer of hope or happiness at the end of the tunnel?

Tansy's early life was not precisely unhappy though, mostly since she had never known any other way of living. But her creator was unhappy for her, and the reader was unhappy for her as well. Harry, able to visualize all too clearly the small docile figure with its shorn hair and shapeless clothing, had to keep reminding himself that this was fiction, for God's sake, it was a story that had existed in the imagination of a man who had lived nearly a hundred years ago. But the setting for Tansy's story was not fiction, and some of the players were probably not fiction, either.

What came most strongly from the dry, brittle pages was the atmosphere of a child's fear and despair, and with it, the kind of surreal, Salvador Dali images that might have scalded a six-year-old's mind. The women who lived in the workhouse... Their faces were like melted tallow candles, Tansy said. As if they had got too near to the stove, and their faces had run a bit. This puzzled Harry for a moment, but then he understood that the lack of fresh air and the unrelentingly hard work would make the women pallid and lifeless, and that they were most probably lumpily fat from the unhealthy food they would be given.

There were overseers—hard-faced women—who walked around making sure everyone worked hard enough. Tansy said they had fingers like whips to sting you with, and if you saw them in the dark you might find that their eyes were red, like rats' eyes were red in the dark. So she knew what rats looked like in the dark, thought Harry, appalled and pitying. And then with an exasperated shake of his own mental processes—oh, for goodness' sake, this is *fiction*! She never actually existed, this odd, shorn-headed child with the bright, original imagination.

The grown-ups who Tansy sometimes sat with to
work or eat had talked about something called the
Speenhamland System, doing so furtively and fearsomely,
stopping at once if any of the rat-eyed overseers or
the beadle came along. Tansy did not know what the
Speenhamland System was, but there was a man who had
explained it to them all one night in the dormitory when
they were supposed to be asleep. It was something about
a village called Speen, where some men called magistrates
had said that poor people should be given more help and
more sympathy.

Tansy had still not really understood, but she had
listened because it was quite exciting to be having this
secret meeting with the grown-ups, and also the man
who talked to them looked a bit like you imagined the
devil would look when he had put on a human disguise
in order to tempt you. The children all knew about the
devil because of church every Sunday, and because of
the Bible class with Mrs Beadle's sister on Sunday afternoons, when there were sometimes biscuits given out. The
devil could be very cunning indeed, so you had to keep a
sharp look-out. But no one thought it was very likely that
the devil would bother to put on his man-disguise and
get himself shut away with paupers, so it was probably
all right to listen to the dark-haired man. He said words
differently because he had lived in another country, which
was interesting. He said they should all band together and
insist on the Speenhamland System being operated here; it
was the law and their right, he said, and he wanted them
to stage a rebellion, but when it came to it nobody was
brave enough. Shortly after this the man vanished, and
Tansy never found out what had happened to him.

Sometimes her friends, the other children, vanished as
well. Somebody said it was because when you were nine
you could be sent to work in the mills and that this was
where the children were taken, but somebody else said, in

a whisper that made Tansy feel very frightened indeed, No, it was not the mills at all, it was because the pig-men took them. Tansy had seen the pig-men; they had thick, coarse skins, shiny with grease from too-rich food, and small mean eyes, and fat hands with rings on, and everyone knew you had to keep out of their way if you possibly could.

The pig-men carried the children off to London to the stews. That was why you had to keep out of their way if you could, although one day the children would do what the dark, devil-man had said, and they would fight back at the pig-men. But nobody could see how that could be done, and even if a way could be found, nobody was really brave enough to do anything.

But Tansy thought that one day somebody would be brave enough, or perhaps it was simply that one day somebody would be frightened enough. She thought that if it came to it—if it was ever her turn and the turn of her friends to be carried off to the stews—she might be sufficiently frightened to fight the pig-men. She thought she might hate them enough to even kill them.

She did not entirely understand about the stews, because stews meant something you ate, and that meant that her friends were being taken away for people to eat them in a hot, savoury stew. She could not think of a way to cheat the pig-men and neither could any of her friends, so in the meantime she made a vow—a proper solemn vow, kneeling down at the side of her bed and praying to Gentle Jesus, meek and mild, look on me a little child— that she would never let the pig-men take her away to be put in the stews. She promised to be good for ever and ever if Jesus would make sure that never happened, and she asked Jesus to help her and her friends to find a way to escape if the pig-men ever came to take them to London and the stews.

The thought of somehow being able to escape was like a strong light pulling her forwards.

The thought of somehow escaping—of getting away from Joe for ever—was the one thing that kept Mel sane, and enabled her to behave normally in Joe's company, and even to discuss the proposed party.

But all the while ideas and plans and strategies were coiling in and out of her mind, until one morning she saw that that she had shaped a workable plan out of them. OK, so now I know what to do. Now it's a matter of coming to grips with the practicalities. Furtive phone calls to letting agents. A few questions to be asked, and the answers to be considered. This was all made much harder because most of it had to be done at Isobel's flat, and all correspondence had to be sent to Isobel's address so that Joe would not find out what she was doing.

'This is something you should have done long since,' said Isobel, who was pretty and lively, with an interesting job in the City and a number of lovers, past, present and potential, and who did not really understand what it was like to marry the wrong person. But Isobel did understand that Joe was spiteful enough to put all kinds of obstacles in Mel's way if he found out what she was planning, and she knew it was vital that Mel simply vanished, leaving no clues to her whereabouts. She was a good friend and she could be trusted completely.

One of the agents had sent details of a little house in a small Norfolk village, which Mel thought might be what she was looking for. Only a small cottage, only two-up-two-down, said the agent, a touch apologetically, but really quite snug and sound. Oh yes, very peaceful. Quite off the beaten track, if you wanted to be romantic about it. Mel did not care about romance, providing the place was far enough off the beaten track to be invisible.

The area sounded all right, but the cottage itself had to be taken more or less on trust, although in the end Isobel made a quick journey there on Mel's behalf, phoning to report when Joe was not around. The place was quite old and a bit basic, she said, but it was by no means derelict and she thought it would fit the bill. There was a largeish garden and no near neighbours, and the village, which was half a mile away, consisted of a scattering of cottages, a church, a village hall, and a small general stores. 'It's a bit bleak because it's so near to the coast, but I think it's as good as you'll get, in fact I think the situation's exactly what you want. And the house is perfectly clean inside, although the furniture's slightly battered, and the kitchen and bathroom are a bit old-fashioned.'

'I don't mind old-fashioned,' said Mel. 'And I don't mind bleak or battered, either. It'll only be for a couple of months until after the operation. After that it doesn't matter if Joe finds out where we are. But until then I want somewhere that's sufficiently out-of-the-way to be safe, but not so remote that there aren't shops and doctors and things within reach.'

Isobel said that Norwich was about eighteen or twenty miles away, and there were odd little market towns dotted around as well. 'And listen, what about money? I know you said you'd scrape along but will you really manage? You won't be able to draw on the bank account, will you, because it'll let Joe know where you are.'

But Mel had a little money from when her parents had died, and she thought that if she was careful there would be enough to live on for three or four months. It had been in a separate account at a building society—her one tiny fragment of independence and she could with-draw it all before leaving, and then open a new bank account in a different name. If you handed cash across a counter people did not worry too much about who you were.

And once in Norfolk she could live very simply; the biggest drain on resources would be the cottage rent. It had been a surprise to find how much people charged for this kind of letting, and she had had to agree to a six-month lease.

'I suppose that's all right,' said Isobel, listening to these plans. 'But you haven't allowed for a car, and you'll need one out there.'

'Cars are almost as traceable as people. I'll manage without one. Masses of people have to.'

'Not on the edge of Norfolk, for goodness' sake,' said Isobel. 'And not with four-month-old conjoined twins to ferry around. Sorry if that sounds a bit brutal, but you've got to be practical. I know you're going to turn into a hermit while you're there, but you'll need to go out for food and fresh air now and again.'

'I'll work something out.'

'I've already worked it out for you. Take my car. It's time I got another one anyhow, and the value of second-hand cars is laughable these days.'

'I can't possibly take your car—' Isobel's car was only three years old.

'Yes, you can. Call it an extra christening present. I'm Sonia's godmother anyway. And it's a hatchback, so you can have one of those collapsible pram things for the twins.'

So Mel had accepted the car, privately resolving to one day find a way to reimburse Isobel, and had gone ahead with the rest of her plans. If by some freak chance Joe did pick up a clue she had overlooked and light on this eastern corner of England, there were so many little villages, and so many odd clusters of houses and cottages along little winding lanes, that it would take him ages to actually find her. Especially with a false name.

A false name. Using Charlotte Quinton's name on the rental agreement sent to Isobel's house and opening the building society account in the name of Mrs C. Quinton had made Mel feel oddly close to Charlotte, and to Viola and Sorrel, who had seemed to slip out of the writers' and the social historians' sights.

There was a sense of adventure at getting into Isobel's car after Joe went off to his office one morning, putting hastily packed cases in the back, strapping the twins' carry-cot carefully in.

As Mel drove away she could not believe how easily she had managed to deceive Joe.

CHAPTER ELEVEN

ROSAMUND RAFFAN HAD thought that she and Melissa Anderson had become really good friends while Melissa was in the clinic having her babies. Roz had worked hard at the friendship and she had been pleased with what she had achieved.

But clearly she had not achieved as much as she had believed, because when the twins were four months old Melissa vanished without so much as a word; going off into the blue, taking the babies with her, and not telling Roz where she had gone. This was disappointing and frustrating until it turned out that she had not even told her husband where she had gone.

Roz was horrified; she could not imagine anyone treating a husband like that. The elderly aunt who had brought her up had always said that if you were lucky enough to get a husband, you should treat him with respect. This was a hopelessly old-fashioned outlook, of course, but even so Roz could not believe that Melissa could be so dismissive and so cruel to Mr Anderson, that kind, selfless man. What a bitch. And Mr Anderson was absolutely distraught over her disappearance. Of course he was. He phoned Roz at her house, telling her what had happened (it was very gratifying to be the repository of his confidence, although Roz did not let him guess this), and then saying he had a request to make of her.

Roz asked what kind of request, and Mr Anderson said it was private and a bit delicate. It would be better if they could meet. He did not want to burden her with his troubles, but—

Roz, unsure what he was expecting of her, thought for a moment, and then rather hesitantly asked if he would like to come to her house. They would be completely private there because she lived on her own. No, it would be no trouble in the least. Any evening he liked. That very evening? Yes, she was off-duty tonight. Yes, seven o'clock would be convenient. Here was the address. No, it was not imposing at all, and she quite understood that he did not like to ask her to come out to his house because you never knew who might be watching.

There was a pleasant and rather flattering flavour of importance about this. It reminded Roz that Joseph Anderson might, before the year was out, be sitting in the House of Commons, shouldering vast and awesome responsibilities, on nodding or even hob-nobbing terms with Cabinet Ministers and Secretaries of State. She remembered that she had been going to have cheese on toast for her supper tonight but in the light of Mr Anderson's visit she called at the supermarket on the way home. He would not expect to be given supper and Roz was not going to be wide-eyed and naïve over this Member of Parliament stuff. But there had better be some-thing a bit more upmarket than cheese on toast to offer if the occasion arose.

She bought fresh chicken and mushrooms in the supermarket, and added a bottle of wine. She was not very knowledgeable about wine: her aunt had not approved of ladies drinking, and although Roz had had a couple of rather half-hearted, lukewarm boyfriends they had both drunk lager so wine was fairly unknown territory. There was a bewildering array in the supermarket, with an astonishing variation in prices, but in the end she bought something called Chianti Classico, because everyone knew about Chianti, and Classico had a reassuring sound. She added a bottle of whisky and some soda, because most men liked a whisky and soda, and bought fresh flowers on the way home as well; flowers always looked nice in a room. The house was a bit old-fashioned because there had not been any particular reason to change anything after her aunt died. But the furniture was nicely polished, and anyway Joseph Anderson was not coming to conduct a Homes and Gardens survey.

She poured him a large measure of whisky when he arrived, and by way of diluting any slight awkwardness, said, 'D'you know, Mr Anderson, until you phoned I truly didn't know your wife had run away. I thought—we all thought—she was staying with her family.'

'That was the official version,' he said sadly. 'And listen, do call me Joe, won't you. Everyone does.'

'Joe.'

He drained the whisky in his glass and set it down, and Roz wondered if she was expected to refill it. Whisky was awfully expensive, but it would not do to appear mean. She poured another, smaller one for him.

Mr Anderson—Joe—was talking about Mel and the twins, and saying he could not leave any stone unturned to find them. So what he had wondered was, whether there might be anything—any clue?—that Rosamund might be able to pick up for him at the clinic? He knew he was probably overstepping medical or ethical boundaries in asking it, but he was at the end of his sanity, he really was. He understood, of course, that Melissa had succumbed to some form of panic and had run away to be on her own for a time, he said. He understood that it was most likely a hormonal thing, as well, following the birth. This was said without any of the embarrassment that men so often displayed when they talked about things like this. Even the so-called New Men could become curdled with awkwardness. So Roz admired Joe for not being embarrassed, and was quite flattered that he felt able to be so open with her.

The most immediate worry, said Joe, was that he did not think Mel had very much money. Certainly she had not withdrawn anything from the joint bank account, so he had no idea what she was living on. He had been torturing himself with visions of her struggling to feed herself and the babies—perhaps not able to afford enough food, or proper heating, cold and miserable and hungry somewhere... He supposed he was just a silly old-fashioned romantic with a too-vivid imagination, but he simply could not bear to contemplate it. Roz saw that he had to choke down a sob when he said this.

Anyway, said Joseph, sitting up a bit straighter, and speaking in the brisk voice of a man determinedly pulling himself together, he had been wondering if Martin Brannan's office might have been in touch with Melissa over some sort of medical check, and if they might have an address or a phone number on record for her. Well, no, he did not like to bother Brannan himself. But he knew Rosamund had been a good friend to Mel, and he had thought she might take a look in the hospital's files. Just discreetly and unofficially. Would it be too much to ask? He looked at her very intently when he said this, and Roz saw that 'discreetly and unofficially' meant secretly and furtively. Looking through patients' records to find an address or a phone number that had probably been given in confidence.

She said, carefully, that it sounded a bit risky. And of course there were quite strict rules about disclosing patients' details.

'I'm asking too much,' said Joe at once. 'I should have realized—' He paused, frowning, and Roz understood that he was trying to master his feelings. He had been seated in the armchair nearest the fire, but he got up and came to sit next to her on the sofa, reaching for her hands. His skin felt hot and his hands were a bit pudgy, but they were still hands that might one day be signing State papers, which was an awesome thought. Roz let him go on holding her hands.

'I'm so sorry,' he said, seriously. 'I've overstepped the mark, I see that. It's just that I'm so upset I'm not thinking very clearly. And I've always found you so easy to talk to. As a matter of fact I've always thought of you as a rather good friend.' His voice sounded different. Warmer. 'I've always thought of you as someone I could come to in trouble, Rosie.'

Rosie. It came out on a sudden note of intimacy and it startled Roz very much. No one had ever called her Rosie before. She had been Rosamund to her aunt, who did not approve of abbreviating names, and she had been Rosamund at school and also to Sister Tutor in the nurses' school, as well. More recently, she was Roz, which was friendly and casual and modern. But she had never been Rosie, not to anyone, not even the half-hearted boyfriends. It almost made her feel like a different person. Someone whom men—even important men like Joe Anderson— might find attractive.

He was still holding her hands in both of his. Roz found she did not mind about this at all. After a moment she said, 'How about the police? Have you thought of asking them to trace Mel—?' But clearly this was the wrong thing to say, because his eyes snapped with sudden anger.

'Oh no, the police mustn't come into this. Not on any account. The publicity could be so damaging.'

'Would that matter?'

'I mean damaging to Mel and the twins,' he said quickly. 'You'll understand that, of course.'

Roz did not understand it at all and she could not see why Joe could not call in the police but she could not very well say this. After a moment she said, 'I'll see what I can find at St Luke's. There might be a clue somewhere. I can certainly look through Mel's records without anyone knowing, and I could talk to Mr Brannan's secretary—I know her quite well.'

'That's a good idea,' he said eagerly. 'Girl stuff. Gossip. Would you do that for me, Rosie?'

Rosie. It occurred to Roz that Rosie might be prepared to do all kinds of daring and adventurous things. (Such as continuing to let somebody else's husband hold her hands...?) 'Yes,' she said. 'Yes, I would. And if I find anything that might help—an address or something like that—I'll phone you, shall I?'

'I'd be so grateful if you would.' He set down the whisky glass and said he supposed he had better be going; he had taken up too much of her evening as it was.

It was Roz who marked his wistful glance at the nicely crackling fire and the comfortable armchair with the evening paper folded nearby, but it was Rosie who said, 'I don't know if you've eaten yet, but you'd be very welcome to share my supper.'

'I don't want to put you to trouble—'

'It wouldn't be any trouble. It's only some chicken.' Pause. Don't rush it, Roz. 'There'll be more than enough for two, and I do think you should have something. The distress of all this— And while we eat, we could try to think if there's anything else I could be doing to trace Melissa through the hospital.'

'You're a very kind girl,' he said. 'Very sympathetic. I'd like to stay to share your supper. It's rather lonely in that big house at the moment. Can I help you with the food?'

It was quite flustering to have a man in the kitchen and he did not really seem very adept with plates and cutlery, but he did open the bottle of wine which was useful. Fortunately, it seemed to be acceptable; Roz had a glass and Joe drank the rest. He was becoming a bit flushed, although Roz thought she might be a bit flushed herself. It would be the excitement of the occasion, of course. Entertaining a man to dinner, and the plan to find Mel. Maybe it would be a bit to do with the wine.

Joe had another whisky after the meal, and talked a bit more about Mel and the twins. 'If I could just know where she is, Rosie— I'm hardly bearing to think of those two trusting babies in some squalid backstreet somewhere.' He broke off, blinking, and fumbling for his handkerchief, and Roz went out to the kitchen to put on a pot of coffee, so that he could master his feelings, the poor man. You did not often see men giving way to their feelings like this; it was flattering to think that someone so important had let the barriers down in front of her.

When she came back she saw that he had poured himself another whisky; it was nice that he felt sufficiently at home to do that. He said he was sorry he was being such a silly old fool giving way to his emotions, but there had been no one he could talk to like this—no one he had felt he could ask for help.

He leaned against the sofa back, and somehow one of his arms slid around Roz's shoulders. He pulled her against him, and bent his head to kiss her. Roz was so thrilled that he found her attractive enough to kiss that she did not in the least mind that his kisses were a bit slobbery and whisky-smelling, or that his hands were thrusting eagerly beneath her sweater. But when his hands suddenly moved down and slid up under her skirt, prodding right up between her thighs, she gasped, and tried to pull away. You did not do this with somebody else's husband—Roz's aunt would have been scandalized to even think about it. For a moment the shadow of her aunt seemed to move in the room, and then Joe mumbled something about loving her and wanting her, and the word 'love' fell on Roz's mind like a blessing. Love. He *loved* her. He had said so. That changed everything: it took it out of the realms of just a tumble on the sofa and into something serious and definite.

She was glad to think that although she had not really had any proper boyfriends at least she was not a virgin. At least she had done it with somebody—well, almost done it. Sort of done it, even if the boy had fumbled and even if it had been at an awful school-leaving party in somebody's rich parents' house, with everybody pairing off as the evening wore on, and going off into bedrooms.

You were supposed to beware of the person who was the leftover in that kind of situation, but it had been a case of either pairing up with the leftover or being looked at pityingly afterwards. Roz had been fed up with being a leftover, and of not having lost her virginity at eighteen, in fact of not even having had a boyfriend.

So she and the leftover had gone into one of the bedrooms, well, actually, it had been the au pair's room, because all the other rooms were taken by that time. There had been the sound of twanging bedsprings and muffled giggles from the next room, and then there had been five minutes of embarrassment, and a further five minutes of groping and panting. When he unzipped his trousers Roz had been surprised, because the upper fourth biology classes did not really prepare you for the reality.

There had been the feeling of hard blunt flesh pushing into her, bruising and tearing, and of hot breath gusting into her face, and just as Roz was wondering if this was all there was to it, and if so, how boring, the whole thing seemed to be rather messily over. They had had to mop the au pair's eiderdown with tissues and then Roz discovered that she had been half-lying on her skirt which was also marked, so that she had had to put it on back-to-front for the rest of the party, and she and the leftover had studiedly not spoken to one another for what remained of the evening. She had thought that if this was the act that the poets wrote about, and that the entire culture of modern-day love songs was based upon, and that people died for and renounced kingdoms for, as far as she was concerned you could keep it.

But Joe Anderson loved her, and he was older and more experienced and this would be different.

It was not different at all. He lumbered on top of her, saying she was being a wonderful comfort, he had been so dismal and distraught and she was so kind. He was a bit breathy from the whisky, and his hands were a bit ungentle. Roz tried not to mind it, and she tried not to mind that he felt heavy and suffocating on top of her. The settee was rather narrow for two but Roz was not sure about the etiquette of suggesting they go upstairs to her bedroom.

Then he seemed to be having trouble getting inside her; for a dreadful moment Roz thought he was not going to manage it at all, because he felt a bit floppy between her legs. She had no idea what you did in that situation. But then he seemed to recover, and he started to move urgently and then even more urgently, so that she had to gasp out that she was not on the pill or anything.

Afterwards he said he was sorry he had not stopped in time but he had been in the grip of such passion. It was brilliant to hear him say that, even though Roz had not much enjoyed what he had done. She said he was not to worry about any of it.

He had another whisky, and Roz wanted to telephone for a taxi because he had drunk quite a lot of alcohol, but he said he would be fine; he was one of those rather rare people whose reactions were actually sharpened by a few drinks.

After he had gone Roz had to get dressed and deal with the washing-up. There was quite a lot of it, and because she had not done it immediately after the meal as she normally did, gravy and fat had cooled and dried on to saucepans. She washed and dried everything, carefully polishing the wine-glasses that had been her aunt's. The one that Mr Anderson had used had a crack down one side. It had not been cracked when Roz got it out of the cupboard, so he must have put it down a bit too sharply on the table. It was a pity because it spoiled the set but they had been fragile glasses to begin with, and you could not expect a man to be dainty-handed.

CHAPTER TWELVE

JUST AS IT had been the daring, dashing Rosie who had invited Joe Anderson to supper, so it was Rosie again who sneaked into Martin Brannan's office after hours and searched his files.

Roz would never have dreamed of doing such a thing: certainly she would not have read confidential information about patients or colleagues, but Rosie got a tremendous kick out of it. Like a heroine out of a spy film. Intrepid and resourceful. Risking everything for the man who loved her.

At first there was nothing to be found, which was a nuisance, not because Roz gave a damn what happened to Melissa, but because of wanting a reason to phone Joe. There would surely be a clue eventually though, and when she found it she would make the call, and she would suggest cooking dinner again for the two of them. She would make it a bit special this time, with something really lavish to eat and the table set with candles and her aunt's crystal wine-glasses—there were still three uncracked ones in the cupboard.

She made an appointment with her GP so that he could prescribe the contraceptive pill for her; it was important to indicate to Joe that she returned his love—that she had liked his love-making and wanted it to happen again without him having to worry about stopping in time. Roz had found that a bit embarrassing. It would be easier to buy condoms than go on the pill but that might be even more embarrassing, especially if she bought them in the small local supermarket where she had shopped for years, and where her aunt had shopped for years, and where the staff knew all the customers and amiably scrutinized people's groceries, and often commented on them. Imagine plunking down a wire basket containing wine and scented candles and contraceptives. The pill would be a much better idea, and everyone was on it these days.

In the end it was three weeks before she was able to phone Joe's office.

'It might not be much,' she said, 'so I don't want to get your hopes up too high. But it might be worth looking into.'

'Yes?' He sounded efficient and businesslike over the phone. Roz visualized him seated at his desk, busy and preoccupied, wearing a crisp white shirt and a dark suit.

'This morning,' she said, trying to match the businesslike tone, 'Mr Brannan had a letter which was marked "Private". His secretary collected it from the mail-room—all the secretaries collect their bosses' mail and take it up to them for ten o'clock each morning. She didn't open the letter, of course, but after Mr Brannan read it he asked her to set up a meeting with one of the paediatric surgeons. She told me about it at lunchtime in the canteen—she's by way of being a friend of mine and we quite often have our lunch together.' No need to say that she had been diligently cultivating the friendship for the last three weeks.

'Mr Brannan didn't say which patient the paediatric meeting was for,' said Roz, 'and his secretary thought that was a bit odd because normally he would have asked her to sort out patients' records and so on, and made sure she would be free to take notes at the meeting.'

'You think it was Melissa who sent the letter?' It was what Roz had thought, but faced with this crisp questioning she wavered. Perhaps after all she had flown to a too-easy conclusion. But before she could speak, he said, 'It's a reasonable assumption, of course,' and Roz relaxed a bit.

Greatly daring, she said, 'If it is Melissa, it sounds as if she's setting up the operation for the twins behind your back, doesn't it?' and this time heard his quick sharp intake of breath down the phone. Ah, she had thought that would get his attention.

But he only said, 'Did you find out any more?'

'Well, yes, I did.' Roz tried not to sound too gleefully triumphant. 'I got the envelope from the waste paper basket before the cleaners went round. And I think I've managed to decipher the postmark.'

'Oh, good girl.'

'It's smudgy, but it's just about readable. Norwich. And there's an E after Norwich, which the post office said means Norwich East. I phoned the sorting office to find that out.' She paused to let this sink in, and then said, 'So I think Mel and the twins are somewhere on the east coast of Norfolk, fairly near to Norwich.'

'Wonderful,' he said. 'Absolutely wonderful.' Ah, *now* there was the warmth in his voice she had been listening for.

'Will you be able to find her from that, d'you think?' she said.

'Oh, I think so. It's not a very densely populated area, the east coast. Not like a big city. I'll get a private detective on to it—' He said this in an off-hand way.

'Mightn't she be using another name?'

'Yes, but my man will be looking for a young woman with two tiny babies who arrived on a specific date.' Again the slight arrogance. My man.

'Yes, I see.'

'It'll be a question of checking new house-lets or even hotel registers,' said Joe, 'although I don't think she'd have gone to an hotel.'

Roz did not think so, either. She said, tentatively, 'Will you want the envelope? For—for your detective?'

'I suppose I'd better have it, hadn't I?' He paused, and Roz waited hopefully for him to say he would call at the house that evening. She wondered if she might manage to squeeze in a lunchtime appointment at the hairdresser's.

But he said, 'I'm quite busy for the few days. This by-election, you, know—'

'Yes, of course.'

'Could you drop it through the door when you're passing?'

'Oh—yes. Yes, I could do that.' Roz was not likely to be passing because the house was quite a long way from the hospital and from her own house. But she said, 'Yes, I'll drop it through your door.'

'You're a star, Rosie. I'll let you know how the search goes.'

She went to bed that night wondering which day she should take the envelope to his house, and what time of day he would be there. Early evening might be a good time, say around seven o'clock. That was an hour when Joe would probably be home from his office, but it would be a bit early for him to have gone out anywhere. Yes, she would go along around seven tomorrow night.

Drifting into sleep, she wondered what kind of place Melissa Anderson had found for herself, and where exactly she was in Norfolk.

The tiny village was called Castallack, and after the first couple of weeks when every creak of the cottage's old stairs made Mel start up out of sleep in fear and when she succumbed to panic at the sight of every stranger walking a dog along the lane in front of the house, or bird-watching in fields behind it, she found it remarkably peaceful.

Castallack was almost on the edge of England's easternmost point, and the cottage was only about half a mile from the start of the coastline. There were several rather intriguing local legends about how this had been one of the ancient sentinel points marked by the Druids, and how the Druids had set guardians—castellans—along the coast in order to guard England from the increasing threats of invasion by Christianity-peddling monks, and from Franks, Romans and assorted Vikings. It might be interesting to read up the place's history in a bit more detail; Mel almost began to regret that she would probably not be here long enough to make a real study of the area.

She had decided that after one month she would feel sufficiently safe to write to Martin Brannan and ask if they could begin the preparations for the twins' operation. She would explain that she had left Joe, and ask him to carry out the operation solely on her authority and to keep it all absolutely confidential. She thought he would understand all that and she thought she could trust him. The letter would have to be sent to him at St Luke's, but if it was firmly marked 'Private' that ought to be safe enough.

As Isobel had said, the cottage was a bit basic and quite small. There was a sitting-room with an old-fashioned open fireplace, a kitchen opening off it, and a twisty stairway behind a door in the sitting-room that led up to two minuscule bedrooms—one with another small fireplace—and a bathroom. This, too, was basic, but there was nothing really wrong with it. The hot-water system was a bit antiquated, but workable. I'm coping and I'm surviving, thought Mel. This is all right.

She liked Castallack, and she liked the huge skies and the clean pure eastern light. Which painter had said that there was no light anywhere in the world quite like that of Norfolk? Turner, perhaps. And the cottage was the kind of place that she would have enjoyed renovating: renewing the worn window-frames and restoring the old brickwork which had softened to tawny red with the years, and which, in the glow of the setting sun, looked as if it was washed by fire. It would have been pleasant, as well, to drive around local antique shops, looking for odd bits of really nice old furniture—carved blanket chests or Victorian sewing-tables with silk pouches under the lid. She did not do any of this, of course. The cottage's condition was the owners' concern, and there was no money to spare for buying furniture. As well as that, she was still frightened to take the twins out more than absolutely necessary in case someone realized who they were.

So she stayed in the cottage most of the time, working in the small overgrown garden with Simone and Sonia lying on a rug on the grass or in their carry-cot, and she read and sketched, and listened to music and watched the small portable television, although the reception was not very good out here. Occasionally she felt sufficiently brave to take the twins' pram for a walk along the lanes, but she was always fearful of meeting someone who might, in rural fashion, want to stop and talk. And the twins were getting plenty of fresh air in the garden in the gorgeous late-summer sunshine, and Mel was getting plenty of exercise in tidying it up. Once she pushed their pram out to where the stretches of marshlands began—Marsh Flats they were called locally and they eventually merged with the North Sea—but it was so bleak a place and there were so many notices warning of the treacherous quicksand nature of the Flats themselves, that she came back.

Milk and eggs and cheese were delivered by a nearby farm, and once a week she drove into Norwich to stock up at one of the large supermarkets. She varied the days for these expeditions, going to a different supermarket each week, bundling the twins up as much as possible and transporting them in the wide carry-cot that fitted on to the collapsible pram-wheels. Her purchases were ordinary and unremarkable, and anyone glancing in the pram would only see two babies sleeping closely together, and would not make any connection between the quietly dressed lady with her babies and the recent Anderson twins who had caused so much interest in the press.

She had opened a building society account in Norwich with her parents' legacy and she had had to use her own name for that but it was a small local building society and unlikely to come to Joe's notice. She had not dared apply for any kind of credit or debit card, and she drew out cash on the first of each month to cover household expenses, asking for a cheque-withdrawal made payable to the agents for the cottage rent, because the tenancy was in the name of Quinton. Other than the shopping trips and the occasional foray into a library or a book shop, she did not go out.

There was no phone in the cottage and Mel did not dare arrange for a phone to be installed in case Joe could track her down through it. Mobile phones were still mainly used by sharp young business executives, but they were becoming a bit more available although they were still quite expensive. Mel bought the cheapest she could find so that she could summon help in an emergency. Isobel phoned her on this every two or three days; Joe, it seemed, had told people that Mel had gone to stay with her family for a week or two, and as far as Isobel knew, he was not making any inquiries about Mel's whereabouts. Which means, thought Mel, he's either accepted my leaving, or he's being very sly indeed about trying to find me. Well, at least any strangers to Castallack would be conspicuous so if Joe sent out private detectives she would know about it.

She had half-expected to be bored, but she was not. She enjoyed returning from the weekly shopping trip, entering the cottage with her own key, putting the carry-cot in a corner of the kitchen, talking or singing to the girls while she stored away the food. They were already responding to her voice, chuckling and waving their little starfish hands. (But it was always Simone's right hand, and it was always Sonia's left hand, because they were still locked in that helpless embrace...) They liked the sound of her voice, and they liked it when she sang. Perhaps they were going to be musical.

Each evening, after the twins had been fed and bathed, she cooked herself a meal before curling up on the battered sofa with music on the small cassette player she had smuggled out when she left. After the first couple of weeks the weather turned stormy so that it was rather nice to close the curtains each evening and build up a wood fire from the little log store outside the cottage, and to hear the rain against the windows. She began to relax properly, to feel safe. Even before the self-imposed month was up she even felt safe enough to write the letter to Martin Brannan. She posted it in the little village post-box the same day. It was absurd to discover that the next morning she woke up with a pleasurable feeling of anticipation, because he might be reading her letter that very day. No, allow for country posts; give it a couple of days. And then another couple of days for him to reply. But perhaps by this time next week she would have heard from him. He

might even drive up here to see the twins. Was it being
naïve and adolescent to think that? Well, she would think
it anyway. He could stay at the village pub if he came, and
Mel might cook dinner for them one of the evenings.

Roz had decided to cook a meal for Joe and to take it to his
house when she delivered the envelope with the Norfolk
postmark. The poor man was still on his own in that big
place which must be very lonely, and he would appreciate
a nice meal. Roz would not push it to stay and share the
meal, but it was fairly certain that he would ask her to do
so. He would be able to tell her how the search for Mel was
getting on: he had promised to do so and she was keen to
hear about it.

Flowers had arrived for her the day after she phoned
about the envelope. A lavish cellophane-wrapped bouquet
of pink and white carnations, with a card written in a
rounded, rather childish hand, almost certainly that of the
florist. It spelt her name wrongly, and said, 'To Rossamund.
Thank you so much for your kindness. Warmest regards,
Joe Anderson.'

Warmest regards. Thank you so much for your kindness. They were not exactly the sentiments you would
expect from a man who had said he loved you, and who
had undressed you and then himself on your own sofa, and
apologized because he had been too far gone in passion to
withdraw before reaching a climax. But of course he led
such a busy life, and there might have been any number
of people in earshot when he had phoned the flower
order through. Roz could understand that. She intended
to behave discreetly and tactfully, although whispers of
the truth might filter outwards from time to time. 'Joseph
Anderson glimpsed with the mysterious lady said to be

a close companion.' That was the kind of thing the more gossipy newspapers printed. It would be romantic.

She enjoyed planning the food to take to his house. She bought pork steaks at the supermarket, secretly pleased by the interested comments from the girls there. 'Two steaks, Miss Raffan? That's unusual for you. Are you having a visitor?' Roz smiled and said, yes, a friend was coming to have supper with her, and had they not any of the puréed apple in stock? Oh yes, there it was on a new shelf. It was nice to think of the supermarket people gossiping after she had gone, telling one another that she was a dark horse, that Miss Raffan, and speculating as to whether the supper guest was a boyfriend.

When she got home she moved happily around her kitchen, cooking the pork in mushroom gravy, and tipping the apple purée into a small container so that it could be heated up. If she did jacket potatoes until they were three-quarters cooked they could be wrapped in foil and finished off in Joe's own cooker. She wondered about a pudding, and decided to make a treacle tart—all men liked treacle tart. She rolled out the pastry in the old-fashioned way her aunt had taught her, using not a rolling-pin but a lemonade bottle filled with cold water, and grated fresh breadcrumbs for the topping. It all smelled very good in the oven.

It was raining quite heavily by the time the taxi came for her. It would be a bit expensive travelling all that way by taxi, but it was two bus journeys to Joe's house, and Roz could not take pork and treacle tart on buses.

Even after all these years there was still a guilty nervousness at the extravagance of the taxi. Her aunt had not approved of paying good money out for things like that. For why had God given you feet, she said, if not to walk? She had not really approved of people being out after dark either, unless there might be a church meeting, or an emergency where you were called on to play the Good Samaritan. But normally, once darkness fell curtains were firmly drawn and doors and windows uncompromisingly locked. The power of Satan was everywhere, said Roz's aunt sternly, but never more so than at night. When night darkened the streets, the sons of Belial wandered forth, flown with insolence; so Rosamund must be very wary of the night. It was not until years later that Roz came across the whole quotation, which was that the sons of Belial wandered forth, flown not just with insolence but also with wine. It was typical of Roz's aunt that she had not mentioned the wine. She had probably not known the whole line, though.

She asked the taxi to drop her off at the end of the road. She had already decided that she would walk the rest of the way in case any neighbours saw her. It had to be remembered that Joe was quite an important man and likely to become even more important soon. It would not do for people to gossip about him—at least, not in a sly squalid fashion. Romantic gossip would be all right.

The taxi fare was eight pounds seventy-five, which was more than Roz had expected. It was to be hoped Joe offered to drive her back home later on because she only had five pounds left in her purse. He might ask her to stay the night, though. Roz did not know if this would be exciting or alarming.

It was still raining quite hard and there was a lot of mud on the road. Roz was wearing her mackintosh and she had tied a rainhat over her hair because she would not be able to manage an umbrella as well as the bag with the food. She could whip the rainhat off before she knocked on the door: she did not want Joe to see her with a plastic hood over her head. But she had put on high-heeled shoes that flattered her ankles but had rather thin soles, and the rain and mud were already soaking through them. The plastic hood had slipped a bit as well, and her hair was getting rained on. Still, once she was in the house she could get dry and warm.

The light was on in the big sitting-room, and Joe's car was parked in the drive. Roz's heart lifted with delighted anticipation and her mind flew eagerly ahead, visualizing Joe opening the door and greeting her with surprise and pleasure; seeing him take her into the warm kitchen and help her to get dry. How nice your hair smells when it's drying, Rosie... Then he would rub her hair with a towel, and bend over to kiss the back of her neck, like people in films did. And, pork with apple sauce, he would say—my absolute favourite food. You are so thoughtful. We'll open a bottle of wine to go with it, shall we...

She had just drawn level with the gate when the front door opened and light streamed across the garden. Joe came out of the house carrying a small suitcase, and closed and locked the door behind him. This had not been in the plan, so Roz hesitated.

She saw him put the suitcase in the boot and slam the lid, and she stepped back into the shadow cast by the thick hedge. Surely he was not going away—surely he would not go away without telling her? The man who had been in the grip of such passion that night that he had not been able to stop in time...?

He was going away, though. He walked briskly across the lawn, and went through a narrow gap in the hedge between his house and the next-door house. Roz, curious and puzzled, crept forward along the road a bit until she was level with the other house. Someone had opened the door, and Joe was saying something about here was the key, and it was good of them to keep an eye on things while he was away. Make sure the milk delivery didn't get it wrong and pile up milk bottles and so on. Open invitation to burglars, wasn't it?

Oh yes, he said, just the couple of days, as planned. Well, yes it was all work and hardly any play at present, still you know what they say about hard work, never hurt anyone, haha. Yes, he would be bringing his wife and the twins back with him; they had been spending a couple of weeks quietly in Norfolk—marvellously peaceful place, Norfolk. The break had done Mel a lot of good, she had been getting a bit wound up what with the newspapers and all the interest in the twins, and then she had been a bit low after the birth, you know how women get, old chap. Still, he would be glad to have her and the girls back, he did not mind admitting it the house had felt like a morgue.

Anyway, here's the key. Thanks very much.

He came back to his own drive, got into his car and drove away.

After a few minutes Roz turned round and began to plod back home. Her feet in the thin, pretty shoes, were sodden, and her hair was plastered against her neck where the rain had got under the hood. It did not matter. It was all part of the dreariness and the misery, and people who wrote about the poetry of the rain, and about walking through it mourning a lost love with rain and tears mingling, had clearly never done so with wet feet and sodden gloves, and a heavy bag with congealing pork and gravy seeping into a freshly-made treacle tart. She dumped the food, bag and all, in the first rubbish-bin she came to.

Joe had tracked down Melissa—the detective must have found her and told him where she was. And now he was going to bring her back. He had not taken the trouble to let Roz know, even though he had promised he would, even though he had said he loved her, and had made love to her that night...

It looked as if she had made a fool of herself. It looked as if her aunt had been right with all those admonitions. Don't make yourself cheap. A man never respects a girl who lets him have his way with her.

It was almost nine o'clock when she finally got home. Joe's red and white carnations were still in the vase on the hall table; the smell of them filled the house, mingling with the odour of roast pork from the still-warm oven. Roz suddenly felt so sick that she had to rush to the kitchen, where she hung over the deep old-fashioned sink, retching helplessly. From now on misery and shame would always smell of carnations and pork and wet dishcloths.

After she had finished being sick and had sipped some water, she put the flowers in the dustbin. Then she fetched the packet of contraceptive pills from the bathroom cabinet and threw them in as well. Waste of good money on a prescription, her aunt would have said. You should have known he'd let you down after you let him maul you about. Maul. Was that all it had been?

CHAPTER THIRTEEN

Mel HAD GONE to bed early after a strenuous after-noon in the garden, taking a long hot bath first to wash away the stiff muscles from bending and weeding. It was nice to have your own bed after the years of sharing one with somebody you did not like very much. Tonight, because there was a definite chill in the air, she had made a little fire up here as well. When she was a child she had always had a fire in her bedroom in winter. It was remark-able how secure it made you feel. She would like to give the twins that memory of warm drowsy safety, if she could.

The flames were sending shadows leaping and twisting over the white-washed walls, and the twins were sleeping peacefully in their cot near the window. Simone liked watching the patterns that the trees and the morning light made on the walls, so Mel had positioned the cot so that Simone was nearer to the window. Perhaps Simone would do something in the art line—painting perhaps or designing of some kind—and Sonia would be the musical one.

She read for a while, gradually growing sleepy. When she reached out to switch off the bedside light the dying fire mingled with a thin spear of moonlight that had slid into the room where Mel had not properly closed the curtains. Nice. She would take the moonlight and the radiance and the scented firelight into sleep with her. She had the feeling that she would have pleasant dreams tonight. Martin Brannan? said her mind, and her lips curved into a smile. That was a treacherous way to think, but still— She might hear from him quite soon. It was just over a week since she had posted the letter.

She was just crossing the boundaries between being awake and being asleep when a sound broke into her consciousness. She was not instantly alarmed; she had learned most of the cottage's sounds by now and the sound had most likely been nothing more than the wind in the trees outside, or a roof timber contracting in the cool night air. No, there it went again. Mel sat up, still not exactly frightened, but listening intently. It was not the roof timbers or the old tree outside, it was more like soft footsteps going round the outside of the cottage. Someone prowling around the garden? She glanced at the bedside clock. Just on midnight. It was probably nothing more alarming than a scavenging fox. And she had locked the cottage doors anyway before coming up to bed. The front door had a strong bolt at the top, and the garden door in the kitchen had a chain. No one could get in. She prepared to lie down again.

The sound came again, and this time there was no mistaking it; this time it was the scraping noise that the gate leading to the cottage's back garden made when anyone opened it. Then there was someone creeping around outside! For a wild, panic-filled moment Mel had absolutely no idea what to do. She glanced across at the twins, who were still asleep.

Surely it could not really be a burglar? There was absolutely nothing in the cottage worth stealing. Yes, but remember its isolated situation, said a voice in Mel's mind. And what if you've been noticed, and marked down as a female living alone, with only a couple of small babies for company...?

She grabbed the dressing-gown lying across the foot of the bed and flung it round her shoulders, trying to think what she should do. She had left the mobile phone downstairs, plugged into the mains to recharge it, but she could get downstairs and summon help inside of a minute: 999, and the police would come screeching out here, sirens sounding and lights blazing. Yes, but remember that the police force covers a wide area out here, and the station is in the next village, seven miles away. Ten minutes for them to get here? Yes, easily that. So what if he breaks in during those ten minutes? But let's be sure of the facts before we start invoking the sirens and the blue flashing lights.

She went cautiously over to the window, and peered through the thin sliver she had left uncurtained. Deep wells of darkness lapped around the cottage walls, and nothing moved anywhere. False alarm? Or had that been a movement just beneath this window? She looked back at the twins' cot. Please don't wake up, twins. You'd only be frightened, and I'd do anything in the world to prevent you being frightened.

There was the crunch of footsteps directly under the window, and the dark outline of a man stepped into Mel's sightline, the head tilted back as if he was looking up at the cottage windows, to see if anyone was there. Mel dodged back out of sight at once, her heart hammering against her ribs. There is someone out there! Oh God, oh God, why did I come out here to hide from Joe! Why didn't I go to live on some large modern housing estate, where everyone's anonymous anyway, but people are within yelling distance!

She glanced round the bedroom. Simone was still asleep, but Sonia had woken up and had turned her head to watch the window. She knows there's someone there! thought Mel. Or she's picking up my panic. Fury rose up in her, because it was monstrous, it was not to be borne, that some greedy, mean-minded burglar should come snooping and creeping around the house and frighten the babies!

The bedroom door was the old-fashioned wooden kind with a latch. No key on it, of course, and there was nothing in the bedroom that was heavy enough to wedge against the door. But there was a heavy earthenware bedside lamp, and the base would deal a pretty hefty blow. Could she use it if he broke in? She looked at the twins again. Yes, she could. OK, let's make that dash downstairs for the phone.

She crossed the room and went swiftly down the narrow stairs, trying to do so quietly, trying not to disturb the twins, because if he heard babies crying he might realize how extremely vulnerable she was— The big bad wolf sniffing round the lambs' pen— Don't start thinking like that!

When she opened the door into the sitting room the tiny current of air stirred the embers of the dying fire, and the charred logs stirred and flickered into life. The crouching shadows moved and for a moment Mel thought he was already inside. But it was only the firelight after all. So far so good, then. The phone was where she had left it, plugged into the socket at the side of the hearth. She was halfway across the room when there was a movement beyond the curtained window. There was a pause, and then the sound of someone knocking on the door.

Mel had been in the act of reaching for the phone, but at the sound of the insistent intrusive tapping she froze, and then turned to stare at the door.

The knocking came again, louder this time. He knew she was in here, of course. But did he honestly think she was going to open the door at this time of night? Or that she was going to behave like some wimpish heroine from a seventies horror film and invite the lost traveller or the stranded motorist into the lonely cottage? 'Car broken down? H'm, h'm, oh dear me, *what* a pity, and oh yes, of course you can come inside and use my phone...'

She had just managed to force her shaking hands to switch the mobile phone on, when there was a scrabbling sound from outside, and to her horror the old-fashioned latch-handle moved. He's trying get in, thought Mel, and for a bizarre moment the famous *Red Riding Hood* scene came into her mind—the part of the story where Red Riding Hood knocks at the door of Grandmamma's house, and is told to pull the bobbin and the latch will go up...

The latch was going up now. It was being slowly lifted from the other side: Mel could see it clearly in the uncertain light of the dying fire. The door shuddered slightly under the pressure. It would not open, of course; it was firmly locked and bolted. But supposing he went around to the kitchen door and managed to snap the safety chain off? Or he might try to break one of the downstairs windows and climb in... But if I can throw off this frozen terror, I can dial the police—

From the other side of the door a voice—a voice that was at once recognizable—called out, 'Melissa? Mel, it's me. I know you're in there. Let me in.'

The terror shifted its patterns and became a fear of a totally different kind. Joe! He's found me! Her hand hesitated on the phone. If I call out the emergency services now, once they realize it's my husband they'll only think it's a—what do they call it?—a domestic. Because Joe can be very convincing when he wants...

'Melissa,' said Joe's voice, sounding so close that he must be pressing up against the door, 'if you don't open the door, I'll smash the window and climb through.'

Still in the fairytale, thought Mel wildly. Only this time it's the big bad wolf, threatening to huff and puff and blow the house down if I don't open the door to him... I'll have to open it, of course. If he does break the window it'll certainly wake the twins, and they'll be terrified. A tiny shoot of anger curled upwards at that, and then she moved to the door, unlocking it and drawing back the bolt. The door swung inwards, and there was the cold, slightly damp scent of the outside air entering the cottage. Joe stood for a moment looking at her; he looked large and menacing.

The silence stretched out, and Mel had no idea how long it was before she finally said, 'How did you find me?'

And Joe said, 'Never mind that. I've come to take you home.'

❉ ❉ ❉

He would not say how he had found her. He murmured something about private detectives and persuasion, and about the tracing of cars, but he looked so spitefully triumphant when he said this that Mel could not ask any more questions.

She said, 'I'm not coming back with you, Joe. I'm really not.'

'Oh, yes you are,' he said, and there was a chilling hardness in his eyes and in his voice. 'I'm not letting you take my daughters away from me, and I'm not letting you subject them to Martin Brannan's mutilation.'

Mel said, 'So it's gone from a surgical procedure to mutilation now? And how do you know it hasn't already been done?'

'I do know,' he said. 'For one thing there hasn't been sufficient time.' He looked round the cottage. 'How many beds are there upstairs?'

'One.'

'Then I'll sleep down here on the sofa. It took longer than I thought to drive up here— I didn't get away from the office until nearly seven, and then there were road-works on the motorway. That's why I arrived so late. Don't try any stupid tricks, will you? I'll hear you if you try to sneak out.'

The rest of the night was dreadful. Mel did not think she slept at all. She lay upstairs, staring up at the ceiling, turning over and over ideas for stealing downstairs and getting into her own little car and driving away. But what-ever she did she had to take the twins with her, and she could not see how she could do that without waking Joe. And even if she did make a run for it, where would she run to?

In the morning Joe sat at the little wooden-topped kitchen table, clearly expecting Mel to cook breakfast for him. When Mel said, shortly, that there was no bacon or sausages because she did not have a cooked breakfast, he said he would have scrambled eggs and toast. He even praised the eggs, which he said were much nicer than eggs bought in the supermarket, you could always spot real free-range farm eggs, and he drank two cups of coffee. It was a pity it was not proper ground coffee, wasn't it, but he would make no objection to instant for once.

It was almost nine o'clock and a thin autumn mist was lingering outside, wrapping ghostly grey fingers around the trees. If Mel had been on her own she would have enjoyed being inside on a morning like this: she would have switched on lights and zapped around the cottage with polish and dusters, with the radio tuned to some bright music.

She had just washed up the breakfast things when Joe said, 'Time for us to set off home, Melissa.'

Home. The place where the glass cage is waiting. Mel was still trying to hit on a way of getting free of him but the grey mist seemed to have got into her brain and none of the half-formed ideas of the night seemed remotely possible.

'Just pack what you need,' said Joe, following her up to the bedroom. 'If you can't pack everything we'll send for the other things later. We'll have to get your car collected, anyway.' So he was not going to let her drive back in convoy with him. It had been clutching at straws to think he would.

Mel had the feeling that there was something odd about the morning but she could not pin the feeling down. She took things out of the wardrobe and the dressing table; she had not brought many clothes up here with her but what she had brought she piled into a case, adding the twins' things. As she dressed the twins she felt even more woolly-headed, and once, bending over to tie on Simone's little bonnet, she had to clutch the back of a chair because the room had tilted and spun all around her. It would be the sleepless night, of course, and the shock of Joe finding her. Once outside her head would clear and she would be able to think of something. She tucked an extra shawl over the twins because of the damp morning. When she put them into the little carry-cot Joe clucked disapprovingly at it, and just for a second or two he was again the man she knew and had married: irritating and old-fashioned and over-fussy about appearances.

But she got into Joe's car which he had parked at the side of the cottage, and sat on the back seat with the twins. The fresh air was not making her feel any better, in fact as Joe drove down the little lane she was feeling very light-headed indeed and slightly sick. The thought of having to endure a three- or four-hour journey home feeling like this, shut into the car with Joe, was appalling. At least the twins were being good; they liked being in a car. Mel usually sang to them while driving; she could see Sonia looking at her, as if expecting it now.

'This is better,' said Joe. 'I'm glad to be out of that frowsty cottage.'

It stung to hear him denigrating the cottage that had been so snug and so safe-feeling. If Mel had felt clearer-headed she would have challenged that one. She wound the window down to let in some fresh air, and then said suddenly, 'This isn't the road to the motorway—'

'No. We're making a detour.' He glanced at her. 'We're going out to the Marsh Flats,' he said. 'Yes, I do know all about them, Melissa. I did my homework on this place before I came up here to find you.'

The cold terror came rushing back. Marsh Flats. The place where people sometimes died in tragic accidents. The farm delivery-boy, when he called for his milk-and-egg money each week, had gleefully related tales of unwary tourists and naturists who had succumbed to the Flats' unpleasant and glutinous embrace. 'Drag you down like quicksands,' he had said, and after that first brief exploration Mel had resolved to steer well clear of the place.

And now Joe was driving her out to them.

She said, with an effort, 'The Flats aren't a very pleasant place for a drive. They're very desolate.'

'I know.' He swung off the road and there ahead of them were the bleak wastes of quagmires and marsh. Mel stared through the car window. The Flats were not precisely the shifting sands of sensational or gothic fiction, but they were not far off. There were patches of loose sand here and there, oddly interspersed with the thick, oozing silt that could suck people into its depths... ('Drag you down like quicksands...')

And now here was Joe—Joe who normally thought the countryside was just somewhere you drove through on your way to somewhere else, and who had never, to Mel's knowledge, even possessed a proper pair of walking shoes—parking the car on the grass verge, and telling her to get out so that they could walk a little way.

'I'd rather stay in the car—'

'No, you won't stay in the car.' Clearly he was prepared to drag her out if she resisted.

'What about the twins—'

'They'll be fine on the back seat for a few minutes. I'll lock all the doors. And we shan't be out of sight of them.'

When Mel got out of the car her legs seemed to have turned to rubber, and she had to clutch the door to prevent herself falling. This was something more than lack of sleep and the shock of Joe turning up. Or was it? But as Joe reached out to put his arm about her shoulders and began to propel her towards the gate leading to the Flats, she suddenly understood. I'm drugged! The evil bastard's drugged me! Something in the coffee at breakfast? She pushed his arm away, but by this time she was so disoriented that she was able to make only the most feeble of flailing gestures.

'You put something in the coffee.' It came out slurred, as if she had had too much to drink.

'I did.' Nodding, as if pleased. 'Six paracetamol. I brought them with me, crushed in an envelope. And I stirred them into your cup while you weren't looking.' Incredibly there was a lick of self-congratulation in his tone. 'It's just enough to make you giddy and weak and drowsy.'

By this time Mel was struggling so hard against the sick dizziness and the engulfing waves of sleep that she was barely aware of him pulling her through the gate, and on to the treacherously narrow towpath that wound through the Flats.

On a spring or summer day the marshes probably looked gentle and benevolent, and they were probably filled with all manner of wildlife and unusual flora, but seen today, on this early autumn morning with the sea-mist lying along the ground, and clinging to the occasional stunted tree that grew out here, they were bleak and slightly sinister. The few sparse trees that grew out here dripped with moisture, like stealthy footsteps creeping along just out of sight. Drip-drip, step-step—

Mel managed to say, 'Joe, what's this all about—?'

'This,' he said, and there was a sudden flurry of movement. His hand smacked into the small of her back, and Mel was propelled violently forward, off the towpath, and straight into the squelching, sucking mud of the Marsh Flats.

CHAPTER FOURTEEN

M EL DID NOT fall headlong, she slithered awkwardly, wrenching an ankle painfully as she tried to save herself, and ending up feet-first and thigh-deep into the quick-sands. It was the most disgusting sensation she had ever encountered. She was wearing corduroy jeans and trainers, but even through them she could feel the thick mud lapping greedily at her legs.

She struggled to climb out at once and realized with fresh horror that she could not: it was as if her feet had been planted firmly in quick-setting concrete. The more she struggled the more the glutinous mud seemed to pull her down. But it would be all right: Joe was on the towpath and there was only about six feet between them. Mel held out her hands to him, expecting him to crouch down and reach out to pull her free. But he did not move. The world began to fill up with panic.

'Joe! For God's sake pull me out!'

A long pause. Then— 'I'll need to think about that,' he said.

'Joe, don't play games! For God's sake get me out!'

'I can't let you interfere with my plans, you see,' said Joe. He was half-kneeling on the path, watching her.

Almost to himself, he said, 'I'm going to be so successful, you know. Parliament, and later on the Cabinet. I'm easily good enough for that. There's no limit. Don't you want to share in all that, Melissa?'

'Yes. Yes, of course I do!' Oh God, you evil monster, I'll share in anything if you'll get me out!

'Then why did you try to take away the best weapon I had?' he said reproachfully.

'Weapon—'

'The twins. So much sympathy there'll be because of the twins. I'll sail through the by-election because of them. Poor good Joe Anderson, bearing such a hardship so bravely. Such staunch religious convictions. Just the kind of man we need in Parliament these days. Just the kind of man for a Cabinet post.'

Mel was hardly believing he was saying all this, even though deep down she had known these things all along. There was a wild moment when she wanted to argue against him: to say, You stupid selfish monster, if you leave me to die you'll never get away with it! And there was another moment when she saw, quite clearly, that he probably would get away with it; he would tell the story of how he had found his poor bewildered wife out here and tried to bring her home where she belonged, but how she had run from him, and had tumbled head-long into the marshes. I tried to get her out, he would say sorrowfully, and he would probably even choke down tears. I tried to rescue her, but she was too far out. He might add that since the twins' birth she had been over-emotional, given to melancholy. He would not use the term post-natal depression, but people would use it for him, and nod solemnly, and say what could you expect, poor dear.

Isobel might put up an objection, and Martin Brannan might support her, but not even Izzy would think that Joe was capable of murder. And so his story would be believed, and even if they recovered Mel's body all they would find would be traces of paracetomol, not big enough to be an overdose.

But I don't have time to argue with him about any of that and I barely have time even to think it, because I've got to get out for the twins' sake I've got to get out... But each time she tried to get free the quicksands pulled her deeper, slopping and squelching as if the marsh were smacking its slabby lips over this unexpected morsel. She was going to die, and once she was dead Joe would have the girls to himself, and he would use them in his campaign, and he might keep using them—over and over again... Oh God, I can't let this happen!

She said, 'Joe, listen, I'll do whatever you want. If you want the twins to stay as they are I'll accept that. I'll try to understand your feelings and—and respect them.'

'Will you? Can I trust you, Melissa? If I really thought I could trust you I might let you live,' he said.

'You can trust me, truly you can!' The mud smelt like wet, creeping mould, and it was gaining a hold on her. This would be a dreadful way to die. One of her hands was caught in the mud now, and the more she struggled the more it pulled her down. Like sticky grey fingers. Like horrid snatching goblins deep below the surface.

'Joe, I promise! I'll agree to anything in the world—'

If there had been a tree root nearby that she could hang on to, she might have managed to get out under her own steam, but there was nothing. Nothing except the swirling mists which were already clearing to show a hazy sunshine, and nothing but desolate wastes of the marshes.

Joe said, as if considering the matter, 'I suppose if you're really promising— And there's a rope in the boot of the car that I could get.' He stood up and appeared to consult his watch. 'I could run back to get it, but I don't know if there's time now— I think I might have left it too late.'

Oh, you fucking bastard, thought Mel who hardly ever swore. You're playing with me! You know to the second how long it will take to get the rope, and you know to the instant how long this murderous mud will take to drown me! Forcing a note of calm into her voice, she said, 'Yes—please Joe—please fetch the rope.' The mud was around her waist now, and her right arm was starting to ache intolerably with the strain of keeping it above the surface. But I must keep that hand free because he'll get the rope and I'll be able to grab it— I know he'll get the rope, really—

He did get it, of course. He had always intended to get it. He went swiftly back to where the car was parked, reaching into the boot for a coil of rope, and returning nimbly along the towpath. Mel managed to watch him all the way there and back. Once she thought he had missed his footing and that he was about to tumble off the path into the marshes' waiting lips, but he did not. He came back and stood looking down at her again.

'There's one more thing, Melissa.'

'What?' The muscles of Mel's right arm and shoulder were screaming with pain. 'Tell me—quickly!'

'We're never going to speak of today,' he said. 'None of this ever happened. If you tell anyone about it, I'll deny it, of course. I might even have you declared unfit. Mentally sick. Yes, I could do that, I think.'

'I understand.' Her right arm was a mass of red-hot agony; any minute she would be forced to lower it, and it would go down into the mud, and then she would be unable to reach the rope that he was still coiling and uncoiling between his hands. Horrid hands. How could I have let those hands anywhere near my body? She said, 'I won't tell anyone about it, Joe. You have my word.'

Precious seconds ticked by, seconds which could not really be spared. Then Joe said, 'OK, here's the rope. Get ready to be hauled out.'

The ancient quicksands did not easily give up their prey. There was a bad moment when Mel saw panic flicker in Joe's eyes, and when she thought, He didn't intend to let me die after all! But he's miscalculated—he really has left it too late!

And then slowly, inch by reluctant inch, the slopping, sucking mud loosened its grip, and with a sound like a wet wound being forced open she was out; she was being dragged on to the towpath, and she was shivering and sobbing and the landscape was spinning around her, and she had to cling to Joe because she could barely stand. But she was not going to die.

He had to help her to walk along the path: by herself she would certainly have fallen on the treacherously narrow path. And then she did fall. She missed her footing or she skidded—perhaps the path or her shoes were slippery from the mud—and she stumbled hard against him.

He fell back, flailing at the air to regain his balance, and went straight into the quicksands where, only moments earlier, Mel had struggled for her life.

He struggled just as she had done. Of course he did. He fought like a thing possessed to get free of the glutinous morass, and with every movement he made he sank deeper in. He looked grotesque, wallowing in the slabby grey mud; he looked like a monstrous human fly trying to drag itself free of a gunked-up flypaper.

Mel sank to her knees, still helplessly dizzy and weak, but looking round for the rope he had used to get her out. Nowhere to be seen. Of course it was not—they had let it fall back into the mud minutes earlier.

Joe was screaming at her. 'Get me out, you stupid cunt! Do something!'

Do something... Yes, something, anything— Mel dragged the narrow leather belt of her cords off, fumbling the buckle a bit because her hands were still slimed with mud and desperately cold, but managing it in the end. 'Joe—grab the end of my belt—'

He made one feeble attempt to reach the belt but missed. 'It's useless! It's not long enough, you mad bitch! Get something stronger! For fuck's sake do something!'

He was disgusting and obscene, panting and spluttering, his eyes bolting from his head in panic. The mud was slopping and licking around his waist, and one of his hands had become stuck in it as well.

'I'll go for help,' said Mel, but when she stood up the world tilted and spun all round her again and she half fell back on to the path. But she said, 'I'll get back to the car— I think I can manage to reach it. Can you stay above the level of the mud?'

'For Chrissake, of course I can't!'

'I've got a mobile phone in the car—'

'There's not *time*—can't you see there's not time! It's pulling me down by the minute—I can *feel* it! Like hands clutching at me—' So he was feeling those hands as well? 'Oh God, *do* something—'

This time Mel managed to stand up properly and to scan the horizon, because surely, surely, there would be someone at hand who could help. But there was no one to be seen, and there was nothing to be done, and he was sinking faster now, because his weight was displacing more of the mud. Once his shoulders went under he would have no chance at all of getting free. How long would it take? Five minutes? More?

In the end it took nearer eight minutes, and those eight minutes seemed absolutely endless. Once he said, 'I'm going to die, aren't I?'

'*No*. I'll get you out,' she said, kneeling on the towpath, fighting off the blurry dizziness, trying uselessly to stretch out a hand to him. 'We'll manage it somehow. Try to reach my belt again.'

But he could not, and there was no longer anything in the world except the mist-shrouded quicksands and the wailing of the seagulls overhead, and the oozing mud and Joe's flailing hand that she could not reach. He had horrid hands. How could I have let those hands anywhere near my body? Yes, but I can't let him die like this...

'Joe, I won't let you go under—'

But he did go under. He sank down and down into the heaving marsh and at the end he began to choke, slowly and horribly, helplessly inhaling the silty mud, frantically trying to keep his mouth and nostrils clear of it, but unable to do so. His face was streaked with the slopping ooze; it was in his eyes, blinding him painfully, and although once he tried to get a hand up to wipe it away he could not. Several times he retched violently, sicking up the mud that was slopping into his mouth.

Even after he had gone completely under the surface it was still possible to hear the dreadful wet gasps for several minutes. Little air-bubbles came up to the surface, but they finally stopped.

After what felt like a very long time Mel recovered suffi-ciently to drive Joe's car back to the cottage. It was a nightmare journey and it was as well there were no other cars on the road because she was barely able to steer straight.

She left the twins lying happily in the sitting-room, and before she did anything else she mixed and drank a pint of warm water with a heaped tablespoon of mustard stirred in. It made her violently sick two or three times over, but although she still felt shaky her head was clearing. She thought she had got rid of most of the paracetamol and the revolting mud, and after this she phoned the local police on her mobile phone to report what had happened.

While she waited for them to come out to the cottage she got into a hot bath and tried to scrub and scour and shampoo away the stench of the marsh.

Joe's body was recovered, of course, although it took two days to do it, and it was a messy, distressing process. But in view of the media interest—which was as much due to the twins as to Joseph Anderson himself—the body had to be got out.

Everyone was very kind to Mel and very patient with her and everyone accepted without question her explanation of an after-breakfast walk and a mis-step on the narrow slippery towpath. Dreadful, they said. And of course they understood that she had wanted a few weeks of anonymity somewhere with her babies, after all the press attention. Perfectly understandable. But how tragic that it should end like this, with her husband dying in such a macabre way on the very day he had driven up to spend a few days with her.

Isobel drove up to Castallack and stayed at the cottage with Mel. God, what a frightful thing, she said. An absolute tragedy. Mel thought she would not have got through it all without Isobel.

There had to be a post-mortem of course, and there had to be an inquest. The post-mortem showed death to have been due to the ingestion into the lungs of wet mud, in fact, in layman's terms, Joseph Anderson had choked to death. An analysis of the stomach's contents indicated eggs and bread and coffee, the digestion process suggesting it had been eaten about an hour before death. Questioned, Mel said yes, they had had toast and scrambled eggs for breakfast.

The verdict of the coroner was the only one possible, given the evidence. Accidental death. The coroner extended sympathy to Mel all over again, and added a rider to the effect that the local authority should make Marsh Flats less accessible to the public. No one expected Mrs Anderson to stay on at the little cottage, and no one was surprised when she and the friend who had come to support her went back to her North London home the day after the inquest, taking the little ones with them.

Mel supposed that when the twins were older she would tell them that their father had drowned in a seaside accident when they were very tiny. Yes, there was enough of the truth in that to be acceptable.

She would never be able to tell Simone and Sonia that Joe had tried to kill her. She would never be able to tell anyone what had happened.

CHAPTER FIFTEEN

SIMONE KNEW SHE could never tell anyone what had happened. She had made a promise not to do so, but the promise was not really needed because she would always be too frightened to say anything anyway.

It had been the year they went to live in Weston Fferna; the summer of her eleventh birthday. Mother had kept the promise about buying a camera as a birthday present; she had said Simone was old enough to understand about looking after expensive things. The camera was a really good one, and Simone had taken about a zillion photographs all through that summer. Mother thought they were very good indeed; she thought Simone showed real talent.

And all the time, lying quietly at the back of her mind, was the image of Mortmain House and the plan for photographing it—not just the outside but the inside as well. The thought of even walking up to Mortmain's door was the scariest thing in the world, but Simone knew there were stories of people who had taken ordinary photographs, and had found things on the developed print that had not been there at the time they took the shots. There was a word—spectral—which meant not-quite-in-the-world and sort of meant ghosts, and Mortmain was surely a place where you would expect to find ghosts.

Ghosts. The pig-men who carried the children off. The little girl with the sly, sooty eyes who whispered inside Simone's mind.

How difficult would it be to get inside Mortmain? Simone and Mother had driven past the place quite a lot of times now and even from the road you could see the gaping holes where the windows had been, and Simone thought getting inside would not be very difficult at all. Even Mother had said, Goodness, what a dreadful place, and never mind about who owned it or did not own it; it was high time it was pulled down before it became dangerous.

Simone waited until a Friday morning near the end of term, and then at breakfast said, as if she had only just remembered, that there was a rehearsal for the end-of-term concert that afternoon.

'I was meant to tell you yesterday, but I forgot. I'm s'posed to stay on if that's all right. Only for about an hour.' It was horrid to lie to Mother—other people seemed to lie to their parents all the time and not care, but Simone hated doing it.

Because she hardly ever told a lie Mother was not suspicious. She said, 'Oh, are you? It sounds as if it's going to be a good concert, doesn't it? I'm looking forward to it. But if you're going to be a bit later than usual I'd better pick you up.'

'Um, well, I was going to cycle home like an ordinary day. Everyone else is. And it won't be dark then, will it? Half past four?'

'No, it'll still be light, although I bet it'll be more like ten to five when you finish. All right. But stay with the others, won't you? And come straight home.'

This was what Mother always said if Simone was doing something after school, like going to somebody's house for tea and homework and then cycling home later. It was not very far to school, and Weston Fferna was so tiny you could practically see everyone else's house from the main street, which meant you all went along to school together in a gang. Mother was pretty OK with that. It was only if Simone was going somewhere by herself that Mother insisted on taking her in the car and fetching her afterwards.

But she always said, Come straight home, and she almost always added, 'And be sure not to talk to anyone on the way.'

Simone said, 'I'll come straight home.'

After the last bell had gone at school, Simone got her camera out of her locker, where she had hidden it that morning. She tucked it carefully in her school bag, between her homework books. There were some arithmetic problems to be done—arithmetic homework was *septic*—but there was also a poem to be learned, which was pretty good on account of you could fit pictures to the words in your mind.

She waited until most people had gone ahead, so that nobody would cycle or walk along with her, and then she pedalled as hard and as fast as she could out to Mortmain House.

Even from the road she felt Mortmain's darkness. She stood at the foot of the track and stared up at the black stone walls for a long time. Can I do this? Can I go up there and photograph this horrid, ugly old house? Up the twisty path with the trees on both sides, and up to the front door, and inside the rooms…? Was she in there now, the little girl who seemed to live in the past, and who knew about the pig-eyed men and the game about the dance of the hangman? No matter where she lived or when, how was it that she could slide inside Simone's mind and tell her all these things? I don't understand any of it, thought Simone. I think I'm quite frightened, but it's an excited kind of frightened. I want to know what this is about.

She pushed her bicycle into the undergrowth so that it could not be seen, but locked the little padlock on to the wheels, so that even if it was seen, it could not be stolen. She left her schoolbag where it was because it was not very likely that anyone would steal arithmetic books although if they did they were welcome to them, but she took the camera out because that was the whole point of being here.

It was ten to four now, and Mother expected her home a bit before five, which meant she had about three-quarters of an hour. She took a deep breath and began to walk up the slope towards the house, the camera in its leather case slung over her shoulder.

The bright, late-summer sunshine felt peculiar. Simone had always thought of Mortmain as a place of darkness and of spooky shadows, like the shadows you got in nightmares. She had always seen it in shades of black and grey in her mind like an old photograph, so it was a bit odd to be seeing it like this, in fact she was almost starting to wonder if she had tumbled into one of the bad dreams without noticing.

By the time she was halfway up the track and the trees were thinning out she could see the house very clearly indeed. It had a lopsided look: the left-hand side was all right but the other side sagged as if something had given it a vicious tweak, and the roof was bumpy so that from this angle the house looked like a hunchbacked giant crawling across the hillside on all fours. Simone eyed it doubtfully, and then unfastened the camera case and removed the lens cover. Focusing the camera made her feel better: it made her feel as if she was controlling Mortmain instead of the other way round. She tried several angles, and then took quite a lot of shots of the house.

So much for the outside. Was she really going to go inside, and try to get photographs of the little girl? Now that she was here she was not sure if she could do it after all. Anything might be in there. Scuttly little animals with scrabbly claw feet and long thin tails. Horrid old tramps—yes, Mother had said tramps came out here. Or gypsies, or even—

Or even ghosts.

Ghosts.

With the framing of the word there was a darting movement at the top of the track, and a blurry whisk of bright colour—something cherry red against the dull stones of Mortmain's walls. Simone blinked and glanced up at the sun, which was the kind of low-lying, late summer sun that sometimes turned quite ordinary things glowing scarlet when it was setting. Then she looked back at Mortmain; at the scrubby grass and the thick old trees behind it. But nothing moved anywhere. Imagination. Or maybe an animal had been in there, and her approach had disturbed it so that it had scampered away. But she did not think it had been an animal: it had been too big. She looked about her again. Was there someone hiding nearby, watching her? A gypsy? But gypsies went around in crowds, and they had dogs and children and brightly-painted caravans and they made a lot of noise. A tramp, then? But tramps did not run in that quick, whizzing kind of way.

And then it came again, the sudden whisk of move-ment, and the impression of someone—something?—going around the other side of the building and vanishing out of sight. Whatever it was it had moved so quickly that its shape had been blurry, but this time Simone had received a half-formed image of someone running in a sort of half-crouch, running a bit lopsidedly, and throwing up one hand.

Throwing up a hand to hide its face? Or—and this was the scary thing—or beckoning to Simone to come up the last few yards of the track?

She's here, thought Simone, her heart starting to thump. The little girl. She's somewhere inside Mortmain, I can feel that she is. She's closer to me now than she's ever been, and I'm as sure as I can be that she was the one who was running around the walls just now. And if I can just see her and ask her to explain all this, and ask her to stop coming into my mind— This sounded stupid. It sounded like something out of a ghost story. But I'll have to do it, thought Simone. This is the best chance I'll ever have of meeting her properly and if I don't go inside now I'll regret it like mad.

But first she sat down on the grass verge to fit the flash attachment on to the camera. She had not yet taken photographs with flash, but she had studied the instructions very carefully before coming out and she thought she had got it right. The little bulbs were in a side pocket; they just screwed in. She saw she had used almost the entire roll of film on Mortmain already, but she had brought a second one with her, so she wound the film carefully back, took it out, and then fitted the new one. So far so good.

She took a deep breath and went up the last few yards of the track, keeping careful hold of the camera so as not to dislodge the flashbulb. She hesitated as Mortmain's bulk came into view again, and then focused the camera to take a couple of shots pointing upwards. They might not come out, not as close as this, but if they did, it would look as if the house was just on the brink of toppling forward. That would be a really interesting view to get.

The huge old door was sagging off its hinges, and it was much heavier than Simone had expected it to be. But she managed to force it open a bit more and slip through the gap. This is it. I'm inside.

There was more darkness beyond the door than she had expected, so that at first it was necessary to grope her way forward with both hands held out in front of her. And what would I do, if a hand suddenly came reaching out of the darkness to touch me? thought Simone and her heart skipped several beats. Because if that really did happen, it might not be a hand belonging to anyone from today: it might be a hand coming out of the past. A dead person's hand. Dead man's hands, like the house's name. Or I might have got into the past myself, without noticing. Don't be stupid, people can't really travel back to the past, not like they do in films! But her heart was performing somer-saults and she had the feeling that absolutely anything might happen to her in here.

But even without spooky old ghost's hands there were other dangers. She might trip over something in the dark and break her ankle or walk into a solid wall by mistake and knock herself out. If anything like that happened she might lie here for days before anyone found her.

Her eyes had adjusted to the light a bit now, and she could see that she was in a big central hall, the size of a very large room, nearly as big as the gym at school. There were two small narrow windows near the main door but they were both boarded up, making it even darker. Doors opened off on each side of the hall: Simone could just make out their shapes, and she thought the rooms beyond those doors would be very nasty indeed. She thought she would not open any of them.

The hall was dirty but it was sad as well. Grass was growing up through the cracks in the floor, and every-where smelt disgusting and most likely there were about a million spiders and scuttly beetles in the dark corners. There was a wide stairway at the back of the hall, but even if Simone had wanted to explore the upstairs parts, the banisters were all hanging off and the stairs looked as if they would come crashing down the minute you stepped on them. Just as she was not going to open any of the doors, nor was she going up those crumbly old stairs.

It was very quiet, but it was not quiet in the way that a really empty house was quiet. Simone listened intently, and after a moment the familiar thought-patterns slid into her mind.

So you're really here, Simone... I knew you'd come, one day... And now we're really together at last...

Simone remained absolutely still. Had it been the inner voice or had the words been said aloud this time? She was not sure because everything felt different in here, in fact she was almost ready to believe that she really had stepped into the past—into the time when the black iron doors had clanged shut every night and the pig-men had prowled through the dark passageways. If she could listen hard enough she might hear the echoes of all those people who used to live here.

But there were no echoes; there was only a faint drip-drip of water from somewhere. If you wanted to give yourself nightmares for about a hundred years you could believe it was a brittle whispery voice, like the tapping of icicles against your bedroom window in winter.

And then it came again. *Come deeper in, Simone... It's time we got to know each other properly... I've waited so long to see you and meet you properly...*

Simone said out loud, 'Who are you? Tell me who are?' Her voice sounded peculiar in the silence. It sounded a bit quavery as well. She said, a bit louder, 'I know you're here. I can feel that you're here. But I can't see you.'

Nothing. Silence. But Simone was still having the fluttery-stomach feeling that you had just before something really tremendous and important. Something's about to happen, she thought. Something that's going to matter a lot.

She removed the lens cover again; her hands were shaking which was annoying, but if she really did manage to photograph the little girl it would act as a sort of weapon. I've got photographs of you, she could say. And if you don't leave me alone I'll show them to people. The little girl would not like that: she wanted to stay secret and mysterious, Simone knew that.

The flash was in place which was good because of the boarded-up windows, and she had only used two of the new roll of film. She would try an inside shot now; it would be great if she could get on film the darkness and the spookiness of Mortmain, and the feeling of all the people who had lived in it.

The people who heard the clanging door that shut them in every night and that shut the world out, and the people who sometimes had to hide from the evil men— Don't think about that.

The flash worked exactly as it was meant to; it went off with a sharp, white flare of brilliance that lit up the dusty old hall so that Simone saw it vividly. She saw the black mouldering stones and the patches of crawly fungus on the walls, and the splintered wooden panels hanging off the walls.

She saw the small figure framed in the doorway near to the back of the hall watching her. Exactly like the nightmare. The little girl with dark, sly eyes.

The flashlight died, and the darkness closed down again like a bad-smelling black curtain. But from out of this clotted darkness a voice spoke. It said, very softly, 'Hello, Simone. I thought you'd never come.'

There was a long silence. Then Simone said, 'Who are you? I don't know who you are.'

'Don't be silly,' said the girl, and she took a step forward. 'Of course you know who I am. Just as I know who you are.' Simone felt the faint familiar tug on her mind. Amusement. She's laughing. And then—no, she's not laughing, she's gloating. She's hugging some secret knowledge to herself. I think what I'll do, I'll just find out who she is, and I'll find out all that stuff about Mortmain, and then I'll cycle home as fast as I can. But she was conscious of a vague feeling of disappointment. All that build-up—all that mystery and excitement—and after all it's just a girl of my own age in a ruined house.

After a moment, she said, 'You know my name, but I don't know yours. What is it?'

'Don't be silly,' said the girl again, and at last she came forward. The shadows slid off her like water streaming away from somebody getting out of a bath. Simone saw that she was wearing a cherry-red pullover with a pattern on the front, and that as she walked one foot dragged a bit and her shoulders were slightly crooked. If she ran or even moved quickly she would do so in a hunching, lopsided way. But other than that—

Other than that it was like looking in a mirror.

'Who are you?' said Simone again.

'I'm Sonia,' said the little girl. 'I thought you knew that.' She smiled, and Simone saw that there was the same small unevenness in her front teeth that Simone had herself. As if a tiny piece had been chipped out.

Sonia put out a hand. 'Come with me, Simone,' she said, and Simone took the outstretched hand.

CHAPTER SIXTEEN

THE HANDCLASP WAS an extraordinary moment. It gave Simone the strangest feeling she had ever had in her whole life, and for several crowded seconds everything else was blotted out, so that she was only dimly aware of where she was and what she was doing here.

Many years afterwards she was to identify it as the feeling of an electrical circuit closing, or of negative and positive forces meeting and fusing, but standing in Mortmain's swirling shadows, staring at Sonia, she was only aware that something important and something tremendous had happened. She did not really understand it and she was not sure if she ever would, but for the moment the nearest she could get was that it felt as if something that had been missing had been found, or as if a final piece of jigsaw had been slotted into place so that you suddenly saw and understood the whole picture. Sonia did not seem especially aware of the fierce emotions zig-zagging back and forth; she was drawing Simone across the hall and through one of the doors near the stairs. 'It's all right, Simone,' she said. 'There's no one here but us.'

And the ghosts, thought Simone uneasily.

'And I think this might be the day I told you about. Remember? Remember how I said that one day we'd meet? And share secrets, so we'd be bound together for always?'

'Blood sisters.'

'Yes. *Yes.* That's what's going to happen today. We've got the thought-talking thing already, but that's a—a shadow-thing. I'd like it if we had something else, wouldn't you? Something in the real world. Something in the daylight world. And there's someone I really hate—someone I really want to get the better of. Remember how we talked about that?'

Simone started to say, 'What do you—' and stopped, because she was not sure she wanted to know what Sonia meant. What she really wanted to do was get away from Sonia as soon as she could, but the trouble was that she would have to think of a way of doing it politely. Sonia was a bit weird and if she got annoyed she might become even weirder. But Simone thought if it had not been for Sonia's hand still holding hers and if it had not been for that insistent feeling of a loop closing, she would most likely have run away there and then, going full-pelt back down the track to where her bicycle was, and then pedalling home at top speed.

But she did not. She walked with Sonia through Mortmain's swirling darkness, trying not to notice that Sonia moved awkwardly because of the squinty slant of her shoulders, and trying not to wonder what had caused it in case Sonia picked up the thought. Mother had always said it was quite rude to wonder about people's disabilities, and it was very rude indeed and probably hurtful to let them see you were wondering. So Simone concentrated on the house: on the long echoing corridors with the black stone walls that dripped with slimy moisture as if a zillion snails had crawled down them, and on the rusting stoves that squatted in unexpected corners and had doors with grinning iron grilles and stumpy little clawfeet. When there was no one around the stoves might come waddling out of their corners and gather in one of the rooms, whispering to one another in clanking rusty voices, making plans to snatch up the next human who entered Mortmain.

Wherever Sonia was taking her she knew the way. Once they went through a long dim room with a scarred table nailed to the floor, and Sonia said, very softly, 'This was where everyone had to come to eat. All of them— children, grown-ups, everyone. The refectory, they called it. There were wooden benches for seats.'

Not everyone could manage to spoon up their food without help...

'And the food was dreadful, anyway,' said Sonia, offhandedly.

'How do you know that? How do you know all this about Mortmain?'

Sonia sent her another of the sideways glances, and then said, 'I know what is and what has been.'

This was no kind of answer at all, in fact Simone was not sure that Sonia mightn't be showing off because it sounded like a line of poetry. Still, the question might as well be asked sooner rather than later, so she said, 'You don't—um—live here, do you? In Mortmain?' Because for a wild moment this seemed entirely possible. It seemed perfectly believable that Sonia might really live here as Simone had once believed; that she might actually sleep and eat and live inside Mortmain, wandering through the empty rooms. (Talking to the ghosts and listening to their stories...? No, that's really stupid!)

'Of course I don't live here. I live in Weston Fferna, though. Well, just outside it. A few miles. But I'm allowed to cycle around places in the afternoons on account of it'll make my legs stronger.' This was said disinterestedly, and because Simone was not sure how to deal with it, she said, 'I've never seen you.'

'No, I only go along the lanes. And there's a back road up to Mortmain. It's closed off from the main road but if you know it's there you can get through, and then you can cycle up the slope. Mostly I use that.'

'What about school?' Because there was only Simone's own school for miles, and Sonia certainly did not go there.

'I don't go to school. I'm different from other people.' It sounded smug. It very nearly sounded as if Sonia liked having a crooked shoulder and awkward legs; as if she thought it made her one-up on everyone else. 'So I have lessons at home,' she said, and sent Simone a quick glance to see how this was received.

'Oh, I see.' Simone did not like to say it must be pretty boring to have lessons at home, and not be able to enjoy things like art lessons and school concerts, and not have the fun of friends to giggle with about the teachers. There were a lot of bad things about school (arithmetic and geography were two of the worst), but there were quite a lot of good things as well.

'I've lived here for a lot of years,' said Sonia. 'In fact—' She stopped and for the first time Simone saw that Sonia was unsure. But then she said, 'I've listened to things people say and stories that they tell. I don't always like having to listen to all that stuff, but I have to listen whether I want to or not. But I probably know more about Mortmain than anyone alive today.'

Simone had the feeling that Sonia had been about to tell her something, and then had changed her mind. She was aware of a small jab of curiosity. I'll stay a bit longer. I'll see what she has to say.

They had reached the end of the corridor, and Sonia pushed open a door and waited for Simone to step through. Beyond the door was a long dim room, with fading sunshine trickling in through the high windows, showing up the dirt and the decay. Strewn messily on the floor were little piles of rubbish, left by the tramps and winos who dossed down here and did not see Mortmain's ghosts, or maybe saw them and were so drunk they thought the ghosts were real people.

The room was dreadful. Simone had never been in such a dreadful place. Even standing just inside the doorway thick suffocating waves of pain and misery seemed to jump out at her, and there was a feeling of something tugging at her mind as if she was being dragged back to the days when people had been forced to live here because they had nowhere else to go and no friends or family to help them.

'Why should you be young and pretty and free?' said this horrid tugging thing. 'We were never pretty, and we were never allowed to be young, not properly... Why should you live in a nice house and go to school and have friends and games and money to spend when we never had any of those things...?'

For several moments the room seemed to fill up with anger and bitterness and Simone had to take several deep breaths before she could go inside. She would not let Sonia know how frightened she was though, she absolutely would not.

But just as Sonia had not seemed to feel the huge surge of emotion that had exploded when they held hands earlier on, now she did not seem to feel the room's anger and pain.

'They called this place the Women's Workshop,' she said, her eyes still on Simone. 'The women came here because they had no money and nowhere to live. If they hadn't come to Mortmain they would have died from starvation. But they all hated being here.'

'That was because of it being a workhouse.' Simone remembered Mother telling her about this. 'It was very shameful to go into a workhouse.'

'They had to work all the time. From when they got up in the morning until when they went to bed at night.

They had to scrub floors and work in the laundry and sew things—horrid things like shrouds for corpses—and if they didn't do it properly they were punished. Locked up or beaten. And some of the people who lived here were mad and sometimes they had to be—what's the word meaning you're tied up so that you don't hurt anybody?'

'Restrained? Confined?'

'Restrained. There're rooms in the cellars with iron doors—they used to lock the mad ones down there until they were quiet.' (Had that been the sound in the nightmares; the clanging of an iron door, followed by sobbing cries of helplessness?)

Sonia had come closer, and her face was only inches from Simone's. It was pretty spooky being this close to the face that was so much like your own. Except the eyes, thought Simone. I know my eyes aren't like that, all mean and sly. I'll try never to have a mean or sly thought ever in my life if that's how it makes you look.

Sonia said, 'Think how it must have been to be so mad you were locked away in the darkness and left there for days and days. But the worst thing of all would be if you weren't mad at all, but people didn't like you or wanted to keep you out of the way because you had found out their secrets. You'd scream and scream, and you'd try to say you weren't mad, but nobody would believe you.'

'Did that really happen? Or are you making it up?'

'I'm not making it up. I told you—I know what is and what has been.' She eyed Simone.

'You said that before. What's it supposed to mean?'

'Don't you know?' In a soft voice, Sonia said:

I know what is and what has been; not anything to me comes strange,
Who in so many years have seen and lived through every kind of change.
I know when men are good or bad, when well or ill,

When sad or glad, when sane or mad...
And when they sleep alive or dead...

Simone thought: she's mad. She's absolutely bats. I'm standing in a haunted house with a mad girl who's quoting poetry at me! At least, I suppose it's poetry—it sounds like it. She looked uneasily about her, trying not to shiver. The ghosts were still here; they were hating the presence of intruders because they were ashamed of having lived in a workhouse, those ghosts, and they resented the two girls from the future who lived normal lives and did normal things. (Except that Sonia was not normal; if she had been here a hundred years ago they would probably have locked her into one of those cellars because they would have said she was mad...)

Simone pushed this thought down at once, and walked determinedly back into the passage. 'What's through that door at the end?'

Sonia's face took on the sly look again. 'Come and see,' she said, and limped across to push it open. There was a grating sound from the warped oak, and then the door swung inwards.

It was another of the dismal, badly-lit rooms, with another of the evil iron stoves watching them from the shadows. Simone hated the stove and she hated the room but she would not let Sonia see this, and so she looked about her, as if she was interested.

One of the windows overlooked a kind of small court-yard. Was it the courtyard where that game had been played about the hanged man? No, that was just a pretend-thing.

Near one wall was a raised area of floor: a large square section different from the rest. At first Simone thought it might be what was called a rostrum: they had one in the gym at school so that the gym teacher could see what they were all doing, and there was one in the little theatre for conducting when the school orchestra gave a recital. It was odd to see one here, though.

Sonia said, 'Help me to move this, then I'll tell you a bit more about Mortmain if you like.' She moved to the raised area and kicked at the edge of it, and for the first time Simone saw that it was not part of the main floor at all; it was a wooden box-structure, with iron handles set into the edges. The wood had rotted in places and a glint of black iron showed beneath.

'What is it? What's under there?'

'It's an old well. I suppose you do know what a well is, do you?'

'Of course I know.' Simone was stung by the faint patronizing tone. 'It's where people used to get water before they had plumbing and bathrooms. You don't usually get wells inside houses, though.'

'It used to be outside. They built this bit of Mortmain over part of an old courtyard,' said Sonia.

'The courtyard out there?'

'Yes. Most of Mortmain's really old and the well's really old as well, only nobody had used it for years and years. But a long time ago—a hundred years ago—they wanted more room and somebody said this was the best place to build, so they just put a cover over the well and built the extra room here. They were only making a bit more room for paupers and mad people and children nobody wanted, you see. That was how they thought of it. They thought it didn't matter to people like that if they had to live in a room where there was a well. They left a small bit of court-yard—that's what you can see through the windows.'

'I don't believe you. Nobody would build a room where there was a well.'

'They did. If you go outside and look at the walls you can see where the bricks are different, and there's a different roof as well.' She was pulling the red sweater over her head like a man will remove his jacket before attempting a strenuous task. She put the sweater, neatly folded, on the ground, and looked back at Simone. 'Are you ready to help me? If you hold that side we can pull the cover off between us. I don't think I can do it on my own, 'cos it's lined with iron and it's heavy.'

I wish I knew why she wants to do this, thought Simone, and I wish I dare ask how she really gets to know all this stuff. I think I'd better help her with the well-cover, but then I'll make an excuse and go. I'll say I'm expected home—that's true anyway. There was a faint, far-off reassurance about remembering Mother waiting for her in the cottage. Tomorrow was Saturday, and they quite often went out for the day somewhere on Saturday. They were exploring the villages and the little market towns, and it was pretty good.

'We have to pull the cover towards us,' said Sonia. 'It isn't bolted down, and it doesn't hinge, or anything like that: it just slides. All right?'

'Um, yes.'

Sonia was already half-kneeling down, grasping the rim of the well-cover. She looked a bit grotesque crouching down like that because of the lopsided shoulders but Simone tried not to notice. She unslung the leather camera-case and put it on top of Sonia's sweater, then she knelt down and reached for the edge of the cover. It was cold and hard and over the years the iron had become pitted so that it felt scaly, like a dead snake. But once it was moved she could say about having to go home.

Sonia had been right about the cover being heavy. At first Simone thought they were not going to manage it, but at the second try it gave way a bit, making the kind of screechy rasping that scraped all the nerves in your teeth. A rim of blackness showed at the far end, and Sonia said, 'Again!' and they pulled harder. The blackness widened, and a faint sighing sound came from within the well's depths. A dank, unwholesome stench gusted into their faces; Simone thought it was almost as if the well had breathed out.

Sonia said, 'One more tug!' and this time the ancient cover slid back and crashed on to the ground with a deafening clatter of wood and iron. Clouds of dust rose up making them both cough, and Simone's heart performed several somersaults because the sound was so massive in this silent old place that surely it would disturb someone or something... But the echoes were already dying away and the dust was settling, and although the stove behind them creaked nastily from its corner as if it were considering coming to life, Simone knew that really it was only that the well-cover had jarred the rusting mechanism.

They both stared at the open well-shaft, while all round them Mortmain sank gradually back into its brooding quiet. Neither of them spoke, and Simone, glancing covertly at Sonia, thought Sonia had not been expecting the well to be quite so creepy. The opening was lined with black bricks and it was not very large—it might be about seven feet across—but everything about it was so extremely old and so dreadfully sinister.

Sonia was still kneeling down, peering into the well's depths. The cold dank light from the bricks made hollows in her face so that there were black pits where her eyes were. Simone had moved back from the well, but even from where she was standing she could see the remains of an old rope looped across the well's mouth. That would be where people had lowered a bucket to bring up water.

'It smells disgusting,' said Sonia, looking up at Simone. 'And it looks as if it's an awfully long way down.' Her words made faint hissing echoes inside the well. An awfully long way down-down-down... An awfully long way, said the well in a black, evil-smelling whisper.

Sonia did not seem worried by this. She said, 'I think I can see water at the bottom. Like a black glint. Wait a bit, and I'll throw something down. A bit of broken floorstone or something—'

The stone dropped silently into the blackness, and after what seemed to Simone a very long time, there was a faint sound that might have been a dull splash or that might simply have been the floorstone hitting a solid floor. Sonia stood up, brushing the dust off her skirt. 'It is deep, isn't it?' she said. 'Anyone who fell down there would never be able to get out again, would they?'

She regarded Simone consideringly, and Simone, horrified, thought, so that's it. She's got me out here to kill me. She's going to throw me down the well, like something out of a stupid nursery rhyme, and then leave me. Except she won't, because I won't let her. She got up off her knees and began to move stealthily across to the door. Because I'm a whole lot stronger than she is, and if I can get to the door I'll run away from her as fast as ever I can—

Sonia laughed, and the laugh was picked up by the well, so that for a moment it spun and shivered eerily all round Simone's head. 'Silly,' she said. 'I'm not intending to kill you. You didn't really think that, did you?

'Um, well, what are we going to do?'

'We've already done it,' said Sonia. 'We've started the secret. You've helped me take the cover off and so the secret's beginning. The pact's being forged.'

I'm missing something, thought Simone. There's something behind all this—I can practically hear her thinking it. It's something to do with a plan she's had for years and years, only she couldn't carry out the plan on her own. She needed help with it—she needed me... For the well-cover? Yes, I think so. I think that's why she got me here.

Sonia was smiling at Simone. 'Once you've made a secret together, you're bound to one another for ever,' she said. 'That's what my—' She stopped abruptly. She was about to tell me something about her home, thought Simone. But she stopped again because she doesn't want me to know where she lives, or who her family are. Well, OK, I don't want her to know where I live or who my family are.

She said, 'But Sonia—um—if we leave the cover off someone might fall into the well.'

'Yes,' said Sonia, her eyes still on Simone. 'That's the whole point.'

'But—but we can't do that! We can't possibly do that!' Simone was already kneeling down again, grasping the well-cover and trying to push it back into place, but without Sonia to help her she could not do it.

'You won't do that on your own,' said Sonia watching her. 'It's silly even to try. I couldn't do it by myself, even though I have to do special exercises for my back, so my arms are probably a lot stronger than yours.' Again the pleased, I'm-better-than-you, I'm-different-to-you tone.

Simone said, 'Sonia, you must help me! We must put it back!'

'No, we musn't. I told you, this is the start of being blood-sisters. We'll each know what we've done, but we'll never be able to tell anyone else. Because if one gets into trouble for it, the other will as well.'

'But it'd be murder!' said Simone desperately. 'If somebody falls in there and dies it'd be murder!'

'Yes, it would, wouldn't it?' said Sonia very softly, and Simone understood properly then that this was Sonia's plan, this was what she had wanted to do all along. She stared at Sonia in horror, and felt the familiar ruffling of her mind that meant Sonia's thoughts were brushing against her own. She blinked, and for a moment, on the inside of her eyelids, there was the darting image of a woman with a rather plain face and straggly brown hair and worried hands. She felt Sonia's hard cold dislike of the woman, as clearly as if she had put her hands inside a freezer and held them there.

That's who she wants to kill, thought Simone in horror. She's been planning it and working it out for years and years. It's someone she hates—so much that it's eating away at her. She tried to see the woman's image more clearly: it was a bit blurry, a bit transparent at the edges, but she could see that the woman looked rather old-fashioned.

And then Sonia said, 'Oh, if anyone falls in it'll only be some smelly old tramp. They come in here or in the Paupers' Dormitory, on account of this is the back of the house and if they make a fire on the stone floors the light can't be seen from the road. If one of them comes in here in the dark he won't see that this is a well; he'll just think it's a patch of shadow.'

Sonia was lying, of course. Simone could feel the lie in Sonia's mind as if she was touching it. It was like touching a hangnail or a blister. She said, 'Sonia, it doesn't matter who it is! It'll still be killing!'

'I know it will.' She moved closer and her hand curled around Simone's again. 'It's going to be a brilliant secret for us to share, isn't it?'

'No—'

'We'll be able to talk about it—the private, thought-talking, I mean. I'll keep coming out here—I told you, I'm supposed to cycle every afternoon—and I'll tell you when we've caught someone.'

Simone said, 'It's the woman with brown hair you want to murder, isn't it?' and Sonia's face twisted with fury.

'How did you know about her?'

'I saw her in your mind just now.' This was the most peculiar conversation to be having, but Simone was not going to be put off. She said, 'You can see into my mind, so why shouldn't I be able to see into yours? I can't do it often, but I can do it sometimes. You don't like her, that woman, do you? Who is she? Is she your mother?'

'No.' It came out angrily. 'She isn't my mother,' said Sonia, and this time there was an unexpected bleakness in her voice. 'But I hate her.'

'Why? Because she isn't your mother?'

'No.' But Simone thought it came out a bit too loudly. 'Because she smothers me,' said Sonia. 'I don't mean she puts pillows over my face—'

'No, I understand what you mean.'

'She makes me listen to lots of old stories— I don't mind that, although she goes on about it all the time. On and on. "Isn't it interesting, Sonia?" she says. "Isn't it nice that we share all this?" And she never lets me go out and see people—I hate that more than anything.'

When Sonia said all this Simone had another of those moments of awareness, and just for a few seconds there was the glimpse of a stifling home, rather old-fashioned, the brown-haired woman always there, always at Sonia's side. Never going out anywhere, never seeing anyone else. The woman thought it was enough, though. We don't need other people, do we? she sometimes said to Sonia. We have all we need here, with just the two of us.

Despite her fear Simone felt a pang of sympathy for Sonia, but she said firmly, 'Listen, though, I can't let you— um—kill someone. I'm going to push this thing back into place.'

'You won't be able to. It's too heavy.'

But the wooden staves at one edge of the well-cover had splintered quite badly when it fell, and Simone managed to grip the iron frame itself. This time when she dragged the cover it yielded.

'Don't!' shouted Sonia, and came forward in a lurching half run. She knocked Simone to the ground and they rolled across the dirty floor, locked together. Simone was perfectly at home with rough and tumble games, and playground scuffles, but for some reason the feel of Sonia's body half on top of her like this felt wrong. Sonia's eyes, staring down into Simone's, were frightening. They were like twin black tunnels, and if you looked into them for too long you might see all kinds of terrible things and you might feel all kinds of dreadful emotions— Simone blinked and tried to look away and found she could not.

'You're not to stop me doing this,' said Sonia in a hoarse angry voice. 'You're not to— It's all right to hate people and to punish them! It is! It's what they used to do—the children in the stories! The children who lived here!'

'Get off me!' shouted Simone, hardly hearing any of this. 'You're mad, I hate you!' She struggled to push her off, but Sonia grabbed her throat and began to squeeze.

'I won't let you stop me!' she said in the same furious half-whisper. Her fingers tightened around Simone's throat: they felt like steel bands and a red mist started to form in front of Simone's eyes. She's strangling me! If I can't get free of her, she'll kill me! I'll die! She had the wild thought that she could not possibly die here—she could not risk dying here—because of the ghosts. Once she was dead the ghosts would pounce on her because they hated her, she knew that already. They hated all ordinary children who had parents and homes, and they would take a revenge on Simone if they could. They would force her to be a workhouse child and make her sew shrouds, and they would lock her away behind the black clanging iron doors every night and even if she screamed and screamed for ever nobody would come to help her... On the crest of this thought she made one last huge effort and this time pushed Sonia backwards.

Sonia tumbled away from Simone, and went rolling and slithering across the floor. Simone had pushed very hard indeed and Sonia slid helplessly across the dusty floor in a jumble of arms and legs, trying to stop herself as she went.

But she did not stop herself. She skidded all the way to the edge of the open well, and as Simone shakily picked herself up from the floor Sonia fell over the edge and went straight down into the sour blackness.

CHAPTER SEVENTEEN

THE SOUND SHE made as she fell was like a night
wind whistling through an ancient cavern, or a train
going through a tunnel in the middle of the night. It
seemed to Simone's horrified senses to go on and on for
an eternity, but just as she was starting to be afraid that it
would never stop it cut off abruptly, and there was a sort
of dull squelching thud. And then silence.

Simone had absolutely no idea what to do. She was
still feeling a bit wobbly from Sonia's attack, but although
she was not hurt she thought that when she could stop
trembling she was going to be very frightened indeed.

And, most terrifying of all, it was not completely
silent in here after all. As she began to walk warily
towards the well she was aware of little sighings and
creakings all round her. She thought that if she listened
hard enough she might hear voices inside those sighings. The ghosts, murmuring to one another like gossipy
old women, or like children giggling and telling secrets
in a corner of a playground? Shall we take this one...?
Yes, she'd do very nicely, wouldn't she...? *Let's take her,
and we'll make her sew shrouds and scrub floors alongside the
rest of us... She looks pampered and properly-fed and nicely-*

clothed—let's show her what it's like to be a pauper, nobody's child, unwanted, unloved...

Yes, if she was hearing anything she would be hearing the ghosts. But I won't listen, thought Simone firmly. In any case ghosts can't hurt you, not really.

Oh, can't we? said the whisperings. *Are you sure about that, Simone...?*

I'm not listening, said Simone in her mind to the ghosts. I'll try to see what's happened to Sonia, and then I'll think what to do next.

What she actually wanted to do was run out of Mortmain as fast as her feet would carry her, and burst into tears in her own house and hear Mother say everything was all right. She was dreadfully afraid that Sonia was dead, but if she was only injured and if an ambulance came out here at top speed— Simone knew about calling for an ambulance; she knew about dialling 999 in an emergency. She tried to remember if there was there a phone box anywhere along the road, and could not.

She leaned over the edge of the well-shaft. 'Sonia?' she said cautiously, and then a bit louder, 'Sonia? Can you hear me? Can you speak?'

The well seized on the words and sent them spinning back at her.

Sonia, Sonia... Speak, Sonia, speak, speak...

And what will you do, said Simone's mind, if Sonia does speak? What will you do if a dead, echoing voice comes whispering up out of the darkness, and says, 'Yes, I'm dead, and I'm dead because you murdered me, Simone'...?

It felt like a very long time before Simone finally managed to crawl back from the well and scramble across the room and out into the corridor beyond. Gasping with fear and panic she ran through Mortmain's empty darkness, and as she ran it seemed that all the ghosts reared up from the dark corners and ran alongside her.

It's no use trying to escape, Simone... We know what you did... We saw everything... We know what is and what has been, Simone... And wherever you run to, we'll catch you... You're a murderess, Simone... A murderess...

Along the narrow corridors with the watching iron stoves in their corners, and through the refectory with its sad echoes— I'm almost there now, I'm almost at the front of Mortmain, and the door that leads outside...

Don't go, Simone... Stay here with us...

The shadows were very dark now; they were like black bony goblin-fingers and at any minute they might reach out to snatch at her ankles... Simone ran on, praying that she was going in the right direction. Once she did take a wrong turning, and found herself going down a passage that did not seem to lead anywhere. Thick swathes of cobwebs dripped from the low ceiling and stirred in the gust of air made by her frantic running; they floated outwards like thin ghost-fingers, brushing her face. She shuddered and pushed them away, and then retraced her steps, this time choosing a passage more or less at random, but then seeing with thankfulness the familiar outline of the central hall, with the decayed stairs, and the cracked floor.

And the half-open door leading out to the hill.

Mother was in the kitchen, stirring a huge pot of what smelt like chili con carne, which was Simone's absolute favourite Friday-night supper, on account of they always had wedges of French bread with it to mop up the delicious sauce.

She looked up to smile when Simone came in, and started to ask how the rehearsal had gone, and then she stopped. Simone supposed she must look pretty awful; she was dirty and cobwebby, and she had torn her school skirt, and she was still shaking so hard she thought she might break into little pieces.

Mother said in her all-time best voice—the voice that shut out all the bad things in the world and made Simone feel safe—'Sim darling, what's wrong?'

And Simone, who had been trying very hard indeed not to cry, sat down on the kitchen chair and put her head on the kitchen table that smelt of chopped tomatoes and spices and home, and burst into tears, and said, 'I've killed somebody.'

It took a long time to explain, and it was quite difficult to tell Mother about knowing Sonia and about talking to her all these years. But she did the best she could, and she talked quickly because of getting help to Sonia who might still be alive.

Mother listened carefully, only interrupting to ask a question here or there. She seemed more interested in the fact that Simone had been talking to this other child inside her mind. When had that started? she said. What kind of things had the little girl said? She did not say much about the fib over the rehearsal, although Simone thought she might say something a bit severe later on, and once she said, 'Oh Sim, why didn't you tell me all this?' and Simone mumbled that she had not wanted to be thought mad because only mad people heard voices inside their minds.

'Not necessarily.' Mother got up to fill the kettle. 'We'd better have a cup of tea and you'd better have sugar in it; sugar's good for shock. And an aspirin or something as well.' She got up and Simone saw that making tea and fetching the aspirin was all to give Mother time to think. When she had made the tea and found the aspirin bottle, she said, 'The thing is that you've got an extraordinary imagination, Sim; you always have had. So it's possible that at times you've mixed up what was real and what wasn't. That isn't a big deal, although we could maybe talk to someone about it—someone who knows a bit more than I do about things like that.'

'I wasn't mixed up about what happened at Mortmain today.' Simone drank her tea and felt a bit better. She felt brave enough to say, 'And I think we ought to get police and ambulances and things out to Mortmain in case Sonia isn't dead—'

Mother had been pouring her own cup of tea, but she stopped in mid-pour and looked across the table, and said in a voice Simone had never heard her use before, 'Sonia? Simone, did you say *Sonia*?'

'Yes, that's her name, didn't I say?'

'No, you didn't. Oh, dear God,' said Mother, and her face turned so white that Simone thought she might be about to faint or be sick. She was grasping the table edge as if she thought she might fall down if she did not cling on to something solid. Simone waited anxiously, and after a moment she said, 'I'm all right.' And then she said it again, almost as if she was forcing herself to believe it.

Simone said nervously, 'About Mortmain—'

'Yes. Yes, we'll go back out to Mortmain shortly, just you and me, but first you'd better wash all that dust away. Have a shower and put a pair of jeans on and a sweater. And then I want to talk to you.'

Simone said impatiently, 'But we haven't got *time* for all that! Talking and showering and jeans— We need to go back to Mortmain—'

'Yes, we have got time.' There was a note in Mother's voice that was not often there, and Simone said, 'Um, well, OK,' and went obediently upstairs.

When she came back down, feeling a bit better again because of the hot shower and the good-smelling soap and shampoo, Mother was sitting in exactly the same place at the kitchen table, staring in front of her at nothing at all. But she turned when Simone came in, and said, in a voice that was still not quite her own, 'Come and sit down. And don't look so fearful, you solemn little owl. I've made you some toast and honey. The chili won't be ready for a while yet, and you'd better have something to eat.'

She waited until Simone had spread honey on a slice of toast, and then said, 'There's something I've got to tell you. I was going to tell you when you were older, but because of what's happened—what you've just been telling me—I think you'd better know now.' A pause. 'When you were a baby you had a sister. A twin sister. But she died when she was very tiny.'

Simone felt as if an icy fist had slammed itself into her stomach. She felt as if something had been jerked out of its place, and then forced back the wrong way round. At last she managed to say, 'Her name was Sonia. That's what you're going to say, isn't it?'

'Yes. But Sonia didn't live to grow up. She's been dead for years.'

The bright cheerful kitchen with the friendly cooking scents seemed to have grown darker as if it was becoming tangled up with the darkness inside Mortmain. Sonia. Sonia. Out of the unreality of this, Simone said carefully, 'If she's dead—'

'Yes, she is dead.'

'Then,' said Simone, fighting down panic, 'who is it who's been talking to me all these years? And what took my hand inside Mortmain this afternoon?'

'I don't know. I can't explain. There are some peculiar things in the world, though. There are a few very special, very unusual people who can—'

'Talk to ghosts?' Simone wished she had not said this, because Mum's face twisted with such pain. So she said, 'Her name really was Sonia?'

'Yes. I named her Sonia for my grandmother, just as I named you for my father—Simon,' said Mother, and Simone thought how really weird it was to hear Mother say the name and talk about Sonia with such complete familiarity. But she listened carefully to the story of how Sonia had died when she was tiny, and to Mother's few small memories of her.

Sonia had been small and pretty, she said, in fact she and Simone had looked exactly alike. They had shared a cot—Simone looked up at this because there had been something peculiar in Mother's voice then—but even though they had been identical in looks, they had had different personalities. Even in those days Simone had liked watching lights and shadows and contrasts, but Sonia had responded more to sounds, to music.

'I used to think you would go for something in the art line, Sim—well, I still think you will—and that Sonia would be musical. I used to make plans about it, and imagine how you would both grow up.'

Mother's voice was so sad and so wistful when she said this that Simone wanted to cry, because Mother had had this dream about Sonia and she did not know that Sonia would not have grown up in the least like that; that she would have been sly and secretive and not really a very nice person. She had gloated over the poor mad people shut away in Mortmain's underground rooms; she had wanted Simone to make a secret with her, and the secret was to be opening up the old well and waiting for someone to fall down into it. But Sonia died, said Simone's mind. She died years and years ago. She couldn't have done any of those things.

'What happened to her? I mean—why did she die?'

Mother hesitated, and then said, 'You were joined, Sim, darling. The two of you were born joined together—'

Joined. Simone stared at her blankly. 'I don't under-stand what you— Oh. You mean—like Siamese twins?'

'Yes, but they call it conjoining now. You were joined at one side—your left side, Sonia's right side.' One hand came out to close briefly around Simone's. 'But it's nothing horrid or ugly, Sim, there was never anything in the least ugly about it, I promise you. You were two very beautiful babies, lying side by side, with your arms around one another. The doctor who looked after us all thought you were so lovely—and the nurses all adored you both.'

Horror was pouring into Simone's mind. I was joined to another human being and that human being was Sonia— Sonia who had those sly eyes and that gloating mouth. I was joined to her—bones and skin and things. And they had to cut us in two so we'd be two separate people but then half of us died—that's what must have happened only Mum might not want to tell me that part—

And maybe I'm not a whole person now, she thought in panic. Maybe I'm really only half of something. Half of a freak. This was unbearable, it was repulsive. But deep inside the horror was the memory of how she had felt when Sonia had taken her hand, and how there had been the tremendous feeling of something locking into its rightful place after a long time of being lost. And even deeper inside that was the memory of how Sonia had looked a bit hunched over, as if her right side was not quite in line with the left.

'It happens sometimes that twins are joined when they're born,' Mother was saying. 'Not very often, but it isn't as rare as all that. There had to be an operation to separate you—'

'That's what the birthmarks are, aren't they?' said Simone, staring at her. 'You always said they were birthmarks, but they aren't, are they?'

'No. You were so tiny when the operation was done, you won't remember.'

'I remember being in hospital once, though. I mean having to stay there in a room by myself, and there were lots of doctors around.'

'They did a skin graft when you were two so you probably remember that. It was so that there wouldn't be too much scarring from the—from the earlier surgery. In another couple of years they can do another graft if it bothers you.'

Simone did not know whether it bothered her or not. She had not thought much about it; it was just part of how she looked. Unless she wanted to wear a bikini or sunbathe nude nobody would know the scars were there. She said, very carefully, 'So she died in the—um—the separation thing?'

It seemed a long time before Mother replied. Then she said, 'She didn't die during the operation itself, but she died very soon afterwards.' Again the pause. 'There was quite a lot of publicity at the time. Newspapers wanting to do articles on you, TV people wanting to make documentaries. I managed to dodge most of it, but it was still a bit intrusive so after a while I altered my name by deed-poll—'

'You did? So what's my real name?'

'Anderson.'

'Oh.'

'And it's mostly why we've moved around so much.'

'Shaking off the journalists?'

'That's quite sharp of you. But yes, that was the reason. When you were smaller they used to turn up from time to time—or,' said Mother rather dryly, 'I used to imagine they did. Maybe I got a bit neurotic, but I don't really think so. It was quite a—a newsworthy thing. There probably isn't much likelihood of anyone trying to make a story out of it any more, although I suppose there's a possibility that some reporter might pick the thing up somewhere in the future. Say, when you're eighteen, or twenty-one, or if you get married. We'll worry about that at the time. And also—'

Mother stopped and Simone looked up from the toast and honey because there had been something in Mother's voice that seemed to suggest there was something else or someone else they might have to worry about. But Mother did not say anything, and so Simone said, as offhandedly as she could manage, 'I suppose that she's—um—buried somewhere, isn't she?' It was irritating to discover that she could not say Sonia's name out loud.

'You mean Sonia?' Mother could say the name, of course, and she said it with the ease of one who has known it for a very long time. It gave Simone a cold shut-out feeling to know that there had been this other child whom Mother had known and loved, and who had as much claim on Mother as Simone.

'Yes, she's buried somewhere, but it's a long way away,' Mother said, and her voice was so dreadfully bleak that Simone knew that Mother had just, only just, managed to tell her all this without flooding over with sadness, and that remembering this mysterious other twin who had died was almost more than Mother could bear. She wondered if Sonia had died at the same time as her father; Mum never mentioned him except to once say he had died in an accident when Simone was a few months old, and she had looked so upset about it that Simone had never liked to ask for details. She had been going to ask about Sonia's grave, and whether they might go to see it sometime, but seeing the look on Mother's face thought she had better not.

Then Mother said briskly, 'So now, Sim, what we've got to do is make absolutely sure that there really wasn't anyone in Mortmain House with you today.' Her hands came out to hold Simone's; they were warm and reassuring. 'I believe everything you've told me,' she said. 'I promise you I do. About the—the little girl who talked to you, I mean. I haven't got an explanation for it, but I don't think it's anything to be frightened of. Odd things happen in the world at times, and there isn't always a logical explanation for them. And twins do frequently have a mental link—a kind of telepathy. That's very well known.'

Even after one of them's dead? thought Simone, but she did not say it.

'If I were particularly religious I'd probably start talking about life after death and about the essence or the spirit of someone living on in other spheres,' said Mother. 'But listen, if we do find that there was a girl in Mortmain with you this afternoon, and if she was killed, then it won't have been your fault. It's very important to remember that.'

Simone thought about this, and then said, 'But you don't think there was anyone, do you?'

'I think what we'll do is to make absolutely sure.'

'Um—both of us, you mean?'

Mother had been turning off the heat under the simmering pan of chili, but at this she turned to regard Simone very thoughtfully. Then she said, 'Yes, I think both of us. It won't take long, and we'll take a couple of strong torches with us.'

She thinks I've imagined it, thought Simone as Mother went upstairs to get a jacket and find the car keys. She wants to show me that there's nothing inside Mortmain.

CHAPTER EIGHTEEN

As MOTHER STEERED the car off the tiny drive in front of the house, Simone said, 'It'll be pretty spooky in Mortmain now, I 'spect. Being dark and everything.'

'It's only six o'clock, it's not pitch dark yet. And it's not as if we're going on a midnight prowl. In any case we've got two large torches, one each, and all we're going to do is walk through the rooms and take a look at the well, and then we'll be back home and eating the chili well before seven.' She slowed down at a junction, and peered in both directions before driving out. Then she said, off-hand-edly, 'You know, Sim, I think that whatever happened in Mortmain—and all those years with the mind-talking thing—I do think it's probably over now. I hope you don't mind that.'

Simone thought it was over as well although she did not know if she minded. She did not say that for the last two hours she had felt as if something extremely impor-tant had gone—something that could never be replaced. She asked, instead, if they ought not to have phoned the police. 'That's what I thought you'd do.'

'Well, we might still have to. But I want to take a look by ourselves first. It would be quite difficult to explain all this if there isn't—if there's no trace of a child anywhere in Mortmain. If we'd brought out the fifth cavalry, I mean.'

'Oh yes, I see.'

'We're going the right way, aren't we?'

'Yes, but you have to turn off along here—just there by that tree.'

It felt odd and a bit confusing to be going back to Mortmain. They rattled up the steep, narrow track, bouncing in and out of the deep ruts and potholes. 'Couldn't you have chosen an easier place to have your peculiar experience?' demanded Mother. 'We shan't have any suspension left on the car— Still, we'll get as near as we can all the same; I'm blowed if I'm going to trek up muddy hillsides in the dark.'

They did not get quite to the top of the track, but they got more than halfway up. They locked the car and set off, Simone holding Mother's hand tightly. A cold wind blew into their faces and the night clouds scudded across the sky, rustling the trees. Simone tried not to think that the trees were sounding a bit like the sly hissing voices inside Mortmain.

Mother did not seem in the least spooked by Mortmain, in fact Simone thought she was quite interested in it. 'It's perfect gothic, isn't it? I'm not surprised you wanted to photograph it. We must get the shots you took developed tomorrow. I wonder when it was built?'

'Don't know. But Mortmain means dead hands.'

'Does it? Yes, I suppose it does. How did you know that? I thought you didn't start French until next term?'

'Um, well, I looked it up,' said Simone awkwardly, but Mother only said, 'Oh, I see. I expect it's got quite an interesting history, in fact— Oh lord, is this the way you went in? Well, all I can say is that you go for the macabre in a big way, you dreadful child. Still, I'd like to know about the people who lived here before it was a workhouse, though, wouldn't you? I expect it was one of those seventeenth- or eighteenth-century families with dozens of children and dogs and horses, and servants and things. It must have looked quite different then. Let's go inside. You take this torch and I'll have the big one.'

The torches cut two sharp triangles of white light through the darkness, and although Simone had actually been a bit worried that she might not be able to find the room with the well—she had even been half-fearful that she might find it was no longer even there—once they had gone through the door near the half-rotting stairs, she recognized the corridor with the Women's Workshop.

Now that Mother was here it was very nearly an adventure to be walking through Mortmain. Mother liked old buildings: she liked finding out about their pasts and what kind of people had lived in them and how they had looked when they were young. Simone had never heard anyone else refer to houses and buildings as being 'young' quite in the way that Mother did. It made them seem different.

But nothing could make Mortmain different. Nothing could blot out the feeling of being spied on or the horrid waddly-footed iron stoves in unexpected corners, or the feeling that this was a place where ghosts might whisper greedily in the darkness and make plots to snatch you up because they hated you for being a modern person with a good, modern life...

As they came up to the door to the Women's Workshop Simone hesitated, because she had thought, just for a moment, that the soft spiteful voices had whispered from the shadows.

We knew you'd come back to us, Simone...

But then after all it was only Mother saying in a cheerful voice something about coming back here one day in summer, and seeing some of the lovely old carving and the panelling, and what a scandal the house had been left to rot like this. Apparently as an afterthought, she said, 'Are you all right, Sim?'

'Yes, only I thought I heard—'

'What?'

'Well, sort of whispering.'

Mother listened carefully, but said she could not hear anything. There was a bit of a wind outside, she said; wind often sounded like whispering, especially at night, especially when there were tall old trees nearby. But when they went into the Women's Workshop she was silent for a few minutes, looking round. Then she said, rather quietly, 'Yes, this is horrid. This feels very bad indeed. I'm not surprised you were a bit spooked by it, Sim. There must have been so much sadness in here.'

'And anger,' said Simone. Had Mother felt the anger as well? 'The people who had to be here would have been angry on account of it being shameful to be in a workhouse,' she said.

'Yes, that's true. That's quite perceptive of you, as well.' Mel shone the torch around, and said, half to herself, 'And nowadays we regard it more or less as a right to be given State assistance, in fact some people boast about how they can outsmart the system and get more than they're entitled to, or how they cheat on income tax. Personally I'm a believer in the old maxim of, "To each according to his needs, and from each according to his means."' Then she said in a brisker voice, 'OK, Sim, let's get this dealt with. If we get back in time we can pick up some French bread from the village shop to have with the chili—they stay open until half past six on Fridays. Is this the room with the well through here?'

'Yes.' Simone knew Mother was saying all this about the chili and the village shop to remind her that there was an ordinary world outside of Mortmain, and that they would very soon be going back into that ordinary world. But as she followed Mel to the inner door, shining her own torch as she went, she knew that even if a hundred ordinary worlds existed beyond Mortmain this was still going to be dreadful. It would be dreadful in one way to find Sonia's body, and it would be dreadful in quite another way not to find it... Which do I really want it to be? thought Simone.

'It's a bit peculiar to have a well inside a house, you know. Are you sure you got that part right?'

'Yes, I did. This used to be part of the outside and so the well was outside, but then they had to have more rooms for the paupers and things so they covered the well up and built the room over it. They didn't think paupers and things mattered, so they didn't care about making them live in rooms with wells— I told you all that,' said Simone a bit desperately.

'Yes, I know you did. It's all right.'

They stood in the doorway, neither of them going into the room, letting the torches move slowly across the dust and the dirt. Simone's heart was thudding loudly in her chest and her stomach kept performing little somersaults of panic, because in another minute the light would fall on the yawning blackness of the open well, and then they would have to look down inside, and then Simone would know whether Sonia had been real or not—

'Is that the well-cover, Sim?'

Mother's voice broke the spell and the fear a bit. Simone started to say, 'Yes, it—' and broke off, staring at what lay in the beam of torchlight. The well-cover. The huge wooden, iron-bound cover that she and Sonia—that she and someone—had dragged clear that afternoon, leaving the well open and evil-smelling. She could see marks in the dust that might have been footprints, but that might as easily have been made by rodents or tramps, or even by little flurryings of wind getting in through the badly-fitting windows. She could see all of this.

And she could see that the well-cover was firmly in place over the well.

For a space of time that she was never, afterwards, able to measure, Simone felt as if she was falling down a long dark echoing tunnel. She felt as if she might even be Sonia, tumbling down and down into the darkness, like Alice down the rabbit hole, or the children falling into one of the Narnia-worlds. She heard a voice that she thought was her own voice saying, 'But—we dragged the cover off. I *know* we did. It shouldn't be back in place like that— I didn't put it back—'

'It doesn't matter. But it looks as if we've got a choice. We can go back home here and now and eat chili—'

'And never really know—'

'Yes. Or,' said Mel, 'we can explore the thing properly and really find out.' She looked at Simone as if she was waiting for Simone to make the decision. In the dimness her face looked pale and her eyes looked like black pits, and Simone suddenly remembered how Sonia had looked exactly like that when she had peered over the well's edge, and said it was deep and that anyone falling in would never be able to get out. Was Sonia lying down there, in the dark?

She said, 'I s'pose now we're here, we ought to look inside. Properly look, I mean.'

'So do I. Otherwise you'll keep remembering and wondering, and I'll keep wondering as well. But I'll do it. You stand just there then you can shine the torch for me.' She was already crossing the floor and setting her own torch down so that it shone directly on the well. After a moment Simone followed her, and shone the second torch downwards. 'That's fine,' said Mother, bending down to drag at the cover. 'Goodness, Sim, this is a situation where I remember I was forty last year— This thing's shockingly heavy.'

Impossible not to suddenly remember Sonia limping across the room with that odd hunched walk, and grasping the cover's edges and saying impatiently that they just had to pull the cover towards them... And how she had said it was all right to punish people, because it was what the Mortmain children had done...

The cover came back easily enough, although there was the same shrieking protest and there was the same rusting-iron shudder from the horrid squat stove in the corner. Simone glanced at it uneasily, and then looked back at the well.

'Give me the bigger torch, Sim—thanks. Wells are quite nasty when they've been abandoned for years and years, but once this one was probably in a courtyard, and the cook would send the kitchenmaid out to draw up a bucket of water, so that they could wash up—' She shone the torch straight down into the blackness and Simone's heart leapt in panic. Which is it? Is Sonia's body down there or isn't it?

Mel said, 'Sim, darling, there's absolutely nothing down here except a few puddles of water and some bits of rubbish.' She held out a hand. 'Come here and you'll see for yourself.'

After a moment, Simone walked forward and peered over the black brick edge into the empty darkness.

So. So although Sonia had once been real—she had been Simone's own sister—the Sonia that had talked in Simone's mind all these years, and the Sonia who had led Simone through Mortmain's spooky darkness, could not have been real, not ever.

Sonia had been a ghost, an echo from Simone's own twin, and if you wanted proof that people lived after death it looked as if Simone had been given that proof. Sonia had died all those years ago—Mum had been very clear about that—but in some odd way she had found, and clung on to, the sister to whom she had been joined when they were both born. It was what Mother thought, and it was probably the only way to think. Simone thought that Sonia might have been angry and bitter at dying when she had been so tiny, and so she had tried to live for a while through Simone. Was that possible? It sort of explained things, but it did not explain absolutely everything. It did not explain all those links to Mortmain, or all that 'I know what is and what has been' business. It did not explain why Sonia had said she had lived near to Mortmain for a lot of years.

They took the roll of film to be developed next day, and when the photos came back Mother thought they were very good indeed. She thought Simone ought to put them into a proper album and keep the negatives somewhere safe; Simone might one day be glad she had done that, Mother said.

It took a bit of the horror out of Mortmain to arrange her own views of it on the thick cardboard pages of the album they bought, and to write the dates in underneath in her best handwriting.

The trouble was that Mortmain would always be a place of darkness for Simone, and it would always be the place she would associate with Sonia. And even though the well had been empty, she still did not know whether Sonia had been a real person or a ghost.

CHAPTER NINETEEN

HARRY WAS BEGINNING to wonder if Sonia
Anderson had been a real person or a ghost.

He had turned up references to various Sonia
Andersons and also to various Sonia Marriots, but
none of the dates tallied with his Sonia's birth. He had
explored every source he could think of to find her-
most of the sources had been official but one or two
had not. Police data banks, the passport office. Under-
the-counter stuff, but you called in favours where you
had to. But even with the favours he had still not found
Sonia, and as far as he could make out Sonia Marriot had
been born as Sonia Anderson, twin to Simone, and then
vanished.

('People died and people vanished...' Markovitch had
said.)

The answer was probably that Sonia had simply
left the country as a small baby, travelling on an adult's
passport and had never returned, or—and this was more
likely—Harry had missed something somewhere. Both
ideas were profoundly depressing, although there was at
least the prospect of being able to say to Markovitch, Sorry,
dear boy, but it looks as if you've backed a loser this time.

There's nothing in the least mysterious to be disinterred about the family.

Liar, said his mind. You don't want to write the feature and you never did, in fact you'd rather starve than write it, but you know quite well that there *is* a mystery, and you're hooked on unravelling it. How about the mother, then? The somehow-shadowy Melissa? Was it possible to find her? Harry considered this.

Any researcher worth his salt knew that you did not just pursue one line of inquiry; you pursued as many as you could, picking up the ends of threads that might lead you to the crock of gold at the rainbow's end, or that might unravel of their own accord and only lead you to a crock of shit or even of bullshit. But there were times when threads that might almost have been the spun gold of the miller's daughter in the old fairytale came sizzling out of the ground and twined themselves around you.

Harry reached the *Bellman*'s office around ten on the morning after receiving Floy's book. He was still thinking about Melissa Anderson—Melissa Marriot—who might be anywhere in the world now, but who might be traceable.

There were several calls on his voice-mail, and there was one that had come in half an hour earlier which main reception had switched through to his phone. Harry listened to it, drinking the coffee that Markovitch thought good enough for his staff.

A rather hesitant female voice said she had read the article about Thorne's Gallery, and she had been so interested to see the photograph of Simone Marriot and to read about her wonderful career and the gallery. She had known the Anderson family very well indeed when the twins were babies, said the voice, but sadly she had lost touch with them. She would so much like to contact them again—was there any chance that a letter sent to Mr Fitzglen, c/o the *Bellman*, could be forwarded? It would mean so much. Perhaps Mr Fitzglen might ring or write to indicate if this was acceptable. Here was her phone number—oh, and her address. She worked at St Luke's Hospital—here was the number of that as well, and her extension. She would be so grateful if he would contact her, and if he rang the hospital he should ask for Sister Raffan. Thank you so much. Goodbye.

Harry dialled the number of St Luke's Hospital straight away.

Roz had always known that one day she would find Simone, and she was deeply grateful to this journalist, this Harry Fitzglen who had written the article on the stupid pretentious gallery. Roz had skimmed the article in her lunch-break, only half-interested, but then she had looked at the photographs with closer attention. Was it Simone? Could it really be Simone? But she had known it was, and light and brilliance had begun to explode inside her head. I've found her! After all these years I've found her! I know where she's working and what she's doing, and I know the name she's using! Marriot, that's her name now. Simone Marriot.

The elderly aunt who had brought her up would have been fastidiously shocked to think that Roz had telephoned a strange man, and even more horrified to think that Roz had agreed to meet him that same evening in a wine bar. Hardly the behaviour of a nice girl, the aunt would have said, thinning her lips disapprovingly, and would have observed that women old enough to be past such foolishness asked for trouble if they ran after men. Roz often thought that it was as well her aunt had died before the wicked 1980s started, and it was certainly a good thing that she had never seen the decadent 1990s.

Harry Fitzglen had said on the phone that he would find out about putting Miss Raffan in touch with Simone

Marriot, but suggested they meet first. Was Miss Raffan likely to be free that evening by any chance? he asked, and Roz had said please to call her Rosie, and that tonight was rather short notice but she might sort something out. She managed to make it sound as if she would have to rearrange another commitment. And where exactly—? Oh yes, Giorgio's would be fine. Yes, she knew it very well. She hoped this sounded as if she quite often called in at Giorgio's, which was a modern and quite upmarket wine bar near the hospital. Before ringing off she remembered to ask how she would recognize him.

'I'll get one of the tables and I'll tell them I'm expecting someone. Then if you ask for me at the bar they'll show you through. Is that all right? Good. I'll see you around eight, Rosie.'

Rosie. It was more than twenty years since anyone had called her Rosie and it gave Roz a jolt to hear it. But just as she had known, within about ten seconds of reading the article on Thorne's Gallery, that she had found Simone, so had she also known that she was going to resurrect Rosie.

It was, of course, Rosie rather than Roz who went to Giorgio's that evening to meet Harry Fitzglen. She was even wearing Rosie's choice of clothes. A red silk skirt— shockingly expensive and what her aunt would have called a tart's colour, but it had been displayed in the window of a small exclusive boutique on her way home that very evening and she had not been able to resist going in and buying it. With it she wore a black silky sweater, and she had fluffed her hair out more than she usually did and had even added big gold earrings. They had been a Christmas present from one of the nurses and she had never worn them, but they would be just right tonight. She felt attractive and altogether good about herself. More to the point, she felt different.

Harry Fitzglen was waiting for her, which was polite of him. He bought her a drink and then said he would be very happy to pass a letter to Simone Marriot, but he had wanted to meet Rosie first, just to be sure who he was dealing with. You got all kinds of weirdos ringing newspaper offices at times—she would understand that, of course.

'Yes, of course.'

'Could I ask you—how well did you know Simone and Sonia?'

Simone and Sonia. The names dropped into Roz's mind like chips of ice, and for a moment the crowded wine bar blurred and there was a roaring in her ears. Stay calm, said Rosie's voice softly. You can deal with this. You have dealt with far worse than this. She sipped some more of her wine, grateful for the cool dry taste, and said, Well, she had known the twins as tiny babies—it had been before the operation to separate them, of course—and she had known their parents as well.

'Their mother? You knew their mother?' He leaned forward, his eyes on her. He was really rather nice-looking when he wasn't frowning at the world. His eyes were that very clear grey you seldom saw, edged with black rims. Roz wondered how old he was. She had originally thought he was quite a lot younger than she was, but she was revising this opinion. He was perhaps about thirty— thirty-two at a push. Not all that much younger after all. Ten or twelve years, maybe.

He was saying, 'I'm sorry, did that sound intrusive? It's just that with this launching of Thorne's my editor's dreamt up the idea of a follow-up feature on the twins—what they've done with their lives, how they coped with growing up. I expect you know the kind of thing I mean,' said Harry, and Roz nodded and murmured that yes, of course, she knew, and how interesting and what a good idea.

It was not interesting in the least and it was potentially an extremely dangerous idea, and it was a very good thing indeed that Roz had nerved herself to make that phone call and to come to Giorgio's tonight, or she would not have known that this was being planned. A magazine feature—actually an article about the twins, with people delving around in the past, and in one particular fragment of the past! Dangerous! Dangerous! This man, this journalist with the beautiful eyes, was clever and perceptive and he might uncover all kinds of things. After a moment Roz said, 'Will you be the one who writes the article?'

'I hope not. Personally I think the idea's crap,' said Harry. 'But my editor's asked me to do some preliminary research to see if there's enough material, and that's the other reason I wanted to meet you tonight.' He paused to drink his own wine. 'I've been trying to find Sonia,' he said. 'The younger twin. But I've drawn a complete blank. As far as I can make out she hasn't died or got married or had children or applied for a passport or a driving licence.'

'It sounds so sad when you put it like that,' said Roz softly.

'Well, if she has done any of those things, she's managed it without getting it recorded anywhere,' said Harry. 'So it occurred to me that if you knew the family you might be able to give me some background. But I do understand you might not have known them well enough.'

He was clearly giving her a polite get-out if she did not want to talk, but Roz could have laughed out loud. How well had she known the family! Oh, only well enough to make love with the twins' father in the prim sitting-room of her aunt's little house. Only well enough that when that cheating bitch, Melissa, ran away taking the babies with her, it had been Roz who had discovered where the ungrateful creature had gone. The past came swooping forward, dark and hurting and viciously unfair.

But none of these things could be said and most of them ought not to be remembered. 'I was at the hospital when the twins were born,' she said, speaking slowly as if thinking back. 'I was only a student nurse in those days, but I remember the publicity and all the fuss. And I went to the house a few times to help with the twins when they left hospital, and I babysat a few times. That's why I'd like to write to Simone now—to say how pleased I am to read about her success.' She hesitated, then said, 'Why is Simone called Marriot now, by the way? Has she got married?'

'No idea. No husband's been mentioned, not that that means anything.'

He was evading the question, of course. The answer was almost certainly that Melissa had changed her name all those years ago; Roz had guessed that at the time, of course, although she had known that one day she would find the bitch. She had not known it would happen like this, though. But she said, 'I wonder if I could find any photos of the family, or letters for your article.'

'Could you? From so far back?' He sounded surprised.

'Oh, I'm a bit of a magpie,' said Roz cheerfully. 'I've got boxes of photos and old Christmas cards and stuff. I'll have a look and phone you, shall I?'

'That would be great. And listen, if you want to let me have a letter I'll pass it to Simone with pleasure.'

'I'd love to see her again,' said Roz, in a wistful voice. 'I didn't quite like to write to that gallery—Thorne's. Not very private, I thought.'

'I understand that.' He smiled at her; he looked completely different when he smiled. 'I'm glad you phoned me, Rosie,' he said. 'Would you like to have something to eat while we're here? They do quite a good lasagne, I think.'

Roz had never eaten Italian food in a wine bar with a man. So it was Rosie—Rosie whose mind was already considering plans and strategies—who smiled, and who said, 'What a good idea. I love lasagne.'

Harry reached his own flat an hour later, too full of slightly acidic lasagne and of nameless red wine that would probably give him a skewering headache tomorrow morning.

He poured a large whisky and then played back the messages on his answerphone. There was one from Angelica Thorne who was full of expensive-sounding plans for going to a really fun-sounding club on Monday evening with a few friends. She wondered if Harry might like to come along, what did he think?

What Harry thought was that at this rate he was going to end up even more insolvent than he had done with Amanda, and from the sound of things twice as quickly. He reached for the phone book to look up details of the night-club, and after this disinterred his last bank and credit card statements. These made glum reading, in fact it looked as if that vow about starving before writing the Anderson/Marriot article was nearer to the truth than he had realized. He then spent ten minutes picturing his exit from the bankruptcy court, haggard and unshaven, brooding on the perfidy of females as he walked to the nearest home-less centre, supping the bitter wormwood of lost love and quaffing the salt-sick gall of angry passion. This random jumble of quotations pleased him so much that he wrote it down in case it could be used some time or other.

Philip Fleury had understood about using good phrases. Harry was rationing himself to reading just a couple of chapters of *The Ivory Gate* at a time, because otherwise he would probably have devoured the book at a single sitting. There was nothing wrong with devouring a book at a single sitting; he had done it many times in the past and it had been one of the traits that had irritated and annoyed Amanda. Living through other people's emotions she had called it, proffering the expression as if it was an original observation of Kierkegaard or Goethe.

But this was not a book that Harry wanted to read in a greedy devouring sweep; it was a book he wanted to read slowly, absorbing the story and its people very thoroughly indeed. He had not yet been able to decide why he had not told Simone about finding Floy. Was it because he wanted to find out more about Floy—even find out who 'C' and Viola and Sorrel had been—and hand the entire package to Simone? To say, Here you are, my dear, this is the man who owned your house, in fact this is a photograph of him—good-looking, isn't he?—and I've found out what happened to him in later life as well. So come out to dinner, Simone, and let me tell you all about it...

As a chat-up line it was about as nauseating as you could get. I suppose, said Harry's mind sarcastically, that you think it's all that's needed to make her fall into your arms or your bed, swooning with gratitude?

There had not been any gratitude in the life of Floy's small heroine, Tansy, but there had been a great many other emotions surrounding her. Predominant among them was hatred and bitterness, but fear was a front-runner as well: the kind of too-vivid nightmare fears that sometimes engulfed small children in sleep, but that always dissolved when they woke to the ordinary daylight world. But most of Tansy's childhood years had been spent actually inside the darkness of the nightmare, struggling with the fear, obeying the rules of the fictional workhouse, submitting to the strict regime.

Hiding from the child-traders when there was a sickle moon, with the path up to the workhouse shrouded in darkness...

Harry had had to look up the expression 'sickle moon', and had found that it was an old country word for new moon. It gave him a curious sense of linking into the past to see this word used so naturally and so carelessly— except, of course, that Floy had probably never penned a careless syllable in his life.

Everyone inside the workhouse had been filled to brimming point with hatred; it had, said Tansy's creator, been so enduring an emotion that over the years it had almost corroded the ancient bricks of the walls, and mingled with the cold gall of despair. Harry liked this phrase about corrosive hatred and the cold gall of despair so much that he made a note of it there and then. Thanks, Philip. And out of copyright, as well, isn't that a bit of luck?

A good deal of the hatred colouring Tansy's early years had been directed at the overseers and at the beadle and his wife, but the deepest hatred of all had been against the men who came secretly to the workhouse on some nights: the pig-men.

There never seemed to be any pattern to their visits, but after a time Tansy noticed that they quite often came on chill, moonless nights when they would not be seen walking up the steep, tree-fringed slope to the workhouse's doors. So on those nights the children in the dormitories kept watch from the narrow windows, and discussed in scared whispers what they could do to escape.

The trouble was that the men sometimes came when no one expected them, entering the long, wooden-floored dormitories secretly and furtively, picking out the prettiest of the little girls, the most attractive of the boys. Tansy knew that sometimes it was a very long time between one visit and the next—so long that you might very nearly forget about watching, or about counting the days to the next dark-moon nights. You simply fell asleep, not thinking about the pig-men, and then one night you woke up with a bump to find the room full of huge shadows with greedy hands and clotted voices saying, Oho and aha, here's a nice pretty little one for us. Into the sack with this nice pretty little one.

One night the pig-men would come for Tansy; and unless she could think of a way to hide from them they would snatch her up and cram her into a bad-smelling sack and carry her away for ever.

Charlotte Quinton's diaries:
1st February 1900
After I had promised the child, Robyn, that we would never tell whatever secrets we were about to see inside Mortmain House (she made us promise thrice over, because she said that to say a thing three times made it a solemn vow), she led us through the dark corridors.

Have to say that this was one of the eeriest parts of the whole thing. Mortmain is a terrible place, filled up with human despair and human hopelessness and a dreadful feeling of *acceptance* by the people who have to live here. As we went along I thought that if ever a place should be burned to the ground and then the ground sown with salt, this was that place.

(If Edward read that last sentence he would smile sadly, and shake his head in that superior way—can't *stand* it when Edward is superior!—and say, Oh dear, my poor misguided Charlotte, one of your flights of fancy again, but Floy would understand at once, because Floy always understood about the dark-nesses in the world.)

As Maisie and I walked behind Robyn I suddenly wanted Floy so much that it was a physical ache, and then I wanted my lost babies, Viola and Sorrel, even more than I wanted Floy. This time last year I was still secretly meeting Floy in the thin tall house in Bloomsbury, and I remembered that this time last year Viola and Sorrel were not even specks of life struggling to form.

I had absolutely no idea what we were about to see, or how Robyn and her friends were planning to 'deal' with the men who came here to get children for brothels. At that stage I think I was still expecting to witness a childish prank; a small rebellion by a handful of children, and I am not even sure I believed in the story of the men either. Patronizing of me to think like that. Devoutly hope that Edward's smugness (also his *mother's*!) has not rubbed off on to me without my noticing it.

As Robyn led us down the dingy passages I kept expecting to encounter someone in authority who would ask our business, but there was no one, and when I asked where the inhabitants were she gave a shrug, and said no one was allowed to walk around, except at recreation times.

'When are recreation times?'

'I don't know times. Recreation's near to bedtime.'

'Where is everyone now?'

'In the Rooms.' The proper noun was impossible to miss.

'The Rooms?'

'Working, of course. This is a workhouse.' It was said with impatience, and I was so angry with myself for asking such a stupid question that I lapsed into silence. Surprisingly, it was Maisie who timidly asked what kind of work people did here.

'All kinds. Whatever's brought. The women have to clean things or sew. Mailbags and such. That's one of the easy jobs.'

'What about the children?'

'We get lessons so's they can say we've been taught to read and write and count. But we have to work in the Paupers' Room afternoons and some of the time we have to help with the babies. That's just the girls. Boys don't look after babies.'

'Babies? You do have babies here, then?'

'Some. They're in a different part from this because they yowl a lot.'

'Are they born here? Or brought here to be found homes?'

'Don't know about born here. Don't know about finding them homes, neither. Usually they're here 'cos nobody wants them.'

I caught Maisie's quickly smothered sob, but before I could speak Robyn was saying, 'Mostly what we have to do is clean things. Sculleries and the wash-house. Then you can sneak away sometimes and not always be noticed. Like now.'

'Yes, I see. And the men? What kind of work do they have to do?'

'Don't know. Don't know much about the men. Somebody said they get taken to break rocks in the quarries.'

We were approaching a partly-open door and Robyn motioned to us to stop. She went forward stealthily, and peered inside, then, apparently satisfied, she beck-oned to us to walk past. Maisie scuttled past it but I looked directly in.

I wish I had not. I suspect that I shall remember for the rest of my life the sight I saw inside that room. It was like a glimpse into hell, but it was a cold, despairing hell and it was truly and utterly dreadful. Rows of women—of all ages—but all stamped with the same helpless, hopeless submission. All with their hair shorn, wearing roughspun gowns and shapeless shoes; all bent over their tasks with a terrible patient humility, and something that might even have been gratitude.

They worked ceaselessly at thick twists of matted, tar-blackened ropes, unplaiting them into loose thin fibres. Even from where I stood I could see how the constant picking at the stained, sticky lumps of hemp had chafed their skin: their hands were scabbed over with old sores, and some were bleeding and raw.

It is almost impossible to imagine that any gathering of women, no matter what task they are engaged on, could be completely silent while they worked. I thought of the charity sewing mornings that Edward's mother sometimes arranges to provide warm clothes for the men in the Transvaal, and all the church and hospital work parties I have attended on my own account, and I thought how the chattering of the women there was sometimes like a group of starlings. But these poor beaten creatures spoke not a word to one another. And then a figure moved into my line of vision—a dreadful ogress-like female wearing a grim grey uniform, and the women nearest her seemed to cringe and then redouble their efforts.

Robyn, seeing that I was still staring into the room, grabbed my hand and pulled me past the door. 'Mrs Beadle,' she said in a vicious hiss. 'If she sees us, she'll have me whipped, certain sure.'

So we went swiftly along the passageways, and I was strongly aware of the small hard hand in mine. It was only when we were out of hearing, I said, 'Robyn—those women. What was the work they were doing?'

'Picking oakum.' Again, there was the scoffing, Don't-you-know-anything? tone. And Maisie, for once in her small life possessed of knowledge I did not have, said, 'It's old lengths of rope, mum. Least, that's what you start with. You have to unpick it and scrape out the tow and the tar, and then it's used on ships and the like. Stopping leaks and seams. Caulking, our dad used to call it.'

I thought: in those women's place I should rebel and demand at the very least decent lighting to work by, and a bit of heat, and the right to talk to my companions if I wished. And then I thought: but would I? What do I know about being homeless and penniless and in danger of starving?

Robyn took us through a long room with a bare wooden floor and windows too high up to admit much light. Narrow beds were ranged down the sides and an iron-barred wall rather sketchily divided the room, with a door at the centre.

'This is where the grown-ups sleep,' said Robyn indifferently. 'Women here, men over there.' Again there was the sideways look from eyes far too old for her years. 'That's so they can't get together and make babies.'

But even without the cage-like wall nothing so joyous as babies could possibly have been made in this room anyway. There was nothing in either section, save the narrow beds. There were no rugs on the floor or pictures on the walls; no ornaments or bedside tables that might contain a few cherished possessions or photographs of loved ones. Nothing. This ruthless obliterating of the inhabitants' identities and the dousing of their private histories was so shocking that I said quite fiercely, 'Maisie, no matter what it costs I shan't let your baby end up here!' And then to Robyn, 'If I can find a way to get you and the other children out I shall do so!'

She regarded me with amusement. 'We don't need you to get us out,' she said. 'We can look after ourselves. Like we're doing now. You'll see. This way.'

'Through here?' I said, for unless I had lost all sense of direction the door she had indicated would surely take us outside.

'Yes.' She stood back to let me step through.

I had been right about it leading outside. Beyond it was a large flagged courtyard—not well tended; there were weeds thrusting up between the flags and a dank, bad-water stench hung on the air. The walls of Mortmain rose up on all four sides, closing the courtyard in so that it had a suffocating feeling despite being open to the sky. For a brief, illogical moment I felt sad for the courtyard which could have been such a pleasant place (Floy once took me to his old college at Oxford, with the sun-drenched quadrangles and the beautiful oriel windows and old, mellowed bricks, and I thought it one of the loveliest places in the world), but then I saw the little cluster of children standing in the deep shadow cast by one of the frowning walls, and I forgot about the surroundings. There were perhaps eight or ten of them, and each one was almost an exact replica of Robyn, with their raggedly short hair and no-colour clothes and wary, defiant eyes. The forgotten ones. Nobody's children.

They were standing close to what looked to be an old well; I could see the low brick parapet and the square outline of the frame rising over it, with the winch for lowering the bucket into the well-shaft.

I looked at all of this, and then I saw that lying on the ground, in an untidy huddle against the black brickwork of the parapet, was the bulky shape of a man.

I said, 'Who is that?' and Robyn looked up at me.

'One of the child-traders,' she said.

CHAPTER TWENTY

Charlotte Quinton's diaries, continued
The children had tied his hands and feet and knotted
a dirty-looking rag around his mouth so that he could
not speak or call for help, but even from where I was
standing I could see the small, mean eyes that glared
with angry malevolence, and the thick coarse skin. I
remembered how Robyn had called the child-traders
'pigs', and saw how apt was the word.

The part I find difficult to explain here (even now,
writing this account in the comfortable privacy and
safety of my old bedroom in the house where I grew
up) is the extraordinary atmosphere of cold, implacable menace that came from the children. There
were ten of them altogether—I had counted by this
time—and although it was difficult to differentiate
the sexes because of the short hair and shapeless
clothes, I was fairly sure there were four boys and
six girls, including Robyn. Most of them looked no
more than eight or nine, but on reflection several of
them must have been older. Workhouse food does not
make for robust health or strong stature. ('Eat your
greens, Charlotte, and eat the crusts on your bread-
and-butter or you'll never grow up to be strong and

healthy...' Remarkable when nursery precepts turn out to be true.)

As we entered the courtyard the children turned to look questioningly at us and some looked truculent (Maisie was still cowering in the doorway—she has a knack of shrinking almost to invisibility when frightened), but Robyn said, 'It's all right. This is a friend and she wants to help. I trust her.' So you'd better do the same, was the implication. 'And she's taken the vow never to tell what she sees.'

(Think a couple of the boys still looked suspicious, so clearly the thrice-times vow not accepted as a guarantee of good faith by everyone, but Robyn said it with a defiant authority and nobody made objection. For which I was *profoundly* grateful.)

The boy who looked to be the oldest, and who had a shock of tow-coloured hair, said, 'Everything's ready,' and I heard that he had a slightly foreign voice. Eastern European, perhaps. He appeared to be the leader, or at the very least the spokesman, and in sharp contrast to his light hair he had dark, angry eyes. I visualized him forcing the other children to fight against the harsh regime, and even whipping them into small rebellions at times.

'Is *he* ready?' said Robyn, and the tow-haired boy aimed an angry kick at the prisoner's ribs. The man flinched and tried to roll out of range. 'He's ready,' said the boy contemptuously.

I said, 'What are you going to do to him?'

'He's going to be punished,' said the boy, staring at me. 'And when the rest of them see what we've done they won't come here any more.' He glanced back at Robyn. 'Are you sure she's to be trusted?' he demanded truculently.

'Yes, I told you.'

I felt absurdly pleased at Robyn's off-hand air of

trust, so I stayed where I was and tried not to interfere with whatever they were doing.

Robyn had joined the other children, and she was
looking at the man on the ground very intently. 'You're
one of the pigs,' she said. 'I know that 'cos I've seen you
in here. You're one of Mr Dancy's people. Matt Dancy.'

With the pronouncing of the name the children
seemed to cringe and the smallest girl glanced
uneasily over her shoulder as if fearful of being spied
on from the shadows. That was the first time I heard
the name of Matt Dancy, and I hated it at once.

'We've all seen you with him,' said Robyn. 'Most of
all, Anthony's seen you. You were the one who took
his little sister away.'

I saw that Anthony was the dark-eyed, tow-haired
boy. He said to the man, 'She hid from you that night.
She hid under her bed and made herself as small as
she could, and prayed that you wouldn't find her.'

'I heard her praying,' said the little girl who had
looked so frightened. 'She whispered the prayers,
but I heard her saying, "Gentle Jesus, meek and mild,
look on me, a little child."' She had a light, polite
little voice, and I imagined her being the much-loved
daughter of some nice people, who had taught her to
say her prayers and always be polite to grown-ups.

'She was eight years old, my sister,' said Anthony,
his eyes still fixed on the helpless man. 'And you
dragged her out, and slung her over your shoulder,
and carried her away. She screamed all the time and
she tried to cling on to the frame of the bed, but you
prised her fingers free and then you took her away.'
His voice held no emotion other than cold hatred,
and I wanted to cry again. I wanted to cry for the
little girl who had hidden under her bed and said
her prayers, and I wanted to cry for all the children
gathered around the old well. But mixed up with the

wanting-to-cry feeling was also the longing to run out from my place of half-concealment and kick the imprisoned man until he screamed for mercy.

Looking back, I can see that it was curious that it never occurred to me to disbelieve these children. But even in retrospect it does not occur to me to disbelieve them. They were certainly all very skilled at lying or cheating in order to dodge the worst of Mortmain's vicious rules, but they had no knowledge of falseness or pretence or sophistry. They knew what they had seen this man—and others like him—do, and they were going to punish him.

Then Robyn suddenly said, 'Let's do it now,' and as if a spell had been set working, the children moved in on their captive.

There was absolutely nothing I could do to help him even if I had wanted to. And in the face of some of the things I had seen inside Mortmain, and in view of what had been said by Robyn and Anthony, I did not want to. The rebellious, angry part of me (the part that Edward does not like to think exists and his mother deplores, but that Floy loved and encouraged) said: let them go ahead and punish this evil creature.

But even the rebellious part was not prepared for what they did.

Two of the girls brought out a thick length of rope—I thought it must be taken from the dreadful room where we had seen the women picking oakum—and Anthony climbed precariously on to the parapet while two of the other boys held on to his ankles. The frame with the winch-and-bucket mechanism was quite large: there were two thick vertical posts supporting a horizontal crossbar above them, and this crossbar was a good three feet higher than the brick surround, so that Anthony had to stand on

tiptoe and lean up to reach it. He was thin and probably under-nourished, but by dint of holding on to
one of the vertical posts he managed to first unhook
the wooden bucket and then knot the rope's end on
to the big iron hook.

The three boys pulled hard on the rope to make
sure it was securely anchored, and then they fashioned a loop out of the rope's free end. No. Not a
loop. A *noose*. And then I became aware that the two
smallest girls were chanting something very quietly,
almost whispering it, but doing so with a fierce
concentration. After a moment I made out what they
were chanting, and a deep horror began to close
round my heart.

> '*On moonlit heath and lonesome bank*
> *The sheep beside me graze;*
> *And yon the gallows used to clank*
> *Fast by the four cross ways.*'

The gallows. The gallows that used to clank by the
four cross ways... I had heard those lines once before,
in Floy's house when a professor who also wrote
poetry had read them to a roomful of people. The lines
were part of a cyclical poem, on the surface pastoral,
on the surface written about this part of England by
an uprooted Shropshire boy. But if you looked below
the surface (and by then Floy had taught me how to
do that), there was nothing pastoral about them at
all. Hearing them inside Mortmain House I saw that
the professor—his name was Housman—might very
well have known about the pockets of darkness in the
world, and might very well have been writing about
one of them. I had thought the verses chilling when
I heard them for the first time, but hearing them
chanted by this group of resolute children, they were

much more than chilling: they were fearsome and grotesque.

Dear God, I thought, I know what they're going to do to him, and no matter what he is, that brute-faced creature, or what he's done I've got to stop this— Or have I?

Anthony and the other boys dragged the man to his feet. He was squirming and struggling to get free, trying to kick out at his captors, but his ankles were bound too firmly. The boy who had helped Anthony to tie the rope over the well-shaft slipped the noose over the man's head and tightened it, and I had the irrelevant thought that whatever these children knew or did not know, this one understood about knots, and perhaps his father had been a sailor or a chandler—

And then thought was cut off abruptly, as the children pushed the man over the brick wall and down into the well-shaft.

He went down feet-first but he did not fall very far. The rope around his neck jerked his body to a grotesque upright position, spinning him around with the momentum of his fall. He hung there, half in, half out of the well's mouth, his waist level with the top of the brick surround, the crossbar of the winch creaking ominously from his weight.

A hundred emotions poured through my mind, but mixed up with them was a tiny voice beating against my consciousness like a hammering pulse. Nothing-you-can-do...They've-hanged-him...They've-hanged-him-and-he's-dead...Serve-him-right, said the softest and strongest voice of all the voices, and an

image of an eight-year-old girl clinging to the underside of her bed, praying to Gentle Jesus that she would
not be taken away, rose up in front of my eyes. Serve
him right.

The children had joined hands around the well,
and they were moving in a circle, not quite dancing,
but not exactly walking either. The only word I can
find to describe their movements is *prowl*. They
prowled in their half-dance, and the eerie thing was
that if the well and its dreadful figure had not been
visible, they might have been any group of children
playing an ordinary childish game.

They all joined in with the chanting of the two
girls.

> *On moonlit heath and lonesome bank*
> *The sheep beside me graze;*
> *And yon the gallows used to clank*
> *Fast by the four cross ways.*

> *A careless shepherd once would keep*
> *The flocks by moonlight there,*
> *And high amongst the glimmering sheep*
> *The dead man stood on air...*

The man's body was still spiralling around, and I
thought: if I were to run across the courtyard now,
could I reach him? Could I cut him down? But into
what? said my mind at once. Straight down into the
depths of the well?

The children were still singing, their hands linked,
circling the well ceaselessly, and now there was
something tribal and even primeval about them.

> *They hang us now in Shrewsbury jail;*
> *The whistles blow forlorn,*

And trains all night groan on the rail
To men that die at morn...

I began to feel slightly sick and dizzy, so I leaned back against the wall behind me, grateful for its solid strength, grateful for Maisie's presence as well, even though she was sheet-white and plainly more frightened than I was. And surely in another minute it would all stop and Robyn and the others would scuttle back to whatever dark corner of Mortmain they were supposed to be in, and Maisie and I could go quietly home. Leaving the children here? Leaving the man hanging? Standing on air...?

And naked to the hangman's noose
The morning clocks will ring
A neck God made for other use
Than strangling in a string...

Their voices were so unchildlike that I remembered the old superstition about possession, and thought that if the old witchfinders could be here now they would swoop on this ragged little group.

(Note: This thought about possession was one I later thought better of, although only slightly.)

And sharp the link of life will snap,
And dead on air will stand
Heels that held up as straight a chap
As treads upon the land...

It was as they sang this line about the heels that had once trodden the land that the worst thing of all happened. The rope was spiralling more slowly now, but as the hanged man swung round to face my part of the courtyard again, life flickered in his eyes and he began to struggle.

A whole new horror scalded through my body.

He was still alive. The shock of the initial tumble had somehow rendered him senseless for a few moments but it had not broken his neck, and now he had regained his senses and he was alive. He was struggling and writhing, dreadful wheezing grunting sounds were coming out of his mouth, and his face was a deep dull red. His eyes bulged so much I had the grisly thought that at any minute they might burst out of the sockets and hang down on his cheeks.

It was the dance of the hanged man, it was the dead man standing on air, exactly as Professor Housman's poem had described, except that this man was not yet dead, he was slowly strangling and we—the children and Maisie and I—were going to see it happen.

Dark patches, the colour of uncooked liver, broke out on his face, and all the time the terrible breathless grunting sounds went on. The sun had gone behind a cloud earlier on but it came out again, casting shadows in the enclosed courtyard. The square shadow of the well's crossbar and what hung from it fell sharply on one of the walls, so that it almost seemed as if there were two men, both jerking and struggling and choking.

The children had not expected this; I saw that at once. They had expected him to die instantly, and although it was an ugly death it would have been more or less instant. Their voices faltered and they stopped chanting. I saw Anthony start involuntarily forward, as if to attempt some kind of rescue, but one of the others—and I think it was Robyn—pulled him back. One of them—and again I believe it was Robyn—began the chant again, a bit raggedly, a bit shrilly, but after a moment the rest joined in.

Time ceased to exist, and the world narrowed to the squirming figure at the rope's end. Once I thought someone approached the courtyard—there was the tap-tap of quick angry-sounding feet coming along one of the corridors on the other side of the door—and I half-turned, although I am still not sure what I would have done if one of the attendants—the ogress-like Mrs Beadle perhaps—had appeared. But the footsteps went on into another part of Mortmain.

The man jerked and grunted in helpless spasm for what felt like several eternities, but was probably about ten minutes. The rags tying his wrists together had worked free and he clawed vainly at the air, feebly trying to reach the constricting rope, once trying to grasp the crossbar. His shadow on the wall clawed and jerked with him. Blood-flecked spittle ran from his mouth and his tongue began to protrude out of his mouth. Urine ran down his legs, soaking his trousers and splashing down into the well-shaft—under normal circumstances I would have found it paralysingly embarrassing to witness this and to write about it now, but it was simply part of the horror and the nightmare.

And then it was over. His body sagged as if a string had been cut and his head fell forward on to his chest. The link of life snapped...as suddenly as if a flame had been snuffed out.

I was shaking as if I had been running very hard for miles and miles, and Maisie was whimpering.

But the children—now that they had done what they set out to do—now that they had achieved their revenge—they were no longer implacable justice-wreakers, they were children again, frightened and bewildered. The tiniest were starting to be tearful, and even Anthony sent scared glances about him. Only Robyn still seemed defiant and uncaring.

I stopped shaking and went forward to them, half-kneeling on the dusty flagstones. ('Charlotte, your *skirt!*' Mamma said later). They turned, half-gratefully, half-warily, and then Anthony said, a bit tremulously, 'I don't think we're sure what we should do—' He broke off, and I saw that he was very young after all. His hair had fallen over his eyes and he pushed it back defiantly and looked at me.

I said, 'How deep is that well? Does anyone ever draw its water?' and saw understanding, and with it relief, shine in his eyes.

It was not quite as simple as I had expected, because I had thought we would be able to release the winch mechanism and wind the man into the well's depths. The iron hook was attached to a thick coil of rope, steel-laced, and on one side of the wooden frame was a handle rather like the one you see on mangles. But when Anthony and the other boys tried to turn it they discovered that it was somehow bolted to the side, and none of us had the least idea of how to release it.

(Note: So much for Edward's mother insisting that no lady ever needs to know anything about machinery, although to be fair to the old bat she could not possibly have anticipated a situation even remotely resembling this.)

I was still half-listening for the return of those tapping footsteps within Mortmain, but I said in as practical a voice as I could manage, 'Clearly the only thing we can do is cut the rope. Has anyone got a knife?' Ridiculous question, of course.

'I could try to get one from the scullery,' said one of the girls rather timidly.

'Very well, but make sure you aren't caught.' As she sped off, it occurred to me that now I was colluding in theft as well, although since I had just colluded in a murder stealing a scullery knife did not strike me as particularly felonious.

We waited in silence. Another of Mamma's precepts was that a lady should never be at a loss for conversational topics, but I defy even Mamma to have thought of a suitable remark to make in this situation.

The little girl returned more quickly than I had dared hope. She had brought a broad-bladed knife, which she handed to Anthony. She seemed quite sure that no one had seen her take it.

And again the children worked together with that tacit understanding of one another's intentions. Anthony climbed back on to the parapet, and from there swarmed up the vertical post, and then sat astride the crossbar. It creaked ominously but it seemed strong enough, and he appeared untroubled by being directly above the well-shaft, and I don't know about the others, but my heart was leaping into my throat with fear, because if he were to lose his balance—

But he worked his way along the crossbar until he was far enough out to reach down and start sawing at the rope. The movement caused it to swing crazily to and fro, and several times the dead man bumped against the black bricks lining the well-shaft. The crossbar was groaning like a thousand souls in torment with Anthony's weight, and my heart was still in my throat in case it should splinter.

But it held firm. The rope began to fray, and the dead man stopped swinging across the well's mouth, and began to spiral again. And then Anthony said, 'It's going!' and the last strands of the rope parted.

The dead man went down into the mouth of the well with a sound like the four furies rushing upon mankind's doom, and after what seemed a dreadfully long time we eventually heard the dull, dead splash of water. It's difficult to describe, even now, how that sound affected me. It was a black, bleak sound, and I thought: even for such an evil creature he's had a terrible death and now we've consigned him to a dank lonely eternity down there.

But I gathered the children around me, and I said, very seriously, 'We must promise—all of us—never to reveal what has happened here. If the man is ever found none of you will know anything about it. You understand that? You may have to lie—' There was a wry smile from some of them at that, and I realized that they would be perfectly used to lying in this place. 'If anyone saw my arrival,' I said, trying to think of all eventualities, 'or saw me talking to you, you are to say that I was a visitor from—from—the Workhouse Commission.' It was a vague definition, but I saw that they accepted this and realized that they were probably quite used to well-meaning ladies on committees and commissions visiting Mortmain. They promised, even the small scornful Robyn. 'I don't suppose you'll come to see us again, will you?' she said, glaring angrily at me.

I knew I would have to return to London and Edward very soon, but I remembered that Mamma was one of the well-meaning ladies on committees, and that Mamma, whatever her shortcomings, can always be roused to crusading anger by a story of cruelty against children.

So I said, slowly, 'I might not be able to come back here, Robyn—I live in London, you see. But there might be ways I can help you from outside. There might be people I could talk to who would look into the—the governing of this place.'

She shrugged dismissively: probably she had heard things like this said before, but I said as earnestly as I could, 'Robyn, please believe me. I will do what I can for you.'

CHAPTER TWENTY-ONE

Charlotte Quinton's diaries, continued
Maisie said, 'Oh mum, Mrs Quinton mum, I can't believe
what we just seen. Those kids— And that man—'
'Neither can I believe it, Maisie.'
'It was awful, wasn't it?'
'One of the worst things I've ever known. But we
have to remember that he was a very evil man.'
(Evil enough to justify condoning his murder?
said the voice of conscience in my ear. Was any
human being evil enough for a fellow creature to
take on himself the responsibility for killing? How
about the Bible's teachings? Vengeance is mine,
sayeth the Lord—remember that one, Charlotte? Of
course I remember it, but if we're quoting the Bible,
hadn't we also better remember the Old Testament
and Exodus? Life for life, eye for eye, tooth for
tooth... But how about the almost certain fact that if
you had tried, if you had really *tried*, between you,
you and Maisie could perfectly easily have stopped
those children?)
None of this could be said to Maisie, who would
probably see the whole thing in terms of black and
white, and who would not understand all the tones

and half-tones in between or the lines that blurred the boundaries between one set of values and another. So I said, 'We have no need to feel any blame, Maisie.' And then, being naturally truthful, I added, '*You* have no need to feel any blame.'

We were outside Mortmain by then; its door had clanged shut and we had stepped unchallenged into the ordinary world once again, although as we crossed the big stone-floored hall we had glimpsed a couple of women. They looked like attendants of some kind, but whoever they were they had not questioned us.

I was trying not to let Maisie see how very shaken I was, and I was trying to walk calmly and composedly down the tree-fringed slope to where we had left the pony and trap. But it was quite difficult. I said, 'I wish I could think of a way to find that man who takes the children, Maisie. Matt Dancy.'

'How would you do that, mum? Where'd you even start looking?'

'I don't know, but there must be some way. Anthony's sister— And all the others—'

'It happens, mum. You can't do nothing about these things.'

('You can't change the world, Charlotte,' Mamma always said. I had always thought she was right until I met Floy, and then I saw that here was someone fully prepared to take on the entire world, and, if not actually change it, at least make a dent in one or two of its shibboleths.)

We were halfway down the track, at the place where it curved sharply around, when I suddenly heard footsteps on the path below us. Whoever was coming towards us was out of sight from the sharp curve in the track and by the trees—even in the winter months Mortmain's trees cluster thickly and darkly around it, but he was coming nearer. Mortmain was so shut away by itself and the path was so lonely that I felt a sudden twist of nervousness.

'There's someone coming, mum.'

'Yes, I heard. But it will only be someone visiting Mortmain,' I said firmly. 'A pity the track is so narrow, but all we need do is bid the person a courteous good-afternoon and go on down to the road.'

'He's stopped,' said Maisie after a moment. 'P'raps he's changed his mind and gone away.'

He had not gone away. As we came around the path's curve he was there, standing quite still as if he had been waiting for us, his coat collar turned up against the wind and his black hair, worn just too long for present fashion, tumbled into disarray. For a moment the landscape tilted and spun all around me, because I had conjured him up in my mind so many times and I had been thinking of him so strongly only moments earlier, that it was treacherously easy to believe we were being confronted by a ghost.

The trees formed a frame for him and the afternoon sun filtered through the leaves, tipping his hair with red. With anyone else I would have suspected him of standing in that exact spot deliberately in order to create an effect, except that he had never tried to create an effect in his life. He had never needed to.

Then he said, 'Charlotte,' and I knew he was real, and I wanted to run forward and fling myself against his chest.

I did not, of course. ('Never make a scene, Charlotte, especially not in front of a gentleman.' I had made many a scene with Floy in the past and some had been passionate and some had been gut-wrenching and some had been merely diversionary, but I was not going to make any kind of scene out here, in the shadow of Mortmain.)

I said, in a polite little voice, 'Floy. Goodness, of all people to meet.'

Maisie gave him one frightened glance and then scuttled on down the track towards the pony-trap. I knew she would wait there, obedient and unquestioning, which meant Floy and I might as well have been alone in the middle of a wasteland. Just as we had found ourselves alone in the middle of a mental wasteland on the day I left him for ever.

'What on earth are you doing here?' I said, in a light, artificial voice.

'I came here to see you, Charlotte.' No one has ever said my name in quite the way that Floy says it. He makes it sound like a caress.

'How did you know where I was?'

'Edward told me.' The smile that was half-saint, half-wolf, showed briefly. 'He was perfectly polite about it, but he does so dislike me, doesn't he?'

'That's because he doesn't understand you.'

'I'm glad. I should hate to be understood by someone like Edward—it would mean we had something in common.' He waited to see if I would react to this, and when I did not, said, 'I called at your house a week after the funeral, Charlotte. I went there as a friend, nothing more, and I was as correct and conventional as you could wish. I said I had come to tender my condolences.' The stiff conventionality of the phrase sat oddly on his lips.

'And Edward said you had gone to stay with your parents for a couple of weeks,' said Floy. 'He was perfectly polite, in fact he invited me into his study and offered me a glass of sherry. I see he still buys cheap sherry.'

'I'm sorry,' I said, forced on to the defensive.

'So then, since you were not in London, and since London without you holds no charms for me whatsoever—'

'I wish you wouldn't say things like that.'

'No, you don't.'

'No, I don't.'

'Since you weren't there I caught a midnight train, and this morning I went out to your parents' house, and said I was a friend of your husband's and of yours, and that I was up here on business and calling to present my compliments. Your mother,' said Floy expressionlessly, 'was utterly charmed.'

'Yes, she would be.'

(Note: In fact, at dinner this evening Mamma observed what a very charming young man Mr Fleury was: how extremely kind it had been of him to call—what a pity you missed him Charlotte—but how *interesting* to meet a writer, your father was quite taken with him. By time we reached the savoury, v. clear to us all that Mamma was basking in a little reflected glory, and revelling in the knowledge that she had actually met *the* Philip Fleury, the one who wrote those rather *risqué* novels. Would not put it past her to have read one or two of them in secrecy, either.)

'Your father's sherry is infinitely better than your husband's,' said Floy, and then without warning the brittleness dissolved and he said in a completely different voice, 'My dearest love, you must have been in agony at losing the babies.'

'Yes, I was. I still am.' I was trying not to let him see that when he looked at me like that I still loved him so much it was a physical pain. 'Thank you for coming to the funeral.'

'Of course I came to the funeral,' he said angrily. 'Don't you have something in your religion about sharing the pain of someone you love? Standing at the foot of the Cross?' This was the pagan side speaking, of course; Floy affects to disdain all religions, but am not sure if he really does. 'Charlotte, when I got back from France and heard what had happened, of *course* I came to be there.'

'I noticed you kept to the back of the church,' I said.

'That was in case lightning struck me.'

Another of the pauses while I sought vainly for something to say. Part of the trouble, of course, was that I was still dazed from what Maisie and I had just witnessed inside Mortmain; it was like coming out of a dark room and being dazzled and made dizzy by bright sunlight. My mind was still drowning in the horror and the ugliness of what the children had done and I could not properly adjust it to Floy.

But I was just thinking that I had handled the situation fairly well, and that in a moment I would say goodbye to him, and go down to the trap, when he said, 'They were mine, weren't they, Charlotte? Viola and Sorrel?'

The words pierced the fragile carapace I thought I had woven against him, and broke apart the darkness that Mortmain and Mortmain's children had spun. For a moment I had no idea how to answer him, and for a moment I was back in the dreadful infirmary ward, and two flower-like hands were clinging to me as if I was the only thing in their small world that they dared trust... Because perhaps the twins had sensed the pitying hostility—they're often said to possess an extra sensitivity, twins—and perhaps they had picked up the sinister intent in the nurse's too-emphatic words that I would be left on my own, no one would disturb me and there was a cushion there if I wanted it...

In a voice I hardly recognized as my own, I said, 'Yes. Yes, they were yours.'

'Oh God, why didn't you tell me?' he said after what seemed to be a very long time.

'I didn't discover I was pregnant until long after you had gone,' I said. 'And it was too late to do anything then. But if I had told you, it would have forced a choice on you. You would have felt coerced. Responsible. And I didn't want,' I said angrily, 'to be anyone's responsibility.'

'You seem happy to remain as Edward's.'

'Edward likes responsibility. He thinks it's what gentlemen do.'

The wolf-look was back in full force. 'Ergo, I'm no gentleman.'

'Well,' I said, 'are you? A gentleman wouldn't have seduced another man's wife.'

'A lady wouldn't have indicated so plainly that she was willing to be seduced.'

I flinched, and then said, 'In any case you wouldn't have wanted conventional domesticity.'

'You didn't give me any opportunity to want it.'

'You didn't give me any opportunity to offer it,' I said at once. 'After that last night we were together you went to Paris, to write and research.'

'And you ran back to Edward and safe, dull security.' He paused, and then said, 'Don't go back to him. Leave him, Charlotte. Come with me now.'

'I can't. Floy, you know I can't. There'd be a scandal—'

'Oh, fuck the scandal,' he said impatiently. (Floy has never troubled overmuch about protecting the delicate ears of ladies with whom he is or has been intimate, which is to say, me and very likely at least a dozen others.)

'In any case writers' careers thrive on scandal,

Charlotte. We can live abroad. I've still got the apartment in Paris. Or we can go to Vienna and Italy. We'll follow the footsteps of Robert Browning and Elizabeth, and of Byron and Shelley. Wouldn't you like that? Wouldn't you like to sit on the banks of Lake Geneva while I write a chilling ghost story, and read it to you every evening by candlelight and wine? Let's do it, Charlotte.' His hair was whipped into witch-locks by the wind, and his eyes were sparkling, and there was a faint colour across his cheekbones. 'We'll take the silk route across Isphahan and walk in the rose-gardens of ancient Persia, and drink mandragora, the love-syrup of the poets...'

The darkness that Mortmain had spun over my mind dissolved a little further, and I saw Floy's words take on substance, as if they had opened up two separate and quite distinct paths. And one of the paths was thorny and uncomfortable and difficult, and the other path was fringed with scented flowers and foaming lavender, with thick sweet grass to walk on barefoot, and I knew I must somehow resist the second and stay on the first.

Floy said, very softly, '"Two Gates the silent house of Sleep adorn/Of polished ivory this, that of transparent horn/True visions that through transparent horn arise/Through polished ivory pass the deluding lies,"' and I jumped because he had not only known what I was thinking, he had picked up something of the mental image as well.

'Well, Charlotte? Which gate are you going to walk through? The gleaming ivory one, where the hopes eventually turn to scorn and where delusions rule? Or the gate of burnished horn where the dreams are true and real? The ivory gate looks so easy, so respectable, doesn't it? But it's a false sheen, Charlotte. And ivory's a cold, unyielding bedfellow.' He took a step nearer. 'Come with me now, my dear love.'

My dear love. When he spoke like that, when he looked at me like that, I wanted to say I would follow him into hell and beyond, and never stop to count the cost. But I knew that I would count the cost. I knew I would be dealing a very great hurt to a lot of people. My parents. That mattered a lot. Mamma would never get over the shame. My two sisters, just emerging from the schoolroom, just starting to be allowed into the adult world, might find themselves ostracized. 'The Craven girls? Wasn't there some kind of scandal a few years back? The eldest girl, was it?'

(Should here record that I don't *like* the way society views these things, but fear it will take a social revolution or an upheaval of unimaginable magnitude to alter people's outlooks.)

And there was Edward. If I ran away with Floy, Edward would be bewildered and devastated. Edward isn't the most exciting husband I could have had (and let's admit in the privacy of these pages that I could have had several other husbands if I had cared to). He'll never quote beautiful poetry to me, or paint exciting and soul-scalding word-pictures with his pen, or walk in and out of my mind as if it was his own bedroom.

But neither will he plunge me into penury, or embark on love affairs that will wrench me apart. (Floy's financial affairs have gone from near-bank-ruptcy to wild affluence and back again at least three times, while his love affairs— Well, everyone knows that his love affairs are *legion*, and I would not trust his capacity for fidelity if he swore it before a hundred altars or on a thousand nuptial couches, I really would not. Do not class Edward's occasional fumbling exploits with maids actually as *affairs*, since doubt he derives much real pleasure from them, and am even surer the girls do not.)

And set above all that is the fact that Edward married me honourably and freely, and I made a vow in church and that isn't something to be set aside lightly.

'I can't do it,' I said at last. 'We've had all this out before, Floy, and I can't do it. And now,' I said, glancing down the path to where Maisie was patiently sitting in the trap, 'I should go.'

'This really is the end, isn't it?'

'Yes, it is. It has to be.' I waited for him to say that of course it was not the end, how could it ever be the end after what we had shared—after Viola and Sorrel, the daughters he had never seen and now never would see—but he did not. He said, 'I won't forget them, you know. Viola and Sorrel. Never.'

I had not expected this, but I said, 'Neither will I.'

'Tell me what they looked like. Make me see them, just a little.'

If I did not get away in the next few minutes I would start crying, and if I started crying I would never have the strength to walk away from him, back to poor, dull, honourable, *deceived* Edward.

But I said, 'They would have been very pretty indeed. Perhaps they would even have been beautiful. They had dark hair, with a glint of red in it, and skin like pale cream. And blue eyes—not like most babies' eyes, but that wonderful dark blue that you so seldom see.'

'Harebells in a wood at dusk,' said Floy. 'Violets and moss roses. Thank you, Charlotte. They're a little more real to me now. And they'll be with me down the years for ever. Like small ghosts.'

His eyes narrowed briefly and I saw that he was already seeing the twins as part of some future book that he would write: something about loss, perhaps, or something about the emptiness of passion, or the intransience of romance that flickered against moonlight and firelight and wine. And—being Floy—there might be something about the dark sides of men's natures as well, and about the cruelties that run just under the skin of the world like sinister swirling currents, or the heartbreaking choices that sometimes had to be made between the ivory gate and the gate of burnished horn...

Without saying anything else he went back down the track, leaving me on my own with the ghosts.

CHAPTER TWENTY-TWO

TWO DAYS AFTER the meeting at the wine bar, Roz phoned Harry at his home.

She apologized if she was disturbing him, but he had given her his home phone number, and she had thought— Well, the thing was that she might have found out something for his research on the Anderson twins. She did not know if it would be of any use, but perhaps they might meet, so that she could explain. What she had thought—and it was only an idea—was that she might repay his hospitality at Giorgio's by inviting him to a meal at her house. Nothing grand, just a bite to eat and a glass of wine. Then she could give him the information she had turned up.

Harry heard himself saying that he would be very interested to know what she had unearthed, but he would not dream of putting her to the trouble of cooking a meal— Oh, her aunt's house? Well, then perhaps— Well, yes, if she put it like that, he would be happy to come out to her house for a bite of supper. Tonight? Yes, tonight would be fine, but please not to go to a lot of trouble— No, he did not have any dislikes or allergies whatsoever. He could eat anything that was put in front of him, and he would see her around half past seven.

She lived in a rather depressing house fairly near to the hospital. Harry approached it with a twinge of apprehension. There was no discernible reason for this; it was just that he had thought he detected a slight over-eagerness in her voice on the phone when she invited him to eat with her, and it had sounded a faint alarm bell. (Oh yes? Think yourself irresistible to all females now, do you?) But the mention of an aunt had been reassuring; he visualized some nice, unmarried lady in her seventies: someone who would fuss at having a Man to supper. An older version of Rosie herself: she had unmistakably spinsterish traits— that reference to keeping letters and old Christmas cards, for instance.

It was disconcerting, therefore, to find himself ushered fussily into a small dining-room, made dark by overgrown shrubbery outside, and to find that there were only two places laid at the claw-footed mahogany table.

'Isn't your aunt—?'

'Oh, my aunt's been dead for years,' said Roz, apparently surprised that he should have thought otherwise. 'She died twenty years ago.'

'Ah. I must have misunderstood you.'

'I lived with her all my life, though. My parents were killed in a car crash when I was a baby, so I came here. She left me the house and all the furniture. Would you like a drink?'

'I would. I brought some wine.'

'Oh, how very nice of you, although quite unnecessary— I'll get a corkscrew. Or you could have a glass of whisky, if you like. Most men like whisky, don't they?'

Harry did like. He accepted the whisky, and asked about the information she had found on the twins.

'I thought I'd save that until we've eaten. I do dislike discussing business things while eating, don't you?'

She was expecting him to seduce her—no, she was *hoping* for him to seduce her. Harry was not sure how he knew this so definitely, but he did know it and he found it deeply worrying. It was only faintly apparent while they sipped their drinks before eating, but it became embarrassingly apparent throughout the roast lamb with mint sauce, and the fruit crumble with cream. ('The apples are from my own garden: I do like fresh food, don't you?')

It became blazingly obvious over the coffee, which was served in the small sitting-room after the meal— 'Now do have a *petit four* with your coffee: I made them myself'— and there, sadly and clumsily, was the brush of her hand against his thigh as the plate was passed to him, and there, pathetically and too-obviously, was the soft press of a breast as she reached across him for the sugar bowl.

Harry was not unaccustomed to being on the receiving end of seduction, and he was certainly not unaccustomed to exerting the technique on his own account, either, but he found Sister Raffan's attempts disquieting in a way he could not analyse. Because she was so much older, was it? Yes, partly that. But it was also something to do with the cloying atmosphere of the room, which was crowded with old-fashioned ornaments and china figures on elaborate side-tables and framed photographs, and with the way she sat by him on the old-fashioned sofa with the cream lace arm-covers.

He set down his coffee cup firmly, and said, 'Rosie, this stuff you found on the Anderson twins—' And hoped her claim to have found information had not merely been a ploy to get him out here, because it would be so infinitely sad, it would be toe-curlingly awful, to have to watch and listen to her trying to explain or make something up.

It had not been a ploy, and she did not have to try to explain or make anything up. She smiled at him and set her own cup down next to his, and said that although she had not found anything of any help in any of the boxes of letters and photos, she had made one or two inquiries at the hospital. 'I was very discreet, of course,' she said. 'I used your article as a springboard, as a matter of fact— I said, Goodness, wasn't this one of the Anderson twins, and, Dear me, it doesn't seem twenty years since they were born in our own maternity unit. That kind of thing.'

'That was tactful of you. And did anyone remember them?'

'Yes, several people. And one of the managers—she was a secretary in those days, but they're all called managers or account executives these days, and she's always been by way of being a friend of mine—she said how nice to see that at any rate one of the twins had done so well—'

'"One" of the twins?'

Roz paused, leaning forward to pick up her coffee cup. 'Yes. She said she had always thought it such a tragedy that both twins hadn't survived.'

There was rather a long silence. Then Harry said, 'So after all, Sonia's dead.'

'Yes,' said Roz, watching him over the rim of her cup. 'Sonia's dead.' She reached for a small envelope on a side table. 'This is quite against the rules, but I got this for you.'

It was a photocopy of a newspaper cutting, quite short, dated about seven months after the twins' birth. It simply said that the operation to separate the conjoined Anderson twins born earlier this year in St Luke's Hospital, had been performed in Switzerland. The newspaper understood that, very sadly, the younger twin—Sonia—had died shortly afterwards from complications following the surgery.

'It was in the old file on the twins,' said Roz. 'I had to ferret around in the records office for ages because it was packed away with the archives but nobody asked any questions. It's not actually an official announcement, is it? But it sounds fairly definite.'

'Yes, it does.' Harry read it again. 'I wonder why Switzerland?'

'Well, as to that I can't say for sure. But I do remember that the family found all the press interest very intrusive.' She gave him a small, rather cloyingly intimate smile. 'They may have gone abroad to try to escape it.'

'It would explain why I didn't find any mention of Sonia anywhere,' said Harry. 'If she died abroad it probably wouldn't be registered in this country.'

'Yes.' Roz paused, and then said, 'I suppose this means there's no story.'

Harry said slowly, 'No, I don't think there's a story.'

'Oh, what a pity.' The smile was still there. 'More coffee, Harry? And—perhaps a glass of brandy with it?'

'I don't think I will, thanks all the same,' said Harry. 'You've been enormously helpful over this, Rosie, and I'm immensely grateful. But it's very late, and I've got an early start in the morning— I think I'd better say goodnight. It's been a great evening.'

Somehow he got himself out of the smothering room, and somehow he got himself down the narrow path with the dark shrubbery pressing in on both sides, and somehow he found his way to the main road and saw, with relief, the light of a tube station at the far end.

He was beginning to wonder whether the game was worth the candle.

It did not really matter that the bed-thing had not come off with Harry Fitzglen; in fact on balance Roz was rather glad it had not, because she did not really find it especially pleasurable. But she had been prepared for it tonight if it would get her closer to Harry and make it easier to keep tabs on his research.

What did matter was that Harry had accepted the facts in the newspaper cutting, so diligently searched for and found in one of Roz's stored-away boxes, artfully photocopied so that it could be presented as part of hospital records.

It had been worth the expense of the meal—a whole joint of lamb it had been and fresh vegetables. Vegetables were not expensive, but they took ages to prepare. 'Fresh peas?' one of the other sisters had said, seeing Roz's lunch-time shopping stored in the locker room. 'Good heavens, I didn't think anyone bought fresh peas any longer. Frozen, that's what my family always eats. Far quicker and easier.'

But Roz had not minded shelling the peas, or scraping and slicing carrots. She had made fresh mint sauce as well, cutting the leaves from the little herb garden near the kitchen window, and diligently chopping them. The fruit for the crumble had come from her own little deep-freeze; Roz and her aunt had always grown their own apples, and stewed the cookers for freezing each autumn. She had used a whole tub of apples for the crumble tonight. (And she had bought condoms on the way home from a large, anonymous chemist, doing so briskly. She was not so old-maidish about buying them these days, and there had been one or two men since Joe Anderson. Never anything really serious, though. It was better, really, to be alone.)

After Harry had gone she felt better. She was as sure as she could be that she had put paid to any disinterring of the past for an article, and she thought she could focus now on the knowledge that after all these years she had found Melissa Anderson—at least, she had found the bitch's daughter!

She could start to lay plans once again.

Harry switched on the electric fire in his flat and threw himself down in his favourite armchair in the sitting-room.

So Sonia, that elusive twin, was dead, and there was no story. Even though he had not wanted to write the story he felt a sense of loss. Markovitch had implied there was a mystery—people died and people disappeared—and Harry had been intrigued, but the answer had simply been that the twins had been taken abroad to escape the media, and Sonia had died. And presumably Melissa had remained abroad and was still there. No mystery about any of it.

He was glad that Rosie had been able to solve things for him, even though the more he thought about her, the more he thought she was an uncomfortable person. Even the name felt wrong. Rosie. The rather attractive, newly-fashionable diminutive sat oddly on her, almost as if a 1940s forces' sweetheart had donned a mini-skirt. She had definitely made a move on him, although he thought he had got out of it with reasonable tact. Oh hell, in addition to everything else from now on call me Heartbreaker as well. Last of the great lovers. Oh sure, said his mind cynically.

Philip Fleury had probably been a bit of a heart-breaker. Harry could easily imagine the passion that had driven Floy's writing spilling over into other areas of his life at times. This could have been a lot of fun for the females in his life, or on the other hand it could not. It would have depended on the particular females.

Harry was about a third of the way through Floy's book by this time, and a conviction was growing on him that Floy might not after all have written this story from his own imagination and his study of the social evils of the day, but out of actual experience. Was it possible that Fleury had known this child, this Tansy, and that what he was really doing was telling her story to the world?

He could not analyse why this idea was taking such a strong hold of him, unless it stemmed from the conviction of Floy's writing. He writes as if he cares very deeply about all this, thought Harry. Yes, but that might simply be because he did care. It might be that Floy had known—or had found out—about the conditions of workhouses and orphanages, and about child prostitution. Tansy's story could simply be a hybrid of all that.

And what about the dedication on the fly-leaf? said his mind. 'C' and 'Viola and Sorrel'? Who were they? 'C' might have been a man, of course; a colleague or a son or a father. And Viola and Sorrel were most likely Floy's wife and daughter or sisters. Simple as that. But I do wonder who he based Tansy on.

Tansy had grown up hating the world, which, considering the world she had lived in, was not surprising. But she thought she might have deserved all the things that had happened to her in her short life.

The children had to go to church on Sundays, and to a Bible class on Sunday afternoons, and they had all learned, by rote, that the way of sinners was made plain with stones and that those who sinned were enemies unto their own lives. Tansy had learned this along with the others but she was not sure if she entirely understood it, except that it meant if you did something bad you were punished for it. She thought she had been quite bad a few times. She thought she might have taken the wrong path once or twice as well—what the Bible class teacher said was the ivory gate. You should never go through the ivory gate, the teacher said; it looked very nice and very pleasing and pretty, but once through it you were on the sure path to the gall of bitterness and the bond of iniquity, and now please to turn to their New Testaments to learn how Jesus had healed the sick.

But if Tansy had not understood about the sinners being their own enemies, or the gall of bitterness, by this time she understood very well about the stews; she understood that they were not things you ate, but houses in towns where men came to lie in bed with little girls and do to the little girls the thing that made babies. She thought the pig-men might lie in wait for children who went through the ivory gate, in fact; you could very easily imagine them hiding just on the other side, ready to pounce on everyone who came through.

But one day she found a hiding place, a secret corner where she could hide when the pig-men came, and she learned the trick of vanishing, silently and swiftly, and of cheating the whip-fingered overseers and fat ratty-eyed Mrs Beadle. It was necessary to do this because Mrs Beadle and the Beadle himself knew all about the pig-men, and they did not mind them at all because they gave money in exchange for the children.

So on the nights when the moon was still a thin paring of cold light, Tansy folded her pillow down beneath the blankets on her bed so that it looked like a sleeping person, and then slipped out before the dormitories were locked for the night. It was easy to wait in the shadows until everyone was asleep, and then to go stealthily through the dark passageways and down the old stone steps to the long grim room below the ground.

Tansy hated this room which smelt of people crying and struggling to escape. She hated the sick smothering darkness of the passages as well. The long room had iron bars at one end, formed into cages, and the other children said this was where you were brought if you were mad or if you did something very bad. You were put inside the man-cages and left there for hours, or even days. Tansy knew this was true, because she could feel the pain and the unhappiness of all the people who had been shut inside the man-cages. There was a story that someone had starved to death down here, and that her ghost walked about when everywhere was dark and quiet. So Tansy was very frightened indeed on the nights when she came down here to hide.

But it was better to brave the darkness and the dreadful swirling unhappiness, and to sleep down here with the ghost and the pain, than to risk being caught by the pig-men.

CHAPTER TWENTY-THREE

THE CHILD-TRADERS had come for Tansy in the end, of course; there had always been a dreadful inevitability about that. And this time they had come on a night when no one had been expecting them—when the moon was full and bright, and Tansy had not thought it was necessary to creep out to her hiding-place. One of the other girls had heard them arrive and had woken everyone up, and Tansy had known, with a bump of terror, that soon she would be crammed smotheringly into one of the sacks and the top tied up so that she could not call out for help, and then carried out to the waiting cart.

The only thing she could think of was to creep under the bed and huddle in the darkness, making herself as tiny as she possibly could and hope they would not see her. But they did see her. They came stomping and clattering into the room, the smell of them everywhere like greasy meat, and they walked up and down, looking at the children one by one. Saying, 'Two little girls wanted tonight—who are they to be?' And, 'A nice plump little boy as well—which one shall we take?'

And then they reached Tansy's bed, and crouched down and peered under it, and saw her. They nodded and smiled so that you could see the stumpy teeth they had, and you could see how their mean little eyes glittered. And then their hands—dreadful thick-fingered hands with huge knuckly bones—were reaching into the cramped space under the bed, and even though Tansy held on to the frame of the bed, they dragged her out, and held her up as if she was a rabbit they had just caught, and chuckled to one another, saying, My word, this is a nice little one tonight. My word, we've done well with this one.

There was the smell of the sack as they bundled her inside—like bad meat, like fish gone off—and Tansy had to fight not to breathe it in. And then they were carrying her, struggling and fighting, out into the night, and there was the feeling of the hard wooden floor of the cart, and then the sound of a horse's hooves clip-clopping on a road.

Somewhere nearby she could hear the sound of a church clock chiming. It would be the church where they all went every Sunday morning, and where they had Bible-reading classes on Sunday afternoons. The chimes grew fainter as the cart clopped farther away from it, and the clopping hooves and the chiming clock formed into a horrid little voice inside her mind. Clop-clop, you're-an-evil-child... You're-going-to-be-punished... Chime-chime, bitterness-and-gall... Clop-clop, punishment...

No matter how evil she had been it was still terrible hearing the chimes of the church clock fading away, because it was the very last link with the place she had known all her life and the friends she had grown up with.

So she listened to the clock chiming for as long as she could, and counted the chimes carefully. All the children had been taught how to count and to read their letters, because the beadle said it was part of his duty to see they were given some schooling, as well as making sure they grew up in the fear of the Lord.

So Tansy was able to count twelve chimes as the pig-men's cart took her away, and she knew that meant midnight. And when the chiming stopped she knew she had gone beyond the reach of her friends for ever.

Harry's mantel clock did not chime the hours, but with eerie coincidence it was showing just on midnight when he closed *The Ivory Gate* at this page.

He went to bed with his mind full of Floy's waif-heroine who had crept into that dreadful hiding-place when the child-traders came, but who had been caught by them despite it. When he dreamed, his dreams were of dark houses and iron man-cages that might have come straight out of *Hansel and Gretel*, and of thin cold moons that stared soullessly down on all manner of atrocities...

And of Viola and Sorrel whose names conjured up the woodbine flowers of Shakespeare's romances, and the scent of autumn rain and woodsmoke... And of 'C', who might be a man or a woman, but who might, in some unfathomable way, be connected with the ill-starred Tansy...

And of Tansy herself who might never have lived outside of Floy's imagination.

Charlotte Quinton's diaries: 8th February 1900
Perhaps one day all this will become dim and faded, and I shall wonder whether any of it really happened, or whether it was all simply a trick of my imagination.

But Maisie's future is reasonably well arranged at last, and when I return to London she will stay in Weston Fferna, as housemaid in one of the neighbouring houses. They are people who own several farms and have what Mamma calls a rather slapdash attitude to house management— 'But *kind*, Charlotte, they are extremely kind.' The great thing about them is they do not mind about the coming child.

Making all the arrangements has helped me to stop thinking about Floy, and about Viola and Sorrel, the daughters he never knew. Telling Mamma a little about Mortmain—just a very little—has helped even more. Mamma horrified and shocked at description of privations and the Paupers' Room, although pointing out at same time that it cannot be made too easy for such people, Charlotte, or they will not want to work for their living at all, and then where should we be? Know that Mamma is a product of her generation and cannot, therefore, be blamed for some of her views, but ground teeth in silent fury at this outlook all the same.

Still, have managed to get her to say she will endeavour to find out about Robyn and try to do something for her. 'And who knows but what we may be able to get the girl into good service, Charlotte.'

Cannot see the small rebellious Robyn in any kind of service, but agree it will be better for her than her present life.

'And,' Mamma said, as I had known she would, 'I will also make some very *stern* inquiries about the governing structure of Mortmain—these things always have a governing structure, Charlotte. There may be a Trust attached to the church, you know. I believe I could consult the rector—yes, that will be a polite way to find out more. I shall invite him for a glass of sherry on Sunday.'

Mamma thinks she may even find a way to get herself on to an appropriate committee somewhere, since clearly something must be done—not acceptable for children to be ill-treated. Somewhere amidst the welter of politeness and the rector to sherry and appropriate committees, at the very least Mamma will ruffle a few feathers. Dear Mamma.

Maisie cried when I told her what I had managed to arrange, and said she would never forget what I had done for her. Gather that from here on her life is to be a model of Christian rectitude and unimpeachable morality. Cannot help thinking this will be v. boring for her (also the child, when it is born!) but perhaps less complicated in the end.

I said truth and purity very admirable to be sure, but I hoped that while Maisie was upholding these strict principles she would also feel able to uphold the story we concocted that she is a widow. If not, everybody's reputation in shreds and tatters in the gutter, not least my mamma's who found Maisie the situation.

Extract from diaries: July 1900
Have had news from Weston Fferna that despite exhaustive inquiries, Mamma has not been able to find Robyn, and believes the child to no longer be living in Mortmain.

Mamma writes that it is possible some of the children have been moved to some other institu- tion—'The laws ruling charitable institutions are very complex, even your father says so'—but I have a dreadful fear that someone discovered what they did that day, and meted out some punishment.

On a happier note, Mamma writes that Maisie was apparently safely delivered of a daughter, and mother and baby are in bouncing health.

Mamma has sent Maisie a gift of baby linen and I have done the same, sending most of the things I had bought and made, or been given, for my own babies... No good being sentimental about smocked dresses or embroidered baby-gowns, although I shed stupid tears over them before briskly packing them into brown paper and taking them to Postal Offices.

Cannot help feeling that straightforward vulgar coinage would have been of more use to the daisie, but although Edward is not precisely mean he does scrutinize the household accounts very closely. Toyed with idea of putting in false entry—purchase of gown or hat—and then sending the money to Maisie by postal order, but regretfully abandoned it, not because have any scruples about such a deception, but because Edward likely to ask indulgently to see gown or hat. Oh why cannot ladies have their own income, completely private and separate from their husbands!

However, Edward not quite so sanguine these days, in fact quite worried over trade situation in Europe. If you ask him, Germany is widening her markets at the expense of rivals, and England will do better to bide her time.

Have absolutely no idea what he means (am not entirely sure he does, either), but do know that he is starting to sound exactly like Father.

Cannot imagine that I will ever be able to forget what happened inside Mortmain House—and think I must continue to try to find out what became of Robyn and the other children, although this may be difficult, since Edward not likely to look kindly on wife making frequent trips to Welsh Marches. But I shall try my hardest.

What I shall never forget is the look in Floy's eyes when he talked about the choice between the ivory gate and the one of burnished horn. He despised me for choosing the ivory gate, of course. But is it really the choice of delusions and falseness? What about the duty one owes to other people?

Those children—Robyn and Anthony and all the others—made a choice that afternoon, although they would not have seen it in terms of Virgilian philosophic poetry. Would not have seen it in those terms myself if it had not been for Floy, who taught me so many things, and opened up doors for my mind that no one else could ever have done, least of all Edward.

Those children saw the killing of the man who stole their friends in such very simple terms. They knew him to be evil—they knew exactly what he and his kind were doing—and so they punished him in order to halt the evil and save their friends. There's a rather frightening artlessness about that.

But if I can find a way to outwit Edward again and trace Robyn and her friends, then I shall do it. All the conventional things—charity dances, luncheons at two guineas a head, seats on committees—do not seem to bear much relevance to Mortmain or its evils, and I am back with the idea of a social revolution to temper mankind's cruelties.

Whether I am able to find, and help, those children or not, I will never forget them, any more than I will ever forget Viola and Sorrel—Floy's moss-rose and bluebell daughters, who are buried so incongruously in a North London cemetery, but whose insubstantial ghosts will always be with me.

CHAPTER TWENTY-FOUR

IT WAS ALMOST seven o'clock on Monday evening when Angelica performed one of her lightning quick-changes in the tiny office at the top of the Bloomsbury house.

'Because there really isn't time to go home to change, and I do think it's far-sighted of me to keep a few outfits here, don't you?'

'Very.' Simone was bent over her desk, trying the effect of different transparencies, one over another.

'You're not staying on, are you, Sim? It's awfully late.'

'I'll stay for a while, I think. I'd like to get a bit further with this if I can. Or at least get an idea where it's going.' A few tenuous threads of ideas were starting to form in her mind and if she did not pin them down tonight she might lose sight of them altogether. 'So don't lock the downstairs door; I'll pull it to when I go. I'll set the alarm as well.'

'All right. It's Mrs Whatnot's night to clean anyway, so she'll be in later.'

They did not open Thorne's to the public on Mondays, but unless Simone was on a photographing trip—what Angelica rather grandly called a field trip—she usually came in. There was generally something to be done: Angelica dealt with most of the actual administration, but Simone often had proofs to be touched up, or developing to deal with. She quite often used a digital camera nowadays, but she still liked the old click-and-develop darkroom method as well. It gave you more of a sense of creating your work.

From the other side of the room, Angelica said, 'Can I look at what you're doing yet, or d'you want to muse on your own for a bit longer?'

'Muse for a bit longer if you don't mind.' Simone said this a bit brusquely, because she was always defensive about her work when it was a new project.

'OK,' said Angelica carelessly. 'Listen, does it look tarty if leave two buttons unfastened on this outfit, or shall I just undo the one?'

'Turn round so I can see— Oh yes, two does look a bit— Just the one undone I'd have.'

'That's what I thought.' Angelica fastened up one of the errant buttons, and then began hunting for earrings in her desk drawer.

'Where are you going tonight? Oh, that Hanover Street place, aren't you?'

'Yes. Rather fun. But you know, I still think you were the one that Harry was really interested in. He talked to you for such hours at the opening, didn't he?'

'Just business stuff.' Simone would have been torn into pieces by wild horses galloping in different directions rather than admit that she also had thought Harry Fitzglen had been interested in her. 'I don't really go for those glowering Heathcliff looks, in fact if you want the truth I don't think I could have coped with him. I thought he was a bit alarming.'

'Oh, pooh, nobody's alarming. All you need is a little panache.'

It was all very well for Angelica, who was disgustingly well-off, despite the scandals and the frenetic socializing, and who was outrageously attractive into the bargain, and loaded with enough panache for a regiment. Also, it was not very likely that Angelica had had to cope with darknesses or secrets much, because, as Angelica always informed everyone, her life was an open book, my dears, and everyone was welcome to know all the things she had done.

But no one knew the things that Simone had done, and that was the problem with getting close to people, well, with getting close to men if you wanted to be exact. If you got too close to a man you might relax and give things away. You might do it in an unguarded moment, not realizing your error until it was too late, or you might even do it deliberately, wanting to tell him all about your life and your feelings. Thinking, If you do love me, you won't care what I might have done or what I might once have been. Foolish in the extreme, of course, and potentially fatal, as well.

Simone had come close to being this foolish two or three times at university, and had been panic-stricken to suddenly find herself on the brink of making disastrous disclosures. The world was a judgemental place and it was best not to trust anyone, which was why Simone tended to back out of relationships if they threatened to get too intense. It had earned her a name for being cold and even a bit prim—and one boyfriend had accused her of being a prick-teaser—but although these names were hateful, there were far worse names you could be called. Freak. Murderess.

So with an air of putting a troublesome matter in its place, she said firmly, 'Anyway, I'm much too busy to be bothered with men at the moment. The stuff for the new exhibition—'

'Oh, rot, darling,' said Angelica, whom nobody would ever call cold or prim (or, heaven forfend, a prick-teaser!). 'Nobody should ever be as busy as all *that*.'

Simone had got up from her desk to put some coffee on to filter. 'I suppose we could ask your journalist to come along to the second exhibition, couldn't we?' she said off-handedly. 'For some publicity.'

'He isn't my journalist.' But the cat-smile showed briefly.

'No? That notch on your bedpost's just woodworm, I suppose?'

'I don't know about notches on bedposts, but I have to say all that damn-your-eyes insolence is *vastly* attractive. Like Sydney Carton, you know. Going scowlingly to the scaffold in Darnay's place, caring for no man and no man caring for him.'

'You never cease to amaze me,' said Simone, who had had to think for a moment who Sydney Carton might be, and who, despite the tortoiseshell glasses that appeared from time to time, had not expected Angelica to be on quoting terms with the works of Charles Dickens.

'Well, I'm not precisely the thinking man's crumpet, darling, but I'm not exactly untutored. And insolence transfers *very* well into bed. All that energy.'

Simone said, 'I don't want to know,' and this time Angelica smiled the smile that made her look like an Italian madonna with a disreputable secret, and said dulcetly that there were some things you never told.

Some things you never told...

Such as murder—the kind of macabre, unintended murder that might have taken place inside a dark old house with revengeful ghosts gossiping in the corners, and a disused well breathing its ancient stench into your face.

But you cannot murder a ghost...

For at least a month after that day in Mortmain Simone had listened carefully to the TV and radio news, because despite what Mother had said and despite that second eerie expedition they had made to Mortmain together, she was still half-expecting to hear about a police search for a missing child. She could watch the six o'clock news each evening if she wanted; it was not a big deal either way, but Mother was quite pleased if she did watch it. It was a good thing to know what was going on in the world, she said, even though a lot of it was depressing. Simone did not understand everything although some of the things were pretty interesting.

But there was nothing at all about a missing girl in the Welsh Marches. There were no trembly-voiced people begging for their daughter or sister or niece to be returned to them, and there were no police appeals for information, or photographs saying, Have you seen this child? After a while she did not listen absolutely every night, and after a while the horror faded a little.

But the memory did not fade and the idea that the dead Sonia had tried to cling on to life using her twin did not fade either. It stayed with Simone, vividly and some-times disturbingly, and the concept of children dying young and unfulfilled stayed with her as well.

In her final Slade year she composed a series of black-and-white-and-grey studies. They were not meant to imply any particular country or culture or time, but each shot had a faint, just-discernible touch of the macabre and the tragic, and each had the theme of lost children or lost childhoods.

One suggested ragged Victorian match-sellers who froze to death on New Year's Eve—but there was a faint overlay of a modern-day Centrepoint and the corner of a copy of the *Big Issue*—while another was a rather eerie setting of a lonely Christmas night, with a half-decorated fir tree and gaily-wrapped presents that would wait in vain for children to open them. A third showed shoes that forced their wearer to dance through frozen landscapes and ice-rimed forests into exhaustion, and whether the shoes were ordinary red shoes, or whether they were red from the blood of their wearer was left to the imagination of the viewer. But the shoes were not classical ballet shoes as in the Andersen tale, they were modern trainers, plastered with designer labels.

It was a series of images that had startled Simone's course tutor who said they were brilliant but dreadfully *dark*, but it had been the series that had won her the coveted Fox Talbot Award, and brought her to the notice of Angelica Thorne who was surprisingly sharp and businesslike beneath the froth and frivolity, and who was just entering her patron-of-the-arts incarnation.

And so, barely a year out of university, Simone had come to the Bloomsbury house with its oddly comforting atmosphere and its feeling that there were stored-away memories, and that those memories might be nearer to the surface than you realized... And that if you could only open the right door or turn a key at the right moment you would unlock those memories and those echoes and see them all come tumbling out around you.

But the memories must be kept in place, both in this house and everywhere else. The past must not intrude: it did not matter and it must not be allowed to matter.

Simone pushed the memories and the echoes firmly away and got up from her desk. Angelica had long since departed for her date with Harry Fitzglen, and the coffee had finished filtering ages ago. She poured herself a mugful and stood at the little window for a moment, looking down into the street. It was dark now, and it was raining as well; she could see the long snaking bead-necklaces of car headlights that were London's perpetual rush hour.

She liked being on her own in this house, and she liked the feeling of expectancy that occasionally seemed to pass through the rooms as night fell, almost as if the house was anticipating the evening ahead in the way it might have done years ago when it had been an ordinary private house, and people had come here. What kind of people had they been? Would it be possible to find out? She remembered that Harry had said he would try to disinter some of the house's history, although it was always likely that he would become so entangled with Angelica that he would completely forget about it.

She went back to her desk, and switched on the small CD player, scanning the little stock of CDs she kept here. When she was working she liked playing music to match the current project. Prokofiev might fit the mood tonight, or maybe Mahler—yes, Mahler would be good. She was quite keen on his music; she had seen the Visconti *Death in Venice* film during her final year at the Slade, and had loved the music as much as the film and had gone on from there. She thought she would play the Sixth tonight; it had that terrific second movement in which you could hear the rhythmic machinery of the factories and the furnace-lit foundries of the late nineteenth century, so that you conjured up images of the machines themselves, unstoppable and soulless and altogether Salvador-Dali-nightmarish.

This all fitted brilliantly with Simone's ideas for Thorne's second exhibition. She was going to link the past and the present again because that was very much her thing and she wanted it to become a real trademark. One day people might look at her work and say at once, 'That's a Simone Marriot, isn't it?'

But this time she wanted to concentrate on people rather than places. Shadowy, sepia-and-grey images of nineteenth-century factory- or mill-workers, overlaid with transparencies of the newest computer-technology and keyboard operators at huge call centres. Yes.

Mahler's gorgeous cadences were pouring into the room, and with them came the images Simone was seeking: the rearing, almost-human-looking machines from the industrial revolutions, and the whirring cotton mills and the clanking foundries and the machinery resembling robotic dragons breathing steel-tainted fire-breath... There was a dark and savage poetry about these images; if only she could pin them down...

Concentrate. Reach down into your mind for the pictures. Diligent spinners and calloused-palmed labourers... Mechanic slaves with greasy aprons and hammers, and sweating bodies, fire-washed amid the dust and the clangour, treading their sordid round... And the sempstresses who had toiled for pittances—'In poverty, hunger and dirt/Sewing at once with a double thread/A shroud as well as a shirt...' Where did I learn that one? It's horridly evocative, though. Sempstresses sewing shrouds... Could I incorporate that image somewhere...?

The dark rhythms of Mahler's music wound onwards and Simone became absorbed, seeing images take shape, hearing the relentless hammers and anvils inside the music, hearing the pounding of iron and steel. How far could you take this idea? Could you have the occasional glimpse of an Armani label against a mob-capped mill-worker? Or an old Arkwright loom that blurred at the edges into a printed circuit board from a computer? Yes, why not? Go for it, kid. Where can I get a shot of an Arkwright loom? Ironbridge? Yorkshire? She broke off to scribble a reminder to write to the various tourist centres.

Delight was gripping her, because she was getting exactly what she wanted—she was conjuring the images up... Thin, workworn fingers tapping out lengths of cloth... Thin, manicured fingers tapping out numbers at call centres—the telecom companies might help there, they might have old publicity stills of switchboards from the forties as well... Might there be a copyright problem with that...?

And then there were the Jarrow Marches, and the General Strike of 1926. Would it work to set sepia shots of those against the Aldermaston Protest Marches? Was there enough relevance between the two, though? What about the miners' strikes from the seventies in Edward Heath's government? Yes, that might be better.

The symphony came to an end and silence closed down. Simone leaned back in her chair, massaging her aching neck, slightly light-headed from the music and the deep concentration. She got up to refill her coffee mug, and she was just switching the filter machine off when she heard something that made her turn her head towards the half-open door that led out to the stair. Someone down there? It had sounded almost as if someone had very quietly opened the inner door that led out of the gallery. She stayed absolutely motionless and after a moment the floorboards creaked softly, exactly as if someone was walking very stealthily and very slowly across the floor directly below.

Was there someone prowling around in the house? Someone who had sneaked inside under cover of Mahler's sweeping music? She waited, listening intently, but there was only the steady pattering of the rain outside, and the faint gurgle as it ran down the drainpipes outside.

Or was it just the rain? Simone set the coffee mug down carefully, trying not to chink it against the desk, and then crossed cautiously to the door. There was a minuscule landing beyond it, and then the stairs which went down to the middle floor, where Simone's photographs were displayed, and then widened out to descend in more leisurely fashion to the ground floor and the main gallery.

She stood irresolute on the tiny landing. The rain was still running steadily down the windows, casting a rippling waterlight everywhere; Simone could see down into the long silent room quite clearly, and she could see that there was no one there. But on the far window-sill was a big spider-plant;

it cast a grotesque, hunched shadow on the walls, and it was moving just very slightly, in the way it always did when someone brushed past it... Or was it only the current of cool air from the windows making it shiver like that?

A churning unease was starting to take hold of Simone and she was remembering that earlier on she had told Angelica to leave the door unlatched for Mrs Whatnot, and of all the mad things to do, to leave a street door unlatched in the middle of London— It would just serve her right if someone had crept in. But there was a buzzer on the door and the music had not been all that loud, and she would surely have heard anyone coming in.

She would certainly have heard Mrs Whatnot who always came in cheerfully and loudly, banging doors, calling out to announce her arrival if there were lights on anywhere, wanting to know if she could make a cup of tea for anyone, exclaiming with uncritical pleasure at anything new that had been put on display since her last stint. Simone waited, hoping to hear the cheerful whirr of the vacuum cleaner start up, or the opening of the broom cupboard under the stairs where the cleaning things were stored, and which Angelica called Little Hell because of its shrieking hinges and black cavernous interior. Nothing. But there had been that soft footfall, she was sure she had not imagined it.

She began to descend the stairs. Nothing moved anywhere, and the middle floor, the floor she always thought of as her own, was shrouded in silent darkness. Simone stood for a moment, scanning the shadows, but everywhere seemed ordinary and unthreatening and exactly as it should be. She went down the last flight, which was wider and easier, and on to the ground floor. Car headlights swept continuously into the showroom, showing it to be empty and innocent, and Simone tried the street door, which was certainly unlatched but which was tidily closed, just as Angelica would have left it. But wouldn't a prowler or an opportunist burglar have closed it anyway to avert suspicion?

The broom cupboard—Angelica's Little Hell—was tucked beneath the stairs. It was deep and narrow, but it was more than big enough for someone to hide. Simone considered it. The door was slightly ajar—there was a line of blackness around its rim. A burglar hiding in the broom cupboard?—oh, for goodness' sake, that's very nearly farcical! But there was a sudden, horridly vivid, image of clutching hands reaching out from the depths of the mops and buckets and dusters, and of angry staring eyes within the shadows... To dispel this picture she walked briskly across the floor and flung the door open. The hinges protested screechingly as they always did, but there was nothing inside except the cleaning things. You see? You really are imagining all this.

Even so...

She went through to the back of the house, to the tiny lobby behind the main gallery where there was a cupboard-sized kitchen, a small loo and washroom, and her own darkroom. But there was no one in the kitchen or the loo, and the darkroom was cool and bland. As far as Simone could tell, nothing had been touched. Imagination after all.

And yet, and yet...

She flipped the latch on the street door, and set the alarm. Mrs Whatnot could easily press the electronic buzzer outside; it would ring in the upstairs office, and Simone could come down to let her in. She went slowly back up the stairs, switching on lights as she went to chase back the shadows. And now the house's warm friendliness closed around her again. Stupid to have been so abruptly jittery. Here was her own floor, with the familiar framed images lining the walls. The shinily-preserved National Trust manor houses, and the forgotten, boarded-up monstrosities. That old grainmill she had found in a Suffolk village, and the remnant of a beautiful medieval keep, crumbling away near to a section of motorway. And Mortmain, glowering sullenly from its corner.

Mortmain...

Something at the back of Simone's mind jumped to attention. Mortmain. There was something wrong with the shot of Mortmain. Was the glass broken? No. But something— Something red where there should only be black, something obscuring the scowling façade...

And then she did understand, and the fear came pouring in with huge scalding waves.

Across the glass front of the frame, in scarlet scrawled letters, were the words, '*The Murder House*'. And underneath it, exactly like a signature, '*Sonia*'.

The *a* of Sonia sloped downwards; in the bright hard whiteness of the overhead spotlights it looked like blood that had trickled down and then dried.

It was lipstick, of course, it was nothing more sinister than bright red lipstick, but it took Simone about three horror-filled minutes to realize this. It took another three to get a handful of wet tissues from the cloakroom and wipe the appalling words away. Even then smears remained on the glass so that Simone had to forage in Little Hell for dusters and spray polish, because it was unthinkable to leave the smallest trace of the words visible.

All the time she was cleaning and polishing away the sinister menacing message, the brightly lit gallery was eddying and swirling with the old nightmares, and the old, remembered echoes were hissing through her mind.

It's no use trying to escape me, Simone... Even if I'm a ghost, it's no use trying to get away from me... Because I know what you did that afternoon, Simone... I know what is, and what has been, remember that, Simone...?

CHAPTER TWENTY-FIVE

THE POLICE, WHEN they arrived, were painstaking and polite, but it was impossible not to think that they were also a bit patronizing.

Could Miss Marriot give any description of this prowler? they asked. Oh, she could not. A pity. Well, had anything been taken? Nothing? And there was no damage to anything anywhere? Simone, determinedly not looking in the direction of the framed darkness of Mortmain, said, No, nothing at all. It was just that she had heard someone creep in—yes, she was very sure about that—and when she went down to investigate she had caught a glimpse of someone running out through the street door. There was some quite valuable stuff in the gallery, so she had thought she ought to report it. Even to her own ears this all sounded like the twittering of an over-nervous female, not used to being on her own and dramatizing some perfectly innocent incident.

But the police said, indulgently, that she had been quite right to call them. Very unpleasant for her, they did not doubt. Now then—had they understood this right?—the street door had been left unlocked, for a while? Oh well, there you were, then. Leave a street door unlocked in the middle of London, and you were asking for trouble. Especially with all these paintings and things on display. A rather disparaging glance at the framed exhibits had accompanied this comment.

The odds were that it had just been a chance intruder, they said. Still, they would file a report, they said, just in case there was a repeat performance. A snapping of notebooks being closed followed this remark, and then as an afterthought, they asked how she would be travelling home. Russell Square tube? Perhaps she might be better to take a taxi on this occasion. Door to door. Not that there was anything to worry about.

Simone locked the door after them and went back upstairs to her partly completed compositions of mills and looms and call centres, because she would not, she absolutely would not, let herself be spooked by Sonia—or most likely by somebody pretending to be Sonia, because clearly that was what this had been. Yes, but how many people know about Sonia? said her mind.

She sat at her desk and considered this. Whoever had played tonight's grisly trick must have known about Sonia beforehand. Yes, that was undeniable. But who, today, knew that Simone Marriot had once had a twin sister called Sonia? There would have been people at the hospital at the time of the birth, and Mother had said there had been a lot of media interest as well. But even though Thorne's had generated quite a bit of publicity—mostly because of Angelica, of course—and even though Simone had been photographed once or twice, no one seeing those photographs could possibly have made the connection between Simone Marriot and a baby called Simone Anderson born more than twenty years earlier. Certainly no one could have made the connection to Mortmain. Mother had known about that but she could certainly be discounted, and no one else had ever known what had happened there all those years ago. Simone suddenly wanted to talk to

Mother very much indeed, but she was still in Canada and it would be a bit thoughtless to ring up and have hysterics over the phone to someone who was several thousand miles away and might be fast asleep anyway. She tried to remember the time difference and could not.

It kept coming back to Sonia. It kept coming back to her. Sonia, who had known what was and what had been... Sonia had known all about Mortmain.

But the thing Simone had seen that day—the thing that had died inside Mortmain's darkness—could not really have been Sonia, because Sonia had died as a small baby.

It was almost ten o'clock when Simone finally set off for home, setting the burglar alarm and locking the street door firmly.

She flinched from the thought of the Underground tonight. It was still comparatively early for London streets and there were a lot of people about. But Russell Square was one of the deep stations, and there was a lift with clanging iron doors and supposing you found yourself shut inside with the person who had written that mad, sinister message...? She picked up a taxi near the British Museum and reached her flat with a sense of relief. I'm safe now, thought Simone, letting herself into the tiny hallway. Nothing can reach me here.

She remembered she had not eaten since lunchtime, and on the strength of this made herself an omelette. After she had eaten it she scanned the bookshelves for something soothing and undemanding to read in bed. An Agatha Christie, maybe; she had quite a collection of those. Yes, she would join dear Miss Marple in the gentle charm of her long-ago world with its vicars and retired colonels and bodies in libraries. Nothing sinister there, and right always triumphed in the last pages. She fell asleep halfway through the first chapter of *A Murder is Announced*.

She awoke two hours later with her heart hammering violently against her ribs and the realization that she was sitting bolt upright in the bed, clenching folds of the sheet in both hands in the classic panic attitude.

OK, only a nightmare, nothing worse. Take deep, calming breaths. After a moment she switched on the bedside lamp, and warm, comforting light flooded the room. Simone leaned back against the pillows, still feeling a bit shaky. The nightmare would take a while to recede because it always did, and the hateful sinister sounds would reverberate in her mind for a while. Childish hands scrabbling in vain against bricks, and fingers worn to bloodied tatters from trying to climb out of a deep dank well-shaft. Tap-tap-tap, get-me-out... And the person who was trapped down there was someone who had sly eyes and a back that was not quite straight...

Sonia.

Simone glanced at the clock. Just on three a.m. Not quite the smallest of the small hours but certainly a time when ghosts might be thought to walk, and when grave-yards might be expected to yield up their wormy dead. Certainly the hour when the darknesses of the past crept out to torment you and slide inside your dreams.

She got out of bed and padded out to the kitchen to fill the kettle for a cup of tea. She had woken, shivering and sweat-drenched, from this particular nightmare too many times not to know the pattern. The sly whisperings would echo over and over inside her mind for several hours yet, and if she went back to sleep they would be waiting for her.

It's no use trying to escape, Simone... We know what you did that day... We saw everything that happened that

afternoon... We know what is and what has been, Simone...
Hateful, sinister voices. *Wherever you run to, we'll catch you,
always remember that, Simone... Because you're a murderess,
Simone... A murderess...*

But you can't murder a ghost, said Simone's mind
defensively. Remember that and hang on to it, because it's
true.

She drank the tea, and then showered and got
dressed. After that, moving quietly so as not to attract any
attention, she carried her photographic equipment out to
where her car was parked on the street, and stowed it in
the back. Then she went back inside, and left a message
on Angelica's voice-mail at Thorne's, explaining that she
was going away for a couple of days. She wanted to drive
up into Yorkshire and Lancashire to look for mills and
looms and remnants of the industrial revolution for the
new exhibition, said Simone; if there was anything urgent,
Angelica could get her on her mobile number. Angelica
would only ring in the event of fire, flood or Armageddon,
and she was not very likely to question Simone's sudden
decision, either. When Simone got back Angelica would
ask if it had been a good trip, and whether the drive had
been hassle-free, but she would leave it until Simone was
ready to talk in detail about what she had done, or display
the gleanings of the expedition. One of the good things
about Angelica was that she never pried.

It was a little after four a.m. by the time Simone
drove away from her flat; it felt strange not to have to
battle with the perpetual gridlock of the streets. London
looked and felt completely different at this hour. Milk
carts and road-sweepers and night-shift workers. Here
and there were prowling cats making for home after the
night's tom-cat run, and there were one or two young
men or girls also making for home after their own
tom-cat night-run, although they were mostly doing so
in cars or taxis.

Harry had left the night-club shortly after half past one, but it was four a.m. before he left Angelica's bed. He walked for a little way before he managed to pick up a cruising taxi, and then spent most of the journey back to his flat trying to calculate precisely how much the evening had cost him, reaching the dismal conclusion that it had cost him far more than he could afford.

His flat, when he reached it, was shockingly untidy; the carpet needed vacuuming and the bedroom was strewn with cast-off sweaters and yesterday's shirt and three pairs of socks. After the hectic glossiness of Angelica's flat Harry was deeply grateful to it for being such a garbage heap.

He stripped off the jacket that smelt of other people's cigarette smoke and hung it on the outside of the wardrobe so that he would remember to take it to the dry-cleaners later on. While he waited for some coffee to percolate he showered, and then made toast which he spread thickly with raspberry jam. Energy, my boy, that's what you need. Get the sugar levels up, because you sure ain't gonna be able to get anything else up for a while after the night you've just had. By way of antidote to the lush plush lifestyle of Angelica and her friends, he reached for Floy's book, and propped it up against the coffee pot.

Tansy had not known about swish Chelsea flats decorated by fashionable designers, or about smoke-filled nightclubs with throbbing music, of course. She had gone from one sleazy house to another.

But although she had been frightened half to death as the jolting cart rattled its way through the night, a tiny greenshoot of hope had uncurled within her mind.

This was bad and it was probably going to become even worse, but at least she was out of the despairing misery of the workhouse. Supposing, just supposing, that whatever lay ahead might be something good? She was still clutching this hope when the cart finally rumbled over uneven cobblestones into a hustling, crowded place filled with shouting, raucous people and mean, narrow streets.

The men who had taken Tansy appeared to be part of the twilight half-world of Victorian brothels, and fairgrounds and freak shows. Tansy had not really understood about that, at least not at the start, but Tansy's creator had understood it very well indeed. The people who owned and ran these child-brothels and these freak shows were a dark and damning stigma on the age, said Floy, and Harry, fathoms deep in Floy's long-ago world, could feel the passion and the bitter anger behind these words. The conviction that Tansy had not been wholly fictional took a firmer hold of him. Floy's sister? His daughter?

The street where Tansy was taken was called Bolt Place, and the house into which she was carried was a thin, squint-faced building, squeezed in between two other similar houses. And despite her determination to see this as an adventure, the first night had been more dreadful than anything she had imagined.

The men took her to a small, sparsely furnished room at the top of three flights of stairs, and gave her a clean shift to put on, bread and cheese to eat and a mug of water to drink. There was a bed in the room, with a pillow and some blankets, and a marble-topped washstand with a chipped ewer containing water. The only splash of colour was a rag rug at one side of the bed, and a small glass jar on the window ledge that someone had filled with meadow flowers—tiny, sweet-faced violets and heart-shaped wood sorrel.

A woman with a hard, grasping face said Tansy was to have a visitor tonight. She must be very kind to the visitor, otherwise she would have to be punished.

The visitor was a man; Tansy had known it would be, of course, and she had known, more or less, what to expect. She had secretly hoped the man might be good-looking and kind, but he had had glittery eyes, like dead fish, and hands with rough nails that snagged her hair and her skin. He had got into the bed with her, and said he hoped she knew what he had paid for. The ugliness and the pain of that night had printed itself indelibly on Tansy's mind for ever, but she had got through it—and through the other nights that followed—by fixing her eyes on the little jar of wild-flowers, and trying to think only about the velvet mistiness of the violets, and the delicate, purple-veined whiteness of the wood sorrel.

Oh God, thought Harry, briefly coming up out of the world Floy had created, you hated not being able to write that scene properly, didn't you, Philip! You took it as far as you could with that stuff about hands and rough finger-nails scraping Tansy's skin, but I'll bet you swore at the censorship laws and cursed the Lord Chancellor because you couldn't properly describe what was done to that poor waiflike creature! An image of Floy, seated in the upstairs room of the Bloomsbury house that was now Thorne's Gallery, thrusting his fingers through his hair in exasperation, rose up vividly before Harry's mind. And yet despite the restrictions, Floy, writing in the early years of the twentieth century, had still managed to paint word-pictures of the seedy house to which Tansy had been taken—he had even put in that glancing reference to violets and wood sorrel—and he had conveyed the pain and fear of Tansy and the other girls, and Tansy's perpetual guilt, which came up from the printed pages like a gust of tainted breath.

The pain and the guilt had stayed with Tansy for a long, long time.

Roz had expected to feel guilty after that night with Joe Anderson, but she had not felt guilty in the least. That would be because he loved her, of course.

She had not been expecting him to leave Melissa and the twins for her (well, not right away), but she had looked forward to the romance and the intrigue that would surely go with being the girlfriend of an MP. Discreet weekends in country hotels; quiet dinners at her house. Even secret journeys in cars with blacked-out windows, with a trusted driver who knew the truth whisking her through the night to be with her lover. It was not overly fanciful to remember Cleopatra smuggled in to Mark Antony rolled inside a carpet in that context. Roz had seen films about that.

But then she had gone out to his house and seen him drive off into the night to bring his wife home; she had heard him tell his neighbour that he had missed Mel, and that had been when she understood that Joe had been making use of her. When she got home, Roz had sat shivering in the familiar sitting-room, the photographs of her aunt and of her parents watching from their frames on the mantelpiece. She thought about Joe and how she had risked her job and her career to find Mel for him, and that made her cry so hard she was sick a second time. Disgusting! Humiliating! And all because of Joe Anderson, the heartless cruel two-faced liar!

Roz's aunt would have been coldly disapproving of such lack of control: she would have called it making an exhibition of yourself over a man, and she would have asked if Roz had no more pride than to sit crying and shivering like this over a man who did not want her? And what of the man's poor wife, she would have said.

Roz had never forgotten her first sight of the woman who was in fact her father's aunt—therefore her own great-aunt. It had been just after her sixth birthday, and she had been taken to the tall thin house, its rooms made dark by the thick shrubbery outside. Her aunt had been seated in a wooden high-backed chair in the room she said was the parlour, and she had studied Roz in silence for what had felt like a long time. Then she had said that this was where Rosamund would live now that her parents were dead, and had asked if she was a good child and loved Jesus.

Roz had not known how to answer this, and she had not known how to cope with being called Rosamund either. She was terrified of her great-aunt, and she was terrified of her aunt's house which was shadowy and unfriendly after her parents' bright modern home. The rooms were full of little whispery draughts that wriggled under the doors and through the ill-fitting windows and made the curtains move, so that if you were in a room by yourself you thought someone was standing behind them.

Every evening at seven o'clock (eight o'clock on Sundays because of evening service), Roz had to go up the unlit stairs to her bedroom by herself, and every evening she heard the stairs behind her creak slightly and knew it was the devil creeping along after her, ready to snatch her up and carry her down to hell. Her aunt said you had to be forever watchful for the devil, who was everywhere in the world. He had cloven hooves which he used to smite sinners. 'I was a sinner,' said Roz's aunt. 'I was a very great sinner, Rosamund, until God put out His arms and brought me home again.'

When Roz was small she had not understood any of this. What she had understood, and what had remained strongly with her, had been the sound of the devil's footsteps slyly creaking on the stairs behind her when she went up to bed. Every night she scurried up the stairs in order to outrace the devil, and bolted into her bedroom and dived under the covers where she was safe on account of the picture of Jesus hanging over the bed. The devil could not bear Jesus, in fact the very sound of Jesus's name made the devil throw up; Roz knew this. Every night she said a prayer to Jesus as she went up the stairs. Her aunt said this was a very good thing to do; prayer was the way to repel the devil.

She said other things to Roz over the years, and the more Roz grew up, the more her aunt talked to her. She told Roz how she had been cheated of her own childhood; an ordinary, carefree childhood was a thing that most people took for granted, she said, but some children had it stolen from them. Some children, by no fault of their own, had to live in dreadful places, under the care of cruel and evil people, and they had to lead lives filled with poverty and ugliness. Sometimes they fell into sin because of those lives; it was not always their fault if they did so, although there was never any excuse for sinning, Roz must remember that. In any case, sinning brought its own heartaches.

Sinning brought its own heartaches... Or did it?

CHAPTER TWENTY-SIX

MEL HAD FOUND the big house unexpectedly unfriendly since Joe's death.

She had never liked the place very much—it was too new and too characterless—but she had never before found it unsettling. Now it seemed to be full of inexplicable sounds—the creaking of a door, the sound of a soft footfall on the gravel path under the kitchen window—and along with all of this was a feeling of being watched. This was patently ridiculous, and it was almost certainly a reaction to Joe's death. There were dozens of stories of newly bereaved people hearing their dead husband or wife returning from an ordinary day at the office, and feeling they were not alone in the house. With a husband you had loved and whom you were missing desperately, such sounds and feelings might be vaguely comforting. But Mel had not loved Joe for several years, and although his death had been appalling and shocking, she was not missing him at all.

She finally acknowledged that the feelings and the occasional sounds were starting to spook her, and she even went as far as having her hearing checked at her local GP's surgery, and booking an eye test with the optician. Everything was absolutely normal of course. Whatever the sounds were, they were certainly not Joe's ghost, returning to haunt her!

But one night, closing the curtains in the downstairs room that had been Joe's study and that Mel had hardly entered since his death, she caught a darting movement in the garden near to the gate, and then a woman's outline—ordinary, unremarkable, wearing a plain dark raincoat—walked quickly down the street. It was definitely not a trick of her own imagination, but it was nothing to fuss over; it was most probably a stranger to the area trying to find a particular house, or someone delivering leaflets. Still, she might see about having one of those security alarm systems installed; if she sold the house and moved somewhere smaller, which was what she wanted to do, it would make a good selling point anyway.

It was a small and pleasant diversion to have Roz Raffan to lunch a few days after Mel glimpsed the raincoated woman. She thought Roz looked thinner and rather pale, but she seemed pleased to see Mel and the twins and to have been asked to lunch. There was a thin December mist outside but the house was warm and bright, and Mel had made a big pot of homemade soup with delicious French bread, and cheese and fruit to follow. They could have a couple of glasses of wine as well, since Roz did not drive. The twins' pram was in the big bay window which was where they liked to be because they could watch what was going on outside. They were still twined in that pitiable embrace, but Simone was delightedly following the progress of birds in the tree outside the window. It was still almost impossible to tell them apart until you remembered that Simone was the one with her right hand free, Sonia the one with her left...

Mel and Roz talked about Castallack and Joe, of course; about how completely bizarre his death had been. Roz asked how Mel was coping, and Mel said, 'I keep replaying what happened that morning—only in the replay, I find a way to rescue him.'

Roz said this was a very frequent reaction to something traumatic. Car crashes and house-fires, things like that. People said, If only I had turned left instead of right, or, Oh, why did I leave the chip-pan on the heat.

'The thing I haven't been able to work out,' said Mel, 'is how Joe found me.' And then, because it no longer seemed to matter about keeping the mechanics of her flight to Castallack a secret, she said, 'I'd been so very careful. I wanted it to be a clean break for everyone's sake, and I thought I had covered my tracks so well.'

There was a sudden silence, and Mel looked up, because there had surely been an odd reaction from Roz. Then Roz said, very slowly, 'But Joe didn't find you, Melissa. I found you for him.'

It came tumbling out, breathlessly and apologetically, but Mel could not help recognizing a note of satisfaction in Roz's voice, almost as if Roz was saying, See! See what was going on, and you didn't know about it!

With a feeling of incredulity, Mel said, 'You and Joe—you and Joe were having an affair?'

'Yes. Yes, we were.' It came out defiantly.

She thinks she's hurting me, thought Mel, staring at Roz. And she's liking hurting me—is that because she was jealous of me? What she can't possibly know is that I wouldn't have given a damn if Joe had slept with half the county. But she was still conscious of surprise that Joe, who had wanted to project that slightly nauseating 'I'm-a-good-husband-and-father' image, had become tangled up with this odd, old-fashioned little creature.

'Joe asked me to look for clues at St Luke's,' Roz said. 'We were having dinner at my house at the time.' There it was again, that sly, I've-scored-over-you tone, and the insistence on a cosy image of Roz and Joe enjoying a warm intimacy. 'And shortly afterwards I found the letter you sent to Martin Brannan—at least, not the letter, but the envelope.'

'And you saw the postmark for Norfolk,' said Mel, slowly. 'Yes, I see now.' And, you poor deluded thing, I also see what Joe was really doing. With the idea of drawing Roz out a bit more, she said, 'I worried about the postmark when I sent that letter, but there wasn't much I could do about it. But how on earth did Joe home in on Castallack? There are dozens of those remote little villages in Norfolk, and Castallack's barely a speck on the map.'

'Dear me, you're quite naïve, aren't you, Melissa?' The animosity was stronger now. 'Once Joe had a starting point—the starting point I found for him—he employed a firm of private detectives,' said Roz. 'They found Castallack.'

'Ah yes, I hadn't thought of that.' Mel paused, and then said, carefully, 'Joe's death must have been a great blow to you. A dreadful shock. I'm sorry— I hadn't known—'

'It was a blow. I thought he cared about me,' said Roz. 'But then he found out where you had gone, and he went straight off to get you and never gave me a second thought. He didn't even bother to tell me he had found you.'

'No, he wouldn't.'

'He used me,' said Roz bitterly. 'I saw that later. He used me to find you.'

'It was more what I represented,' said Mel. 'Conventional family image—supportive wife, children—I don't know that there was much love lost between us.'

'So much for the grieving widow.'

Mel had been holding on to her temper fairly well, but at this she said sharply, 'Oh Roz, for goodness' sake, Joe was a selfish cheating bastard, you must have known that! And he wanted the twins back even more than he wanted me—he was going to use them in his wretched campaign.'

'Yes. The twins—' Roz went over to the pram standing near to the window, and as she stood looking down at Simone and Sonia, Mel had to bite back an involuntary protest—'Don't touch them!'—because it was surely only the cold grey light from outside that made Roz's face look suddenly hard and cruel. Even so, Mel had had the absurd feeling that Roz was about to snatch the twins up and run out of the house with them.

Then Roz said, 'You're so very lucky. To have these two—'

'Yes, I know.' There's something wrong about all this, thought Mel. There's something wrong about Roz. She said, 'Roz, I'm sorry for you if you got hurt by Joe, but I think it would be better if you left now.'

'After I understood that Joe had made use of me to find you,' said Roz, as if Mel had not spoken, 'And after he went off to Castallack to bring you back—' She stopped, and Mel waited.

Roz said, 'I found out that I was pregnant.'

'I don't know if this will be good news or not,' the GP had said, glancing non-committally at Roz's left hand with its absence of a wedding ring. 'But I can tell you that you're definitely pregnant.'

'Yes, I thought so.' She had, in fact, been watching the calendar anxiously for more than a week, counting the days up. She had been sick when she got home from Joe's house that night in the drenching rain, but that could have been from shock and distress. And how likely was it to conceive on a single encounter? Minimal, surely? Yes, but remember the final moments: remember what he said to you afterwards? 'I'm sorry I didn't pull out in time, Rosie, but you made me so aroused...'

She looked back at the doctor, and smiled. 'It's good news,' said Roz.

'Sure?'

'Yes, I am sure. It's very good news indeed.'

It had been the best news in the world.

Walking back from the doctor's surgery she thought she would cope all right with a child: her nurse's salary was not huge but her aunt had left her the house and some modest investments, and there were a couple of insurance policies from the deaths of her parents. Financially there would not be too much of a problem. Socially there would not be too much of a problem either; it was the 1980s by then and people had long since ceased to care about single-parent births.

Her aunt would have cared, of course; she would have been scandalized to think that Rosamund had behaved in such a sinful way. A bastard, she would have said, thinning her lips in the way Roz hated and feared. Making yourself cheap with a married man—no wonder he cleared off and left you.

But Roz's aunt had also talked about what she called her own lost childhood and there had even been the occasional wistful note in her voice when she did so. She had rocked back and forth in the old wooden-framed rocking-chair where she liked to sit in the evening, and she had unrolled the memories for Roz.

'You should write all this down,' Roz said once when she was thirteen. 'Write it all down, so that people can read about it.'

But her aunt had said, no, she would not care to do that, letting strangers know such things about her life. Roz was different; she was family. And in any case, said her aunt, her life had been written about once already, a long, long time ago, and people did not want a twice-told story. She said this sternly, but Roz had picked up the bitterness, and she had not liked to ask any more questions.

She felt the presence of that indomitable old woman as soon as she unlocked the front door. She felt her aunt's disdain and disapproval, hard and cold and abrupt, like walking into a clenched fist, so that a headache smacked across her eyes as soon as she entered the house. But she remembered again about her aunt's lost childhood, and she remembered the austere years of her own childhood in this house, and she thought she would make it very different for her own child. The headache persisted a bit and in the end she took paracetamol which dulled it to a low sad ache that spread through her entire body.

The headache finally went but the other low-down ache remained. It went on hurting for the best part of a day and a night, and at three a.m. it suddenly resolved itself into a dreadful clenching agony that came and went with frightening regularity. Roz lay in bed, clutching the sheets, trying not to cry out, trying to take deep, calming breaths, not knowing how serious the pain was, not knowing whether she should try to summon help or not.

But by the time it was growing light outside—a grey, dispirited, wintry light—and by the time she heard the cheerful clatter of milkmen and postmen and people going off to work, she had started to bleed quite badly. This time she managed to get to the phone to call her GP's answer-service, asking if an emergency visit could be made to her house. No, she could not possibly get down to the surgery. But please to hurry.

The GP arrived an hour later, but by then the child had bled itself out on to rolled-up bath towels from the airing cupboard and her aunt's second-best eiderdown.

'I lost the child,' said Roz expressionlessly to Mel. She was still standing in the window, still watching the twins. 'It died—it bled out all over the bed—'

'I'm so sorry, Roz,' said Mel rather helplessly. What could one say in the face of this? 'It's a desperately sad thing to lose a child, and an unborn one is no less of a tragedy. Had you—had you wanted it?'

'Oh yes. Oh yes, certainly I wanted it. It was going to put the balance right, you see. It was going to replace a childhood that had been lost.'

'Your childhood?' Roz had never said very much about her family, but Mel had always had the impression of a bleak, rather lonely childhood.

'No, not mine. Someone else's.'

'Oh,' said Mel, not understanding, but not liking to ask any questions.

'But then I lost it that night. But you,' said Roz, staring at the twins, 'you had two babies together. Double yolk. And from the same man who fathered mine. That's not really fair, is it?'

'Well, put like that—' Mel was starting to wish Roz would go. She was starting to feel extremely uncomfortable at the look in Roz's eyes. Sadness, was it? No, something stronger than that.

'In fact,' said Roz, turning the hard dark stare on Mel, 'in fact, looked at in one way, it could almost be said that you owe me a child, Melissa.'

And then Mel identified the look in Roz's eyes.

Hunger.

'Did she really say that?' demanded Isobel, having listened to Mel with growing concern. 'That you owed her a child?'

'She did.' Mel had not been able to get warm since Roz's visit. She had gone round the house turning up all the heating, but it was an inner coldness. 'She said it and then she stood looking at the twins for a while longer, and then she went out. I haven't heard from her since.' But she knew Roz was nearby; several times she had sensed Roz's presence, and twice she had got up in the night to see to the twins, and caught sight of a dark figure standing in the road outside the house. Looking up at the lit bedroom window...

'She's probably a bit unbalanced, I suppose,' Isobel was saying.

'When she was staring into the twins' pram, there was a look—a kind of greed—I can't begin to describe how sinister it was.' Mel twisted her hands together, and then said, 'I'm truly sorry for her. I really am.'

'But you're also a bit frightened of her,' said Isobel shrewdly.

'Yes. Just a bit. Well, more than a bit.'

'OK. So what are you going to do about it?'

'I'm not sure yet,' said Mel. 'I don't think she's violent or dangerous or anything like that. But I'm still thinking I'd like to sell this house and move to a different part of London. Try to shake off all that press interest and give the twins a normal life—'

'You do think she's dangerous?'

'Not really. And I've wanted to move house since Joe died, you know that. But I can't do it until after the twins have the separation. And since that's something that will probably churn the publicity up all over again—'

'Yes?'

'I'm wondering if I could ask Martin Brannan about the possibility of having the twins' separation carried out somewhere abroad. Quietly and anonymously.'

'You're frightened,' said Isobel, almost accusingly.

'No. No, I'm not really,' said Mel.

❀ ❀ ❀

But she was frightened, of course. Every time she remembered that hunger in Roz's eyes, and every time she remembered Roz's words—'It could almost be said that you owe me a child, Melissa...'—she was increasingly aware of a compulsion to lock the twins away somewhere safe, out of reach of those cold avid eyes.

She began to check the twins' pram at too-frequent intervals, and she took to getting up in the middle of the night to make sure that doors were bolted and windows locked. Several times in the week after Roz's visit, driving home from the supermarket with the twins bundled into anonymous shawls and bonnets, she took absurdly circuitous routes in case she was being followed. This was ridiculous and neurotic, of course: Roz did not possess a car, and Mel did not think she could even drive. But then, once back in the house, she found herself going into all the rooms. This was the most neurotic thing of all, because Roz could certainly not get into the house. And yet, and yet...

You owe me a child, Melissa... And there had been those nights when she had seen Roz standing in the street outside, watching the house...

She spent the next Sunday at Isobel's flat, enjoying Isobel's careless lavish hospitality, and the pleasant untidiness of Isobel's big flat which consisted of the upper half of a big old Victorian house. Several of Isobel's colleagues turned up towards the end of the afternoon—Mel thought one of the men was shaping up to be Isobel's latest lover. Good for Isobel. Wine was opened on the grounds that the sun was already well over the yard-arm, and Mel ended up staying longer than she had intended. The twins slept happily in Isobel's bedroom, and it was nice to be with ordinary people again.

It was dark by the time she got home, but the time-switches that Joe had so diligently installed had all kicked in, so that there were lights on in the downstairs rooms. The house looked friendly and welcoming, and Mel was relaxed from the company and the cheerfulness. She stopped the car on the drive and got out to open the garage door, leaving the engine running, the twins safely inside. She had just got the garage door open and she was turning back to drive the car in, when a shadow fell across her and she spun round to see Roz standing close behind her.

'You've been out somewhere,' said Roz, without any preamble. 'You've been with nice people and you've enjoyed yourself. I can see that you have.'

'Yes.' Dear God, thought Mel, what is she going to do? She glanced across to the car, wondering if she could get to the twins and get them safely inside. But Roz was between her and the car, and there was a glitter in her eyes that was quite frightening.

'You've got so much, haven't you?' Roz was saying. 'Friends and a nice house to live in—and you had a husband. And even when he died you had everyone's sympathy. Poor Melissa, people said. Such a tragedy— we'll have to help her through this. Nobody said, Poor Roz, though. Nobody helped me.'

Mel was hearing the dangerous note in Roz's voice very clearly by this time, and so in as gentle a voice as she could manage, she said, 'That must have been a dreadful time for you.'

'It was. I had to keep everything secret—losing the baby—everything. I told them at the hospital I had stomach flu—they believed me, of course. Good old Roz, nothing in the least questionable about her life, never had a boyfriend, even.' She half-turned her head to look at the twins and Mel tensed her muscles to spring forward, but Roz turned back and the moment was gone.

She said, 'Roz, I'm truly sorry about it all. Weren't there any friends you could talk to—?'

'There wasn't anyone. There never has been anyone. It's easy for you to talk glibly about friends. It's easy for you to pretend to be sorry, as well. You've come out of Joe's death very nicely, I should think. Insurances and pensions— Joe was the sort of responsible man who would make sure his family was looked after. You might be a tragic widow, Melissa, but I'll bet you're a well-off tragic widow.'

'I'm not really—'

'I think you are. It's all a matter of luck, isn't it? Some people get it all. And even though the twins were born as they were, there's no joining of any vital organs, so they can be operated on and they'll be very nearly perfect. What a lot of luck you've had, Melissa.' Again there was the swift darting glance towards the twins, and again Mel had to fight down the impulse to run forward and snatch the twins up. Unthinkable to involve them in any kind of struggle. And Roz looked so wild and sounded so unstable, Mel was afraid of triggering a much more dangerous situation.

And then a car came swinging around the curve of the road—one of the neighbours returning home—and the headlights picked out the two of them, and Roz blinked at the glare, and seemed to suddenly realize where she was. Mel saw that the wild glare had faded from her eyes.

But Roz said, 'Remember everything I've said, Melissa. Remember that I was cheated of what should have been mine.'

A child...

'Remember I'll be watching you, Melissa,' said Roz.

'You've been watching me for quite a while, haven't you?'

Incredibly Roz smiled. 'Yes, I have. Did you know I was around?'

'Yes. I saw you a few times. Sometimes I just knew you were there.'

'Good. I wanted you to know. And I'm going on watching you, Mel. And watching the twins. I'm waiting until after the operation that will divide them.'

She turned and went back down the drive and along the road.

❀ ❀ ❀

Mel sat in the warm comfortable sitting-room of Isobel's flat and tried to stop shaking.

'She means it,' she said. 'She really does. Once the twins have had the operation to separate them, she'll try to take one of them. She won't care which one—she just thinks she's owed a child—she thinks I owe her a child, because she thinks she was cheated.'

'But that's the maddest thing in the world.'

'I know. But if you had seen her and heard her— I've got to get out of her reach as soon as I can. Sell the house and move away, and just—well, vanish.'

'Isn't that a bit drastic?'

'I've intended to do it ever since Joe's death. You know that. I've even thought of changing my name so that there wouldn't be any more media attention in the future. I'd only be bringing it forward a bit.'

'Well, don't move away from me, will you?'

'No, of course not. I can't imagine how I'd have got through any of this without you. But listen, I think I'm going to talk to Martin Brannan. He might be bound by all kinds of medical rulings, but I think I can trust him and one thing he might do is arrange for Roz to have some help. Psychiatric help, I mean.'

'That's very generous of you.'

'It isn't really. I'm frightened to death of her if you want the truth, but I'm eaten up with pity for her as well.'

Isobel seemed to study Mel very intently for a moment. Then she said, 'Fair enough. Let's work out exactly how you're going to vanish.'

'You'll help me?' Mel had not expected this.

'Of course I will. I'm Sonia's fairy godmother anyway, remember?'

'If you help with this you'd be giving her one hell of a christening present.'

'Yes, I know. Much better than a prick in a lonely turret,' said Isobel deadpan, and despite herself, Mel laughed.

Martin Brannan, discreetly invited to a modest lunch on the other side of town, listened carefully to Mel's story. 'This is a tricky one,' he said at last. 'I agree with you that Roz needs help, but until or unless she does anything that's a danger to anyone—including herself—I don't think we can force any kind of treatment on her. I'll make some discreet inquiries about that, though. You're convinced that Roz really means to snatch one of the twins?'

'I'm sure she does.'

'It's not unknown after a miscarriage, of course,' he said, and Mel was deeply thankful that he appeared to accept her judgement, and that he seemed to take it for granted that he would help her. It ought to have felt peculiar to be with him like this in the relaxed friendliness of the small wine bar, but it did not.

'Where will you disappear to? When the operation's over, I mean?'

'I don't know yet. I'll probably just stick a pin in a map. The house can be sold—I'll give my solicitor the keys and ask him to instruct a firm of agents. I can get a furnished house for a few months and once a sale goes through I expect I can buy something. Probably I'll change my name by deed-poll. This has got to be long-term, I think. It would only take one reporter with a good memory to do a tacky follow-up story sometime in the future, and the whole thing would blow up all over again. I don't just mean Roz, I mean all the media intrusion.'

'You'll be all right for money?'

There was no reason to feel suddenly embarrassed by this. For God's sake, thought Mel, he's had his hands inside my body more times than I can count! She said, a bit brusquely, 'Yes, perfectly all right, thank you.'

'I'd like to know where you go,' he said. 'Write to me, will you? I'll give you my home address. Or phone me?'

'Yes. Yes, I'll do that.' She would probably replay that part of the conversation several times when she was on her own. Like an impressionable teenager, said her mind jeeringly.

Martin said, 'First things first, then. The twins' operation. What are we doing about that?'

'That's the part where I need your help most of all. Is there any way it can be done secretly?'

Martin appeared to think about this for a moment, and then he said, 'Would you be prepared to take them abroad?'

'I'd take them to Alpha Centauri if it meant they were safe.'

Between them, Mel, Isobel and Martin worked out a plan. 'It's feeling a bit James Bond-ish or Le Carré,' Isobel said at one point. 'But I don't think we're overreacting. We've got to assume that Roz is watching all the time.'

I'll be watching you, Melissa... Mel repressed a shudder, but Martin said, 'I've talked to the Swiss clinic twice now—it's an excellent place, in fact I know one of the surgeons from university. He's phoning me at home this weekend, but I'm fairly sure they'll be able to take the twins. It's a question of logistics—of how soon they can assemble the right surgical team.'

'Might they manage it before Christmas?'

'I'll do what I can to push them, but I can't promise.' He looked at Mel. 'I'd rather they had the operation in this country,' he said, 'but there are only two or three hospitals here that could cope with it, and we'd never keep it secret.' He paused, and then said, 'If I do get you into the Swiss place how would you get there?'

'I've talked to Isobel about that. We thought flying would be a bit public, and probably not very comfortable for the twins either. So we'll go in Isobel's car. She can get a longish leave from her company—she's on one of those short-term contract arrangements with them, so she can organise things to get a month or so between two jobs. We'll take the ferry at Dover, and drive across to Switzerland.'

Martin considered this, and then said, 'That's quite a good idea. Even if anyone did recognize you all you're doing is dodging the journalists, which is understandable in anyone's book. It'll be a much longer journey than if you went by plane, but you could take it in easy stages.'

'We thought we'd make two overnight stops,' said Mel. 'One in Reims and then one in Dijon. They're both big enough places for us to be anonymous, and there are several large hotels—Travel Lodge types.'

'You and Isobel would share the driving?'

'Yes.'

Martin said thoughtfully, 'I've driven in France and Spain quite a bit, so I'm used to the right-hand side of the road. Would you like a third driver?'

'Yes,' said Mel staring at him. 'Yes, I think we'd like that very much.'

'I'd have to let the GMC know,' said Martin. 'Because you and the twins are still officially my patients. But I don't think they would object. We could let it be thought that Isobel's a girlfriend of mine—that's she's helping you with the twins and I'm coming along partly in case they develop any problems en route. A working holiday. I'm due some leave anyway, and I think I can re-arrange my clinics. Isobel and I could drive to Dover with the twins, and you can travel down there by train. We'll hand the twins back to you for the actual boarding so they can go through on your passport. They're still below the age for needing their own, aren't they?'

'Yes. I could apply for passports for them,' said Mel. 'But I don't think there's time.'

'Roz doesn't drive, does she?'

'No. So even if she finds out where we're going she won't be able to follow us, not at such short notice, and certainly not on the same ferry. And she couldn't possibly track us across France and into Switzerland. I think it'll work,' said Mel.

'So do I.'

It would have to work. Mel could not begin to think what she would do if Roz eventually found her.

CHAPTER TWENTY-SEVEN

THE SMALL NEWS item in the weekend paper was not very informative. It simply said that the conjoined Anderson twins had been taken abroad for the operation that would separate them: the family did not want the venue disclosed, but it was known that a team of specialists had been assembled, so presumably the operation would take place soon. Roz, reading this, knew at once that despite all her care, Melissa had slipped out of her grasp, taking the twins with her. Or had she...?

That night she began to weave her plans. She thought her aunt would have approved of what she was doing: God punishes where it is required, and rewards where it is deserved, she had said. *Reward*. The replacing of the child—the little lost thing—that had trickled sadly and despairingly out of Roz's womb in that grey dawn.

The first priority was to find out where Mel had gone. It took a while for Roz to decide how to go about this, but after a night's consideration she focused on Martin Brannan. Where was he in all this? In fact, where was he literally, because he was not at St Luke's at the moment, that was for sure. He was where? On holiday? Until after the New Year? Well, how interesting.

Roz had kept up the lukewarm friendship with Martin's secretary at St Luke's, not because she particularly liked the woman, but because you never knew who might come in useful. The friendship came in useful now.

Mr Brannan was in France, said Martin's secretary, and added, in the smug, I-am-in-the-know tone that always jarred on Roz, that he was not alone. A lady friend, said the secretary coyly. Well, they all knew what Mr Brannan was, of course. Quite a lot of girlfriends he had had over the years. But this latest trip had all been arranged in secrecy—a surprise for the lady apparently, wasn't that romantic? A ferry crossing, and then a drive down into Southern France.

Roz did not care if Martin Brannan shipped an entire harem across the English Channel, or held orgies all the way from Dover to Provence and back again. What she did want to know was the identity of the 'lady friend'. Could it possibly be Melissa?

But it was not. Roz was aware of a stab of disappointment because it would have fitted so well. Melissa and Martin would have driven quietly down to Dover to get on the ferry, the twins travelling on their mother's passport. Two babies, well wrapped up in a carry-cot, would not have been especially remarkable.

She said, casually, to Martin Brannan's secretary, that hadn't Mr Brannan been seen with the French actress, Anne-Marie St Clair?

'*Has* he?' said the secretary, saucer-eyed and wholly unsuspecting.

'Perhaps I got it wrong— But when you said France—'

'Mr Brannan isn't in France with Anne-Marie St Clair, that I do know,' said the secretary, and then, unable to resist sharing the rest of the gossip about her boss, and remembering that Nurse Raffan, so quiet and mouselike, never gossiped, she said, 'It's a lady called Isobel Ingram.

I know because the travel agent sent the ferry tickets here by mistake.'

Isobel Ingram. The name smacked across Roz's consciousness. *Isobel Ingram.* Melissa Anderson's closest friend. Roz had met Isobel at St Luke's when she had visited Mel, and several times during her babysitting stints for Mel and Joe at the house. Isobel Ingram. The one person in the world whom Melissa would trust after Martin Brannan! Roz saw at once that what Mel had done was to give the twins into the temporary care of Isobel and Martin Brannan for the journey to France. Probably Melissa had followed them a day later, or had even travelled on the same ferry, but separately. Once in France it was anybody's guess where they had gone, although Roz was inclined to think it was Switzerland where there were so many private clinics. Money again, you see! It smoothed all paths!

There was absolutely no way that Roz could follow Melissa and the other two even if she had known their destination. She would have to wait until they got back, but that was fine; waiting would help her to sharpen up the finer points of her plan. It would let her imagine for a little longer the culmination of the plan—it was remarkable how much pleasure she was deriving from that.

But the plan was going to be carried out, that was for sure. The balance had got to be redressed. Melissa would be trying to evade Roz from now on, which meant she might not return to her own house. Roz thought Mel would probably put it up for sale, and go to live somewhere else.

But where?

The phone book listed three Ingrams with the initial *I*. Roz rang all three numbers that same evening. The first was a man, and although the second was a woman she was definitely not Isobel. To both people Roz said, crisply, that she was a British Telecom operator checking the line for faults. The third number rang out a few times, and then an answerphone clicked on and Roz heard Isobel's voice asking the caller please to leave a message. In case the machine had detected someone calling and maybe even recorded the number, Roz again said she was ringing from BT engineers' department, checking the lines in the area. If there were any problems, please telephone fault inquiries between nine and five.

So far so good. She had Isobel's phone number and also her address from the phone book. She consulted a street map, and then caught a bus to Isobel's house. She had been careful to put on her dark raincoat, and to take with her a collecting box for one of the hospital's many charities. She was an indefatigable helper for all of the various Support Groups. Good, dependable Roz. And nobody ever looked twice at someone going from door to door with a collecting box.

Isobel lived in part of a converted Victorian house—No. 22b, the phone book had said. It was a tree-lined street, rather quiet and fairly prosperous-looking. No. 22 was halfway along; it stood a little way back from the road, in quite large gardens. The house itself looked quite large as well. It would be rather nice inside: probably it would have those large high-ceilinged rooms. Roz glanced up and down the street, and then advanced cautiously through the gate and down the gravel path. No. 22b was the top half, of course. There was a main doorway which was plainly shared by both flats. It was closed and locked, but it had two oblong panes of coloured glass let into the oak and Roz managed to peer through one of them. Yes, there was the door into the ground floor flat on the right-hand side, and straight ahead was a staircase winding upwards. It looked as if the main hall was shared; it looked very clean, and there was a well-polished hall table with a large asparagus fern on it.

There were curtains at the downstairs windows but there was a deserted feel to the place, and when she peered through one of the windows she saw that there was no furniture in any of the rooms. The ground floor flat was empty.

'It's been empty for about three weeks,' said the woman at No. 24, in response to Roz's deliberately timid inquiry. 'But I should think it will have to be sold. A youngish woman's got the first floor—I think she's away at the moment or I'd suggest you knock on her door to ask if she knows what's happening. But the old chap at 22a died recently, I do know that. He was in hospital for a longish time so the place has got a bit neglected. His family will probably redecorate before they sell. So as to get a better price, you see.'

Roz explained that she was looking for a flat in the area. Someone had told her about 22a so she was taking a look from the outside. She thought it looked a bit small for what she wanted, but she might ask the agents about viewing it.

Martin Brannan was not expected at St Luke's until after Christmas and the New Year holiday. He would be back by the fifth of January for certain because he had a clinic on that day. The paragraph about the twins had appeared in early December, so if they came back with Mr Brannan, or perhaps shortly afterwards, they would have had about a month in the clinic, wherever the clinic might be. Roz was not very knowledgeable about time scales for this kind of surgery, but she thought four or five weeks did not sound an unreasonable recovery time.

Just before Christmas she asked a large firm of estate agents about renting out her own house; she might be taking a job in the north for a few years, she said. No, she did not want to actually sell the place; she would most likely be returning to it. Could they arrange a tenancy—a furnished let for two or three years? She would want someone responsible who would look after the place, but she would take advice as to the amount of rent to charge. She would not be greedy about that, although she would hope for a reasonable income from the property.

The agents were sure they could find a suitable tenant on this basis, and probably without too much difficulty. There was the nearby school of languages, they said. Oh no, they were not suggesting renting to students, but there were very often foreign lecturers who came there on a one- or two-year contract. That might fit the bill very nicely. Such people quite often liked to bring their wives over with them, so they did not mind paying a reasonably generous rent. Yes, certainly the rental monies could be paid directly into a bank for her; that was a perfectly normal arrangement.

'I'll let you know in a couple of weeks if I get the job in the north,' said Roz.

She had some leave due to her for Christmas, which she spent on her own. There was a nurses' party at St Luke's to which she could have gone—beer and fruit punch in the canteen, it was—and then one of the other nurses invited her to a New Year's Eve party at her home, but Roz had never gone to any hospital parties in the past and she did not want to do anything out of pattern in case it drew attention to her. So she said she would be having a quiet family Christmas, thank you.

For most of the holiday she watched television and listened to the radio or did crossword puzzles, and when she was not doing that she was working out the details of her plan. At times she was awed at the vastness of it, but Rosie thought it was the right thing to do. It was a good plan; parts of it were flexible, and parts of it depended on other people and on events coinciding. But Roz thought—and Rosie agreed—that it would work.

She strung Christmas decorations in the front sitting-room window because people might notice if she did not, and on Christmas Day she cooked a turkey, eating part of it for her Christmas dinner, and slicing and jointing the rest for the freezer. The neighbours on both sides of her house were away, and it was very quiet indeed. Roz did not mind; she was able to focus all her attention on what was ahead. She was used to being quiet, and in any case Christmas was really a time for children.

Ah, but this time next year—

The agents dealing with the house where Isobel Ingram lived were a much smaller firm than the ones Roz had approached about letting her own house. This was fortunate, because it was important to keep all the different parts of the plan separate.

The agents were helpful and efficient. They would be more than happy for the quietly-dressed lady to view the ground floor flat. It was not strictly speaking on the market yet because they were still waiting for probate to be granted. But they had the keys, and if she was interested they could let her know the asking price when it was fixed. Oh, and she would have to allow for the current condition of the rooms, which were a bit grubby. But it was amazing what a lick of paint and a few rolls of paper could do to a place.

'Yes, of course I'll take that into account. What about the keys? The thing is that I'm a nurse at St Luke's and my current shift means I don't finish until half past eight in the evenings. I couldn't really get out there until nine.'

The firm's rule these days was that all viewings had to be accompanied, but there was no furniture in this particular flat, and surely to goodness a nurse ought to be trustworthy. And nobody in the office really wanted to turn out for a nine p.m. viewing of an empty flat on a winter's evening. If they let her take the keys for viewing the place tonight, could she bring them back the following morning?

'What I could do,' said Roz, pretending to think about it, 'is put the keys through your letter-box later tonight, after I've had a look at the place. That way you'd have them first thing the next morning. Would that do? And I'll be very careful about locking everywhere up.'

This was all quite acceptable. The electricity was still on, because of leaving a bit of heating in the place during the cold weather—frozen pipes, you know—so perhaps Miss Raffan would make sure that all lights were switched off when she left?

There were no problems about any of it. Miss Raffan even telephoned the next morning to make sure that the keys had been found. No, the flat was not quite what she had been looking for, after all. But you had to check, hadn't you?

As the year gradually died, the small flutter caused by Simone and Sonia Anderson's birth died as well.

Shortly before Christmas there was a brief announcement that the operation to separate them—the operation their father had considered against God's wish—had gone ahead. Hard on the heels of this came a second announcement that the younger twin—Sonia—had died from respiratory arrest on the operating table. This was followed by a slightly different announcement in another newspaper that it had been renal failure, and that Sonia had not died until nearly a week later. There was next a report that Mrs Anderson would not be returning to England, and although one or two feature-writers optimistically requisitioned travelling costs and booked half-page spreads, as one editor gloomily pointed out, the world was a big place and even if you narrowed it down to Switzerland, which was the likeliest country, there were any amount of private, discreet clinics in Switzerland, and where did you start?

Martin Brannan, recently back from a holiday in France, was tracked down and questioned, but he gave no help at all. In any case he might be leaving gynaecology altogether, he said; he had been offered a research fellowship in Canada, which was a very attractive prospect. Yes, certainly he had seen the reports that Sonia Anderson had died somewhere abroad, but he knew no more than anyone else. No, he had not been involved in the operation to separate the twins; it was a very specialized field of surgery, wholly outside his province, and in fact the twins and their mother had ceased to be his patients for quite some time. Yes, of course he had recommended one or two specialist paediatricians to Mrs Anderson after the twins' birth, but it would be a breach of medical ethics and patient confidentiality for him to disclose any of those names. No, he did not know where Melissa Anderson and the surviving twin might be now. His tone said that even if he had known he would not have divulged it.

The journalists ferreted around for a further week or two; some of them ferreted longer than others and some of them ferreted deeper than others, and a young man called Clifford Markovitch, who was trying to raise the finance to start his own gossipy, celebrity-slanted magazine and who considered himself more far-seeing than many of his colleagues, added the name of the Anderson family to the rather complex card-index he was compiling.

But in the end, since nothing is so stale as yesterday's news, and nothing is so saleable as tomorrow's scandal, by the third week of January the twins and their story had more or less faded from the public's mind.

In the mind of one person it had not faded at all. Roz did not believe these rather contradictory reports of Sonia Anderson's death. She had a very good insight into the twists and turns of the bitch's mind, and she believed that these reports about Sonia were false, partly intended to throw journalists off the scent, but mostly intended to fool Roz herself. She kept watch on both Isobel Ingram's flat, and on the bitch's house. Just as she had thought, in the week following Christmas, a 'For Sale' board appeared in the garden of Mel's house, with a sticker saying that viewing was strictly by appointment with the estate agents. As with Isobel's flat, Roz took careful note of the position of curtains, and saw the mail pile up on the other side of the glass-panelled front door, although she did not think Melissa would come back here.

But on the second Saturday in January the curtains of Isobel's flat were pulled all the way back, as if someone had wanted to let in light and air. Two of the little top windows were open, and a car—a smallish hatchback, the kind that a lot of women drove—was parked on the drive. In the back of the car was a child's safety seat.

Just one child's safety seat.

The agents' keys to the empty flat in Isobel's house had, of course, only fitted the ground floor. Roz had not expected otherwise. But on the key-ring had been a key that unlocked the main door of the house. It could not have been otherwise, of course; the occupants of the two flats would need to secure the outer door against prowlers and cats, and they would each need their own key to it. Roz had duplicates of all the keys made in one of the big, while-you-wait, key-cutting places in the town. It was a busy lunchtime, and nobody would be likely to remember the small, ordinary transaction.

As for the other transaction—

You did not work in a large hospital without getting to know a bit about all the other departments. Roz had been on the staff of Martin Brannan's maternity clinic for two years, but she had worked in the men's surgical ward before then, and she had also done a stint in Casualty— what was beginning to be called Accident & Emergency.

She did not know everyone who worked in St Luke's, of course, but she knew a lot of people by sight, and a lot of people knew her by sight, which meant she could go pretty much anywhere in the building without being questioned. But could she go into the morgue? Could she openly consult the fatalities list that was posted on the notice-board outside? Yes, why not?

She went along calmly and unhurriedly the next morning. She was in uniform and she carried a hospital folder, and if anyone challenged her she was going to say she had been asked to help with some new NHS statistics that were wanted about juvenile deaths. But no one did challenge her. Right was on her side, and the stars fought in their courses for her and for two days running she was able to go down to the semi-basement where the morgue was situated without being stopped.

She had been afraid that she might have to wait a long time for a suitable death, and this had worried her quite a lot because although she could probably get away with three or four expeditions, more than that might attract attention. But on only her third trip to check the notice-board there was a new entry. A little boy, the victim of a cot-death. JDF/2841/M, and a date of birth three months earlier. How sad. The autopsy had taken place two days ago and the funeral would be the following Tuesday. A boy, a three-month-old boy. Roz considered carefully. Could she take the risk with a boy? But she might wait months for a girl. This was as nearly perfect as she could hope for. She would do it, and she would do it at once.

A child for a child. JDF/2841/M. J was probably for John, or James. But it was better not to wonder about a name; it was better not to personalize the child in her mind in any way.

She got through the rest of her shift, and then waited until mid-evening—the hour when shifts were changing over and people were too taken up with coming off day-duty or going on night-duty to notice much else. She carried a little pile of clean pillowcases, and she consulted her watch anxiously as she went. I'm in a tearing hurry and I can't stop for anyone—if I don't get this laundry back to the ward in the next five minutes Sister will go into orbit.

Here was the door leading to the morgue itself. It had been nerve-racking enough to come down here on those other occasions but it was a hundred times worse now that she was going inside. But do it as if you've got official business in there, Roz. Walk inside confidently and firmly. That was Rosie saying that, of course. Rosie was encouraging Roz every step of the way.

It was cool and quiet inside the morgue and no one was around. Roz had counted on that; at this time of day the place was hardly likely to be a hive of activity. The big autopsy room was closed and locked, and the small administration area was deserted, with covers on all the typewriters and the phones put through to the main switchboard. There was supposed to be someone on duty here all the time, but at this hour whoever it was would most likely be in the hospital canteen. It was a lonely, rather eerie place, the morgue. That was all right by Roz; she wanted it lonely, at least for the next ten minutes. She advanced warily into the room.

A dim light burned from overhead, but it was enough to read the name-labels on each of the metal shelves. Roz's heart was pounding with nervous dread by now, but she went steadily along the rows, checking each one. Had JDF/2841/M been moved out already? It had said the funeral was next week, but— Ah, no, here he was, a little way along on the left. She made a mental note of the setting on the little thermostat at the side, so as to set her own fridge at home in exact accordance. It was quite a lot colder than a normal fridge temperature, but it was not freezer-level.

Even so, the metal handle of the drawer was very cold, and when she pulled the drawer out it made a screech of sound that sent her already-taut nerves jangling like bells on wires. She waited, holding her breath, expecting someone to come marching in to demand to know what she was doing, but no one appeared and the place remained quiet and still. She looked at what lay in the metal coffin-shaped compartment. JDF/2841/M. Not in the least frightening or grisly; only rather sad. Three months old. Still, that's the way life goes, JDF, and we can't all live to be a hundred. Roz did what had to be done, then closed the drawer, which was now empty. Five minutes later she was walking back through the hospital, still carrying the little stack of pillow-cases.

She caught her normal bus home that evening. The bus conductor was quite often on this route; he exchanged a joke with Roz, and commented on the heavy shopping bag she was carrying. All work, wasn't it?

'I'm afraid so,' said Roz, getting out at her usual stop. 'Goodnight.'

She remembered to turn up the setting on the fridge, but it was necessary to take the wire shelves out of the fridge, and to store the cheese and butter and last night's cold chicken in the old-fashioned walk-in larder. Fortunately the original marble slab was still in there so everything should stay fresh. A pity if all that good food had to be thrown out. The milk would be all right; it could stay in the fridge's door compartment.

At first she thought JDF was not going to fit in, even with all the shelves removed. But at length, by dint of propping him into a sitting position, she managed it. She had to beat down a little stab of sadness at the flicking off of the fridge's inner light when the door closed on him.

After this she made a pot of tea, and sat drinking it. Tea was very reviving; her aunt had held strongly by the virtues of a properly made pot of tea.

It had been an unpleasant thing to do, and what she would be doing tomorrow would be even more unpleasant, but it was all necessary if Roz was to have what was rightfully hers.

A child for a child.

The next day was a Saturday, which might be an advantage, or then again, might not. Before ten o'clock Roz went out to the nearby shopping centre, and bought two or three sets of baby clothes in one of the big department stores. These were suitable for a six-month-old baby, were they? It was a present for a friend's little girl—she did not want to get the size wrong. She paid cash for the clothes, and bought two packs of disposable nappies in a busy branch of Boots.

Back at home she made sandwiches from the cold chicken, which she wrapped in greaseproof paper, and also put coffee in a vacuum flask. It was a bit disconcerting to open the fridge for the milk, and see what was in there, sitting hunched up. For a heart-snatching second or two she thought it had moved, but it was just her imagination.

She caught the bus to Isobel's house just after lunch, being careful with the large wicker cat-basket she carried. Two tins of cat-food were prominently on display in a separate shopping, basket, and anyone looking her way would think she was travelling to a vet's surgery to collect a sick pet.

She would have preferred not to be doing this on a Saturday, but the day had been chosen for her by finding JDF yesterday. Still, Saturdays were often shopping days for people. She could watch the house from the semi-concealment of the trees on the other side of the road. If the upstairs flat stayed stubbornly and permanently occupied she would simply wait until it was dark, and then slink inside very quietly. But luck favoured her, and when she reached the house there was no car parked in the drive.

She let herself into the main hall with the duplicate key. There was a faint scent of polish as if someone had been cleaning, and there was a scattering of letters on the hall table. Roz looked at the addresses in case there was anything worth noting but they were only circulars. She visualized Isobel picking them up from the mat, and putting them down again to be thrown out.

The empty flat did not smell of polish; it smelt of unaired rooms and stale dust. Roz flicked down the security latch on the door, because there was a small possibility that the agents might send or bring someone to view the flat, especially on a Saturday afternoon. If that happened they would not be able to get in, and they would most likely assume that whoever had been here last had bungled the mechanism, and a locksmith would probably have to be called out. That would all take time.

She put the cat-basket down on the floor. It had been quite heavy to carry and her shoulders were aching. After consideration she took up a position behind the window at the side of the building where she could not be seen from the drive. She would hear the sound of a car turning in, and she would hear anyone coming in through the outer door.

As well as the chicken sandwiches and the flask of coffee, she had brought a couple of paperbacks, and a book of crossword puzzles. She still had no means of knowing if it would be Isobel or Melissa who would come back here, or even if it might be both of them. Melissa might be staying with Isobel. But Roz did not think that was very likely. The car she had seen had only one child-seat in the back. She thought they had split the twins up to fool people—to fool Roz herself, of course, but probably the press as well. It was a clever idea, but it was not quite clever enough.

Roz did not mind which of the twins was living here, and she did not mind how long she had to wait for the occupant of the top flat to return. It would not matter if she had to wait until tomorrow or the day after: there was no one either at home or at the hospital who would miss her before Monday morning.

And she would not be on her own while she waited because Rosie would be with her.

CHAPTER TWENTY-EIGHT

Isobel GOT BACK to her flat shortly after four o'clock.

She had enjoyed the afternoon; the shopping centre had been crowded but it had been cheerful and colourful and Sonia had loved it. Isobel had enjoyed Sonia's pleasure. She would not want a child permanently—too much of a career girl!—but she was liking having Sonia for these few weeks. Being a godmother would be fun.

She and Mel had been a bit worried that the girls might be confused or fractious after the separation, but once they were over the physical trauma they had seemed entirely untroubled. But Isobel had noticed that on several occasions, if they were in different rooms, one or the other of them seemed to be listening to something very intently, and she had wondered if they might turn out to be a bit telepathic. Twins often were. She was not sure if Mel had noticed this, but she had not mentioned it because Mel had enough on her plate without coping with telepathy or sixth sense complications.

At least Sonia seemed perfectly content in Isobel's company, although both the babies were very used to Isobel, of course, and perhaps at this age babies' priorities were simply to be fed and cuddled and kept warm and clean.

She parked at the side of the house, got out to unlock the main door, and went back for Sonia's carry-cot, leaving the door open. She loved this house. She was hoping that whoever bought the ground floor flat would not be noisy or untidy or intrusive; the man who had just died had been a dear old boy, he and Isobel had got along very well. But it would take more than an untidy neighbour to make her leave; she loved living here, and she loved the high-ceilinged rooms, even though the stairs were a bit of a pain if you had heavy shopping to carry. They were a bit of a pain for carrying Sonia up as well, but it could not be helped.

She got the carry-cot upstairs and set it carefully down on the floor so that Sonia could not tip herself out. It was odd how different the house felt and sounded now that the ground floor was empty: she had not noticed it before but it seemed to be full of peculiar little rustlings and creakings. It was to be hoped mice had not got in.

She went back down to the car for her shopping. There were a couple of carrier bags of food for the weekend; she lifted these out and then reached on to the front seat for the two extravagant purchases she had made for herself: a moss-coloured, ankle-length woollen skirt, and a silk shirt the colour of autumn leaves to go with it. The shopping centre catered for the commuter population and both garments had designer labels. They had cost the earth, but they would be terrific for the winter. Isobel enjoyed giving small supper parties—her sitting-room was huge and she had made a dining area in the deep bay window that looked out over the gardens.

She thought she might invite Martin Brannan and Mel to a meal one evening; the three of them had got quite close during that bizarre journey across Europe. Isobel liked Martin, but she had a suspicion that Mel liked him even more. Good for Mel, it was time she had a bit of luck in her life. She thought Martin quite liked Mel as well, but it would not hurt to give him a bit of help. Yes, she would invite them to a meal—it was time she got back into circulation anyway—and she would add a couple of other people so that it would not look too blatantly like match-making.

She would have to wait until they had got Mel safely and unobtrusively established somewhere. Mel had gone back to Norfolk when they returned to England—in view of Joe's death, Isobel had found that slightly peculiar, but Mel liked Norfolk. She liked the light and the loneliness. You could come to terms with things in a place like that, she said. She had found a small bungalow that could be rented for a couple of months until the house was sold and she could look for somewhere permanent. She thought she might move nearer to London again then.

Isobel had the feeling that Mel might move more than once in the next few years, and she thought Mel had been more unnerved than she had let on by that business with Roz—that was understandable, of course. It would be as well to keep a discreet eye on Mel, to make sure she did not lose money on buying and selling houses; Isobel felt a bit responsible for Mel, who was like the younger sister she had never had. It was a good friendship, although there were one or two no-go areas—one of these was money. The only reference Mel had ever made to money was when she had said, in an off-hand voice, that there was one good thing to be said for Joe: he had had a number of quite good insurance policies that had all paid up unhesitatingly when he died.

Isobel had not told Mel yet, but before they left for Switzerland she had made a new will, leaving her own bit of money and this flat to Mel. It was not a fortune, but if Isobel died suddenly Mel would get everything, and the twins would have an extra layer of financial security. If they had not worked out that last bit of subterfuge over Sonia, Isobel would have left everything to Sonia outright, godmother to god-daughter. But neither she nor Mel knew yet how that part of their plan would pan out, and Mel had still to sort out the legalities of changing her name. It was as well Martin had gone back to England before they had sent those carefully worded, deliberately contradictory announcements of Sonia's death to the British press; it would probably have been wildly compromising for him as a doctor to even have known about it.

Isobel was deeply thankful that the operation was over, and that it seemed to have gone all right. Mel said the surgeons thought Sonia might have a more pronounced limp than Simone, and Simone had more scarring on her left side than they would have liked, but as Mel said, this could be lived with and in time there could be other treatments. Skin grafts for Simone; physiotherapy and orthopaedic treatments for Sonia. The important thing was that the twins could start living ordinary lives; before much longer they could do ordinary things.

'They'll be able to do pretty well everything,' Mel had said. 'Sonia's spine isn't absolutely straight and her right hip's a bit askew, so she'll need special exercises. They think swimming will be particularly good, and also cycling. And they don't think it'll be too noticeable if it's looked after early enough. She might not be able to dance, though.'

'That'll be a pity when she's older,' Isobel had said. 'But after all this I shouldn't think you care if she never dances a step.'

'No, I don't. They're separate people. That's the best feeling in the world.'

Isobel went back up the stairs to her flat, her mind moving ahead to what she would give Sonia for supper. You got a whole new perspective on things when you suddenly had a small baby to feed. Instead of thinking on the lines of pasta or salad, you found yourself wondering whether to serve puréed vegetables or minced chicken, with rice pudding for afterwards.

She dumped the food shopping in the kitchen, set the kettle to boil for a cup of tea, and poured out a beaker of orange juice for Sonia. While she gave it to her, she told Sonia about the idea for a supper party. 'Because your mum's a very classy lady, and your pa was a slimy toad, so it's a good thing that he's out of the way. And I think it'd be great if we got her together with Martin Brannan, don't you?'

The house *did* feel peculiar tonight. Probably it was because she was still mentally in Switzerland, or perhaps it was because Sonia was here. But it might be mice she was hearing, or even—horrid thought!—rats. She shook this thought off, and leaving Sonia in the kitchen went through to the bedroom to change into jeans and a sweater. Her purchases, laid out on the bed, looked just as good as they had done in the shop. She was taking a pair of old jeans out of the dressing-table drawer when she heard what sounded like a furtive creak quite close by. She looked round at the door at once, but there was only the little hall, and beyond it the big sitting-room, softly lit by table lamps. Imagination. Even so, she checked on Sonia again, and then went out to the hall to make sure she had locked the door. Yes, of course she had. And it was a good, stout door, so that even if someone was prowling around outside—

Of course there was no one prowling around outside. For one thing no one could get in through the outer door downstairs, at least not without a great deal of smashing and bashing, which Isobel would certainly have heard. This was just a vague attack of nerves. Probably something to do with the unfamiliar responsibility of having a tiny baby here. Yes, that would be it. She stepped out of the skirt she had been wearing, dropped it into the linen basket, and pulled on the jeans. She went back to the kitchen, and she was just setting out Sonia's little dish of carrot purée when she heard something that made her heart leap. She turned her head towards the bedroom, listening. It was almost certainly her imagination again, but it had sounded exactly like the wardrobe door in her bedroom being slowly opened. Or was it? Yes, that was exactly the slow hissing creak the hinges made.

Isobel hesitated and then, glancing at Sonia, went back across the hall to stand in the bedroom doorway, her eyes on the wardrobe. Whoever had planned this flat had made quite good use of space: the wardrobe and a dressing-table unit had been neatly tucked beneath the steeply sloping eaves on this side of the house. The dressing-table was narrow, but the wardrobe was directly under the roof and it was deep and wide. It was more than deep enough for someone to hide inside.

There could not actually be anyone in there, of course. The flat had been locked all day, and the main door had been locked as well. What she had heard—what she thought she had heard—was probably a draught causing the door to move. Or she had not closed the door properly when she went out earlier in the day. But as she stood there, staring at the wardrobe, the sound came again and this time, unmistakably, a rim of darkness started to appear around the door, as if it was slowly being pushed open from inside.

Isobel began to back away, tensing her muscles for a quick sprint to the door. But she would have to snatch Sonia up on the way. And then she would have to unlock two doors—the door to this flat and the main door downstairs. Her handbag, with the keys inside it was on the kitchen table. Would there be time to grab the keys and get Sonia as well? There would have to be. There was an intruder in here—some sinister prowler who had somehow got into the flat while she was out, and who had hidden himself in the wardrobe. Illogically she remembered getting partly undressed in here a short while ago. Had he watched that?

Her mind was working at full pelt. Should she make a run for it, snatching up Sonia and the keys, and trust to luck that she would get outside before the intruder caught her? Or would it be better to walk slowly and unconcernedly, hoping that he would not know she had seen him? If she had been on her own she would have made a dash for it, but there was Sonia to think about. The slow, nonchalant stroll, then. But before she could move the wardrobe door suddenly swung wide and banged hard against the wall on one side.

For a blessed moment Isobel thought she had been wrong, because after all there was nothing inside the wardrobe except her own skirts and jackets and shirts on their hangers, and after all it must have been a freak draught of air that had dislodged the door-catch, or maybe Isobel had not closed the door properly when she went out, or maybe even somebody's cat had got in—

And then the dark folds of a long winter coat stirred, and a figure appeared and stepped out into the bedroom. Roz Raffan. Isobel recognized her at once from visiting Mel in St Luke's and from all those babysitting sessions. Her heart lurched in panic, because despite all their care—despite all the subterfuges and plots—Roz had tracked her here and somehow got into the flat. She was after Sonia, of course, the poor mad thing—Mel had been right about her being unbalanced; you had only to take one look at her eyes to know it.

Isobel was very frightened indeed, but she was damned if she was going to let Roz know. She had no idea how best to deal with this, but she summoned all her resolve, and in a sharp voice, she said, 'Roz? How dare you sneak in here like this! Get out at once!'

But Roz was already lunging forward, her face twisted with such blazing intensity that for a moment she looked barely human. Isobel flinched and instinctively threw up a hand in defence, half falling back into the hallway. She looked wildly about her for some kind of weapon, but Roz was already upon her, and before she could defend herself, she was knocked to the ground. Fingers that felt like steel bands were closing around her throat, forcing her head back. Isobel gasped and struggled, striking out almost at random but although her fist connected with soft flesh, the pressure on her neck did not lessen. Through the panic she heard Sonia start to cry, a thin, frightened cry, and she fought to get free. But Roz's hands were like a vice around her throat, and she was lying half on top of Isobel. It was disgusting and repellent to feel Roz's body pressing down on her, and to smell Roz's body-scents. Isobel renewed her struggles, but by this time jagged lights were starting to zig-zag across her vision, and a tight band was closing agonizingly and inexorably around her head. If she could just get one breath of air into her lungs, she could put up a real fight against this creature, this baby-stealer, just one breath, that was all she needed—

A crimson mist flooded her entire vision, and she was sucked down and down into a whirling black nothingness...

Roz would have liked to kill Isobel by smashing something down on her head—she had not overmuch cared for the physical contact that strangling had necessitated, and she knew the vulnerable places in a skull. The temples, or possibly the base of the neck, were the places to go for. But she could not risk it; any splintering of the skull might later be regarded as suspicious, and this was a death that absolutely must be put down to a sad accident.

She checked Isobel's vital signs meticulously as she had been taught in her training. Yes, Isobel was definitely dead. Very good, everything was going according to the plan.

She picked up the baby, who was crying with fright and bewilderment, and spent a few minutes calming her down. She sponged the tears away, and because she still did not know which of the twins this was she unfastened the little jacket, and saw that there was a large surgical dressing on the right-hand side, covering most of the ribcage and shoulder. Then this was Sonia. Would she keep that name for her? She thought she would; the child might already be recognizing it, and Roz rather liked it.

Don't cry, Sonia; from now on you're going to be mine. You're going to live with me—we're going away together tomorrow morning—the world's our oyster, really—and I'll look after you, and you'll be such a privileged little girl. We can deal with that surgical dressing on our own; I can take out stitches so that they don't hurt a bit, and I can look after you. And when you're older I'll tell you all the stories about my family, and sing you the songs my aunt taught me, and you'll get to know the people in the stories so well they'll be like your real family.

She found Isobel's keys, which were in a handbag in the kitchen, and then she wrapped Sonia up as warmly as possible, and picked her up, remembering to be careful of the dressing over the operation wound. But as she carried Sonia down to the big main hall it felt almost unbearably good to be holding this living child: Roz was wearing the thin surgical gloves she had put on before entering the house just in case the plan misfired, but she wanted to rip them off so that she could feel Sonia's soft plump little body properly. Sonia had stopped crying, and she was warm and rosy and wholly unafraid. Roz thought she was even curious about what was happening and where she was being taken. There was a clean, baby-powder and soap smell about her, and Roz had to struggle not to hug her too hard for fear of hurting her.

She put Sonia on a cushion just inside the downstairs flat, and collected what had to be collected. The cat-basket and what lay curled up inside it, and the shopping bag with the other things. The cat-basket was not particularly heavy but it was large and awkward to manoeuvre, and several times she banged it against the stair wall. Sorry, JDF, and sorry about what's ahead of you as well, but you've been dead for several days and you won't care what happens to your body.

She put JDF down in Sonia's carry-cot, and covered him with a blanket. Should she actually dress him in some of Sonia's things? No, it was not necessary. She unscrewed the small can of lawn-mower petrol she had tucked into the cat-basket, and sprinkled the contents over the carpet and curtains, careful not to get any on herself. Enough? No, perhaps a few drops should be used in the kitchen. Fires in houses nearly always started in kitchens.

She left the door of the flat open, and carefully unrolled a ball of thick string, tying the end around the door knob, and then winding the rest down the staircase, wiping the last dregs of the petrol over sections of the string as she went. It was important to be sparing with the petrol at this stage but it was also important to make sure that the string caught fire strongly enough. On the half-landing she left a little bundle of rags and newspapers.

Sonia was where Roz had left her. Roz waved to her, and it seemed that Sonia waved a little hand back, a bit uncertainly. She picked Sonia up, and with her free hand felt in her jacket pocket for the small disposable cigarette lighter she had bought. Holding Sonia firmly against her left shoulder, she used her right hand to light one of the fire-light tapers from the shopping bag. It glowed steadily and

Roz bent carefully down to set it to the string's edge. It was very thick fibrous string, thicker than parcel-string, in fact it was very nearly rope thickness, and once it caught light, it would burn steadily. There was a heart-stopping moment when she thought it was not going to catch, but then a bright flame crackled up the stairway. When it reached the bundle of rags and newspapers it flared up very strongly.

Roz did not dare wait to see any more: when the flames picked up the petrol on the first floor the whole house would go up like matchwood. With Sonia still held against her shoulder, she kicked the main door closed, and went as quickly as possible down to the drive and out on to the road.

She paused for a moment, waiting for the fire to take hold of the house properly. That was when she would know that her plan had succeeded. She stood in the deep shadow of a tree halfway along the road, watching. Please let it burn, and please let it burn *fast*—

As if responding to this last frantic thought, angry flames shot upwards into the night sky, and showers of sparks cascaded over the adjoining gardens. There was a soft whooshing sound as the fire caught stronger hold, and the timbers and old bricks began to burn in earnest. The smell of smoke and heat was filling up the entire night, and there were shouts and running feet as people came out of their houses to see what was happening. Roz stayed where she was for another moment, taking everything in. Somebody would certainly have called the fire brigade by now and the fire engines would get here quite soon, but by the time they had doused the fire and been able to get inside, the two bodies in the upstairs flat would be so badly burned they would be barely recognizable.

She turned and began to walk away, in the direction of the town. It was quite a long way, and Sonia was heavier than she had expected, but she did not mind. She would have carried Sonia for a hundred miles if she had to.

In the event, she carried her to the high street, which was still quite busy at this hour of the early evening, and went across to the big taxi rank on the far side of the town. She was an ordinary Saturday-afternoon shopper with her daughter, and—wouldn't you know it!—her daughter's pushchair had been caught by a motorbike while they were in a shop, so she had to get a taxi home. She was anonymous and ordinary, and she was one of at least a dozen fares the taxi-driver had had that day.

She would pack her things tonight, along with the things she had bought for Sonia, and in the morning she would telephone St Luke's to say that a family illness had called her away, and that she would not be at work on Monday morning. After about a week, she would write to the personnel department, tendering her resignation on family grounds, offering to forfeit her month's pay in place of working her notice. St Luke's was such a large place, it was no big deal if one of the junior nurses left unexpectedly.

She would also write to the agents she had interviewed about letting her house. She could send them a set of keys by registered post, and give them her bank details for payment of the rent they collected. Other than this, there was quite a lot of her aunt's money, and also her parents' money, all stashed in a deposit account, and the interest on it was quite good. Roz thought she could live off that, together with the rent from the house, reasonably comfortably. It would not be riches, but it would be enough for the next few years; certainly enough to rent a house somewhere. And when Sonia was a bit older, Roz could probably go back into nursing if she had to. When Sonia was a bit older... She tried the phrase out again in her mind. It felt good to look down the years and see herself with Sonia, her very own daughter, the two of them living comfortably and happily together. They would have a nice house, and Roz might even take driving lessons and try to afford a little car. It would be very useful to have a car, particularly if they lived in the country.

Roz knew she was perfectly safe and she felt entirely confident about everything. It was not very likely that a connection would be made between the macabre loss of a small baby's corpse from St Luke's Hospital, and the charred bones found in the remains of a fire in an old house at least twelve miles away. And even if it was, it would not matter because by then Roz would be out of reach. Her house would be occupied by respectable tenants, and she would be living many miles away. Under an assumed name? Yes, why not? She would open a new bank account and one connection that would certainly never be made was the one between the rather prim, rather mouselike Nurse Raffan who had never, so far as anybody knew, even had a boyfriend, and the brisk young single mother with her tiny daughter, living in—

A smile curved her lips. Living in a place called Weston Fferna, the place where once her great-aunt had lived, all those years ago. Because life's a circle, and that's where I want to be—in that place where all those tales happened. All those tales, told by an ageing woman to a small fearful child who hated the darkness and the sadness of the stories, and who was frightened by the grisly song about the hanged man in the moonlight, but who could not avoid listening.

Roz knew she had meted out a just punishment tonight, and she thought she had redressed the balance for her aunt's childhood. She had got Sonia for herself, and as far as that bitch, Melissa Anderson, was concerned, Sonia was a heap of charred bones inside a burned-out flat. Melissa would believe Sonia to be dead—she would grieve for Sonia of course, but she would not be able to instigate any inquiries because she had already told people that Sonia had died in Switzerland after the separation. She would be hoist with her own petard, and serve her right.

But Melissa would never know the truth about what had happened to Sonia. No one would ever know the truth about what had happened to Sonia Anderson.

CHAPTER TWENTY-NINE

T HERE HAD BEEN times in the house in Bolt Place when Floy's Tansy had been afraid she was going to die and no one would ever know the truth about what had happened to her.

After she had been in London for a while she found that the men always came to the house at night, just as they had done in the workhouse, so that when twilight started to fall you began to feel panicky and fearful, just as you always had done. It was terrible to find that you had not left this twilight-fear behind you after all: that it had followed you all the way to London. In stories twilight was the time when good things happened: it was a purple and violet word, full of soft scents and magic and secrets. But twilight in the house in Bolt Place was not like that in the least. It was a creeping, oozing darkness, it was black goblin-juice bleeding into the sunshine, showing up the dirt and the decay of the houses, and the poverty of the people.

The men who came to the house were mostly navvies and merchant seamen on shore leave, or men from one of the nearby street markets or abattoirs. They left their rancid body-smells in the rooms and the beds—Tansy hated this. The children in the workhouse had been taught strict cleanliness—it was next to Godliness, Mrs Beadle had said. Once a week they had had to scrub themselves at large stone troughs in a long room, and there had been bars of lye soap and bits of flannel to dry yourself on afterwards.

But the withered house did not have a bathroom of any kind; there was a pump in the yard and an earth closet at the far end of the cat-ridden garden, but these had to be shared with eight other houses and the woman who let the men into the bedrooms and took money from them said she could not be tramping up and down stairs with jugs of hot water for tarts and moppets, her back would not stand it. So most of the time it was impossible to wash the smells away; Tansy hated that, but sometimes the older girls took her to a public baths where you could immerse your whole body in water, and even wash your hair. It cost twopence each to do this, but if you were careful you could easily take twopence—sometimes a bit more—out of a man's pocket while he slept. Tansy became quite good at this after a while, because she had small, deft fingers.

Harry, reading this, felt the nod that Floy was giving in the direction of Dickens, and also Henry Mayhew. He read how, after a while, Tansy began to adopt the ways of the other girls; how she started to redden her lips with a crushed geranium petal and streak her eyelids with kohl, and he had a sudden heart-breaking image of Tansy, probably no more than eleven or twelve, already beginning to adopt the ways and the appearance of a whore.

Once, when one of the men was very drunk and sick over his own boots, one of the older girls managed to take as much as six shillings without getting caught, and six shillings was quite a lot of money. It was enough for a music hall for all of them, with a jellied-eel supper afterwards. It had to be a Sunday night, on account of the men not usually coming to Bolt Place on a Sunday, and somebody said the acts were not quite as naughty as they would have been on other nights, but it was a good outing, all the same. Tansy had been a bit bewildered at first by being in such a huge room, with so many people laughing and singing and drinking, but the others said it would make the return to Bolt Place, and the smelly rooms and rumpled beds, easier to bear, and so it had done.

But Tansy knew that even though the smells could be washed away and the men who came to her room most nights could be partly forgotten in a furtive outing to a music hall, her sins and her guilt were building up, and she was still beyond the sinful ivory gate. She was a thief and a harlot, and she was well along the path to the gall of bitterness and the bond of iniquity, and one day there would be a reckoning. It might not come until after she died, but it would come, as sure as sure.

And even if there was no reckoning in this life—even if the reckoning and the punishment were being stored up for her in the next life—she knew that the memories and the images of these years would stay with her for ever.

Extract from Charlotte Quinton's diaries:
10th August 1914
It's quite astonishing how the memories and the images stay with one down the years, so that even when one thinks they have been successfully tidied away, they occasionally jump out to disturb one in the most painful way.

Viola and Sorrel are memories that have been very constant indeed, of course; Edward has never understood that, and I have tried not to be tedious or lachrymose about my lost babies. Perhaps if there had been other children, I might have been able to forget them—*no*, not forget them, never that, but perhaps I could have *accepted* their loss a little better. But I have not conceived again, and there does not seem much prospect of it now—I have to remember I am thirty-six after all. A dismal prospect, *I* think, but—

A mere girl, says Edward indulgently. He is still quite fond when he remembers to be (which is usually on Saturday nights when it is not necessary to get up early for his office the following morning).

On the other hand, his mother (who appears to be positively indestructible and has never been fond in her whole life) points out that in Biblical calculations thirty-six is halfway to three score and ten, and therefore I am a middle-aged woman who should behave more circumspectly.

Someone (and I think it was George Eliot) said that happy women have no history. Perhaps bored women have none, either. My life has been a bit too full of ghosts to be happy but it has certainly been boring, so much so that for the last few years I have scarcely bothered to record anything in my diary. Occasional accounts of charity committees (Edward's *mother*, oh, how that evil old witch tries to regiment my life!), and luncheons with the wives of Edward's business colleagues or weekends at their homes.

These last are nearly always in houses considerably grander than our own: Edward possesses a keen sense of the social register and is v. discriminating about which invitations we should accept. These things are important in business, he says; you would not understand, Charlotte. Personally, I would not give a *hoot* where we went or how humble the company, providing people interesting or hospitable, but this is what Edward wants and I do my best to conform. And have to say, it has been extremely pleasant to stay in the houses of the wealthy, and to be part of grouse shoots and lavish dinners or trips to race-meetings, especially in the years when Edward

VII was alive, disgraceful old goat. I was seated next to him at dinner on two separate occasions (!) and have to say his style of conversation was v. racy—what Mamma would call rather *warm*—although not if Alexandra was present, of course (which was not often, poor soul). And if one has to have one's rear end stroked beneath the table while playing after-dinner bridge, suppose it might as well be stroked by the King of England as anyone else!

In complete contrast George V seems an amiable, honourable man, although will reserve judgement on May of Teck who looks a bit starchy and unapproachable.

But now, with German troops violating the neutrality of Luxembourg—which Edward says is an act of outright aggression if ever there was one—and the refusal of von Bethmann-Hollweg to pledge respect for Belgian neutrality, war has been declared between this country and Germany. We are at war—it's rather frightening, rather awe-inspiring to set those words down.

Edward says it will be all over by Christmas and probably it will, but I think I am going to start writing about this war, and about what is happening in the world. (*So* good for the character to think of things bigger than oneself—I can hear Mamma saying it!) Edward is inclined to look indulgently on the idea, and has even asked if I am hoping to become another Paston or Pepys—should not have suspected Edward of even knowing the names of Pepys or the Pastons, for to my certain knowledge he has not opened a book (except account books) for the last seventeen years. People are full of surprises.

Edward's mother is not full of surprises, though; she thinks any war a great waste of time and human life, and considers that writing about it is an even greater waste. I would be better employed in doing something useful, such as knitting balaclava helmets for our brave boys on the battlefields, as she and her mother did when we fought the Boers and the Zulus.

Cannot help thinking knitted helmets not much use to our brave boys in the kind of war currently being predicted, and would much prefer to do something more active than knitting anyway. Did not say so.

Charlotte Quinton's diaries:
10th September 1914
Once I wrote in these pages it would take a social revolution or an upheaval of unimaginable magnitude to alter people's outlooks and women's standing in the world. Now I think we may be seeing the beginning of that upheaval.

The German cavalry has already reached Ypres and Lille in France, and that makes the war suddenly seem frighteningly close. I have *been* to Lille for heaven's sake, in fact Clara Wyvern-Smith took a house there one summer and Edward and I were invited for a couple of weeks, although Edward v. grumpy most of the time, since he does not like Abroad. Personally, I always believed Wyvern-Smith's real goal was the seduction of Edward VII—he was always rather partial to France, particularly after he met Sarah Bernhardt, and he stayed at Wyvern-Smith's house more than once.

(NB. Would not be surprised if Clara W-S had achieved her aim, because let's face it, Edward VII never took much seducing.)

Asquith is predicting huge losses in men in this war, and there is much talk of what they call trench warfare, which sounds terrifying, and of the need to raise a large British army, which sounds terrifying in quite a different way. Edward is not sure that Asquith is the right man to lead the country: mark his words we shall see the Chancellor of the Exchequer, David Lloyd George, moving into the war arena before long! A good thing too, what we need in wartime is a Prime Minister with some fire and stamina, although in light of recent events, perhaps a pity Mr Lloyd George must needs have modelled this National Insurance arrangement on the German plan.

Edward quite vehement, but suspect he is secretly rather relieved that he is too old to be regarded as fit for active service. So easy to go around saying, My word, I wish I could be over there fighting those Huns, when you are forty-nine next birthday.

Edward's mother is knitting for dear life, and my Mamma is organizing charity events to raise money for all the poor young war widows that will shortly flood the country. Caroline and Diana are helping her—Caroline's husband will probably be sent to France with his regiment quite soon, so unless she goes back to live with Mamma at Weston Fferna while he is away, may have to invite her to move in here for a while.

Meanwhile, I am secretly making inquiries about the war work that the Queen is setting up for women but have not yet told anyone about this.

Charlotte Quinton's diaries:
20th September 1914
Am becoming more and more convinced that the social revolution really is beginning. The signposts

are more than half visible, not least of which is Mrs Pankhurst's current activities, although when you consider the matter, unthinkable that Mrs Pankhurst would *not* be in the forefront of any social revolution. The indomitable lady was doggedly conducting her campaign for Women's Votes from her current sojourn in prison—think this time it was for complicity in bomb outrage on Lloyd George's house, an act I never wholly understood since Lloyd George appears to me something of a social reformer on his own account what with Old Age Pensions and National Insurance and so on. Should have thought he and Mrs P practically soulmates.

But immediately war was declared Mrs P informed the government that she was prepared to cease all her militancies, and put the services of her Women's Social and Political Union at the country's disposal. The government have accepted—cannot decide if this indicates they value the energy and intelligence of the female sex in general and Mrs P in particular, or if they are just grabbing at any life-rafts that are offered. But whichever it is, they have released all ladies who were in prison for suffragist offences.

Edward views this with disapprobation, but thanks God Women's Votes unlikely to be allowed in *his* lifetime. Ladies do not understand politics, he says, and does not know what the world is coming to. I reminded him of the famous quotation about war educating the senses and calling into action the will (Emerson?—must look up exact line in public library), upon which he said I had clearly been wasting my time reading radical literature again instead of giving my mind to my proper duties, and why had he no clean socks in the correct drawer?

In the face of Mrs Pankhurst's dedication had been starting to feel quite ashamed of my own tranquil

life, but then this morning I received a letter in reply
to my request for war work. It seems that ladies all
over England want to help in this war, and the Queen
is very keen to harness all this energy, in fact she
strongly believes there is a place for today's woman
in a war. (Am rapidly revising my image of a starchy
ice-queen!)

It would, says the letter, be extremely generous of
me to devote some of my time to the war effort, and
my offer is most gratefully accepted. Convalescent
homes—partly hospitals, partly rehabilitation
centres—are being set up wherever seems appropriate for the wounded men sent home from the
Front, and there will be several in London. Nursing
is not at present a problem, but there is a sad lack
of people prepared to cope with the practicalities of
administering these places. The letter does not quite
say it is a rather mundane area of work and not one in
which heroines are likely to be made (one inevitably
remembers Florence Nightingale in the Crimea), but
it implies it, with a faint air of apology.

Have never grappled with administration of
anything on this scale but have run this house and
the servants for fifteen years, and also served on
innumerable charity committees, so feel this is something I could usefully manage. Do not think I am the
stuff heroines are made of anyway, so have agreed to
give two hours a day to helping run a large East End
centre which has been converted from an old music
hall into a hospital.

Edward is appalled, but he has just been given an
appointment in a minor War Office department (something to do with the accounting systems for supplying
the troops with food, right up Edward's street, of
course), and he is too taken up with the importance of
that to give his mind to what I am doing.

My Mamma and my sisters are twitteringly anxious about the entire project, although I suspect Caroline of being slightly envious. I always had great hopes of Caroline as a kindred spirit, but she has married a dull and conventional Army officer (just as I married a dull and conventional keeper of balance sheets), and as a result has become rather staid and matronly. And Diana's two daughters are worthy and dutiful pillars of the local church, just like Diana.

Edward's mother is shocked to her toes at my venture, and does not scruple to say that it will end in disaster. She cannot think what Edward is doing allowing his wife to go off to such a place, since ladies do not fight wars by working in East End infirmaries, in fact ladies do not fight wars at all, and all we can hope is that I will be dealing with officers rather than common soldiers. Came away from her house in a rage and said several *truly* unladylike words on way home. Felt much better for it.

Ordered several sets of new clothes—hobble skirts clearly impossible for this kind of venture, so have ordered what they are calling tailor-made outfits—plain jackets and skirts, v. practical and not at all unflattering, especially since jackets can be worn over rather fetching silk or cotton blouses. Felt even better for that, and do not see why wars cannot be fought with some semblance of style.

But clearly I have neither sympathizers nor supporters for this venture. Do not care, however; I am going ahead with it and am setting off for the disused music hall in London's East End first thing tomorrow morning.

CHAPTER THIRTY

Tansy had no idea how long she would stay in
the house in Bolt Place, but she thought it would probably be a long time. Once or twice, she wondered about
leaving and earning a living somewhere on her own, but
London seemed so vast and so noisy that it frightened her.
Since the pig-men brought her here she had never been
outside the house by herself and she did not know how
to set about finding somewhere else to live or how to get
work. One of the older girls said it was all very well to say
bravely that you were going to leave, and that you were
going to earn your own money; it was not so easy as that.
Unless you wanted to sleep in the street you had to find a
room, even if it was only what they called a two-pair back,
and the only work you were likely to get was as a skivvy,
perhaps in a tavern. But the wages for work like that were
cruel and the hours even crueller.

There was street-selling—flowers or watercress or
bootlaces—but you had to have a few shillings to buy your
stock, and you were out in all weathers, and even if you
made a penny or two there was always the rent to find.
Leastways in here you were sure of your room and a bit of
bread and meat or a kipper to your supper, and cheerful

company. Tansy was feeling a bit glum, that was all. How about planning a treat? They could all lift a few coppers from tonight's visitors and treat themselves to the music hall again on Sunday? They might go to Dancy's this time; it was only just down near the River.

Dancy's, thought Harry, his mind detaching from Floy's story for a moment. It's the first time he's used any actual place names—except Bolt Place, which could be anywhere. Was Dancy's a real place, I wonder? One of the dozens of little halls and supper-rooms that flourished in London in those days? How could I find out?

Tansy had worn a blue cloak on the outing to Dancy's—one of the girls had given it to her—and she thought she looked nice, but she had not enjoyed the evening very much. She had liked the other music hall to which they had gone even though it had been so noisy and hot, but Dancy's was different. There were one or two acts with people singing or dancing, but the evening seemed to be given over mostly to what were called speciality acts. 'Freak show,' said the girl who had advised Tansy not to run away from Bolt Place. 'People lap it up, but *I* think it's cruel on the poor things. I don't think I'd have come if I'd known they were doing that tonight.'

Tansy would not have come either. She sat quietly in her seat, her eyes on the small lit stage, and tried to shut out what she was seeing. First there were midgets—small men and women—who danced and capered about, and this was not too upsetting because the midgets seemed lively and cheerful, and when the audience shouted things to them they shouted back, grinning hugely and making rude gestures with their hands. After this were two people with the man skeletally thin and the woman monstrously fat, and this was not too upsetting either. They sang the song about Jack Sprat Could Eat No Fat, His Wife Could Eat No Lean. Tansy knew the song; it was one she and the other children sometimes used to sing.

But then came a man who was announced as the 'Half Man of the World'—he had no legs and a very short torso so that he really did look as if he was only half a man. He was grotesque and pitiful, and there was a pretend-thing of sawing him in half on a table which Tansy found dreadful although most of the people around her were laughing and calling out encouragement.

Last of all were two girls who were introduced as Siamese twins—their bodies were joined together at the waist. Even from where she sat near the back of the long room, Tansy could see that they were very young, not much older than Tansy herself, and that they were very pretty, with sweet faces and bright eyes and smiling mouths. Their arms were around one another the whole time, and they sang a song about All the World's in Love with Love, which everybody joined in and which was so lovely you wanted to dance around the room to it, and then they sang one called Three Little Maids from School Are We.

They had beautiful voices, sweet and clear; Tansy thought they sounded like birdsong in the early morning. While they were singing they might just have been two ordinary girls, but when they had finished singing they performed a dance, and Tansy had to clench her fists and bite her lip so as not to cry, because it was unbearable to see them moving so crookedly and awkwardly, with everyone watching. Until then she had thought the man who was only half a man had been the worst thing she had ever seen, but she thought these two pretty girls doing this ugly, distorted dance was the most pitiful and tragic sight in the world.

Twins, thought Harry, staring down at the page. Conjoined twins—what Floy's time would have called Siamese twins. That's an extraordinary coincidence to come upon.

On the way back to Bolt Place Tansy and the others had bought bags of jellied eels and winkles to eat. The other girls thought they had had a real good evening out, but Tansy had hated it.

Tansy's creator had hated it as well. Floy, using the character of the older girl who had befriended Tansy, said that once upon a time, and not so long ago a time as all that, deformities had been accepted; such unfortunates had been part of the community, and every village had had its idiot, or its holy fool. Accepted. Tolerated. Even, occasionally, venerated. Because earlier ages had been more used to Nature's mistakes, was that? Or simply because people had been more tolerant? Whichever it was, it was undeniable that the nineteenth century, and even the brave new world of the twentieth, was cruel and venal. It no longer accepted these flawed creatures as part of ordinary life; it put them on show, and it exploited them unforgivably.

Harry considered this premise and found it fairly sound, although not absolutely watertight, because exploitation had always existed all through history. But at least the twenty-first century, with its sleek, slick surgical technology, did not deal in freak shows. Or did it? Well, of course it does, you cretin, said his mind at once. Nature still gives the occasional vicious tweaks to the human race, and every time it happens the media fight to get pictures and make TV documentaries of them. A year or so back there had been a man in America who had sold video rights to the operation to separate his twin daughters, and then had used the money to buy drugs.

Floy had hoped the world had been changing for the better, but Harry was not sure that it had. We still sightsee nature's mistakes, he thought. We still pry and snoop, and get a vicarious kick out of human tragedy. And I'd better stop feeling smug because I'm not much better myself, in fact if I had a dram of decent feeling I'd kick Markovitch and the *Bellman* into the gutter where they belong and refuse to have any more to do with this Anderson-Marriot story. Because there isn't a story, not any longer. Sonia died abroad, it's as simple as that.

But he would continue with Floy's book, because he was intrigued by Floy, who had lived in the tall, thin Bloomsbury house—the house that Simone Marriot had been so strongly drawn to—and who had created this odd heroine-waif in his book, and written with such passion about the appalling cruelties meted out to pauper-children.

And about the exploitation of freaks in late-nineteenth or early-twentieth century music halls.

Charlotte Quinton's diaries: 15th October 1914
Antwerp has fallen, also Zeebrugge, and we are getting casualties from the Ypres battles. Some of their wounds are *dreadful*, and some are wounded in their minds as well—do not think doctors entirely understand this. But it is starting to be clear that this war is not going to be the death or glory business the poets write about, or the heroes of literature and myth make stirring speeches over. Perhaps no war ever is, and perhaps poetry and literature will take on a different flavour when this is over. If ever it is over. Edward is still insisting that it will be over by Christmas, but even he is sounding a bit doubtful, and I suspect he does not entirely believe it any longer.

My work at the convalescent centre is something of a housekeeper's role—partly overseeing the paying of bills and receiving of governmental funds that do not always reach us when they should—but mostly taken up with ordering supplies and ensuring that the kitchens keep proper accounts and records. It is a little daunting trying to feed so many people, but we buy huge ham bones and vegetables to make really nourishing soup, and bake our own bread (Mrs Tigg has given me several excellent recipes for this, and I have persuaded her to come to the centre every Monday to help out). We also try to get chickens to make broth for the weaker men; there are several chicken-farmers not too far out of London who will supply us.

But sometimes I go into the long room which is now the main ward, and which was once a raucous cheerful place of entertainment, and see if there are any little commissions I can undertake for the men. I write letters for them to their wives or sweethearts, and read the replies if they cannot read them for themselves. The letters—and the replies—are almost always heartbreakingly sad.

Today one of the men, who had been blinded by a shell explosion, felt fumblingly for my hand, and when he had found it, held it hard and said, 'You have the most beautiful voice in the world, Mrs Quinton,' and I came home and howled into my pillow for the sheer pity of it all.

18th October 1914
Today we heard that the main British force has been moved to Flanders, and that although Zeebrugge and Ostend look like falling to the German armies, the British are determined to keep hold of Calais.

Tomorrow more men are expected from Ypres. Somebody said the man escorting them home was a conscientious objector—devoutly hope not, since he will create no end of trouble among the soldiers who will jeer and hand out white feathers if they can find any. But then someone else said, no, it was one of the stretcher-bearers. Rather a mystery.

20th October 1914
It is not a mystery at all, and the man is very definitely not a conscientious objector, in fact if he had been only a few years younger, he would certainly have been in the front line, fighting the Prussian armies with every fibre of his being.

He came into the room where I usually work in the mornings, wearing an aged herringbone coat with a hem that trailed carelessly on the ground, looking as if he needed a haircut and a shave and a bath.

It was nearly fifteen years since I had seen him and although he was older, just as I was older, beneath the ragged unkemptness he had not altered so very much. He was thinner and more intense-looking, but he still had the air of a man prepared to take on the world and refuse to be defeated by it.

He stopped dead when he saw me, and the light flared in his eyes, in the way it always used to. Then a faint amusement lifted the corners of his mouth, as if he might be thinking: I should have known you'd do something like this. I stared at him, unable to speak (in fact I had to grip the sides of a table to stop myself from falling down), and after a moment he said, 'Charlotte,' making it a statement. 'What the devil are you doing here?' His voice was exactly as I remembered it: smooth and soft, but with the remembered spikiness underlying it.

'The same as you, Floy,' I said. 'Fighting the war.'

In two strides he was across the room and I was in his arms, and the fifteen years—the dull, struggling years of trying to be Edward's wife, and trying to be conventional and well-behaved—melted into nothing.

There were a number of theatre museums in London—the best-known was housed in Covent Garden's old flower market—and there were also a great many people listed in the various phone books who described themselves as theatrical historians. It was impossible to know how much reliance to place on these descriptions, but they would all have to be checked. On top of all this there was a plethora of bookshops in and around the St Martin's Lane area who dealt in theatrical memorabilia.

Harry made careful lists, and began working systematically through them. Finding an East End music hall ought, in theory, to be a breeze, in fact compared with chasing the Holy Grail or the White Unicorn or discovering the drowned city of Lyonesse, it ought to be child's play. The trouble was that Dancy might never have actually existed, and even if he had existed and had owned or run a music hall in London's East End, the place would have been demolished years since. Between looters and developers, to say nothing of the German Luftwaffe, the rubble of Dancy's Hall would lie beneath the concrete foundations of some ugly office-block. Lancelot and Gawain and the rest of their gang had had it easy when you remembered they only had to get on a horse and ride vaguely around Logres until a descending cloud or a vision pointed them in the right direction. Then all they had to do was embrace celibacy for a while, possibly along with poverty and extreme deprivation, and the Grail materialized in their hands.

On this last thought, Harry broke off his quest to deal with several phone messages left on his voice-mail. There were really only two that needed an immediate response: one was one from Rosamund Raffan, who was wondering

how his research was getting on and whether she had
been of any help, and perhaps they might meet again
to discuss it. Any night this week would suit her. It was
impossible to miss the implication that any night between
now and the Third Millennium would suit her, and Harry
decided to delay calling back.

The other message was from Angelica Thorne, who
apparently thought it would be great fun if they went to
the theatre that evening with a few friends, and then on to
a club. Since the celibacy requisite in most quests seemed
unachievable at the moment, but since poverty and deprivation were clearly beckoning from the near horizon,
Harry rang Angelica back to accept.

Charlotte Quinton's diaries:
22nd October 1914
So after all is said and done, I have resumed my
harlot status. I am a sinner and a fornicator and an
adulteress, and a war is raging half across Europe
with people dying wholesale, and I have never been
happier in my life.

When I said all this to Floy, lying in the upstairs
room of his house in Bloomsbury—so dear and so
familiar and welcoming, that house!—he laughed and
said, Did I honestly mean to tell him I had been abid-
ingly faithful to Edward for the last fourteen years?

Well, I have not been faithful to Edward, of course,
but there is a difference between unfaithfulness with
the body (which do not think necessarily counts
so very much), and unfaithfulness with the mind
(which, as I see it, counts very deeply indeed).

So I said to Floy that I had been unfaithful to
Edward once or twice (actually it was six times, unless

you count the sweet young boy at Clara Wyvern-Smith's that time, and that was only one afternoon when everyone else was out shooting, and in any case he was a virgin, poor child, and embarrassingly grateful afterwards, so do not really feel it qualifies).

'But I don't suppose,' I said to Floy, 'that you have precisely lived the life of a monk these past years?'

'I have not.'

'I thought not,' I said, a bit waspishly. 'It's practically a religion with you, isn't it, seducing unwary females?'

Floy said, 'Some to Mecca turn to pray, and I towards thy bed, Yasmin.'

'Oh rot,' I said. 'You pray to books if you pray to anything. Your own and other people's.' I turned my head on the pillow to look at him. We were lying in the big wide bed in the room that looked down on the jostling London streets, and his hair was an untidy tumble of black silk against the white sheets. There was a faint sheen of perspiration on his skin from the frantic love-making earlier on, and I loved him so much that I was not sure if I could bear it. So I said, in a much gentler voice, 'Tell me about the war.'

His expression changed at once, so swiftly that it was as if a light behind his eyes had been abruptly snuffed out.

'Charlotte, it's going to be appalling. It's dreadful now, but it's going to become much, much worse. I don't think there's ever going to be another war like this one.' He paused, and I waited. 'Officially I'm attached to Reuters, although I've sent stuff to the *London Gazette* and *Blackwood's* on my own account, but it all means I've been allowed very near to the front lines of battle. Sometimes I've been near enough to help with the casualties—there're some conscientious objectors doing a lot of that work, did you know?'

'No.'

'I helped a bit where I could,' he said. 'Especially after they moved the main British force to Flanders—you knew about that?'

'Yes.' I had been able to follow quite a lot of the war's progress, reading articles in *The Times*, talking to some of the men brought to the centre, even listening to some of the things Edward brought home from his work in the War Office. The thought of Floy going into the thick of it all, helping to carry the wounded or the dead into the Red Cross huts, sent a panic-stricken pain through my body.

'I've seen so much in these last months,' he said. 'And all of it bad. The Ypres battles— They're so impossibly young, those soldiers. That's one of the most heartbreaking things, their youth and their—the only word I can think of is *innocence*. None of them have any idea of what they're going into, you know. They walk out of their homes—they walk away from all the familiar things of their lives. Meadows and country lanes and perhaps sweethearts. And they're going from that into a—a darkness. Battles and fear and pain. Half of them end up drowning in mud that's like thick, evil-smelling ooze, with machine guns relentlessly spitting in their faces.' He moved restlessly in the bed, as if pushing the nightmare images away. 'I keep seeing those boys, Charlotte. I keep seeing them walking down country lanes with primroses in the fields and bluebells in the woods, perhaps singing one of these cursed jingoistic songs as they go. And all the time having not the least idea that they're probably marching straight into their own squalid deaths.'

When Floy talks like this, it's dreadfully easy to visualize it all: the spoiled fields, and the fierce rainstorms that turn the battlefields into swamps. It's dreadfully easy to see those boys dying in pain and terror, with people and horses screaming all round them, and mud trying to suck them down, and blood puddling everywhere from the dead and dying...

But I listened without interrupting, and I thought: one day he will write this all down and it will be a kind of purging for him, in the way that nearly all his writing is a purging. I did not say this because there are areas of Floy's mind where it is never possible to venture—just as I suppose there are areas in anyone's mind where it is never possible to venture. I let him talk, and held him against me, and we made love again, this time more quietly but with such intensity that I wept for sheer joy and love, and afterwards we went downstairs and ate a meal from the food he had bought in one of the street markets near the hospital centre that morning. Beautiful fresh mushrooms and cheese, and there were a dozen eggs and a slab of butter on the marble slab in the deep larder downstairs. We beat everything up into an omelette which we cooked over the stove, and ate it at the kitchen table with wedges of crusty bread, thickly spread with butter. Should like to see Edward cooking omelette or anything else and should like to see him eating at a kitchen table as well!

While we ate he said he would probably sell this house: the government were asking for properties in London so that numerous war departments could be set up.

'You'll hate losing it,' I said. 'You love this house. So do I.'

'Yes. I will hate it.' He smiled at me. 'But I shan't give it away, Charlotte, I'm not that altruistic. And there will be other houses when this is all over.'

Other houses. Did he mean he and I would share one? And when the war ended, would that be the time that I could finally leave Edward?

Deeply thankful that Edward presently in the north, organizing his interminable lists of wartime supplies. Could not have faced Edward tonight— could not have faced anyone tonight.

I left Floy and walked home slowly through the gathering twilight, my mind in turmoil.

CHAPTER THIRTY-ONE

Harry SAT AT the dining table of his flat, and stared at the foxed, ragged-edged playbill spread out in front of him.

He had spent the last week searching for evidence of Dancy's Music Hall, and in that time he had met Dickensian-visaged gentlemen who kept obscure bookstores in curious little pockets of London and who wore fingerless gloves like Uriah Heep; earnest librarians who offered specialist search services; bright-voiced girls who clearly had no idea of the stock they were selling and wanted him to go on our mailing list, it's really good; and several sharp-eyed salesmen who attempted to talk him into attending pseudo-sounding auctions for dubious-looking *belles lettres* and questionable first editions.

He had hunted through what felt like hundreds of boxes of old theatre programmes, drawers-full of sepia postcard prints of actors and actresses from the Naughty Nineties and the Roaring Twenties and all the years between, and had sifted innumerable stacks of old and extremely dusty playbills.

And then, just when he had been on the verge of giving the whole thing up—you could only take quests so far, for pity's sake!—in a little narrow street near to St Martin's Lane he had found the rather grimy bookshop with its 'All books £1' table hopefully positioned outside its squeezed-up façade. Inside, amidst turgid autobiographies of Victorian actor-managers and colourful memoirs of ladies who had acted with Irving and played with Tree, had been a cardboard box which had once contained baked beans and was now full of old music hall programmes.

Hardly daring to hope for anything any longer—you did not expect to discover the very fragment of the past you wanted inside an old baked-bean carton—Harry had knelt down to sort rather perfunctorily through the contents. And there, halfway through, had been the single tattered sheet announcing Matt Dancy's Music Hall, London's Finest Supper Club, Every Sunday night a Dazzling Array of Speciality Acts. The paper was brittle with age and frighteningly fragile and shreds of it flaked off it as he lifted it out.

There was no address for the hall; Harry supposed that would be too much to hope for, and the playbill had probably been given out to people who were already inside Matt Dancy's Music Hall. But if there was no address there was a list of acts.

The Lilliputs—a family of midgets from Germany—were billed as dancing, singing acrobats, and after them had come the 'Living Skeleton', weighing just over four stone, and his wife, the Fattest Woman in Europe, who weighed an incredible forty-five stone. They were called Peter Robinson and Bunny Smith, and they sang nursery rhymes. Nursery rhymes. Such as, Jack Sprat Could Eat No Fat…?

There was a Half Man as well: billed simply as 'Mr Johnnie', but described as having a body that ended just below the waist. Harry, reading this last, was aware of strong repulsion at the faint whiff of prurience that came up from the words.

Last of all, in what had probably been regarded as the equivalent of star-billing, were listed two sisters—'The Gemini Songbirds'. This was printed in an elaborate typeface, larger than the other names, and was adorned with many printer's flourishes and curls. Beneath it were the names of the Gemini Songbirds.

They had been called Viola and Sorrel.

Viola and Sorrel. Harry sat back on his heels, no longer aware of the tiny bookshop with its wares spilling over on to the floor, and the musty shelves filled with nameless publications.

Viola and Sorrel. And Floy had dedicated *The Ivory Gate* to 'C' and to Viola and Sorrel. It was an enormous leap of faith to think he had found Floy's Viola and Sorrel, but surely there could not have been two sets of girls with those names in that era. But did this mean that Floy's Viola and Sorrel had been Siamese twins, performing in what sounded to be a fairly seedy music hall?

At last he got up, paid for the purchase of the playbill, which was £7.50, watched jealously as the proprietor slid it into a manila envelope, and went back out into the hustle of the Soho streets, the envelope clutched in his hands. By the time he got back to his flat he was wholly unable to remember precisely where the bookshop had been.

He rooted out an old photograph frame that was about the right size, discarded the unimportant contents of it (himself and Amanda at some meaningless charity bash), and put the playbill in so that it would be protected by the glass. Then he sat looking at it for a very long time, almost as if by doing so he could draw from it the essence of those long-ago people. Viola and Sorrel. OK, so where do I go from here? How do I go about finding some more?

And why bother? demanded his mind sneakily, kicking in with its opinions as usual. What's the point? No point at all. Aha, said his mind: Simone Marriot again? Oh, shut up, said Harry to the annoying voice, getting up to reach for *The Ivory Gate* in case there were any more pointers leading back to the past. He might as well finish it in any case.

Floy wound up the story of his small sad heroine neatly and satisfactorily. He gave Tansy a happy ending—at least, he gave the reader the strongest possible hint that a happy ending finally awaited her. Harry was absurdly pleased at this.

One of the children—a boy called Anthony with whom Tansy had grown up in the fearsome old workhouse-cum-orphanage, and who had made brief appearances in the early years in a supporting role—had left the orphanage and come out into the world. He had done so to find work, but also, it appeared, to find Tansy, and there were a couple of quite tense chapters telling how the boy—now a young man of twenty or so—had scoured the twilit half-world of the greedy brutish men who stole children for brothels. Inevitably his search had brought him to the house in Bolt Street, and inevitably when he got there it was just after Tansy—by now sixteen or so—had summoned up sufficient courage to walk out, and had found work in a small flower shop near Covent Garden. Out through the deceiving ivory gate at last and forging a new life among the flowers and the sweet-scented flowering herbs. Violets and wood sorrel. What else? thought Harry.

But Tansy's new life was to include Anthony, of course, and with help from the older girl who had befriended Tansy in Bolt Place, the story wound its way on to an emotional reunion. Harry, reading this scene critically, was again aware of Floy's annoyance at not being able to get his two main protagonists into bed together. No sex please, we're still in the early twentieth century, you know.

The book ended with a deeply satisfying confrontation with the rascally owner of the Bolt Place brothel, and this time there was no doubt about the writer's enjoyment; Floy had relished every syllable of his villain's ignominious end.

Tansy had seen the confrontation; she had accompanied Anthony, and she had watched as Anthony had cornered the man, accusing him, threatening him and then finally losing his temper and beating him to a pulp. Harry quite expected her to faint or succumb to hysterics, but heroines in those days—at least, Philip Fleury's heroines—appeared to be made of sterner stuff. Tansy watched it all from just inside the door, and although several times she had to cram her fist into her mouth to stop herself from crying out, she did not do anything to prevent the man's punishment. When finally he slumped back on the floor, blood trickling from his mouth, his head lying at an unnatural angle to his body, she knew that he was dead and the lines of a song that the children used to sing ran through and through her mind.

On moonlit heath and lonesome bank
The sheep beside me graze;
And yon the gallows used to clank
Fast by the four cross ways.

A careless shepherd once would keep
The flocks by moonlight there,
And high amongst the glimmering sheep
The dead man stood on air...

Harry did not recognize the lines, but he thought the meaning was clear enough. Retribution. The justifiable killing of an evil man.

And naked to the hangman's noose
The morning clocks will ring

A neck God made for other use
Than strangling in a string...

And sharp the link of life will snap,
And dead on air will stand
Heels that held up as straight a chap
As treads upon the land...

The image of the hanged man was startlingly vivid. Harry understood that Floy was saying, as clearly as if he had written it out, that the killing had been deserved; that turned over to the authorities the man would have been sentenced to death anyway. He was not sure he could subscribe to Floy's outlook but he could not fault Floy's logic.

The shock came at the end of the chapter, four pages before the end. Tansy's abductor, the man who had spun the evil, sticky spider-web network of brothels and child prostitution, was the same man who ran the music-hall with the heart-breaking speciality acts. Matt Dancy.

Charlotte Quinton's diaries:
2nd November 1914
If my mind was in turmoil after that afternoon when Floy so unexpectedly came back into my life, the feeling is a drop in the ocean compared to the soul-scalding emotion now engulfing me. Am not even sure I can write it down with any degree of coherence but if I do not do so, think I may burn up with the intensity of it.

My babies are alive. Viola and Sorrel are *alive*. And even though I have written that down on this page, and even though I have spent a long time staring at the words, I still find it difficult to accept. Had thought I would be able to record my emotions tonight and find relief in it, but I cannot; the tears are blotting the page and I must break off...

Later
Midnight, and I am still not able to find words to describe the crushing weight of emotion. But incredibly, somewhere mixed up in the confused tumble, is guilt, because I should have known, I should have *sensed* that my babies weren't dead—what kind of a mother am I that I did not know they were alive somewhere in the world! But there was the funeral that day and that heartbreaking coffin, and Edward said they had died—

Edward said they had died. That is the thought to which I keep returning.

2.00 a.m.
Am not a great deal calmer, but think am at least calm enough to try to write down all the events. (And will I one day be able to show these pages to Viola and Sorrel? The prospect terrifies me as much as it fills me with delight.) So I have wrapped a woollen shawl around my shoulders, and I am sitting at the little desk under the window. Clary (Maisie's replacement as maid-of-all-work) had lit a fire for me, and the glow from the embers is still warming the room. The light is not enough to write by though, so I have lit a small lamp and placed it on the desk. It's very quiet

outside and in here is only the measured ticking of the mantel clock and the occasional settling of coals from within the dying fire. I feel as if I'm the only person awake in the world.

Today—no, yesterday, for it is already long past midnight—began like any other ordinary day, except that no day which might contain Floy could ever be wholly ordinary. But when I went along to the hospital centre everything felt ordinary. It was cold and sharp—the kind of autumn day I love—and I took a tramcar to the centre. Edward finds it shocking that I do this, but I like tramcars; I like looking at all the people on them and wondering about their lives. Also, it is a quick and convenient way to travel across London (although rather rattly, and dusty, so I wear a motoring hat with a chiffon scarf).

Floy was at the centre ahead of me, talking to one of the men who had been in the group that he had helped bring back from France. When he saw me he came across the long room towards me, and said, without preamble, 'Charlotte, there's something you must know at once. Where can we be private?'

So we went into one of the tiny rooms that had been the performers' dressing-rooms when this was a music hall, and that is now an office, and he made me sit down, and then—unusually for Floy—seemed not to know what to say next. At last he knelt down in front of me and took my hands in his. Then he spoke, and his words sent the entire room spinning crazily around me.

'Charlotte—my dear love. It's Viola and Sorrel.'

'What about them?' I said, my heart starting to thump with apprehension.

Floy hesitated again, and then said, 'They're alive.'

At least I didn't faint or cry although have to say it
was a near thing on both counts. What I did do was
to cling to Floy's hands like some ghastly, die-away
Victorian heroine, while I waited for the room to stop
whirling madly around me. After what seemed to
be a very long time, I was able to say, 'They can't be.
There was a funeral. There was a coffin— They were
buried, Floy!' I had to break off there because I was
having a nightmare vision of the twins lowered into
their graves while they were still alive. Not dead but
only sleepeth...

'Something was buried that day,' he said, and then
seeing my expression, 'No, I don't mean anything
macabre, Charlotte. I think the coffin was probably
weighted with stones or something. But Viola and
Sorrel weren't inside it.'

'I must be dreadfully stupid, Floy, but I don't
understand—'

'I've had longer to think about this, Charlotte,' he
said. 'In fact I've had all night. Listen now, is it possible
that Edward lied to you about the twins' deaths? Is it
possible that he bribed people at the time?'

'You mean paid them to say the twins were dead?'
The room had stopped tilting like the deck of a ship
in a storm but I still felt very odd. Like being in a
dream where nothing is quite what it seems. 'He
might have done, but I don't see why.'

Floy was still kneeling in front of my chair, his
hands still holding mine. 'My poorest love,' he said
in a voice that was suddenly very gentle. 'You're so
honest, Charlotte, you're so absolutely all-of-a-piece
all the way through. Not everyone's as straightfor-

ward as you are, or as—as full of light. People have
darknesses in their natures—even I do at times. And
Edward certainly does. And he's pretentious and
shallow—he's puffed up with his own small achieve-
ments, and he thinks nothing matters so much as
possessions and social standing.'

Floy was perfectly right about this, although at that
point I ought by rights to have defended Edward.

'The birth of the twins put Edward in a dilemma,'
went on Floy. 'His vision of what he wanted for himself
and his family—his vision of how he wanted people
to perceive him—didn't include two flawed children.
Edward belongs to the pitiful section of society that
regards anyone outside the norm as an embarrassment. Even shameful. And he saw the twins as a very
great embarrassment—maybe even as a slur on his
manhood.' He gave me the sweet, infinitely intimate
smile. 'He wasn't to know they weren't his anyway,' he
said.

'No. Go on, please. Tell me it all.'

'This is all supposition,' he said, 'but I can't see how
else it could have happened. I think that as soon as the
twins were born Edward conceived the plan to put them
into an institution. But he knew that you would never
have agreed to it—'

'Of course I wouldn't!'

'Edward knew that, so he simply didn't allow the
question to arise. He told you the girls had died, paid
several people to keep quiet—doctors, nurses, church
authorities, God knows who else!—and then got the
twins away to a children's home of some kind. It's the
only possible answer, Charlotte.'

'An orphanage,' I said, staring at him. 'He put them
in an orphanage.' Against my will a dreadful image
of Mortmain House and all its darkness and sadness
rose up before my inner eye. People have darknesses,

Floy had said, but buildings also have darknesses sometimes. Had my beautiful babies been taken to a place like Mortmain?

'Floy,' I said, 'where are they now? Viola and Sorrel?' I realized I was still clutching his hands so hard that it must have been bruising him so I pulled my hands free and held on to the wooden chair-arms instead.

'They're in London,' he said. 'I haven't been able to trace exactly what happened to them—we can do that later—but they're here in London, Charlotte.'

'Where—?'

Floy's eyes were filled with the most intense compassion I had ever seen. 'They're in the hands of a man called Matt Dancy,' he said. 'Why did you jump when I said that?'

'It doesn't matter for the moment.'

'Dancy owns houses of ill-repute—'

'He owns brothels,' I said angrily. 'Whore-houses. It's not like you to use euphemisms, Floy.'

'I'm sorry. Dancy's brothels are the worst kind,' he said. 'Children and young boys. But Viola and Sorrel aren't in one of them; Dancy has other interests, Charlotte. He puts on music-hall shows.'

I looked at him blankly. 'The twins couldn't be in a music hall, Floy. They're *children*! They're fourteen!'

'Dancy's put them in a freak show,' said Floy, and that was when the sick darkness came down again, and this time I really did faint.

5.30 a.m.

It's barely light outside, but I can hear Mrs Tigg and Clary moving around downstairs—there's the chink of crockery and the rasping of the stove being raked out. In about an hour—perhaps a little longer—I will go downstairs and there will be a pot of tea made and they will give me a cup. Mrs Tigg will exclaim to see me up and about so early, and blame it on this nasty war, upsetting Christian ladies so that they can't sleep properly in their beds, and why not let me bring a nice breakfast tray up to your room, mum.

At least a merciful Providence has decreed Edward is still away, compiling his inventories for the army. I have absolutely no idea how I am going to face Edward after this, in fact I have absolutely no idea how I am going to be able to go on living as Edward's wife after this. I can forgive a great many things, but if Floy's suspicions are proved right I can never, *never* forgive Edward.

I have no idea what I shall do next, but I know I am going to find my babies, I *am*.

If Floy had administered a shock to his twenty-first-century reader by naming Matt Dancy as Tansy's abductor, he had kept the biggest shock of all to the very end.

Double whammy, thought Harry, staring down at the closing pages of *The Ivory Gate*, reading for the fifth or sixth time how Tansy and Anthony had taken a final journey together, not quite hand-in-hand into the sunset, but not far off.

It was a journey Tansy had never thought to make and it was a journey she would never, left to her own devices, have made. But Anthony had wanted to do it; he had wanted to chase away any lingering ghosts for them both so Tansy had agreed.

They had travelled on a train, which was an adventure all by itself, and at the station they had hired a pony and trap— Tansy had been proud of Anthony, who knew about things like this, and who knew that even though you paid people for this kind of journey you always gave them a penny or two over the cost. The man had doffed his cap as they got down, and said, Bless you, guv, you're a toff.

The trap had taken them through the winding lanes with fields on both sides, and along to the four cross-ways with the little pointy signpost so that if you were a stranger you would know which road to take. They slowed down to take the left-hand road, and Tansy caught sight of the church across the fields.

There were a lot of trees now—tall dark shapes standing up against the sky, like sentinels guarding the way to the past... Because the past is a place you should never seek to enter: you should leave it alone and you should leave its ghosts to walk their sad dusty mansions by themselves...

But there was one mansion that you would never be able to leave alone, because your mind would pull you back to it over and over—

The trap jolted its way around the last curve of the road, and there ahead of them, brooding on its hillside, was the place where Tansy and Anthony and the other children had lived for all those harsh, sad years.

Mortmain House.

Mortmain House...

Harry closed Floy's book and sat motionless for a long time. So Floy had known about Simone's nightmare mansion. He had known about the place Simone had photographed when she was a child. And Viola and Sorrel had been real people, and Matt Dancy had been real, as well. What about Tansy? Had Tansy been real?

After a moment he reached for the phone and dialled

the number of Simone's flat. It was annoying to find that she was not in, and it was impossible to explain all of this to an answerphone. In the end he simply left a message saying he had disinterred some quite interesting information about the Bloomsbury house, and perhaps they could meet for a drink so that he could tell her what he had found.

CHAPTER THIRTY-TWO

Roz SUPPOSED IT had been a bit childish and a bit melodramatic to scrawl that macabre message on the photograph of Mortmain House, but it had given her a good deal of satisfaction to do it. You had to seize opportunities as they arose and the opportunity that had arisen to get inside the stupid pretentious gallery and deliver a psychological blow to Simone had been too good to ignore.

She had gone out to Thorne's on her next off-duty day, deliberately waiting until late morning when the streets would be crowded and she would be unnoticeable. She still had Rosie's cunning to draw on if the occasion required it!

She had consulted the *A-Z* to find the exact location of Thorne's, but in the end it was quite easy. It was quite a busy area, and there were a lot of shops and little restaurants and coffee places, which was good because it meant no one would give Roz a second look. The house, when she found it, was nicer than she had expected it to be: one of the elegant Georgian buildings you saw in the classier parts of London. That would be down to Angelica Thorne, of course, although Roz did not care to think how the little whore had got her claws on the money!

The gallery itself was pretty much as she had expected: meaningless, over-priced pictures and photographs pretending to be great art. But what she had not expected was the huge surge of emotion that engulfed her when she saw Simone. It was just after one o'clock, and Simone came out of Thorne's and went quickly along the street. She was wearing a long dark-coloured trenchcoat and she had wound a vivid amber-coloured scarf around her neck. The sunlight caught her hair so that it glinted with red lights like copper wires, and she walked with an eager step as if she found life good and as if she expected good things to be waiting for her everywhere.

Roz stared at her from the half-concealment of a shop doorway, and felt as if something had slammed a clenched fist into the pit of her stomach. This, then, was how Sonia would have looked if she had lived to grow up. This was what Sonia would have grown into. For a moment Sonia was with her again, in that cosy world they had shared, all-in-all to one another, as they had been since Sonia was a baby. Roz had seen to Sonia's every need during those years, teaching her all her lessons, protecting her from a world that might have been cruel to her, devising exercises to help strengthen her legs and her back—Sonia would never have been able to walk with Simone's happy hopeful step, of course.

She had returned to Thorne's the following day, doing so in the afternoon this time, moving from shop to shop, buying a newspaper in one place, having a cup of tea in another, but keeping Thorne's in her sight all the time. The lights were on inside the place until quite late, and it was just on seven when she began to think she really could not linger very much longer. And then Angelica Thorne—unmistakable figure to anyone who had ever read a newspaper or watched TV!—came out, leaving the street door unlocked. Roz had time to notice that Angelica was dressed up like a Piccadilly tart, but she gave Angelica only the most cursory of glances, because her heart was pounding with sudden anticipation. Was Simone in the house on her own, then? It seemed probable. Angelica hailed a taxi—no tubes or buses for *that* lazy little madam!—and Roz walked briskly across the street and stepped inside the door of the gallery. If anyone was there she would say she was looking at the pictures— Oh— Was the gallery not still open to the public at this hour? And even if Simone saw her it would not matter, because Simone had never seen Roz.

But everywhere was quiet, and after a moment Roz went up to the second floor. And there, facing her, had been the monochrome photograph of Mortmain House and whatever else you might want to say or think about Simone Anderson—Simone Marriot—you would have to admit that she had captured the exact atmosphere of despair and secrecy of the place.

She had felt Sonia's presence as she rummaged in her bag for her lipstick and wrote that message—*The Murder House*, with, beneath it, *Sonia*, like a signature. That would make the bitch writhe! Roz had felt very close to Sonia in that moment; fanciful and stupid, of course—Sonia was dead, and the bitch who had killed her was walking freely about London, carving out a career for herself, making friends, making money. The unfairness of it welled up in a scalding hurting flood, because this murderous harpy had gone unpunished for too long. Retribution, remember that? Thou shalt give life for life, that was what the Bible said, clearly and unequivocally, and it even dotted the *i*'s and crossed the *t*'s by adding that you could take an eye for an eye and a tooth for a tooth and a hand for a hand if you were so inclined. Roz had learned it all in her aunt's house, and it was a good feeling to know she had Old Testament approval for what she was doing.

But when you boiled it down what she was planning was an execution, perfectly justified. Simone had killed

Sonia, she had committed a murder, and people who committed murders must forfeit their own lives.

You cannot murder a ghost, but nor can you ever really escape a ghost, either.

Simone had tried very hard not to think about the ghosts while she was away from London, and on the whole she was pleased with the results of her trip. She had discovered a working Arkwright loom in a very good museum near to Preston and the curator had been helpful about letting her photograph it. She had stayed in the area for a couple of days, booking into a small pub, and the curator had taken her out to dinner on the second night.

Next morning she had driven back through the Midlands, just because it was a different route, enjoying the glimpses of the old iron and steel foundries from the motorway. It had been raining quite heavily with a misty drabness everywhere so that Simone had the feeling of having stepped back into a Lowry painting. Rain and greyness and the feeling of a treadmill—clocking-on at eight and clocking-off again at five, part of a huge relentless machine...

On an impulse she had taken the motorway exit into Stoke-on-Trent: sometimes called the Potteries, home of good china and ceramic—Wedgwood and Royal Doulton and Minton—but also home of Anna of the Five Towns. She had wandered around for the better part of the afternoon, and got several terrific shots of old kilns and cooling towers.

Delaying reaching home? her mind had said, sneakily, at one stage. Putting off the time when you have to go back into Thorne's, and when you have to wonder who left that message on the Mortmain shot? Of course not. Liar, said the voice. You know what you've got to do when you get home, don't you? I'm not listening, said Simone to the voice.

She reached London in the early evening, and drove straight to Thorne's. There was no on-street parking, but there was a narrow side street a few yards along where you could sometimes get a space in the evenings if you were lucky. Simone got one tonight and carried her cameras and light-meters and tripods into the main gallery. She unlocked the street door, remembering to disable the alarm when she got in, and then locked the door behind her.

There was a message on her voice-mail from Harry Fitzglen. Simone had forgotten what a nice voice he had. He was phoning to let her know that he had found out one or two intriguing bits of information about a previous owner of the Bloomsbury house. He thought she would be interested in what he had found—was there any chance of them meeting for a drink to talk about it?

There was no reason not to respond to this call, which was a business thing as much as anything else. Simone was still keen on the idea of a display showing the Bloomsbury house's past; potential customers would like it and it would make a good talking point for casual callers. She scribbled down Harry's number; she would definitely phone him in the morning. It was rather a friendly thing to come home to his voice and his invitation.

She went slowly back downstairs. What now? Should she simply leave her stuff here and go home? There would be a lot to do tomorrow—she was interested to see how the Arkwright loom shots had come out on the film. She ought really to go straight home and have something to eat and an early night. Stupid, said her mind: you know quite well what you're going to do now. Why don't you just get on with it? Simone frowned, and then after a moment went across the main gallery to the back of the building.

The Bloomsbury house had a big square kitchen which was slightly below ground level, so that even on a sunny day it was rather dark. At this time on an autumn evening it was very dark indeed. Leading off the kitchen, down six shallow steps, was an old larder, and it was this larder that Simone had annexed for a darkroom. It was a cool oblong-shaped place, windowless and with a stone floor and unplastered walls. There was a deep old sink at one end, and wide, marble-topped shelves all round the walls which had probably been used for storing churns of milk and wheels of cheese. It meant there was masses of room for the enlarger and the guillotine that Simone used for cropping and trimming prints, and for the stop-bath and the baths for developing fluid and fixer. The renovations had had to include new electrical wiring, which had been expensive and messy, but it had meant that power and light could be installed in the scullery. If you had wanted a tailor-made darkroom you would not have got one much better than this.

She closed the door, and switched on the main overhead light, and after a moment she opened a small drawer and reached inside.

She had tried very hard to accept her mother's explanation about Sonia's presence in Mortmain that day—that there was some sort of telepathic link between Simone and Sonia and that it was something that had lingered on, even years after Sonia's death. If you wanted proof of an after-life, Mother had said, here it was, and she had looked so shiningly happy at this idea that Simone had never been able to say anything to spoil it for her, not then and not since. And it was true that when they went back to

Mortmain there had been no trace of Sonia. Nothing here, you see, Mother had said, reassuringly.

But Simone knew there had been something in Mortmain that day—something that had seemed alive and ordinary and that had talked to Simone and led her through the bleak echoing corridors of Mortmain. Something that had screamed as it fell into the echoing blackness of the well, and something that had returned to her in dreams ever since, scrabbling vainly at the bricks of an ancient well-shaft in an attempt to climb out...

And whether it had been Sonia or only Sonia's ghost, Simone had left her to die all alone down there in the dark.

At the time it had not seemed like that. At the time it had felt as if Simone had stayed in the dreadful room for a very long time and had done all she could to rescue Sonia.

She had scrambled to the edge of the well after Sonia fell and had knelt there, peering down, panic-stricken and terrified. But however frightened she was, it was not possible to leave Sonia who might be bleeding to death, or lying there with her legs or arms broken, alive but unable to call for help. There might even be a ledge a few feet down that had broken her fall, and Simone might be able to reach her and pull her out.

As she leaned cautiously over, the sour clammy breath of the well came up into her face. She tried not to notice it, and she tried to peer inside the thick darkness. But although the light from the room trickled down a little way, showing up the brick-lined shaft and the row of iron rungs sticking out on one side like a makeshift ladder, after that solid blackness took over so that it was impossible to see more than a couple of feet down. If only there was a way of shining a light down there—

A light. The word exploded in Simone's mind. There *was* a way of shining a light, of course there was! There was her camera with the flash-attachment. She could position the camera over the well's mouth and take a photograph with the flash, and in the split-second when the flash worked she would be able to see what was at the bottom.

The leather case had still been lying on Sonia's sweater where Sonia had left it. Simone took the camera out, slinging the case over her shoulder. There were two flashbulbs left, which meant she had two chances of seeing into the well. She fitted one carefully in; it was quite difficult to do it in the dimness, but she thought she had got it properly in place.

Then she leaned out over the well's mouth again. She was quite frightened of losing her balance, but in the end she half sat down on the ground so that most of her weight was firmly on the floor. The bricks were cold and hard against her legs. Simone positioned the camera so that the shutter was facing directly downwards; it ought to be easy enough to operate it with her right hand, and keep hold of the brick wall with her left, and she did not need to be looking through the lens; she only needed to flick the shutter and look down as she did so. There would be a half-second chance and maybe even less than that, but it should be long enough to show up what was down there.

It was enough. The flashbulb exploded into a split-second of white brilliance against the darkness and then the darkness closed down again, thick and impenetrable. Simone sat back on her heels, clutching the camera, feeling trembly and a bit sick.

The dazzling flare of white light had printed itself on her vision, so that she had to blink several times before it began to fade. But also printed on her vision—on a much deeper vision than just her eyes—was something that she thought might never fade. The image of Sonia's figure, looking small and impossibly far off, lying still, and broken... Sonia's left shoulder—the one that had been a bit crooked—lying at a hideously *wrong* angle to the rest of her... Splintered sticks of bone protruding from both her legs...

But worst of all, far far worse than broken legs or smashed shoulders, was Sonia's head, lying half in and half out of a puddle of black, greasy water. Or had it been only water? Mightn't it have been blood, dark and sticky, seeping out to mix with the well-water so that you could not tell which was which...? *Because blood turns black in the darkness, didn't you know that, Simone...?* For a moment it seemed as if the whispering voices pressed in on her again. *Blood turns black in the darkness, Simone, we know all about that, you see...*

Whether it was blood or not, Sonia had fallen on to her back and her head looked as if it had been seized by giant hands and wrenched to one side. Dreadful. *Dreadful.*

That had been when Simone had tumbled across the room and, sobbing and terrified, had run through the old house and down the tanglewood path to cycle home.

There had been no real need to keep that roll of film. Mother had shone the torch down into the well later the same evening and Sonia was not there, and although the explanation was a bit weird, it should have been possible to regard the whole thing as over.

But Simone had kept the film. She had wound the camera back that night and taken the film out, being careful not to expose it to the light. Then she had tucked it at the back of her dressing-table drawer, wrapped inside a woollen scarf. She had had the first roll developed—the ones with the shots of Mortmain's exterior—and Mother had seen them and been quite impressed by them. It had been one of those shots that Simone had used in the exhibition—a vanity thing, she had said to Harry Fitzglen, but really, of course, it had been an attempt to dilute the nightmare.

They had left Weston Fferna pretty soon after that afternoon at Mortmain: Simone had thought they probably would, and she had not been in the least bit surprised when the very next week Mother had started to telephone estate agents, and talk about them being gypsies again and wonder whether it might be better for Simone if they moved nearer to London. Neither of them had actually come out and said they were leaving the place where Simone had had that creepy experience, but Simone thought they both knew that this was the real reason.

She had never told Mother that there had been a second film with two flashlit shots on it. Over the years she had often thought about destroying the roll of film from Mortmain, but she had never done so and it had gone with her when they left Weston Fferna and moved to the North London house, and then to the flat she had shared with two other girls while she was at the Slade. It was a sort of talisman in reverse; something that might, despite all the evidence, one day prove what had really happened in Mortmain that day.

Since Thorne's had come into being the film had lain in a small drawer in the darkroom. If you want to hide a leaf, you do so in a forest. If you want to hide a roll of film you do so in a photographer's studio.

Simone took the film from the drawer, and looked down at it for a moment. Then, in the crimson glow from the filter-light, the light that was like the light in her nightmare, she began the developing process.

In the early days of photography primitive people had found it a frightening process; they had believed that the camera had the power to steal souls and they had shied away from it in terror. In a curious distorted echo of this, some psychic researchers held the theory that supernatural entities could be caught on film, although they more often utilized the process to unmask fakes rather than to prove the existence of ghosts.

Simone had never ceased to be fascinated by the gradual forming of pictures on blank surfaces, and even though she understood the chemical processes by now, there were times where it still seemed almost magical. It seemed magical tonight as she bent over on the workbench, waiting for the images to lift themselves out of the paper.

The first two—the ones taken just outside Mortmain, pointing upwards—had come out surprisingly well. Simone studied them for a moment. Yes, they had clarity and lots of contrast, and from a technical point of view they were not at all bad.

She turned to the next one, which was the one she had taken just inside Mortmain's central hall. Here were the shadows and the rotting staircase... And the ornate plasterwork of the crumbling stone arch... Simone's heart skipped a beat, and then resumed an uneasy pitter-patter. There's something there; something on the right-hand side, just on the edge of the field of vision. She bent over the workbench, narrowing her eyes. Yes, there it was: a definite blur of colour, as if something had suddenly darted across the camera's range. Something that had been wearing a cherry-red sweater, but that had moved so fast the camera had not been able to capture it. Like a smudged fingerprint, like your own reflection in a steamed-up bathroom mirror. Simone stared at this out-of-focus shape for several moments, then turned to the final one.

This is it, she thought, uncomfortably aware that her throat was dry from nervousness. This is the moment when I crawled on to that evil-smelling brick parapet and pointed the camera straight down. The flash lit up the whole well-shaft like a spear of lightning, and I saw her lying down there—Sonia. But am I going to see her now?

The well-shaft came sharply and distinctly into focus; it looked like a long narrow tunnel, lined with dry black bricks. And there at the bottom lay a small, broken figure, jagged bones sticking up from both the legs, the head twisted around in that sickening, *wrong* angle that Simone had seen all those years ago and never really forgotten. Half of the head was turned towards the camera, one eye staring accusingly and sightlessly upwards. The other half of the head lay in a pool of clotted smeary blackness. *Because blood turns black in the dark, remember that, Simone…?*

Simone realized she had been sitting hunched over the workbench for so long that her neck muscles had cramped. She leaned back, trying to ease them, her eyes still on the photograph. The camera could lie, of course, and frequently did, but it was not lying now. Sonia had been in Mortmain that day, and she had died there—here was the proof of it. Mother had said Sonia had died soon after she was born—just after the operation to separate her from Simone—but either Mother had lied for some reason or she had not known the truth herself. Simone could not decide which was the likelier of the two. I'll have to tell her, she thought, appalled at the idea. I'll have to phone her as soon as I get home, and somehow I'll have to find a way to tell her that it really was Sonia that day and that I really did kill her.

And then a small voice said, But when you went back to Mortmain that day, Sonia was no longer there. And dead bodies don't pick themselves up and climb out of well-shafts. Sonia could not possibly have got out of the old well by herself. Simone considered this fact, and a small voice inside her mind suddenly said, Of course she couldn't have got out. But someone could have got her out.

Who?

The woman you saw in Sonia's mind. The dowdily dressed woman with brown hair and anxious hands whom Sonia had wanted to kill.

Simone had remembered the woman's face vividly, even though she had only glimpsed her through Sonia's mind. But that glimpse had stayed with her, and the woman whoever she was—had become one of the ghosts and part of the memories.

CHAPTER THIRTY-THREE

Charlotte Quinton's diaries: 10th November 1914
All these years I had kept the memory of Viola and
Sorrel as those two tiny curled-up creatures, warm
and safe and loved in their crib. It's been a good
memory, one to hold on to. But now I have to face that
the memory has changed into a nightmare, and that
it's a false memory. Viola and Sorrel were stolen away
from that safe warmth, almost certainly by Edward,
and they were taken to Mortmain House. Were they
there the day Maisie and I went to Mortmain, the
day Robyn and Anthony and the other children dealt
out their dreadful vengeance to the child-trader? The
dead man standing on air...

But whenever they were taken to Mortmain they
must have lived there for years, shut away behind
those grim walls. They would have lived as one
of the ragged orphans, nobody's children, forced
to work, to scrub or scour, or pick oakum... Oh
God, did they find any happiness at all during
those years? Did they have friends and were they
ever shown any kindness or pity? And did they
understand what was happening when they were
snatched up by the child-traders, the men Robyn

called pigs, and put into a freak show for people to pay to stare at them?

If it were not for Floy, believe I might go mad thinking about all this, or sink into a decline. And *then* Edward would regretfully put me into an institution of my own, and people would say, Oh dear, poor Charlotte, the war quite unhinged her, you know: but then of course she never really recovered from the deaths of those poor afflicted children... And Edward's *mother* would tell everyone it was a great tragedy, still, what can you expect; Charlotte never had any stamina, only look at how she never even gave poorest Edward a son... If I think about the part Edward's mother might have played in this I think I *will* go mad, because I will never believe the evil old besom was not part of the whole wicked plan!

Floy has only the sparsest of information about Matt Dancy, and what he does know comes from one of the soldiers who was in the convalescent centre for a while with shrapnel wounds. The man came back to visit one of the other patients, seemingly, and mentioned a travelling group (or should it be troupe?) of performers. The twins had sung several songs at the end, he said, but for his part he had not much enjoyed seeing them; a bit cruel, he thought it, this business of putting such unfortunates on show, although the two girls had very sweet voices. (I *know* this is being supremely illogical, but I am aware of a jealous rage every time I think of Dancy or one of his revolting minions teaching my babies how to sing...)

One of the ironies about the situation is that the convalescent centre where I am working was apparently leased by Dancy himself and used as a music hall and supper club until the War Office requisitioned it. Since then Dancy has taken his performers on the road (think this is the correct term), and is trav-

elling the country with them. The twins are billed as
the Gemini Songbirds, which I find truly dreadful.

Floy has questioned the soldier carefully, but so far
has only managed to elicit the information that Dancy
and his performers have been touring the outskirts of
London—places like Hackney and Hoxton—but that
they left London a week ago.

Charlotte Quinton's diaries:
15th November 1914
Was reading over breakfast an article in *Blackwood's*
about Government plans to revive compulsory mili-
tary service. For the moment it will apply only
to unmarried men between eighteen and forty—
cannot help feeling *agonized* for all those boys being
summarily sent out to fight, and cannot help remembering Floy's recurring images of the mudfields and
the relentless shelling like iron rain beating down,
and of all those heartbreakingly young boys dying in
pain and confusion, and horses screaming in terror.
One day Floy will write about it, I think, and if he
does it will make scalding reading.

The morning post brought a letter from Edward who
is grumpy at being given what he calls inferior billet-
ing—believe that when he volunteered for this War
Office post he saw it in terms of proper servants and
featherbeds, and civilized drinks before dinner with
the Colonel. He says, irritably, that this is a very inef-
ficiently run war; there was not all this nonsense about
short rations and Jack's-as-good-as-his-master when we
fought the Boers. He does not think his digestion will
comfortably support the kind of food he is being given
either, which he knows will cause me great concern. It

does not cause me any concern at all, in fact I hope he is suffering the torments of *hell* from his digestion.

However, Edward is convinced that the war will be over by Christmas, and a good thing too if you ask him. He will be coming home this weekend, and looks forward to seeing me. Fondest love.

I will see to it that Edward has no love, fond or otherwise, from me ever again.

2.00 p.m.
It is not my day for attending the convalescent centre, and I have felt guilty at being in the comfort of my own home for a few hours. Spent the morning writing letters, and checking household stores with Mrs Tigg. There are shortages of a great many things now: Mrs Tigg does not know what the world is coming to, and will I have a nice baked egg for my lunch today?

I was just sitting down to the baked egg, when a note was delivered by special messenger. Floy's writing. Absurd that the sight of it still sends my pulses racing.

Floy writes that he must speak to me urgently—can I possibly come to his house right away? He has found Matt Dancy and his performers. They left London three days ago, bound for the Welsh Marches.

9.00 p.m.
I have thrown a random assortment of garments into a portmanteau, and I am writing this in my bedroom while I wait for Floy to collect me in a hackney. (Mrs

Tigg horrified that I am going anywhere in a hackney, never mind to that nasty draughty Paddington railway station—whatever can you be thinking of, mum?—but I am beyond caring. I would go after my daughters in a wheelbarrow if it was the only means available.)

Just under two hours ago Floy and I held a snatched conversation at his house. Dancy seems to be heading back to Mortmain House, which seems odd to me, but Floy thinks Dancy might be fleeing from some kind of police pursuit. He is such a villain he has probably transgressed any amount of laws, and Mortmain would make a very good hiding place for him—especially if he is in league with the beadle.

But when Floy said he would confront Dancy on his own I stared at him incredulously. 'Without me?'

'Yes.' He paced the length of the room restlessly a few times, and then said, 'Charlotte, this could be extremely awkward. We don't know the legal situation. I suspect Dancy could have legally adopted Viola and Sorrel—Edward might have signed some sort of contract renouncing all claim on them. And if Dancy is some kind of criminal escaping justice he might be violent—'

'I don't care how violent he is,' I said. 'Floy, you can't expect me to stay in London while you go after Viola and Sorrel. You *can't*!'

'The whole thing could be so distressing for you—' He broke off, thrusting the fingers of his hand through his hair, and I said that if he did not take me with him I would simply travel to Weston Fferna on my own, and search for Matt Dancy by myself and very likely end up shooting him.

'My dearest love,' said Floy, with infinite tenderness, 'do you even so much as possess a shotgun?'

'No, but if necessary I'll steal one.'

We stared at each other, and then with a gesture of exasperated resignation, Floy said, 'All right. We'll travel together. I believe there's a train from Waterloo at ten o'clock. Can you be ready at nine if I collect you in a cab?'

'Of course.'

'What about your family? Your parents and your sisters? They're still living up there, aren't they? Will you feel it necessary to stay at your father's house?'

'No.' I had already thought about this. 'There's no need for my family to know any of this—at least, not yet.'

'But there are people you might want to call on?'

I thought about Maisie, living in respectable mediocrity with her small daughter: I had visited her a couple of times while staying with my parents, and her little girl was a pretty, although rather oppressively well-behaved child. But Maisie had embraced her repentance with such zeal and lived such an austere, Bible-driven life, that there had been an atmosphere of cold disapproval towards me all the time I was there. Then I thought about Robyn and Anthony who had vanished so completely and whom I had never been able to trace.

I said to Floy, 'There's no one. For the purpose of this journey I'm a respectable married lady travelling on an urgent errand in wartime. No one will raise any eyebrows but if anyone does I shan't care. We'll book two rooms at The Bridge.'

'What if you're seen? Recognized? Charlotte, you spent your childhood in that part of the world, and if we're travelling about the countryside trying to find Dancy—'

'I'll wear a veil,' I said in desperation. 'I've got one of those motoring things. It's as thick as a shroud, for goodness' sake! And if anyone speaks to us, I'll—I'll pretend to be foreign. A Belgian refugee from the war.'

Floy threw up his hands in resignation, but then said, 'What about Edward?'

'Oh, bother Edward,' I said, although in fact I used a much stronger word than bother, which I feel is inappropriate to write down here. 'Edward's still away, fighting the war from an office,' I said. 'So he's not likely to even know I'm away as well. But if it troubles you, I will leave a letter for him implying that I have travelled home to see my sisters.'

It was eight o'clock when Simone finally came out of Thorne's. She set the alarm and locked the door carefully, conscious of extreme tiredness. Facing ghosts was a fatiguing business, it seemed.

Ghosts. Whatever had happened before or since, Sonia had not been a ghost that day, she had been a living, breathing entity. Simone was still grappling with the prospect of phoning her mother later on, although she could not begin to think how she would tell her. But she would make the call as soon as she got in. Maybe she could write out what to say before phoning—yes, that might make it easier. But however she put it and however she did it, there was still going to be that appalling moment when she had to say that it looked as if after all she had killed Sonia, and they had better try to think who the brown-haired woman might be, because clearly she was mixed up in all this—

She was glad that she had her car here for once, and that she could drive straight home; she reached her flat, parked outside the building, and got out, locking the car door. She was just turning to go up the narrow path to her own door when a figure stepped out from the shadow of the adjoining building and stood in front of her. Simone glanced up with an automatic stab of apprehension, because you never really felt safe from muggers and handbag-snatchers in London, even though this was a fairly quiet street.

It was not a mugger and it was not a handbag-snatcher either, and for several wild seconds Simone thought she had tumbled straight into the nightmare and not realized it—or even that Time had somehow wound itself back, because although this was a set of features she had never, to her knowledge, seen before, it was a set of features she knew and recognized. Brown hair, in no particular style, plain features with rather hard little eyes. A little plain brown sparrow or a wren, unremarkable except for the mouth which was thin and might merit the description rat-trap, and except for the hands which were unquiet and nervous... Simone recognized her at once as the woman she had glimpsed in Sonia's mind that day: the drab, rather dowdy woman whom Sonia had hated so fiercely and who had become part of Simone's own recurrent nightmare.

There was a moment when Simone stared, her mind whirling with confusion, and there was another moment when she thought that it was not so much that Time had wound itself back: it was more that it had wound itself forward, because now there were lines of age around the woman's eyes and mouth that were not there in the dream, and that was somehow the most frightening part of all because surely ghosts did not age, surely they stayed frozen in their own fragments of time and space and infinity...?

She thought she started to say something although she had no idea what it would have been, but before she could frame any words the woman had reached out a gloved hand, and there was a glint of something and then a sudden sharp skewering pain spiking down into Simone's arm. The familiar street with her own front door only yards away tilted and spun, and for a moment she thought she was going to faint.

'You won't lose consciousness,' the woman said, as if she had picked this up. 'I've given you chlorpromazine—enough to make you more or less helpless, but not quite enough to knock you out altogether.'

Simone managed to say, 'Why—?' but the woman was already taking her arm very firmly, and propelling her along the street. She felt immensely strong.

'My car's just along here,' she said. 'And what's going to happen is that we're going to get into it—you'll be in the back seat, but you'll be strapped in and I'm going to bind your wrists and ankles so you won't be able to do very much. And if anyone questions us before we reach the car I shall say you've been taken ill and that I'm a nurse and I'm driving you to hospital. I really am a nurse anyway,' she said, 'so it's likely that I'll be believed. Here we are now. In you go.'

Simone had been hoping that someone would come along and that she could appeal for help, but the woman's car was only a few steps along the street and this was not a time of day when many people were around. The car was a small hatchback—Simone was pushed on to the back seat, and the woman leaned over her. There was the feel of something being snapped around Simone's wrists—twine or some kind of thin tough plastic. The sort of thing they put around your wrists in hospital with an identity tag on it. She remembered that the woman had said she was a nurse. But everything was feeling so distant and blurry that Simone was not even sure that this was actually happening any longer. Perhaps it was a new twist to the familiar nightmare, and if so she might wake up in a moment. 'And now your ankles,' said the woman, reaching down. 'Good. Last of all the seat-belt. I don't want to be stopped by the police because we aren't both properly belted in.'

She clicked the seat-belt around Simone's waist, and then straightened up, closed the rear door and got into the driver's seat. Simone struggled against the wrist bindings, but whatever the woman had given her—chlorpromazine, had she called it?—was making her so impossibly weak that even to move a finger took a huge effort.

'There's no point in trying to get free, Simone,' said the woman, and glanced at Simone in the driving mirror. Her eyes were like hard little pebbles. 'Oh yes, I know your name,' she said softly. 'I know a very great deal about you, Simone. I've been watching you on and off for quite a while now and I've been waiting to meet you for years. I know far more about you than you can possibly realize.' She fired the engine and the car moved off.

'Where—are—you—taking—me?' Getting each word out was like climbing a mountain but Simone finally managed it.

'We're going on quite a long journey, Simone,' said the woman. 'Tonight we're going to Mortmain.'

Charlotte Quinton's diaries:
16th November 1914
This morning we are going to Mortmain, Floy and I.

I was all for going out there directly we arrived last night, but Floy pointed out (with maddening male logic!) that it was already well past midnight, and not a good idea to approach any house, least of all that house, at such an hour.

So I have had to contain my soul in as much patience as I can muster for the last seven or eight hours, and have managed to eat a little breakfast (a cup of coffee and a slice of toast), and now I am ready, wearing a plain tailor-made (brown twill), over a cream silk blouse. Realize it is wholly frivolous to be recording this sartorial information when in a very little while I may be meeting my dear lost daughters after fourteen years, but refuse to lower standards on these matters. Also, writing about my clothes helps to fill up the time until we can decently set out for Mortmain. Brown twill costume, small brown hat with bronze trimming, buttoned boots, amber beads and brooch, cambric handkerchief, sprinkled with lavender...

I think I am more terrified than I can ever remember being in my entire life, but I shall not let anyone guess.

9.30 a.m.
My bedroom is at the front of the Bridge, overlooking the roadway (quite a small room but v. cosy and pleasingly furnished), and I have just opened the window to listen to the morning. The air always smells so different in the country to London, and I do so love the autumn scents—golden brown and copper scents, all mixed in with soft rain and chrysanthemums and bonfires...

Down below I can hear Floy arranging for the pony and trap that serves the Bridge's guests to be brought round for us at 10.00. So in an hour's time— perhaps two hours—I may be on the other side of the most momentous meeting and the most extraordinary event of my life.

CHAPTER THIRTY-FOUR

Charlotte Quinton's diaries:
20th November
It is now three days since we arrived in Weston Fferna,
Floy and I, and we began our search early on that first
morning, taking the Bridge's pony and trap out to
Mortmain House and asking the man to bring it back
to collect us at midday. (Would not have thought of
this, but Floy sometimes unexpectedly practical.)

We had no very precise plan, only that we would
go up to the house and ask to see the beadle, and then
inquire of him whether twin girls, their bodies joined at
birth, had been brought here in the first weeks of 1900.

'It's a very long time ago,' I said doubtfully to Floy
as we got down from the trap, and walked the last
few yards to the house.

'Fourteen years. That's barely a speck in the infinity
of time. Hardly the weight of a microcosm floating in
the seas of eternity.' When Floy is at his most flip-
pantly lyrical it is usually because he is hiding his
feelings. I knew he was hiding them now; his voice
was light but I saw how his eyes went to the house,
still a little way ahead of us on the track, and I
thought he flinched just very slightly.

I had been hoping that this time Mortmain would be less forbidding, but of course, I was wrong. Mortmain was, and is, enough to make anyone flinch. For all these years I had remembered it as a place of lowering darkness, but today there was bright sunshine and a lovely golden haze from the autumn trees. None of this helped Mortmain to look better; even on a sunlit day it's a terrible place. It ought not to have any reality outside of brooding midnights, in fact it almost ought not to exist at all in daylight.

We walked silently up the track, but as we drew near, Floy said, 'Charlotte, I think you had better take my arm as if we're a married couple, although perhaps—'

'Perhaps we had better be as strange as if we had been married a great while, and as well-bred as if we were not married at all?'

His mouth lifted slightly, but he only said, 'My, my, someone has been attending to your education while I was away, Charlotte.' He paused and looked down at me, and then in a very different voice, said, 'Ready, my dear love?'

I was not ready of course, and I probably never would be ready for this encounter, but when Floy looks at me like that and calls me his dear love in that caressing voice, I become convinced that I can climb mountains and swim oceans. So I said firmly, 'Yes, I am ready,' and with a feeling that I had tumbled backwards into a dreadfully familiar nightmare, I reached up for the door knocker and let it fall on the dull oak of the door.

We were received by a rabbit-faced maid who eyed us nervously, twisting her hands in her apron, and then bobbed a nervous, awkward curtsey and scuttled away to apprise someone of our arrival. Five minutes later we were seated in a small study, facing a jowly, small-eyed man with a female seated next to him. I thought she was the woman I had seen in the Paupers' Room all those years ago—there was the same rat-trap mouth and cold eyes—but I could not be absolutely certain.

'So you see,' Floy was saying urbanely, 'we are here to trace the two girls who came here fourteen years ago.'

'Not possible.' The words came out like little hard pebbles, and I saw Floy's lips tighten momentarily. But he only said, 'The children's legal family are extremely anxious to know their whereabouts.'

'Took their time being anxious, didn't they? Fourteen years.'

'The family were told the children had died,' said Floy, and an angry edge had crept into his voice. I glanced at him and thought: don't lose your temper, Floy, please don't, because this is one of the rare occasions where I don't think it will do any good—

Either he caught the thought or he had reached the same conclusion himself, because when he spoke again he seemed to have the anger more under control. He said, 'We know—and the family's advisers know—that certain illegalities were committed when the babies were taken. Our inquiries have brought us here.' A pause, the space of four heartbeats. I was watching the man and saw that the mention of 'advisers' had struck an unpleasant chord with him. If either of these two were to break, it would be him.

'Mr Dancy was involved in the babies' abduction,' said Floy. 'We do know that.'

A look passed between the two people behind the desk, and then the man said, 'We might know Mr Dancy. We wouldn't say we didn't know him.'

'In the way of business,' said the woman.

'Ah.' Floy leaned forward. 'So you know Dancy. And the girls? You know what happened to the girls? Come now, this will probably need to become a police matter. It would be better for you to co-operate with me.'

Again the exchange of looks. It was clear that neither of these two people knew what status to accord Floy, and also that neither of them quite had the courage to ask who he was.

Then the man said, 'We was given proper legal rights all those years back. All in order. As for abduction, there was no such thing.'

'Guardianship given into the hands of the Trust,' said the woman righteously. 'Signed by the father in this very room, and sworn to by a justice.'

Signed by the father. By the *father*... I had already known it, but even so there was a deep sad pain at this final proof of Edward's cruel deceit. It was no consolation to know that Edward was not, in fact, the twins' father.

Floy was saying, 'Where are the girls now?'

'With Dancy.' It came out sullenly. 'He takes the ones he thinks suitable.'

'For his music hall? Or for his brothels?'

'We don't ask questions. We're answerable to the Trust, no one else.'

'It must be a very strange Trust indeed if it allows children to be handed over to a man who runs a freak show and a brothel,' said Floy. He was still keeping his temper but it was a near thing.

'Dancy *is* the Trust,' said the man. 'Mortmain belongs to him. It's his money as runs it and the children who come here are made over to him. He takes guardianship of them. Mostly they're orphans or bastards. Not wanted anywhere else. All legal. So what he does with them when they're older is his right.'

I said, 'But the women I saw working here some years ago? They were adults.'

'Oh, we take paupers as well.' This was the woman, speaking off-handedly. 'That's Poor Law requirements. Mortmain has to obey the Poor Law requirements.'

'In return, presumably, for certain benefices from the church authorities? Yes, I thought that was what you meant.' Floy considered for a moment, and then said, 'Where is Matt Dancy now? Does he live here?'

'He has a room here,' said the woman unwillingly. 'But he's not here so very often. Mostly he's in London.'

'He's not in London now. He travelled up here almost a week ago.'

The man glanced at the woman, and appeared to shrug. 'He's taking his performers around the towns for a week or two,' he said.

'London too hot to hold him, was it?'

'I wouldn't know as to that. He came here a night or two, and talked about going around some of the towns hereabouts. All in the way of business. *His* business. There's many a tavern will pay well for a travelling show.'

Many a tavern will pay well.

This part of England is a maze, a spider-web of little villages and hamlets, and although, as Floy had pointed out, I had spent my childhood here, I knew it would be difficult to track Dancy down to any one place.

'Difficult, but not impossible,' said Floy. And then, frowning, 'Charlotte, oughtn't you to stay in the Bridge while I search?'

But we hired the Bridge's pony and trap as a permanency—only real means of transportation in the area—and began going doggedly from village to village and town to town. I think the boy driving the trap thought we were mad or possessed, but Floy paid him well and he did not ask any questions. We returned to the Bridge each evening, dined in the small coffee room, and slept the sleep of exhaustion.

Floy was tireless. Several times I broke down and cried from fatigue or despair or both, and he was unfailingly patient. But it was a bizarre chase we were engaged on, and towards the end there was a nightmare quality to it—the sort of nightmare where you are desperately hunting something across an alien landscape, and where you never quite manage to catch up with your invisible quarry.

But the quarry was not completely invisible; in villages where Dancy had taken his performers he had left his smeary spoor. Yes, they had seen the concert, people told us in the lovely lilting voice of the region. A bit sad they had thought it what with those poor creatures on display—not what you'd really call entertainment, was it, but there you were, you did not get so much entertainment out here, and it made a change, didn't it? Take the children and everything. And lovely singers there had been at the end, as well. It was a beautiful thing to hear good singing.

It is ten o'clock on the evening of the third day, and we have dined on the Bridge's very good mutton and apple pudding with cider syllabub to follow, and tomorrow evening we are to travel to a little cluster of villages near to Machynlleth. For it is there that Dancy seems to have taken his performers. They will be giving two shows in one of the old barns once used by travelling players and now a local hall for local choirs and children's concerts, and Floy thinks this is where we shall finally reach Dancy. The villages are further south than either of us had expected to travel but Floy has consulted a map and it is not so very long a journey. Twenty miles or so.

I would not care if it were a thousand times the distance. I would travel barefoot through flood and tempest, and scale the iron walls of Milton's fire-drenched Malebolge in order to reach Viola and Sorrel.

The journey was quite a long one, but Roz would have driven far longer distances to mete out punishment to the creature who had murdered Sonia.

Still, she was not used to driving for so long a stretch, and there was also the worry that she might not have judged the chlorpromazine shot accurately. Supposing Simone managed to get free of the plastic tapes around her wrists and ankles?

But Rosie was urging her on, and the journey was achieved without any trouble whatsoever, with Simone remaining in the helpless half-daze in the back of the car. Roz saw she had been silly to panic about that: had she really not trusted herself to administer a properly calculated drug, after all these years of nursing? As for the rest—when it came to it, she had lost none of her old cunning.

A lot of planning had gone into tonight, and with

it the careful working out of a timetable. By means of keeping a careful watch on Simone Roz had managed to establish the pattern of her days, and she had decided that Friday evening should be the night. Friday. Her heart bumped with nervous tension at the realization of how near she was to her goal. Friday.

Since Sister Raffan could not suddenly absent herself from her duties without prior warning, at the start of the week Roz had requested four days' holiday, to begin at the end of Thursday evening's shift. She was sorry it was short notice, but it was a family crisis, she said sadly. She would try not to be away longer than two or three days, so she might even be back on Monday morning. There had not been any problem because she hardly ever took her full entitlement of holiday; the nursing director was happy to grant the request and the other theatre sisters were willing to organize cover while she was away. She was so conscientious, good, reliable Sister Raffan. No real private life, of course, wonder what she does with her spare time, wonder what she does about sex...

And then—would you believe it!—just with everything nicely arranged that artful bitch, Simone, had suddenly vanished! Her car was no longer parked outside her flat, and the flat itself was silent and deserted each night—Roz had checked the place every evening. This had been worrying, but eventually Roz had telephoned Thorne's and asked to speak to Simone.

Angelica Thorne, snooty cat, had taken the call. She had said Simone was away at present, she was out of London.

Away! Out of London! All the crime stories—fiction and truth—said there was almost always one small detail the criminal overlooked, and Roz had smiled at this because she had believed she had provided for every eventuality. Now it seemed she had not.

Angelica asked if there was any message she could

take for Simone, and Roz had been ready for this. She said, 'It's about her dentist's appointment. There's been a muddle about the dates, and we're trying to sort it out.' This was a ruse she had seen used in a TV film, and she had thought it quite a good one. She added, conscientiously, that it would be easier to speak to Miss Marriot direct. Did Angelica know when she would be back?

She waited, her heart beating too fast with nervous tension, but Angelica was unsuspicious. In her cool expensive voice she said Simone would be back on Friday—probably not until early evening, after the gallery had closed. But she could leave a note on Simone's desk if that would help.

'I wonder if that would be best.' Roz pretended to think. 'No, look, I won't trouble you to do that, I'll put a little note in the post to her, that's what I'll do. Thank you so much.'

Friday. Simone would be back on Friday. She was expected to check in at Thorne's, after which it sounded as if she would go on to her own flat. Excellent. The plan did not even need to be altered.

Roz calmly worked her normal turn of duty on Thursday evening—two routine scheduled gastroscopies, and an emergency appendectomy on a small boy brought in just after lunch. Nothing very demanding about any of them. She left the hospital shortly before seven, and drove home to pack a small suitcase and leave a note cancelling the milk for the weekend. She did not want to return to a doorstep full of sour milk.

When Roz had gone back to St Luke's after Sonia's death most of the nurses she had known had left or moved on, but the nursing director had been so pleased to have someone with a few years' training, no matter how long ago it had been, that she had welcomed Roz with open arms, and allowed her to take a refresher course before assigning her to theatre work again. It was easy to slip back into the old life: her tenants had left her aunt's house, and now that she had a regular salary again she had afforded that car she had always promised herself, and a course of driving lessons. No one had asked much about what she had been doing in the intervening years and it had been easy to give the vague impression of elderly, sick parents who had needed her support for a few years. It was a situation easily associated with someone like Roz.

Life was a circle, anyway. She supposed it had been inevitable that she should return to St Luke's. She supposed it was inevitable that she should return to Weston Fferna and Mortmain House, as well: in the end all roads led you back there; they all led back to the shameful, soulless workhouse, whose dark despair and whose sad, bitter memories Roz had absorbed as a child.

Her aunt had told her that once you had lived inside Mortmain—once you had known Mortmain's sadness and its memories—you never really escaped from it. Roz knew her aunt had never really escaped, and because of it, Roz herself had never really escaped either. She had told Sonia the stories when Sonia was old enough to understand, and Sonia had listened with absorption. She had liked hearing about Mortmain and about the children who had lived there, and the songs they had sung. She had understood that even though you might go to live hundreds of miles away, in your mind you would never really escape.

And now Simone, who had killed Sonia, and who had achieved the life that had been denied to Roz's aunt, would never escape from Mortmain House, either. There was a symmetry and a rightness about Simone dying inside Mortmain.

Roz reached the lonely stretch of road and parked on the grass verge, swinging the car well off the road so that it would not be noticed by some officious motorist or inquisitive AA man. It was just after midnight. She opened the glove compartment for the two torches she had brought, tucking one into each pocket, and adding the spare batteries as well. Details, you see. You had to allow for every eventuality.

Then she got out and opened the car's rear door to drag Simone out. Simone was still barely conscious from the chlorpromazine; Roz had judged the dosage very accurately indeed. Just enough to keep the bitch helpless for the length of the journey, and just enough for it to start wearing off once she was inside Mortmain.

The ghosts were clustering around her as she began the climb to the house. Rosie was one of them, of course. She could not have done any of this without Rosie, that strong wilful lady that Joseph Anderson had summoned into being all those years ago. ('*You made me so aroused, Rosie...*') As she went up the narrow track, half-pulling the stumbling helpless Simone with her, Roz was glad to have Rosie's strength once again.

Sonia was here as well, of course, for where else should Sonia's ghost be except in the place she had loved and in the place where she had died? Sonia was pleased with what Roz was doing tonight: Roz could sense it. Sonia was glad that Roz was meting out this punishment to the creature who had murdered her.

Lastly and most importantly, Roz's aunt was here. The spirit of the indomitable woman who had lived through such nightmare years, and who had never really shaken the nightmares off, was with Roz as she approached Mortmain. It was very late now—almost midnight—and although there was only a thin sliver of a new moon, several times Roz saw the unmistakable outline of her aunt's figure walking along beside her. She saw the two sticks her aunt had always had to use because she could not walk very well, and she saw the unmistakable skewing of her aunt's shoulders. Sonia had had almost the exact same skewing. You did not come unscathed out of the kind of fearsome operation that Sonia had had, and the even more fearsome operation that Roz's aunt had endured.

Roz could even hear her aunt's hissing venomous voice inside the night wind: the voice that had talked and talked of her dreadful early childhood, and of the later months when she had fallen into the clutches of an evil, venal man who had touted his collection of sad misshapen performers around the countryside...

Aunt Viola walked steadily with Roz as they went up the track by the light of a sickle moon.

CHAPTER THIRTY-FIVE

MORTMAIN HOUSE WAS wreathed in darkness, but this did not frighten Roz in the least. She knew all about Mortmain's darkness, and she knew precisely where she was going. Once she was through the main door she had to cross the central hall and go along the corridors and rooms on the right-hand side. Through the Paupers' Ward and across the well-room, and down the twisting stone steps to the underground rooms.

Viola had known about those rooms, of course; she and her sister had never been taken there, but all the children at Mortmain had known about them. Cages, they had said, whispering the word fearfully to one another. Cages for punishment.

'Dreadful,' Viola had said, seated in the wooden-backed chair, her face set and austere, her eyes bleak. 'On some nights we had to pull the sheets over our heads to shut out the screams of the people carried down there, and locked into the cages. For we could hear them crying for help, on and on, until you thought your head would burst with the sound—' And then the bleakness would vanish, and the hard bitterness would show. 'But they were sinners,' Viola would add. 'Sinners in the Lord's eyes, for why else would

He have sent such a punishment to them? Just as He sent punishment to my sister and to me. I learned about punishment when I was very young—I learned a great many very hard lessons when I was very young, Rosamund, and you must learn them as well. Above all, you must never forget that God punishes. He has His instruments in this world, and He makes use of them.'

God has His instruments... Roz was God's instrument now, guiding Sonia's murderess along the dim echoing passages of the place where Viola and her sister had spent that dreadful childhood. Through the Paupers' Ward where tramps sometimes spent the night, and into the courtyard room with the old well. As the torch beam cut a triangle of white brilliance through the dust and the dirt, showing up the rotting wooden cover over the well, for the first time Simone struggled. Roz tightened her hold at once and quickened her step in case the chlorpromazine was wearing off. Four to six hours, that was the rule of thumb, but you could never be precise about it.

The worn shallow steps were thickly covered in dust, and as they reached the foot Roz's torch showed up the thick festoons of cobwebs like layered veils. When she reached up with the torch to brush them aside they shrivelled at her touch.

The cages were directly in front of the steps: iron bars, formed into oblongs, each one about as tall as a fully-grown adult, and half as deep. They were set against the wall and there were eight or ten of them. At the front of each one was a door, fashioned from the same iron staves, but made to swing outwards. There was a small catch on each one, and a padlock. Even from this distance Roz could see that the padlocks were all rusted beyond use but that did not matter, because she had brought one with her, carefully purchased from a large, busy hardware store one lunchtime.

It seemed as if she had timed the chlorpromazine absolutely right. Simone was struggling harder now—it was a frail kind of struggle that would not have harmed a kitten and would certainly not prevent Roz from completing the plan—but she was certainly coming out of the drug-induced haze. There was no time to waste. Roz dragged Simone to the nearest cage and pushed her inside, giving the bitch a shove that sent her tumbling forward. Then she slammed the iron-bar door and taking the padlock from her pocket, snapped it into place before Simone could escape.

She paused at the foot of the stairs, shining the torch on the cages. Simone had crawled to the front of the cage, and her fingers were curled around the iron bars. In the livid light from the torch her eyes were wide and terrified, the pupils still pinpoints from the chlorpromazine. Her hair was tumbled and her face was white with fear and panic. As Roz brought the torchbeam back to the steps she was glad that the chlorpromazine had worn off sufficiently for Simone to understand what had happened to her.

Clustering shadows lay across the narrow track as she walked back down to the road, and Roz quickened her step, trying not to hear the soft rustlings and the faint whisperings, determinedly not looking at the dense blackness of the trees on each side of the path.

Sonia's ghost was still with her, of course. Sonia had loved Mortmain and she had never been afraid of it; she had never minded the swirling echoes or the eeriness. If there were any ghosts there, she had said, they were the ghosts of people from the stories. How could those people be frightening when she knew them so well?

But Roz had told Sonia, over and over, to stay away from Mortmain: you had to be careful of such places, she had said. Supposing Sonia met an old tramp in there or a gypsy? Supposing she fell down and broke her leg or her arm? But Sonia had only turned away angrily, and said she hated being fussed over. If ever she vanished, Roz would know where to come looking for her, she had said. Sonia could occasionally be wilful, of course; she could even be hurtful as well, saying that she hated living with Roz, she hated not being let to go to school or do the things other girls did. Roz had never minded it when Sonia said this; she knew that it was important to protect Sonia. Sonia was so special, so precious.

Then had come the day when Sonia had vanished, and Roz had gone looking for her, She had seen Simone run out of Mortmain as if the furies were pursuing her-there had been a moment when she had thought it was Sonia, of course, but Sonia had never been able to run like that, or to move so swiftly and so easily. When Roz eventually found Sonia's body she had known, instantly and for certain, what had happened. She had known that somehow the twins had found one another (how had they done that?) and she had known that the bitch's whelp had killed Sonia. Clambering down inside the well-shaft and bringing out Sonia's poor, broken body, Roz had made a vow that one day she would find Simone—God would arrange that she did so—and when she. found her she would kill her.

To begin with she had thought it would be easy to track Simone down—she had found the little house where that bitch, Melissa, had brought Simone to live, and in the middle of the anguish and the grief there had been a tiny consolation in knowing that one day those two would pay for Sonia's death. But before she could make any kind of plan Melissa had vanished from Weston Fferna, leaving only a house agent's sale board in the garden and no forwarding address anywhere in the village. Sly, you see! Sly as a snake! But there would come a day of reckoning for the creature, Roz had always known that, and now the day was here.

As she went down to the road the thin moon came out from behind a patch of cloud and she looked at her watch. It was a quarter to one. Much too late to book into some local hotel, and in any case she did not want to draw attention to herself. She would drive back to the motorway and check in at one of the service motels. She had never done that before but she knew they were impersonal and therefore anonymous.

Then tomorrow she could drive back here to check on Simone's cage. It might take the creature a day or two to actually die. Roz wanted to be there when it happened.

Charlotte Quinton's diaries: 21st November 1914
It is a few minutes after midnight and although I am so tired I can barely hold a pen, I know I will not be able to sleep until I have set down what happened this evening.

I have no recollection whatsoever of our journey to the village near to Machynlleth, although I think Floy cursed our driver several times for going too slow, and at least twice for taking a wrong turning. (One forgets at times that Floy has travelled so much, and that he has spent the last few months moving around France and the Low Countries, gathering stories for his newspapers, and sometimes helping the wounded men from the battlefields.)

Even though there were two box lanterns hung on the sides of the trap, and even though there were no clouds and the night was clear and still, the narrow country roads were dark and difficult. High hedge-rows shut us in on both sides, and after a while I began to feel as if we had been jogging rhythmically through the darkness for ever and that we would go on doing so for ever. At one stage I began to wonder if this was the purgatory that Catholic priests warn of, because it felt as if we were caught in an endless grey misery, stuck between two worlds, unable to go forward or backwards.

But even worlds sometimes end, for eventually we came to lighted buildings and some semblance of life and movement, and ahead of us was a village green with a rather ugly iron cross at its centre depicting something or commemorating someone. On the far side was a long, low-roofed building, probably once some kind of tithe barn, brightly lit from within, with a number of people going inside it.

We paid a fee and were shown to uncomfortable wooden bench seats—could not help thinking it a dreadful irony that the first time I would see my daughters properly would be from a wooden seat in a village barn. All around us people were laughing and talking and there was an air of pleased expectancy. A man was seated at a badly-tuned piano, rather dispiritedly playing snatches by Léhar and Strauss, and the room was getting hotter and hotter, and filling up with various bucolic smells.

I remember very little about the first part of the performances, although I know the audience displayed some unease at the sight of the dwarfs and then of a grossly fat woman and a skeletally thin man who sang a duet. My heart—that unfailing and often infuriating indicator of emotion!—was beating so fast and so furiously that I was afraid I might swoon before the twins appeared, and there was the feeling of something hovering directly over my head, beating huge invisible wings. In a very few minutes I would see them, I would see my babies...

And then the pianist began to play the light, vaguely Oriental tune of 'Three Little Maids from

School Are We', and without warning they were there. Sorrel and Viola, the two furled-up beings who had lain together in their cradle... I had named them for harebells and wood sorrel, and the first time—the only time—I had seen them, they had been lying into that helpless embrace and their tiny hands had curled trustfully around my fingers...

They were still in the embrace, but it was no longer the curled-up rosebud embrace I had kept in my memory. It was ugly and unnatural, something to pity and be shocked by. Their voices as they sang were sweet and true and heart-breakingly young, and as long as they remained still there was nothing much out of the ordinary about them. But towards the end of the second song they performed a short dance, and I think that if I live to be a hundred, and if the world freezes and hell burns itself to a cinder, I shall never—*never*!—forget the sight of that dance. I cannot possibly describe it here, it would be disloyal to my babies. But it was the most piteous, most appalling thing I have ever seen, then or since.

The audience felt it as well; a shiver of pity and repulsion stirred them, and some of the women turned uncertainly to their husbands. I thought: I cannot bear this, I simply cannot bear it, but I was aware of Floy taking my hand and I remembered that it had to be borne, because *they* had to bear it. I clung to Floy as if he was the only sane and good thing left in a vicious, splintered world.

But when the performance was over the twins stepped back behind a curtain, and the small audience was ushered politely but firmly outside, and before either Floy or I could do anything about it, two big covered carts mounted on drays were driven away, and we realized that Dancy's performers had gone off into the night.

I said, in a voice numb with misery, 'We've lost them. Oh Floy—'

'No, we haven't lost them,' said Floy, softly. 'Stay with the people. Move around and listen to what's being said. Pick up the clues, Charlotte.'

He moved across the square and I did the same, going to stand near to a small group of women, not precisely eavesdropping, and certainly not *appearing* as if I was eavesdropping (unpleasant practice), merely looking as if I was waiting for my husband to rejoin me. But listening to everything, absorbing all that was being said, just as Floy was doing.

And within a half hour we knew that Matt Dancy had taken his people to a village a few miles on Machynlleth's south side. 'Staying at the Pheasant Inn,' said one of the women in my group, busily informative. 'My sister's girl, she helps out there of an evening, and the boss told her to make up extra beds. Quite pleased, they are. Brings a bit of prosperity to the area, see.'

'We'll go out to the Pheasant first thing in the morning,' said Floy as the little trap was jogged back along the moonlit lanes. 'Yes, my love, I know you'd like to be hammering on the doors right away, but it'll be midnight before we find the place and I'd prefer not to confront Matt Dancy in the middle of the night.'

I did not speak, and he glanced at me. 'Charlotte, it will be better this way, I promise you. I don't want Dancy slithering out of our reach under cover of darkness.'

He's right, of course, even though it kills me to admit it. And now, writing this in my room at the Bridge, even though I have found Viola and Sorrel, I think I am more desolate than before. I cannot bear knowing that they are being exploited in this pitiful way, and I am terrified that when Matt Dancy knows who I am, he will find a way to spirit them away again.

Unless I can think of a way to outwit him.

Simone came out of the chlorpromazine gradually.

Her head was aching, and she felt weak and slightly sick. But her senses were clearing, and she understood that the hard-eyed woman who had brought her to Mortmain had shut her in here and left her.

She was still by no means sure that she was not inside the nightmare, because this was how it must feel to be buried alive, trapped fathoms down in the earth. Above her was Mortmain, and she had the feeling that its immense weight and the grim echoing emptiness of its rooms was pressing down on her.

But I will get out, said Simone determinedly. I think this might be really happening, and of course I'll get out. I'll be able to snap the lock or force one of the iron bars out. Or if I can't do that someone will miss me and start looking. But how long would it be before that happened? And would anyone think of looking inside Mortmain House?

The blackness was so absolute that she could not make out the time on her watch, and she had no idea how long she had been here because time seemed to move at a different rate when you could not see. She huddled into a corner of the cramped space and tried not to hear the little whisperings and scufflings all around her. They were pretty spooky sounds, but they were ordinary and explainable. Rats and bats and ravens and owls. All of them a bit dark and sinister, no matter how much you tried to ignore them. The spectral owl, dwelling in his hollow in the old grey tower—night's fatal bellman, Macbeth had called him, and if Macbeth did not know about fate and its heralds, then no one did. And the raven with his dreaming demon's eyes trailing his own lamplit fantasies in his wake... Yes, owls and ravens were undoubtedly creatures loaded with the macabre, and bats and rats had never had a good press, of course. Not to be thought of in this situation.

But the ghosts were impossible to ignore. Simone could hear them and she could feel them. Sonia had once said, in her sly way, that the children who had lived here had sometimes been taken by dealers in child prostitution—she had said they used to hide down here to try to fool the child-traders—and for a wild moment Simone could hear the heavy stomping tread of the child-traders searching the house for their prey. She listened carefully, in case there really was someone walking about overhead, but it was only the pounding of her own blood in her veins she was hearing.

I'm delirious, she thought, sitting up as far as possible, and forcing herself to breathe calmly and slowly. It's something to do with—what do they call it?—sensory deprivation. It's as black as pitch down here, and as silent as the grave— No, I won't use that word. But I do wish it wasn't so silent.

But the ghosts were not silent. Simone could not see them but she could feel their presence and she could hear them. She could hear the long-ago children scrabbling to escape the child-traders, and she could hear their small hands beating uselessly against the door.

Nails scratching against iron... Hands beating against bricks...

She came back to full awareness to discover that she was beating frantically against the iron bars of the cage, and that it had been the frantic beating of her own hands that she had heard and felt.

CHAPTER THIRTY-SIX

'I T'S PROBABLY ABSOLUTELY nothing to worry about,' said Angelica's voice on the phone. 'But there's this thing that's happened, and the more I think about it, the more I find it just a small bit worrying. So I thought I'd see what you thought about it.'

Harry asked what was a small bit worrying.

'Well, it's Simone. She seems to have—this is going to sound frightfully melodramatic—but I suppose you'd say vanished. I haven't seen her since Monday—that's not the worrying thing because she left me a message to say she was going off on a field trip for our new exhibition, and wouldn't be back until Friday night—'

'It's only Saturday afternoon,' Harry pointed out. 'She's probably still on the field trip.'

'No, I don't think she is. We were due to meet someone for lunch today—an idea I had about including some paintings on silk for the next show and we were going to have a look at the artist's portfolio—and Simone didn't turn up. That's so unlike her, she's very nearly old-fashioned when it comes to keeping appointments and being on time and things like that.'

'Perhaps she's not well. Flu or migraine or something.'

'I don't think so. I've phoned and *phoned,*' said Angelica. 'And it's just the answerphone at her flat—well, it's not even that any longer because the wretched machine's reached the end of its tape and it just bleeps at you now, *very* rude it sounds, I do wish they would make these things more *harmonious*— So then I drove out to her flat, and here's the thing, Harry, her car is there so she must have got back from her trip all right, but there're bottles of milk on the step and mail on the mat. You can see it through the door and it looks like several days of mail.'

'There might be any number of explanations.' But Harry could not, for the moment, think of one. He felt a small jab of unease.

'So *then,*' said Angelica, 'I came back to Thorne's, and I went into her darkroom. I *never* do that because it's by way of being her sanctum and I never pry into her work. But I thought there might be a clue to where she was, so I broke the rule this time.'

'And was there anything?'

'I'm not sure.' For the first time Angelica's voice lost some of its colour and affectation. 'I found something she'd been working on—from the look of it she did come back here yesterday, because she developed some film.'

'Yes?'

'This is the part I'm worried about,' said Angelica. 'Listen, Harry, is there any possibility that you could come over to see the prints she developed, because I don't quite know what to do about them.'

'Those two are Mortmain House, of course,' said Harry, standing in the narrow darkroom with Angelica and staring down at the four prints lying on Simone's workbench.

'Well, I do *know* they're Mortmain House for heaven's sake, we've got that *grisly* view of the place upstairs, perfectly gothic although utterly brilliant of course, and we've sold several prints of it—' She trailed off as Harry picked up the last image.

'This is the one, isn't it?' he said after a long time.

'Yes. I don't even know what it is.'

'It looks as if it's a tunnel of some kind,' said Harry, frowning. 'Somewhere narrow and very old—'

'The child's dead, isn't she?'

'Oh yes.' Harry went on studying the print. 'She looks to be about ten or twelve,' he said at last. 'Is there any way of knowing when this could have been taken? Any date-stamp anywhere on the film, or anything like that?'

'I don't know. I haven't a clue about that kind of thing. And I haven't dared disturb things in here. Those were lying on the workbench, face up. But I think this is the original film over here.'

'It's quite an old one,' said Harry, taking it. 'I don't think you can buy that make any longer.'

'And the shots aren't trimmed,' said Angelica. 'Simone always trims her prints as she develops them—she's amazingly neat and organized. I'm pretty sure she must have developed this last night when she got back.'

Something was tugging at Harry's mind, and it was something he could not quite grasp. Something about the child lying in her own blood on the photograph— Something he ought to be able to identify—

'This will sound utterly mad,' Angelica was saying. 'But when I first saw that shot of the dead child, I thought it was Simone. I've seen a couple of photos of her as a child, and that's exactly how she looked.'

The thing in Harry's mind that he had not been able to grasp came sharply into focus. He said, 'Oh God, of *course*. Angelica, it isn't Simone. It's Sonia.'

'*Sonia*? The sister? The twin who died—?'

'Yes.' He laid the print down very carefully. 'Have you got any really good maps of England and Wales?'

'Well, I daresay I could find one, or there's the AA, *so* useful— Why? Are we going to call the police or something? Or Simone's mother—oh wait, though, she's still in Canada.'

'We aren't going to call the police yet,' said Harry, although at a different level his mind was saying, Canada! Then *that's* why I couldn't track down Melissa! 'I don't think we need to worry Simone's mother until we know there's something to be worried about,' he said. 'What we are going to do though, is find Mortmain House.'

'You think that's where Simone is?'

'I don't know. I'm going purely on instinct. But these shots are of Mortmain, and that's Simone's twin, and I'd like to take a look inside the place before we call in the cavalry.'

He borrowed a car for the journey from one of the sub-editors at the *Bellman*; the car's age was honourable but its suspension and staying-power were questionable, and the sub-editor had been dubious about its ability to ever reach its destination. If it did not blow all the gaskets by the time Harry got off the M25, he said glumly, then it would most probably develop carburetor trouble, in fact the likelihood of either Harry or his passenger or the car ever being seen again was pretty remote. Still, here were the keys, and please to remember that if you had to smack the foot-brake hard for any reason, you then had to lever the pedal back into place with your toe on account of there being an airlock somewhere in the hydraulics.

But the car did not fall victim to any of the ills predicted by its owner. It bounced spine-jarringly over the various roads and it drank petrol with vampiric greed, but it reached without mishap the part of Shropshire that the map designated as the Welsh Marches. The names on the signposts altered gradually along the way. Childs Ercall and Morton Say. Whixall and Whorthenbury and Threapwood. And then the start of the inevitable *Ll* names, and the Mawrs and Bryns.

'Nice,' said Angelica, leaning back luxuriously on the battered passenger seat and looking out of the windows. 'Living in London one forgets about things like fields and farmlands and hedgerows.'

'And smudgy blue and purple hills, and tractors and churches with lych-gates, and village pubs.'

'Dear me, you aren't a thwarted romantic by any chance, are you, Harry darling?'

'Perish the notion,' said Harry, but he thought: one day I'll write a book with all this as the setting, and with the history and the legend of these places somehow woven into it. Tudor bastard princes and Owen Glendower rebelling against the House of Lancaster... The Book of Taliesin and the Mabinogion, and the Severed Head of Harlech that presided, undecayed, over revelries... And an old, old house named for an ancient law that had been created in the Middle Ages...

He was roused from this reverie by Angelica, who had been map-reading for the last thirty miles, pointing out a turning off the bypass that they had better take. 'And Weston Fferna's about five miles along from the look of things.'

'OK. Yes, there's a signpost to Weston Fferna. You're sure, are you, that this is the right place?'

'Yes, I told you. Simone lived in Weston Fferna for a while as a child. That's when she took that shot of Mortmain House—the one in the gallery. Oh, and the hotel guide says there's a place called the Bridge where we can stay.'

The Bridge was larger and more comfortable than Harry had been expecting, and, since it was Angelica's choice, probably quite expensive. He was beyond worrying about this, however.

They were given two rooms at the front of the building. There were deep comfortable beds with huge puffy eider-downs, and chintz curtains and padded window-seats. If you opened the casement windows you looked directly on to part of an old coach road which had meandered through the countryside before the brash dual carriageway was gouged out.

'*Very* nice,' said Angelica, coming in five minutes later. She did not comment on the separate rooms. Harry was grateful for that.

He said, 'What time is it? Half past eight. OK, I'm going downstairs to do a bit of prospecting.'

'Would you like me to come with you? Or shall I stay up here and change for dinner—although I have to say that the *jumble* I threw into my case in London—'

'Never mind the jumble,' said Harry. 'But you'd better stay up here. You'll only confuse matters.'

Downstairs the small dining-room was serving a few tables with the evening meal. Harry wandered through to the bar, and by way of opening negotiations, requested a whisky and soda. The barman, who seemed to also be the landlord or even the proprietor for all Harry knew, accepted the offer of a drink for himself and was amiably disposed to chat. Yes, this was a fairly quiet time of year for visitors, although they were always very busy during the spring and summer months. Tourists, of course, and romantic weekends. And they did a good trade in bar lunches for people passing through.

Harry said, 'I'm here with Miss Thorne to carry out a bit of research in the area.' He prayed no one had recognized Angelica, and then said, 'We're trying to track down a place that was once an old workhouse or an asylum. We haven't got much to go on except the name, and I'm not even sure if we're looking in the wrong part of the county. But I wonder if you'd know of it?'

'Can but try, you know, sir.' It was said with a faint lilt, not quite Welsh, but getting on that way.

Harry said, 'It's called Mortmain House,' and the barman-cum-landlord set down his own glass of beer, and said, bless us all, sir, everyone hereabouts knew Mortmain House, shocking old ruin it was. So now then, what Mr Fitzglen and his secretary had to do was to take the main road heading for the bypass, turn off sharp left before actually hitting it, and then go on for three miles. They would see Mortmain House high up on the side of the road. You could not, said the barman-cum-proprietor cheerfully, miss it.

I bet you can't, thought Harry, buying the man another drink, and then going back upstairs.

Angelica, told she was Harry's secretary, only grinned, but when asked whether she wanted to come out to find the nightmare mansion there and then, promptly said, well of course she wanted to come; what did Harry think they were there for?

They found the house with ease, and Harry pulled the car off the road, and sat staring up at it.

So this was Simone's nightmare house and Tansy's bleak workhouse, set amidst desolate fields and dark watchful trees. This was the legend-drenched place built around the early seventeen hundreds, named for the ancient law of Dead Man's Hand...

'Are we going up there?' asked Angelica, sounding a bit fearful.

'We are. At least, I am. You can stay in the car if you'd prefer. If you lock the doors you'll be perfectly all right.'

'No, I'll come.' But Angelica cast a doubtful glance at Mortmain's outline. 'I daresay there might be a few ghosts in there, but what's a ghost or two among friends? I refuse to be daunted by ghosts anyway.'

'I don't believe in them,' said Harry firmly. 'Although I'll admit that something probably lingers in there.'

'It'd be odd if it didn't,' said Angelica with one of her unexpected flashes of seriousness. 'It was a workhouse, wasn't it, and people used to see workhouses as a lurking menace. A bogeyman.'

'And now,' said Harry, 'instead of that we've got the Welfare State and Centrepoint-type hostels, and the I'm-owed-a-living mentality.'

'Dear me, I had you down as a sweet old-fashioned romantic.'

'There's nothing romantic about Mortmain's ghosts.'

'I thought you said you didn't believe in ghosts.'

'I don't. Let's just run the car into that patch of shadow under those trees, shall we?'

'Why d'you want to do that?'

'Because I think we should keep our visit as unobtrusive as possible.'

'All right. How do we get up there, does anybody know?' demanded Angelica, as they emerged from the car a few minutes later. 'Because I can't see how on earth— Oh no, wait, there's a sort of track over there.'

As they began to climb the sort of track, Angelica said, 'I do feel as if I might be performing the classic act of every wimpish heroine in every hackneyed thriller film.'

'Tripping guilelessly up to the dark old house on the hill?'

'Finger perplexedly to lips,' agreed Angelica. 'Do we have a plan for this wild escapade?'

'Not really. I just thought we'd walk round the place first. We can do so perfectly quietly.'

'In case there are any black-cloaked counts holding an annual convention of vampires?'

'In case of any drugged-up teenagers,' said Harry.

As they neared the top of the track a sharp wind blew into their faces, sending the night clouds scudding to and fro across the moon. Above them Mortmain seemed to swim in and out of the shadows.

'Are we actually going inside?' demanded Angelica, surveying the place dubiously.

'Yes, because I want to try to identify the places on Simone's prints. I've brought a couple of torches—here, you'd better take one. It'll be as black as the damning drops from the denouncing Angel's pen in there.'

'Really? As black as all that?' said Angelica, deadpan, and Harry smiled despite himself.

He said, 'Yes, but it's not the darkness that worries me.'

'I know it isn't. It's the ghosts.'

'It is. How did you know?'

'It's the ghosts that are worrying me as well,' said Angelica.

After a time Simone became aware of a faint thread of light coming from the stairs. Did that mean the night had passed, then? There was still not enough light to see her watch, but there was a different feeling.

She felt weak and quite odd, although she thought she might have slept for a while, drifting in and out of an uneasy, uncomfortable half-consciousness. Her mind had swung violently between panic and a creeping despair. You'll never get out, said the whisperings and the scufflings. Never, ever get out... You'll die here in the dark, just as Sonia died here in the dark...

She had clung firmly to the belief that either someone would come searching for her, or the hard-eyed woman would come back. This seemed perfectly likely; people did not shut complete strangers away in ruined old houses and leave them to die. It was some bizarre punishment, or the woman was in the grip of a mad fixation. Simone remembered the woman's eyes and the strength of her hands as she had pushed her into the cage, and shuddered.

To keep these images at bay she had tried to recite poetry, but with the perversity of the mind all she could remember was Lovelace's ode about stone walls did not a prison make nor iron bars a cage... The poetry did not really shut out Mortmain's ghosts, either. It did not shut out the scufflings and the scratchings all around her. If a rat gets in here, thought Simone, her skin crawling with horror, I think I'll go genuinely mad.

The scufflings did not get any quieter with the coming of the faint curl of grey light, and after a time Simone thought they might even be growing stronger. Were they rats or ghosts? She half-turned her head listening, because just for a moment she had thought there were voices inside the scufflings. But it had only been her imagination, after all—

Or had it? This time there were more definite sounds, and they were definitely neither rats nor ghosts. Footsteps. The woman coming back to free her? To say it had all been a mistake, or a joke, or a bet? No, surely there was more than one set of footsteps? Yes, they were directly overhead, and Simone was sure she could hear voices as well. People were inside Mortmain House.

Dredging up every ounce of energy, terrified that they might go away without finding her, Simone drew in her breath, and shouted at the top of her voice. But her voice, weakened from the drug, dry from the hours without water, came out in a cracked, feeble croak. Oh God, no! Oh God, let me find a way to let them know I'm here! Don't let them go away without finding me!

She clenched both fists hard, and began systematically banging them on the iron bars of the cage.

❀ ❀ ❀

Harry shone the torch slowly across the dereliction of Mortmain's main hall, recognizing parts of it from Simone's photographs.

'We're in the right place, at any rate,' said Angelica, nodding in agreement.

'Yes. But I don't know if we're going to find anything. I told you I was going on instinct.'

They went deeper in, carefully negotiating the intersecting passageways. The sad smells of worm-eaten timbers and mouldering stones closed around them, and there was the acrid stench of urine—human or animal or both. Their shadows, cast into sharp relief by the torchlight, walked with them: it was fanciful to imagine that occasionally the shadows did not quite walk in step with the two intruders. Harry had to make a conscious effort to shake off the feeling that Floy's small Tansy was among those walking shadows.

The torchbeam cut its livid swathe through the darkness, showing up the crumbling bricks and the crusted dirt of years. Spiders and black beetles scuttled out of their way, and as they went deeper in, towards the house's heart, the shadows were thicker and the stench was almost overpowering. Harry was aware of Angelica fumbling for a handkerchief to put over her mouth, but after a moment, she said, 'Fortunately, I practically *bathed* in *Joy* before we came out. I think *Joy*'s winning, don't you?'

'It usually does,' said Harry, suddenly inexpressibly grateful for Angelica's presence. And then he stopped and Angelica stopped as well, because somewhere inside the old house was a faint sound. They both stood still, hardly daring to breathe. Nothing. Imagination, probably. And then it came again, light, frail. There was a faint rustling in one corner and Harry felt his senses leap, and he shone the torch. A small furry body with a long thin tail scuttled out of sight.

'Oh God,' said Angelica. 'The one thing I hoped we wouldn't see. Harry darling, do a Pied Piper act, or something, and *get rid of it*—'

'It's all right, it's gone. You can have a nice noisy bout of hysterics after we've got outside. In fact would you rather go back down to the car and wait there?'

'And miss the chance to tell this story around a dinner table afterwards? Darling!' said Angelica reproachfully and Harry grinned.

'All right. Onwards and upwards.'

'In any case, you've wanted to do a romantic knight-in-shining-armour act with Sinione ever since you met her, haven't you?' she said shrewdly, and Harry glanced at her.

'You're mixing me up with someone who possesses a heart, Angelica.'

'I don't think I am. And as a matter of fact I think you'd be rather good for Simone.' She glanced at him, and said, 'Harry, *darling*, did you really think I didn't know it was Simone you wanted all the time?'

'Well—'

'But we've had a lot of fun together these past few weeks, haven't we?'

'Angelica,' said Harry, 'you're unique. I can't think of another female who would stage a farewell scene in a situation like this. In fact, in all my experience—'

'Stretching over many nations and five continents?'

'You know,' said Harry after a moment, 'if you don't get rid of that habit of quoting, people will start to think you might be intelligent.'

'Or,' said Angelica levelly, 'that I'm hiding a heart behind the cynicism.'

Before Harry could think how to answer this, she said, 'We'd better finish exploring Karloff Castle, hadn't we? I don't know about you, but personally I'm extremely glad that I'm absymally ignorant about history: I wouldn't want to even start *thinking* about the original purpose of most of these rooms, would you?'

'I'm trying not to.'

Near the back of the house they found a long dim room where the stench of human misery was so strong that it was like walking into a solid wall. There were high, barred windows, and a rotting, worm-eaten floor.

Angelica said in a whisper, 'And there's something on the other side that looks like a lid—'

'It's a well-cover,' said Harry after a moment. 'Oh God, yes, of course it is! It's a *well*, Angelica. That was what Simone photographed! The inside of a well!'

'Yes, I see that. But does it,' demanded Angelica, 'get us any further? I mean, actually? And should we look inside, because—' She broke off. The sound they had both heard earlier—the sound they had thought was the scuttling rat—had come again. And this time it was unmistakably coming from below.

'It's someone banging on a wall or something,' said Harry, after a moment.

'Someone trapped? Simone?' They looked at one another. 'Could it be?' said Angelica.

'I don't know, but we'll have to track it down. Through here, I think.'

They found the stone steps a few minutes later, and went cautiously down. The walls were dripping with damp and condensation, and when Harry moved the torch upwards for a moment there were pale blind fungoid growths on the ceiling.

They reached the foot of the steps, and there, in the torchlight, were rows of iron bars, each one roughly four feet high and two or three feet deep, set against the wall. There were eight or ten of them at least, each one linked to the next.

Cages, thought Harry. Iron cages. For a brief, sickening moment he was back in Floy's book, with Tansy stealing fearfully down to this very room, to hide from the child-traders...

The cages were rusting and discoloured like decaying teeth, and they were filled with rubble and dead leaves. But in one of them something was moving... Something that was huddled inside an iron cage, and something that had bruised and torn hands from perpetually beating against the bars to attract their attention.

It took ten minutes to break off the padlock, but by dint of smashing into it with a partly-crumbled edge of floorstone Harry finally managed it.

'Knight in shining armour after all,' murmured Angelica, but when he paused because his fingers were cramping, she snatched the floorstone off him and took over.

As Simone, half-blinded from the hours in complete darkness, covered in dust and dirt, fell forward into Harry's arms, Angelica, who was nearest to the steps, looked round, and said, 'There's someone coming.'

'Rot,' said Harry, 'you're imagining it. I can't hear anything.'

'No, wait, she's right.' Simone had struggled into a half-sitting position. 'Listen—'

This time Harry heard it as well. Someone was walking quickly through the rooms overhead.

Simone, her eyes distended in purest fear, her hands clutching Harry's, said, 'She's coming back. The woman with brown hair. She's coming back to kill me.'

❋ ❋ ❋

If Harry had been driven by instinct for the past five or six hours, now something even deeper took over. He said, urgently, 'Listen, Simone—can you possibly bear to go back into that thing for about ten more minutes? Because if we're going to lay a real trap—'

In the light from the torch, his face was white and intense. His eyes held Simone's. She said, 'Yes. Yes, all right.'

'Good girl,' said Harry. 'We'll both be just over here, you'll be perfectly safe. Kill the torchlight, Angelica, for God's sake—'

'I am killing it,' said Angelica in a whisper. 'Simone, darling, you're an absolute heroine. I promise we'll crack the most expensive magnum of champagne together when we get out of here.'

CHAPTER THIRTY-SEVEN

Even with the knowledge that she had been rescued and that in a very short time she would be outside and the ordeal behind her, the sudden dousing of the torchlight sent Simone back into the nightmare of the last hours.

It took a great deal of resolve to scramble back into the loathsome cage, but she did it, pulling the iron bars of the door behind her, and crouching in a huddled position against the sides. Her heart was thudding with apprehension and she had absolutely no idea what was going to happen in the next few minutes. But tucked deep in her mind was the memory of the look in Harry's eyes, and the feel of his arms catching her and holding her hard as she had tumbled out on to the stone floor. She supposed that at some point she would find out how he and Angelica had found her, but for the moment it did not matter.

The footsteps were getting louder. Simone's heart was beating so furiously she thought it might burst out of her body. Supposing it was not the woman after all? Supposing it was just some chance passer-by, or a wino looking for a night's doss-down, or— She's at the top of the stairs, thought Simone, tensing, and with the thought a triangle of torchlight suddenly lit up the stairs. It was to be hoped Harry had some kind of plan: Simone had not the remotest idea of what to do.

The torchlight was coming nearer. Would the woman expect her to be dead by this time? Simone was pretty sure she had been down here for nearly twenty-four hours; she was ragingly thirsty and hungry and she felt as if she was in the middle of a bad attack of flu, but she was nowhere near dying and if the woman really was a nurse she would surely know that. Then she's coming back to finish me off, thought Simone, and panic swept in again.

When the woman stepped into the stone underground room there was a sense of surprise, because for the past hours Simone had been building her up as a monster, and the reality was so different. She had not realized how small and how almost insignificant the woman was. You would pass her in a crowd fifty times and never notice her. Plain, a bit dumpy, dressed in drab clothes... But the eyes were the hard, cold eyes Simone had looked into yesterday, and the hands were as she remembered them: unstill and nervous.

She came up to the cage and knelt down so that her face was on a level with Simone's. 'Still alive, Simone?' she said. 'I thought you would be. But I don't suppose you've had a very good few hours, have you? That was all part of the plan, of course. You had to be frightened and you had to know you were going to die.'

Simone said, 'Am I going to die?'

'Oh yes.' The woman was pulling something out of her coat pocket that glinted. A syringe? 'You'll die quite quickly, Simone, and I'll be here to watch you do it. And then I'll take your body to the hillside where I buried Sonia. I think it will be a nice touch to put the two of you together, don't you?'

'I think it'll be a lousy touch, Rosie,' said Harry's voice, and he stepped out of the shadows, Angelica at his side, and switched on his own torch.

She backed away at once, her eyes bolting from her head in the glare of the torch. Simone, consumed with fear but also with a terrible pity, thought she looked exactly like a small unattractive animal caught in car headlights on a dark night.

Before Harry and Angelica could pounce—certainly before Simone could crawl out of the cage again—Roz had whipped round and was running back up the stone steps. Harry went after her, hurling himself across the room, but Simone could hear that the woman had already reached the top of the steps, and that she was running hard across the rooms above.

Simone was not at the time aware of scrambling out of the cage, but she must have done so, because she and Angelica were running hard after the other two, and Angelica had switched on her own torch.

'Darling, are you sure you're all right—?'

'Never better,' said Simone, who was feeling so weak and light-headed she was not at all sure she would be able to reach the top of the steps.

'Shouldn't you be lying down—blankets and brandy and things—?'

'We can do all that afterwards. Don't fuss, Angelica.' And miraculously she had reached the head of the stone steps, and they were crossing to the room that Sonia had once called the Paupers' Room, and the ghosts were back in full force now, because they had never really gone away in the first place, those ghosts—

It was not until they reached the central hall with the cold spears of moonlight sliding across the ground, that they caught up with Harry. He was standing in the doorway, staring out into the night; his hair was untidy from the chase through Mortmain's rooms and he looked pale and angry. He said, 'I've lost the bitch. Either she's hiding out somewhere in this wretched ruin, or—'

All three of them heard, faintly but definitely, the sound of a car starting up on the road below, and driving off into the night.

'We've lost her,' said Harry, and swore profusely.

Charlotte Quinton's diaries:
23rd November 1914
I have lain awake for most of the night, and now, this morning, I am convinced that Floy's idea to have a straightforward interview with Dancy is wrong. Dancy is twisted and warped and evil, but I have the strongest feeling that he could also be extremely cunning.

And the only way to outwit cunning is to meet it with more cunning.

So, as soon as I have finished the coffee and toast brought up to me by the chambermaid, I shall ask them to have the pony and trap ready earlier than Floy had arranged. The young man who drives it is acquiescent and unquestioning: suspect he may be what the locals call a 'natural', but perfectly good-humoured and trustworthy. Floy has, of course, already paid for his services in driving us around, but I shall reward him with a couple of sovereigns as well after this is all over. And if luck is with me I shall be able to set off before Floy even realises I have gone.

(Am distinctly unhappy at practising this deceit on Floy, although have no qualms *whatsoever* about practising any kind of deceit at all upon Edward.)

However, needs must when the devil drives, and if ever the devil drove anything, he will be doing so today...

24th November

The Pheasant Inn turned out be be rather a sleazy place—Edward would have apoplexy at the thought of his wife entering such a place, and suspect Floy would not be too pleased about it, either. I asked the driver to wait for me, and went inside.

The main door opened directly on to what I thought was a tap-room (although I have no idea how to recognize a tap-room), and a slatternly-looking female asked, politely enough, how she could help me.

'I wish to see Mr Dancy, if you please.' I used Mamma's most commanding voice, and was glad to see it had its effect. Also, was wearing a very authoritative hat, which may have helped.

Either the hat or the voice, or possibly both, worked, because within a few minutes I was shown to a room on the first floor, overlooking a cobblestoned yard at the rear. Beyond the small window I saw the covered drays, and my heart began to thump erratically. Were Viola and Sorrel in there? I was just wondering if I dared go out of the room and across the yard, when the door opened and he was there. The man I had for the past three weeks been hating with an intensity that frightened me.

I had visualized him as a semi-ogre—a huge blustering red-faced man with mean little eyes and greedy hands, and the reality was not so very much different, except that his voice—this was a shock—was much quieter than I had expected.

He said, in this soft, nearly-cultured voice that sat so oddly on him, 'How can I help you, Miss—Mrs—?'

I had kept my gloves on so he could not see my wedding-ring. I said, with an attempt at efficient sprightliness, 'Miss Craven.' (Did not dare use real name in case he recognized it from the twins.) 'I am from *Blackwood's Magazine*, Mr Dancy, and I should very much like to talk to you about your work. For an article, you know.'

He liked the word 'work'; I saw that at once. Men are ridiculously easy to flatter. He waved me to a seat on a greasy-looking sofa, and sat next to me. How extraordinary, he said, patting my hand, to find a young lady in this branch of work, although, of course, the war made it necessary for ladies to take on men's work.

I am actually thirty-seven next birthday so by no stretch of the imagination can I be called young, but this was a promising start, so I said, 'That's very understanding of you, Mr Dancy. I saw your performers last evening, and thought them quite an extraordinary group.'

He leaned nearer, smiling down at me, and told me about his music hall and his travelling show. I was waiting for him to refer to the twins, but he did not, although he recounted, in a voice full of self-congratulation, how he had come by some of the other poor creatures whom he showed to the public.

I scribbled notes, more or less at random (had brought my travelling notebook for the purpose), and in a very short time he was not only patting my hand but holding it in his, and eyeing my figure. It took him another five minutes to make his pounce.

It was the most utterly loathsome experience to feel this repulsive creature's hands pawing my body, but it was what I had planned and angled for.

I instantly donned an air of outraged, but over-awed, innocence, with—God help me!—a coy understanding beneath. 'Oh, Mr Dancy, whatever kind of girl do you think I am...' (Had practised before leaving, and think it came out quite well.)

But it was necessary to manoeuvre him into a position in which I would have greater physical dominance, so I set my teeth throughout the next few minutes, and allowed him a few fumbling intimacies. He slobbered kisses over my neck (will never be able to wear any of these clothes again!) and slid his free hand up under my skirt, forcing me back so that I was half-lying against the sofa's back. He was half on top of me, his thick body pressing into me so that I could feel his arousal thrusting insistently against my legs: a thick blunt hardness like a battering ram. He would prob-ably use it in just that way, as well—have noticed more than once that a man's character is frequently reflected in his sexual organ.

His face was flushed an unbecoming crimson and he was breathing harshly. I waited until he had fumbled at the fastening of his trousers and pushed them down around his knees, and then I reached into my jacket pocket (so useful, these tailor-mades!) and brought out the long-bladed breadknife I had taken from the Bridge kitchens when I took my breakfast tray down.

In a voice quite different from the one I had been using, and far more like Mamma's ringing committee tones, I said, 'Please don't move, Mr Dancy, for if you do I will stick this knife straight into your kidneys and I believe that is a vastly painful way to die.'

Do not think I have ever felt an erection dwindle so speedily. He became still at once, but his mean little eyes darted to my face like a watchful snake. He said, in a poor attempt at bluff archness, 'And now what game are you playing, Miss Craven?'

'My name isn't Craven,' I said, coldly. 'And it isn't "Miss". I'm Charlotte Quinton.' The flush faded from his cheeks, leaving a blotchy pallor. 'I see you know who I am,' I said. 'That makes everything much simpler. No—don't try to resist, because I'm very tempted indeed to kill you outright. And if we can't come to an agreement I may have to do so anyway.'

'What do you want, you bitch?'

'My daughters, of course,' I said. 'The twins.'

'Oh no,' he said. 'Not those two. They're mine—all legal and above board. Your own husband signed them over to the Mortmain Trust—'

'Let's not play with words. We both know that you're the Mortmain Trust. I suppose Edward paid you to keep quiet about his deception, did he? Yes, I thought he must have done.' I felt him move slightly as if he was about to jerk away, so I dug the point of the knife very slightly into his back. It penetrated his coat and scraped his flesh so that he gasped with sudden pain and surprise. 'I will kill you if I have to,' I said. 'I promise you that I really will. You're an evil animal, and I find you utterly disgusting and I would kill a hundred people to free my daughters.'

'They'd hang you for it, you bitch.'

'I'll risk that. Now tell me where the adoption papers are, so that I can destroy them and take my daughters home.'

He was sweating so profusely that I could smell it—a horrid yeasty stench that made me feel sick. But he said, 'In the portmanteau,' and indicated a worn-looking carpet bag in a corner of the room. 'I take my papers with me when I travel.'

'Stand up,' I said. 'But remember that when you do,

this knife will be in direct line with your repulsive genitals.'

'You wouldn't do that, my dear— Come now—' Incredibly his voice was sliding back into the treacly patronizing note of earlier.

'Oh, I would,' I said. 'And I would enjoy it.'

He stood up slowly, a ridiculous figure with his trousers around his knees. He made to pull them up but I stopped him because it was an effective way of hobbling him, and so he shuffled awkwardly to where the bag was, and reached inside. There was a bad moment when I feared that he might snatch something heavy—a plantpot or one of the hideous china ornaments from the mantel—and fling it at me, but he did not. He rifled through a sheaf of papers, and then sulkily held out two sheets, covered in lawyers' copperplate.

'Good,' I said, and like a fool I reached forward to take them.

It was what he had been waiting for, of course; within four seconds he had kicked his trousers off over his boots and launched himself at me. He knocked the knife out of my hand and pushed me back on to the sofa, one hand clasping itself around my neck, half throttling me.

'You stupid cunt,' he said. 'Did you really think you could get the better of Matt Dancy? I don't let any woman get the better of me and certainly not you.' His other hand was already circling both my wrists. I struggled against him, kicking his shins and trying to bring my knee up to jab into his groin but he was too strong.

'You won't have your precious brats,' he said, in a hissing voice, his breath hot and fetid in my face. 'They're for me. They're money-spinners, those two. People *pay* to see them sing and dance on a stage.

And there's something else.' His face swam nearer to mine, red and exultant and ugly. 'In another couple of months I'm going to fuck them, your precious daughters,' he said. 'I've been saving them up for that. And afterwards—after I've taught them a trick or two—there'll be many a man will pay to have them in bed.'

I stared up at him in horror, and he laughed. 'They're freaks, you stupid whey-faced bitch—*freaks!*—and there's plenty of men who get a hard-on just thinking about being in bed with a freak! Women too.'

At that I sank my teeth into his hand, and he swore and smacked me hard across my mouth. 'Cat,' he said. 'You'd better be taught a lesson. You don't come in here with your fluttering eyes and your soft white skin, and give a man a stand like a telegraph pole, and then draw a knife on him—not without being punished for it, you don't.' Incredibly one hand came up to stroke my face. 'White skin,' he said in a voice suddenly thick. 'And a ladylike voice. I've always been partial to the ladylike ones,' he said, and I realized with horror that he had become aroused again.

I fought him for all I was worth but he was strong and heavy and I was no match for him. Then I yelled for help, but he only laughed. 'Scream away, my soft white bird,' he said. 'No one here pays much attention to a screaming female.'

He jerked my legs wide and tore aside the thin underclothes I was wearing, so that there was the repulsive heat of his body against mine—coarse skin and hair, and the hot stalk of masculinity against my thighs. I yelled again, and thought that somewhere down in the tavern a door opened and closed. But it was already too late, he was already starting to force himself inside me.

The door opened and he turned his head towards

it instinctively. I saw his expression alter, and incredibly he released me. There was a darting movement from the door and I struggled to a sitting position, and turned my head. And then I saw who was standing in the doorway, and I saw the horrified understanding on the two young faces.

Viola and Sorrel. My lost babies, seeing me for the first time in the grotesque embrace of this evil monster.

They moved across the room, and I saw Viola snatch up the discarded breadknife. Viola, whose left arm had to be around around Sorrel's waist, but whose right hand was already raising the knife—

I think I cried out but it was already too late. Viola brought the knife plunging down and drove it deep and hard into Dancy's thick neck.

He staggered back at once, his eyes bulging, blood spurting from his neck. He flailed helplessly at the air, and tried feebly to pull at the knife, but before he could reach it he crashed to the floor. His body jerked and twitched and froth appeared on his lips, and then he was still.

After what seemed to be a very long time, I raised my eyes and looked at them. They were watching me with Floy's eyes, but I could see, as I had not done last night, that they had my cheekbones and my too-wide mouth.

I managed to pull my skirt down and tug my jacket into some semblance of order. I said, as calmly as I could, 'Is he dead?' My first words to my daughters.

'Yes, he's dead.' Viola again.

'Do you know who I am?'

'Oh yes,' she said, and Sorrel nodded. She's gentler, I thought, and I looked at her, wanting to hear her speak. She said, 'Anthony saw you last night—he told us he saw you. He met you once before. He said you looked exactly like us. So we knew then.'

'Anthony?' We were talking about things that did not matter: I was aching to rush forward and wrap my arms around them both but I did not yet dare.

'Anthony Raffan,' said Viola. 'He was at Mortmain—he met you there one day years and years ago. He told us.'

'He told us that you swore on our names that you'd never tell what he did to one of Mr Dancy's men.'

Memory flipped upwards and I was standing in Mortmain again, facing the ragged little girl called Robyn. 'Promise on the thing you hold most sacred in the world,' she had said, and I had at once said, 'I promise on the memories of Viola and Sorrel that I'll never tell.'

'Anthony told us about it,' said Viola, watching me. 'That's how we know who you are. He followed us when Dancy took us away. He said one day he would help us to escape.'

'We knew you'd come one day,' said Sorrel.

'I thought you were dead. Your—my husband told me you were dead.' I glanced across the room at Dancy's body, and Viola said, at once, 'It's all right about Dancy. No one will guess we did it,' and I saw that she did not in the least care that she had just killed a man, and when I thought about it—when I thought about what Matt Dancy had done, and about all the children he had taken and abused and forced into prostitution—I discovered that I did not care either.

'Are you going to take us away?' said Sorrel, and I saw that she was on the verge of tears.

'Would you like that? Would you come with me now?'

'Oh yes,' they said together.

But would there be anything to link the twins to Matt Dancy's death? Viola killed him, said a small voice somewhere inside my mind. It was Viola who did it.

I said, 'Listen, this is what we're going to do. We're going to walk out of here, quite calmly and quite normally, and we're going to get into the trap that's waiting for me just along the road, and we're going to make a normal life for you.'

That was when I crossed the room and put my arms round them and when I felt, for the first time, their soft cheeks pressed against mine.

Roz knew she had only escaped Harry Fitzglen because she knew the layout of Mortmain House and he did not. So she had been able to run through the rooms and along the passageways until she came out into the central hall. Aunt Vi had been with her, to see that she found the way, and Sonia as well, and behind them had been all those long-ago children from Mortmain.

Once she was in the hall she had gone out into the night, and back down the hill like a thin shadow.

She drove back to London, hardly noticing the roads, hardly aware of her earlier fatigue. In front of her mind was the look in Harry Fitzglen's eyes when he had stepped out of the shadows. Pity. Contempt.

She had no idea whether Harry and that little alley-cat, Angelica Thorne, were following her, but she thought they were not. She reached her own house around one a.m., and went inside, switching on lights and locking all the doors and windows. Aunt Vi had always kept doors and windows locked; it was better to shut out the world, she used to say.

But Roz would not be able to shut out the world. Harry Fitzglen knew how to find her: he knew where she worked, and even though he had looked at her with that pity, he would tell people what she had done and there would be a police investigation and a charge of attempted murder. And before very long Roz would be shut away as a punishment.

'There's always the punishment,' Aunt Vi had said. 'I sinned once—a great, great sin, Rosamund, the worst sin in the world—and because of that I have lived my life alone. Sorrel left me after the doctors had finished with us—she married Anthony and they went away. They were your grandmother and grandfather, Rosamund.' She indicated one of the silver-framed photographs on the mantelpiece. 'They had a son together—Charles, his name was. He was your father, Rosamund, and he was my nephew, but I never knew him. They all lived in France, and then they died in a car crash when you were small. I never had anyone except you.'

Roz could hear Viola's voice very clearly tonight as she sat in the room that had been Viola's sitting-room, the photographs that had been Viola's staring down from the walls and the mantelpiece. Family photographs, cherished and polished, several in silver frames. All of the faces familiar to Roz. All of them looking at her now with the same pity and the same disgust as Harry Fitzglen...

Her head was beginning to hurt, and the pain seemed to be slicing through her mind, splitting it agonizingly in two. One half of her—Rosie's half—knew that there ought to be some means of escaping Harry, who would certainly hunt her down, but the other half knew there was no way of doing so. In her mind she was already seeing the humiliation of a trial, seeing herself convicted of trying to kill Simone. Perhaps they would even find out what she had done to Isobel Ingram, and how she had stolen the baby from St Luke's and left it in Isobel's flat to burn, and taken Sonia. But she had lost Sonia as well, and with the thought she saw Viola nodding and saying, Yes, that was what happened when you had committed a sin: you lost everything that was most dear to you.

They'll shut you away for ever once they know what you've done, Roz... They'll say you're mad, that you can't be allowed to live in the world ever again... You'll be put behind heavy clanging doors, exactly as Viola and Sorrel were put behind heavy clanging doors... Exactly as all those children were—those children who sang the song...

> *And naked to the hangman's noose*
> *The morning clocks will ring*
> *A neck God made for other use*
> *Than strangling in a string...*

Strangling in a string...

It was not so very long since people had been hanged for murder. Viola had murdered someone but she had not been hanged because her mother had smuggled her and Sorrel away. Viola had told Roz about that one night, saying that at the time she had not thought that what she had done had been wrong, for the man she had killed had been evil. But then afterwards—yes, afterwards, she had seen her act for what it really was and she had come to see that although she had escaped the justice of men, she had not escaped that of God. God had punished her by taking Sorrel away from her, and by never allowing her to meet a man to marry and have children with.

They would send Roz to prison, or perhaps to some grim bleak institution where they would prod and pry into her mind, and try to understand the things she had done. I can't face it, thought Roz. There must be a way out of this.

It was as if Viola and Sorrel—Sonia too—had come to be with Roz properly at last, and as if they were looking at her with pitying eyes.

There is a way out of this, Roz, there IS...

She had almost forgotten Rosie, but suddenly Rosie was with her, and she turned her head slightly, the better to hear what Rosie was saying.

You can cheat them, Roz, you can, you CAN...

Can I? How can I?

You already know...said Rosie inside Roz's mind. You know how it has to end, Roz... You do know, don't you...?

She got up from the chair, moving very slowly and very quietly. A way out...

People would be shocked; they would say, Roz Raffan? Good, unexciting Sister Raffan? Surely not. They would talk and speculate for a while, and then they would forget.

Do it now, Roz... Do it quickly, for there isn't much time...

Yes, whispered Roz. Yes, I must do it quickly. And I must do it *right*. She went into the kitchen where she had prepared supper for Joe Anderson and later for Harry Fitzglen, and from the cupboard under the sink she took a length of clothes line. Then she climbed the stairs to the landing with its railed banisters around the deep stairwell. She wound one end around the banister, and tested it. There was a faint creak, but the wood held, and the clothes line was tough and strong.

She looped the other end around her neck, and then climbed on to the banisters. It was what the ghosts all wanted her to do: Viola and Sorrel and Sonia. And there was someone else there with them as well now: a thin-faced woman whose face Roz did not at first recognize. Who—? And then she realized who it was. Isobel Ingram. Isobel, whom she had murdered more than twenty years ago, and whom she had not thought of for years. Punishment, you see. Retribution. Yes, it was right that Isobel should be here tonight to see that Roz did what had to be done.

But as she climbed up on to the banisters, her last thought before she jumped down into the stairwell was of Sonia. Would Sonia be waiting for her?

CHAPTER THIRTY-EIGHT

THE HOUSE WAS at the end of a narrow lane, on the very edge of England's east coast. The clean pure light of the North Sea was everywhere.

The house was not quite what Harry had been expecting—it faced out to the sea, but it was modern and almost streamlined. Its owner was not quite what he had been expecting, either.

'I'm so glad you're here,' she had said when he arrived. 'Simone's told me quite a lot about you. You saved her life, of course. I don't know how to begin to thank you for that.' There were no polite preliminaries: no, how do you do, did you have a good journey, stuff. Straight in with, Thank you for saving my daughter's life. This, then, was the woman at the heart of the twenty-year-old legend Harry had spent the past weeks trying to unravel.

'It was Angelica who found the photograph of Mortmain that afternoon,' he said. 'All I did was help her put two and two together. And if I'd done that sooner, we might have saved Simone the night inside Mortmain.'

'If you had done it later,' said Melissa Anderson, 'Simone might not have lived to tell the tale.' She smiled at him, and Harry, who had been thinking she was quite ordinary-looking, suddenly saw why her memory had brought that odd look of wistfulness to the face of a cynical hard-bitten Fleet Street hack. She had a quality, Markovitch had said, commissioning Harry to write the article about this family. There had been something about her that made her stick in your mind. Simone had the same quality.

'I'm glad you could come,' Mel was saying. 'It's so remote here, not everyone wants to. But it's a nice kind of remoteness, isn't it?'

'Yes. Tranquil. Something to do with the light.'

'It is, isn't it?' She looked at him eagerly, as if pleased to hear this. 'I lived in Norfolk for a while when Simone and her sister were very tiny—in a village just a few miles along the coast road—and I fell in love with the whole area. I always wanted to come back.'

'To dodge the journalists?'

'Partly. Not you. I don't want to dodge you. I'm glad you're here. Simone's glad as well.'

'Is she?' Harry was annoyed to find that this came out a bit anxiously. What happened to the narrow-eyed cynic and the sardonic heartbreaker?

'I've given you the little room at the back—I think you'll be comfortable,' said Mel. 'It's quite snug, and— Oh —this is Martin. You haven't met, have you?'

'No,' said Harry. 'We spoke on the phone, though.' He shook hands with Martin, and then said, 'This is actually quite an odd experience. In a way I've lived with you both for the last few weeks, even though you didn't know about it. So I feel as if I know you very well. But there are still bits of the jigsaw that I don't know.'

'There are bits we don't know, either,' said Martin. 'That's one of the reasons we wanted you to come; so that we can fit them together. Simone's gone for a walk along the coast—she often does that when she's here. She'll be back quite soon. Come in and have a drink. Is that your case? Good. You can unpack, and when we've had supper we'll make a start on the jigsaw.'

'It took a while to fit together the pieces I've actually got,' said Harry, as they sat in the low-ceilinged room with the transparent Norfolk light flooding the house. 'But in the end I managed it.' He looked at Simone who was curled into a chair by the window. The light turned her hair to spun bronze. 'One of the really curious things,' he said, 'is the links with those other twins—Viola and Sorrel Quinton.'

'It was Sorrel who was Roz's grandmother?' This was Martin.

'Yes. I think,' said Harry, 'that Roz saw a parallel between the two sets of twins—I think it attracted her to your family very strongly, although it wasn't a healthy attraction. I think she resented that you had given birth to twins whose condition mirrored that of Viola and Sorrel and that you had done so in an age when there was a good chance that it could be dealt with.' He looked at Mel. 'But I'm on thin ice as to exactly what happened between you and Roz.'

'To begin with I thought she was a friend,' said Mel slowly. 'I even felt sorry for her because she seemed so alone in the world, and she seemed so very attached to the twins— And then one day, quite out of the blue, she began talking about being owed a child.' She glanced at Simone. 'It sounds so melodramatic to say it now, but she wanted you or Sonia for herself.'

'That's mad,' said Simone, and Harry saw her shiver and glance towards the door as if she was afraid someone might be standing outside, waiting for her.

Mel said, 'She was seriously disturbed of course, but none of us realized that until it was too late. There had been a bit of an affair between her and Joe—my husband—and Roz had apparently become pregnant by him and then miscarried.'

Simone leaned forward at this. 'Didn't you find that dreadful?' she said. 'You never talk about my father, but you must have been devastated to find he'd been unfaithful with someone you thought was a friend.'

'No, I wasn't devastated,' said Mel, meeting her eyes. 'He was not a very easy man, your father.'

Harry thought she faltered, and at once Martin said, smoothly, 'As for Roz, it's not unknown for women to flip after a miscarriage, and try to steal other children.'

'I knew that at the time,' said Mel. 'And was desperately sorry for her. I thought she was unbalanced, although I didn't realize how mentally disturbed she really was. None of us did. So I made a plan to get you and Sonia away. Once we were out of England—once the operation had taken place and hopefully you had both survived it—Martin was going to try to get psychiatric help for Roz.'

'So you decided to just disappear?'

'Yes. I wanted to escape Roz, but I wanted to escape the press, as well.' Mel looked at Harry. 'They had been very intrusive.'

'I can imagine.'

'So,' said Mel, 'we smuggled the twins into Switzerland for the operation. A close friend of mine—Isobel Ingram—came with us, and afterwards she brought Sonia back and I brought Simone. We crossed to England on separate ferries—we reasoned that one woman travelling with a single baby wouldn't attract any attention.'

'Yes, I see that,' said Simone.

'The plan was that we'd let the dust settle for a few weeks—Sonia would stay with Isobel during that time—and eventually I'd vanish with both of you. Change my name and go to live somewhere else. We'd become an anonymous family—a widow with twin daughters. Completely unremarkable.'

'But before any of that could happen,' said Martin, 'Isobel's flat burned down with Isobel and Sonia inside—at least, a child we assumed to be Sonia.'

'Only we couldn't tell anyone we thought it was Sonia, because we had let it be believed that Sonia had died in Switzerland after the operation,' said Mel. 'I was absolutely distraught at losing Sonia—as I thought—but as well as that I was still desperately afraid of Roz.'

'So you did everything possible to get beyond her reach,' said Harry.

'Yes. From a practical aspect it wasn't too difficult. There were insurances from Joe's death, and then I found out that Isobel had left me her flat and some money. So I sold the house and left London, and changed my name. And by then,' she said, looking at Simone, 'you were all I had. I didn't dare draw attention to myself, and I didn't dare draw attention to Martin, either. He had already sailed very close to the wind by condoning the conspiracy that Sonia died in Switzerland. So I ran away.'

'It took me a very long time to find her,' said Martin. 'She moved from place to place like a grasshopper. But in the end, I did find her.'

Harry had the sudden impression that mentally and silently they smiled at one another.

Mel said, 'I didn't know that Roz had got Sonia all the time, of course. I keep thinking that if only I had known, Sonia might have turned out differently—she needn't have died—'

'Didn't you check on Roz?'

'Yes, because I thought I might need to warn Simone. But St Luke's said she had left—that she had taken a job in the north to be near family, and I thought she had probably got over the miscarriage, and that she was making a fresh start somewhere. I thought the danger was over.'

'But,' said Harry, 'the child who died in your friend's flat—'

'There was certainly a child's body there,' said Martin. 'A baby of around the right age. But the body was badly charred—both bodies were badly charred—and conventional identification wasn't possible. And this was more than twenty years ago remember, and there was no DNA testing then.'

'I took it at face value,' said Mel. 'I accepted that Sonia was dead. Whether Roz engineered the fire at Isobel's flat, I don't know.'

'But later on,' said Harry, thoughtfully, 'Sonia began talking to Simone, and years afterwards they met in that Welsh village.'

'Yes.'

'I still find that a bit spooky,' said Simone.

'It isn't really,' said Martin at once. 'Telepathy isn't so uncommon between twins.'

'I meant the way she knew so much about Mortmain,' said Simone. 'But I see now that that was all from Viola's memories.'

'Viola had actually lived in Mortmain with Sorrel,' said Harry. 'She probably talked to Roz about it quite a lot. And Mortmain was a workhouse of the worst Victorian kind. For a child to live there would scar it deeply. I think Viola was scarred by those years—I think she passed a lot of the—the *darkness* of it all on to Roz.'

'That's your side of the jigsaw, isn't it?' said Simone. 'Viola and Sorrel.'

'Yes. Roz is dead, so a lot of it's guesswork,' said Harry. 'But I worked backwards from Roz, and also—' He paused, and then said, 'I managed to talk my way into getting inside her house after the inquest.'

'Friends in high places?' Martin said it with a grin.

'One or two favours called in,' said Harry. 'Probably vaguely illegal, but it meant I got a look at a lot of documents before they were taken away. Roz's grandmother was Sorrel Quinton. I ransacked hospital archives for the first twenty years of the twentieth century, and although I didn't find the record of their birth, I did find that the Quinton twins were surgically separated just after World War I ended—they were seventeen or eighteen. There was a brief record of it in the archives of Thomas's Hospital.'

'It would have been a barbaric procedure,' said Martin. 'Anaesthetics were still quite primitive then.'

'But both the twins survived the operation,' said Harry. 'And later Sorrel married a man called Anthony Raffan. There was a marriage certificate in Roz's desk in her bedroom, and there was a birth certificate for a son born in 1925. Charles Raffan. From there on it was quite easy to trace them all.' He paused again, and then said, 'I'm seeing Sorrel as relatively normal. I think she had quite an ordinary, happy marriage and life.' Careful, said his mind. You're letting the hard-bitten cynical act slip again. 'But Viola never married,' he said. 'I don't know if that was because she came out of the operation more—well, more damaged than Sorrel. I don't necessarily mean physically. And then Sorrel's son died in a car crash when Roz was four or five—there was the death certificate for him and his wife—and that was probably when Roz went to live with Viola.'

'Why Viola?' This was Martin. 'Why not Sorrel, who was married and living an ordinary life?'

'And who was also Roz's grandmother,' put in Mel.

'Sorrel died in the late 1950s,' said Harry. 'I can't remember the exact year, but there was a copy of a death certificate among the documents in Roz's house. I should think Roz hadn't even been born then.'

'So that when Roz's own parents died, Viola was the only one who could take her,' said Martin. 'Yes, I see.'

'It's so easy to imagine Viola pouring out all her anger and bitterness to Roz, isn't it?' said Harry. 'All her memories of the years spent inside Mortmain.'

'All the memories Roz passed on to Sonia,' said Simone.

'Oh yes.'

'It's no wonder Sonia hated Roz,' said Simone thoughtfully. 'And she *did* hate her, you know. She hated the—the weight of the sadness and the burden of sadness that Roz kept laying on her. Sorry, I'm interrupting the story. Go on about Sorrel and Viola.'

Harry said, 'When they were in their early teens they were sold to, or stolen by a man who had one of those appalling freak-shows. They were toured around the country.'

Martin said slowly, 'Straight from a workhouse into a freak-show. That's something you might never recover from.'

'I don't think Viola ever did recover from it,' said Harry.

Simone was leaning forward, her expression absorbed. 'How do you know all this?'

'Because,' said Harry, 'a man called Philip Fleury who lived at the same time knew about them. He knew a very great deal, and I've picked up a lot of clues from him. And this is where we hit the only real coincidence in all this. The Bloomsbury house that's now Thorne's Gallery was once owned by Fleury. I found him when I was tracing the house's history.' He glanced at Simone, and then said, 'Fleury—Floy he used to be called—wrote a book about a little girl who lived in Mortmain House when it was a workhouse and an orphanage: a little girl who was there from the time she was a baby, and who was taken by a child-trader to a London brothel when she was twelve or so. At the end of his book Floy refers to Viola and Sorrel, and to their appearance in a touring show managed by a man called Matt Dancy. At first I thought it was just part of Floy's story, but he had dedicated the book to Viola and Sorrel. So then I managed to dig up an ancient playbill from 1914, and sure enough Viola and Sorrel Quinton were once exhibits in a freak show owned by a man called Matt Dancy.'

'I found a reference to those twins,' said Mel. 'To Sorrel and Viola. Before my twins were born I read up a few cases of other conjoined twins—d'you remember suggesting that, Martin? It was only a brief reference in one of the books, but it stuck with me.'

Harry reached into the battered briefcase at the side of his chair. 'This is Floy's book,' he said. 'It's called *The Ivory Gate*, and it's really the story of Viola and Sorrel's childhood, I think. The dedication is to them, and also to someone Floy only called "C". But it's a truly remarkable story, and I think if it belongs to anyone, it should belong to you.' He handed the book to Simone.

CHAPTER THIRTY-NINE

Final extracts from Charlotte Quinton's diaries
26th November 1914

We reached London midway through the afternoon; Floy had somehow managed to acquire a motor-car to bring us back, which was better and more private for the twins.

They sat quietly in the back, not saying very much, but watching the scenery slide past. Sorrel enjoyed it—I could see that, but Viola seemed wary and suspicious. Will have to remember what happened in that tavern room when she picked up the knife, and I think I will have to go very carefully with Viola.

Floy took us to his own house, and made tea for us all. (Am not sure how I shall cope seeing the twins eating and drinking, each using their free hand, passing things to one another, and clearly doing so without needing to think about it.)

The girls will stay with Floy in Bloomsbury for the moment; there is a big bedroom at the back of the house where they can sleep and be as private as they want. They will have to be brought into the ordinary world so gently and so gradually, and there will need to be discussions with doctors, to see if there is any way of alleviating their condition.

It was late by the time Floy finally put me in a cab, but we had talked, he and I, and we are agreed as to what must now happen. Floy has sent a note by special messenger requesting an interview with Edward later this evening.

Later

Edward sulky when I reached home. A fine thing when a man's wife is not at home to greet him after a business absence, and why must I need go off to see my family at such a time?—could I not content myself with the running of my home like most women? He had provided a comfortable home for me, and he had rather thought I would like to stay inside it. I said, as quietly as I could, that I was sorry he had missed me, and he countered this after dinner by saying he supposed my gallivanting was to blame for the poor quality of tonight's dinner.

(Dinner, in fact, was a soup made from leeks and potatoes from our own garden, followed by one of Mrs Tigg's delicious steak and oyster pies—have not *dared* ask how she obtained the meat!—and castle pudding with blackberry sauce to finish. Edward drank the best part of a bottle of claret. What does this deceitful, conceited man *want*, for pity's sake!)

Over coffee, he said, disgruntled, that as if all his other problems were not enough, now here was this man, Philip Fleury, calling without invitation, and what did he want, Edward would like to know. A mere acquaintance, that was all Fleury was.

I came upstairs, pleading a headache, and I am sitting in my bedroom waiting for the sounds of Floy's arrival, and I am frankly frightened to death at the thought of what is going to happen.

Midnight
This is going to be appallingly difficult to write, but I shall try.

Floy arrived punctually, and was shown into Edward's study. After a moment I went downstairs and joined them— Edward v. surprised— No need for you to be here, my dear; a little bit of business to discuss, just between men, run along now.

But I stayed, of course, and I listened as Floy related the facts of Viola and Sorrel's birth, and how they had endured all those years in Mortmain and then been taken by Dancy for his freak show.

Edward was inclined to bluster and order Floy from the house—Can't see what any of this has to do with you—but Floy simply waited until Edward had huffed and puffed himself into silence, and then said, 'Quinton, it's useless to adopt that attitude. I know what you did and I have proof of it. You sold your own daughters into the most appalling misery, and you let your wife and the rest of your family believe they were dead. You even arranged for a false funeral—and a revolting piece of over-sentimental theatre that was! How many people did you bribe to stage it, Quinton? Quite a large number, I imagine. You do know, I suppose, that quite apart from the rest, that fake funeral was a criminal offence?'

He glanced to where I was seated, and before

Edward could respond, said, with a formal politeness that I had never heard him use before, 'Forgive
me for this,' and then stepped back into the hall, and
said to someone waiting there, 'Come in, please. He's
in here.'

In the doorway stood two men, one dressed in
plain dark clothes, the other wearing the uniform of
a police constable.

In the same remote voice, Floy said, 'That is the
man I wish you to arrest. You will have your own
language for the charges, but in broad terms they will
be for deception, bribery, and the unlawful trafficking
in minors.'

And so now they have taken Edward away to
their cells, and tomorrow morning he will face a
charge—several charges. The irony is that it seems
unlikely that he can be made to answer for giving
the twins into Matt Dancy's care—as their legal
guardian it is possible that the court will rule that
he acted within his rights. (Nothing to prevent
a parent selling a child into almost any kind of
slavery, it seems—not so long since hundreds of
poor mites were given to chimney-sweepers).

The policemen explained some of the formalities to
me, but I had gone beyond understanding properly
by that time. But I think Edward is going to have to
answer to charges of various forms of deception and
fraud: the pretence at that grisly funeral, the bribery
of several people at the hospital where the twins were
born, and a surprising number of church authorities.

I know I agreed to all this, and I know it was the
right thing to do. But when I think of what is ahead—

When I think of Viola and Sorrel perhaps having to give evidence in a courtroom—

28th November 1914
It is over.

This morning Edward was brought before magistrates, and his solicitor (who was v. shocked and disbelieving) requested he be released on bail.

I sat in the public gallery—I wore the thick veil I had worn in Western Fferna, and do not think anyone recognized me. Edward looked small and oddly shrunken in the dock, as if someone had jabbed a thick pin into him and let out all the bombast and the selfish conceit. He was so pale his face looked grey.

The solicitor asked that he be released on the surety of £5,000, and appeared to think it was only a formality, and that of course Edward would be granted this bail. The magistrates—there were two of them and they looked very severe indeed—consulted for a moment in whispers. I leaned forward to hear what they were saying, but I could not.

Then one of them said, 'We are reluctant to grant bail to your client, since we feel—'

That was when Edward seemed to stagger forward almost as if he had been pushed hard in the centre of his back. From being pale he was suddenly and shockingly flushed—his face turning dark purple, the veins on his forehead standing out like cords. He put up a hand, whether in supplication or defence it was impossible to tell, and then pitched forward over the front of the dock.

For a truly dreadful moment nothing happened, and then one of the ushers sprang forward, and somebody called out to get a glass of water for God's sake, and a sort of muted panic broke out.

I had absolutely no idea what I should do, but before I could do anything at all, the usher who had come forward and who was bending over Edward straightened up, a look of shock on his face.

'Is he all right?' asked the elder of the magistrates. 'Is it a swoon?'

The usher looked up at the high bench. 'It's not a swoon, sir,' he said. 'He's dead.'

That was when I slipped out of the door at the back, and somehow found my way home.

Clary, silly wench, has been in floods of tears all evening. Mrs Tigg has merely said, All will be well in the end, madam.

'If I said I was sorry it would be false,' said Floy to me. 'I can't be false with you, Charlotte. But we will observe the conventions, my dearest love.'

15th December 1914
I have observed the conventions very carefully, and so has Floy.

There has been a postmortem examination, of course, and the word apoplexy has been used on the death certificate. It is as good a word as any; I do not know if Edward died from fear of the disgrace and humiliation that lay ahead of him, or if he died from a sudden, shamed realization of what he had done. I shall try to believe the latter, but I am not sure.

The funeral was private, of course, and people have condoled with me, but with an eager curiosity that I find repellent. I do not really want condolence, and I wish I could feel grief or shock or compassion for Edward, but I cannot. I can only think that he was guilty of that monstrous deceit, and that he condemned Sorrel and Viola to a childhood lived in Mortmain. I shall try to make it up to them—they are still with Floy, but when he goes back to France I shall take them to live quietly in the country somewhere until this war is over, and until I can talk to doctors about an operation for them. It would be a difficult and dangerous thing and I do not know if it would even be possible, but I believe it must be attempted.

I am getting to know my daughters a little now. Sorrel is open and confiding and I think she will be unscathed by what she has been through, but Viola—Viola has alarming spells of silence and there is sometimes a hardness in her eyes that ought not to be in the eyes of any fourteen-year-old girl. Yes, Viola will have to be very gently handled.

Anthony Raffan has been to visit the girls—I see Sorrel blushing very attractively in his company, which makes me even more determined to talk to doctors about the twins' condition.

I would like to think I can trace that child, Robyn, as well, but Anthony says she was taken from Mortmain soon after my visit there and he never heard what happened to her. I think he believes she vanished into that evil half-world of brothels and freak shows ruled by men such as Matt Dancy, and I don't think we shall find her.

Floy has already begun to write Viola and Sorrel's story; he thinks he will do so as if they are one person, which he says will have a better impact, so his heroine will be fictional. But the story of Mortmain, and the story of Viola and Sorrel, will be real.

He will return to France next week, to the writing of his war articles, and to his help in the Red Cross tents which are being set up to treat the wounded. I have no idea when I shall see him again, or even if I shall see him again.

But we are almost at the start of a new year—1915 —and perhaps the war will end very soon, and then Floy and I can at last be together.

It was not until the evening after the discussion in the white, light-filled house that Harry and Simone walked along the coast path and down a narrow shingled track to a stretch of pale beach. It was cold and sharp and they were both wearing anoraks and scarves, but it was a good kind of coldness.

'I love it here better than anywhere in the world,' said Simone, pausing at the top of the narrow path. 'My mother came here after I went to university—I think she felt free to do what she wanted by then, and Martin had finally turned up. He had worked on a research fellowship in Canada for quite a number of years, but he came back to England when I was eighteen. That's when they got together, and bought this house. They still spend a bit of the year in Canada, but they're here for quite a lot of the time. This is where I used to come for holidays and weekends. Martin's the best thing that ever happened to my mother.'

'I think you were the best thing that ever happened to her,' said Harry. 'I think you're the best thing that's ever happened to me, as well— Oh shit, I can't believe I said that. Give it another twenty-four hours and I'll start quoting poetry at you!'

'I wish you wouldn't be so cynical.'

'I wish I wouldn't, as well.'

She turned to look back up at him at that, and quite suddenly smiled. Without realizing he had been going to say it, Harry said, 'I love your smile.'

'Did you like Angelica's smile as much?'

'No, nowhere near as much,' said Harry, taking this one absolutely straight. 'Angelica started out as a means to an end. She was a way of getting close to you. But I got a bit tangled on the way.'

'So I understood,' Simone said dryly, and Harry studied her for a moment.

'I'm not an angel, Simone.'

The smile showed again. 'I know. I'm rather looking forward to you not being an angel.'

'Well, I hope you don't want me to not be an angel out here, because I'd really rather wait until we're somewhere more private— Is this the path down to the beach?'

'Yes, it is. It's usually a bit slippery, so we'll have to go carefully.'

'You'd better hold my hand, then.'

They went down the shingled path until they were on the stretch of beach.

'God, it is steep isn't it?' said Harry. 'Don't let go of my hand: I don't want to lose you—'

'On the slippery path?'

'Or at all, I suspect.'

'The sun's just beginning to set properly now,' said Simone, after a moment. 'This is my favourite time of day.'

'Mine too.'

'But we'll have to wait about another ten minutes before we go across to that stretch of the beach, because at this time of the day you find you're walking straight into the light and it's quite dazzling.'

Hand-in-hand into the sunset? demanded Harry's inner voice, but he only said, 'OK. Let's sit on this bit of wall for a while until the sun's a bit lower.'

The wall was warm from the day's sun. 'I started to read Floy's book last night in bed,' said Simone. 'It made me cry in places, but it's an extraordinary piece of work. I don't want to stop reading it.'

'It affected me like that as well.'

'D'you suppose it would ever be possible to get it reprinted? Properly, I mean, so that it could be on sale in bookshops?'

'It would be nice, wouldn't it? We can try to find out.' He hesitated, and then said, 'Simone, as well as the book I brought this for you,' and reached into his anorak pocket for the padded envelope containing the small, silver-framed photograph he had taken from the mantelpiece of Roz Raffan's house while no one was looking.

It was an oblong frame, rather old-fashioned, and the silver was slightly tarnished. But the inset photograph showed two people standing close together: one a dark-haired man perhaps in his early or mid forties, thin-faced, with narrow intelligent eyes. His arm was around the woman. She had high cheekbones and a slightly too-wide mouth. It was difficult to know her hair colour from the faded, sepia photograph, but it was possible to see that she had the matt creamy complexion that often goes with chestnut hair.

Simone stared at this for a long time, and then turned it over. On the back, in the spidery writing of an earlier era, was written, *'Philip Fleury with Charlotte... France. October 1920.'*

'Floy,' said Simone at last, making it a statement.

'Yes.'

'He looks a bit like you.'

Harry had not expected this. He had not seen any particular resemblance between himself and Floy. But before he could say anything, Simone said, 'And—Charlotte? Was she the "C" in the dedication?'

'I think so. It's a reasonable assumption.'

'Floy's wife? Were they married to one another?'

'I don't know. They look as if they're very together, don't they?' said Harry. 'But I don't suppose we'll ever know if they were married to one another.' He stood up. 'The sun's almost in the sea. It looks quite safe to go down there now. Come with me?'

Simone paused, studying him, and then said, 'Into the sunset?' 'Why not?' said Harry, and held out his hand.